REDEMPTION

Also by Heather Burnside

The Manchester Thrillers
Guilt
Blackmail
Redemption

The Working Girls Series
The Mark
Ruby
Crystal
Amber
Sapphire

The Riverhill Trilogy
Slur
A Gangster's Grip
Danger by Association

The Manchester Trilogy
Born Bad
Blood Ties
Vendetta

HEATHER BURNSIDE

REDEMPTION

HEAD
ZEUS

An Aries Book

First published in UK in 2023 by Head of Zeus,
part of Bloomsbury Publishing Plc.

Copyright © Heather Burnside, 2023

The moral right of Heather Burnside to be identified
as the author of this work has been asserted in accordance with
the Copyright, Designs and Patents Act of 1988.

All rights reserved. No part of this publication may be reproduced,
stored in a retrieval system, or transmitted in any form or by any means,
electronic, mechanical, photocopying, recording, or otherwise,
without the prior permission of both the copyright owner
and the above publisher of this book.

This is a work of fiction. All characters, organizations, and events
portrayed in this novel are either products of the author's
imagination or are used fictitiously.

9 7 5 3 1 2 4 6 8

A catalogue record for this book is available from the British Library.

ISBN (PB): 9781801107976
ISBN (E): 9781801107952

Cover design: Matt Bray

Typeset by Siliconchips Services Ltd UK

Printed and bound in Great Britain by
CPI Group (UK) Ltd, Croydon CR0 4YY

Head of Zeus
First Floor East
5–8 Hardwick Street
London EC1R 4RG

WWW.HEADOFZEUS.COM

In memory of all the estate kids who didn't make it.

Prologue

May 2011

'Eh, you'd still be first on my list, Aggie, if I didn't have a missus,' Macca called back as he left the late-night convenience store.

The smile remained on his lips when he walked past the shopfront, noticing the debris that littered it. There were cigarette butts, sweet wrappers, and the odd used condom, all soil-stained and with the smell of dank urine polluting the air. It was something he wouldn't have spotted at one time but now it was all too apparent.

It didn't stop him grinning as he thought about Aggie. She was in her late sixties now but still kept herself trim. Her age showed in other ways though: the white roots that occasionally poked through her dyed black hair, and the tramlines that coursed her overly made-up face. No amount of war paint could hide so much wear and tear.

Macca could still remember her from when he was just a kid. She must have been in her thirties at that time and was a stunner. She hadn't worked in the convenience store then but in another smaller grocer's on the estate, and she wouldn't tolerate any nonsense from anyone. He even remembered getting a clip round the earhole from her when he'd tried to pinch some sweets.

Macca felt sorry for her in a way. Despite her age, she took up every opportunity to flirt with much younger men, probably trying to relive her heyday. Macca was a prime target, aged forty and with a toned physique that compensated for his lack of stature at only five eight. He enjoyed the banter with her, knowing that it probably made her day.

He was still thinking about Aggie when he turned the corner at the end of the row. Here there was a bridge-like structure that spanned from the end of one row of shops to another. It formed an open tunnel, which led to the car park and to the estate further on. In the daytime it seemed light and airy as it was about five metres in width. But at night it could become menacing to those more vulnerable than him.

Macca was halfway through the tunnel when two youths approached, one tall and gangly with dirty blond hair and the other a similar height to himself and dark-skinned. He'd hardly noticed them before they were on him, the smaller one throwing aimless punches while the other was reaching inside Macca's jacket pockets in search of his valuables.

'Give us your fuckin' money!' he yelled.

It took Macca only a moment to react. He threw a right-handed punch at the dark-skinned lad who staggered back clutching his chin, his face a mask of shock. Then Macca laid into the other one, jabbing with his left and following up with a strong right hand.

It was a particularly heavy thump to the tall lad's stomach

that left him doubled over and panting for breath. The first youth had now recovered from the blow to his face and his hand was no longer clutching his swollen cheek. He was about to come back at Macca but, on seeing his friend in obvious pain, he hesitated.

'Come on, lad,' urged Macca. 'Show us what you've got.' He nodded at the lad's friend and chuckled. When he received no response, he said, 'I hope you've got more than your mate anyway.'

The lad's eyes drifted to the expensive watch Macca was wearing and Macca laughed. 'You didn't think I'd be wearing a watch like this round here if I couldn't handle myself, did you?'

Then the lad surprised him by pulling out a knife. 'Right, stop fuckin' about. I want your watch and your fuckin' wallet or else.'

Macca's response was immediate. No longer jovial, he aimed a sharp roundhouse kick, which struck the lad's hand, sending the knife spiralling through the air and landing some distance away with a clunk as the metal blade hit the paving stones.

'Don't even fuckin' think about it!' yelled Macca, grabbing the lad before he had chance to recover the knife.

Once he had him in his clutches, Macca gave him a good pasting, thumping his face and torso till the lad yelled out in pain and slumped to the ground. Macca waited till both lads were out of action then he spoke again.

'So, is this what you kids get up to nowadays? In my day it was house break-ins. Or shops. Either way, we netted more than you'll get from muggings. Who told you that was a good idea, anyway? Most of the people round here haven't got enough fuckin' cash for themselves and their own families, never mind for a pair of muppets like you.'

It amused Macca to see the reaction on the lads' faces as they looked at him in awe, so he carried on. 'You're not the first to get up to no good, y'know, and you won't be the last. But me and my mates didn't always need knives. Our reputations were enough to scare anyone.'

The taller lad was standing up straight now and the smaller one was off the ground but neither of them made a move. Instead, the smaller of the two asked, 'What the fuck are you talking about?'

Macca sighed and said, 'You can't surprise me, lads. I've done it all in my time. But if I'd have known at your age what I know now, I never would have got involved in any of it.'

'Why? Who are you?' asked the dark-skinned lad who seemed to be the most talkative of the two.

'I'm just a guy who was once like you. But I'm telling you now, lads, give it up. It might seem like a quick earner, but it'll get you nowhere in the long run. Believe me, I was one of the lucky ones, but some weren't so lucky.'

The taller lad finally spoke. 'You from round here?'

'Yeah, brought up a few streets away.'

'What's your name?'

'Doesn't matter. It's not important but what I'm telling you is... get on the straight and narrow before it's too late. Keep your heads down and stay out of trouble. And get yourselves a decent job.'

'Why, what's your job?' asked the smaller of the two. 'Are you wadded?'

'I do alright,' said Macca, smiling.

Then he drew a bunch of notes out of his wallet, split it in two and handed a pile to each of the lads.

'What the fuck's this for?'

'It's for whatever you were gonna buy after you'd mugged me, as long as it's not drink or drugs. Take it home with you. Treat your mum. But stay out of fuckin' trouble.'

'Cheers, Mister,' said the taller of the two, running off.

His mate followed suit and Macca stared after them as they made their way to the run-down estate. Stupid lads – they obviously had no idea what or who they were dealing with. He felt no bitterness towards them knowing that they probably weren't all bad. They'd perhaps had a difficult start in life and didn't know any better.

He carried on in the same direction as the lads. Although his car was in the car park he wasn't going home yet. There was someone on the estate he needed to see: Todd Brown. An old mate he'd known since they were a similar age to the two lads he'd just come across.

The lads had reminded him of himself and Todd in a way, always up to no good and on the make. That's why he hadn't felt bitter towards them. On the contrary, they'd given him food for thought and reminded him of how it was all those years ago.

25 YEARS BEFORE

I

June 1986

Mark (Macca) McNeil heard the fight before he saw it. He was walking along the school corridor with his mate, Chris Spinx, known as Spinxy, when they heard the jeers of 'Fight, fight, fight, fight!'

It drew their attention, and they peered over the railing that bordered the quadrangle, a rectangular yard set at a lower level. A large crowd had gathered and Spinxy became animated.

'Look, Macca. There's a scrap. Let's go and have a look.'

Macca caught hold of his jumper before Spinxy had chance to get very far. 'No, stay here,' he said. 'We won't be able to see fuck all in the yard. There's too many people watching.'

Spinxy peered over the fence. 'Oh yeah,' he said. 'We've got a better view from here.'

They adjusted their positioning slightly to get a better view, and both watched intently. 'Eh, it's that new lad, Todd Brown,' said Spinxy. 'Fuckin' hell! He can scrap.'

Macca heard Spinxy's sharp intake of breath as they watched Todd pummelling the other lad. Macca was surprised to see that Todd's opponent was Mike Finch. The two were in the year above Macca and Spinxy but Mike Finch was someone they tended to avoid. He was known as a tough lad and a bully, especially to those in lower years.

Todd had only been in the school a couple of weeks and Macca was surprised that Todd had been transferred to their school so late in the school year. There were only a few weeks to go till the school year ended and Macca wondered if Todd must have done something really bad at his previous school to have been sent to this school now.

After a while Todd stopped pummelling Mike Finch. Instead, he drew his face up close to him.

'What the fuck's he doing?' asked Spinxy. 'Kissing him or what?'

'Shush,' said Macca, who was busy taking it all in.

Macca had always been able to handle himself and was getting a bit of a reputation for fighting although, unlike Mike Finch, he wasn't a bully. But he was always wary of the older lads. Anybody who was regarded as a bit handy presented a challenge to them, and Macca had felt for some time that Mike Finch had him in his sights.

'I'm fuckin' glad he's getting a pasting,' he said to Spinxy, checking first that no one was listening.

'Me too – he's a twat.'

Macca's eyes were still glued to the scene when he heard an agonising scream from Mike Finch and a roar from the crowd. It wasn't so much a cheer as a wave of revulsion, and some of the girls turned their heads back as though they couldn't bear to look. This had Macca even more intrigued as to why Todd had drawn up so close to Finch's face.

As they watched, Todd pulled away again. He said something to his opponent before giving him a last kick in the groin, picking up his school bag and walking away with a swagger.

Mike Finch stayed on the ground for some time as Macca and Spinxy carried on watching. The crowd dispersed apart from two of Finch's mates who handed him his coat and backpack when he got up off the ground. Blood was now pouring from Finch's face, and he gazed around awkwardly, aware that everyone had witnessed his defeat.

A group of girls walked towards Macca and Spinxy, and Spinxy swung round. Assuming they had come from the crowd watching the fight, he asked, 'What happened?'

'He bit his fuckin' ear off, that's what happened,' said one of the girls.

Shit! thought Macca. *This new kid must be a right hard case.*

'I'd watch him if I were you,' added the girl. 'He was thrown out of his old school for beating people up there too.'

Spinxy let out a roar of amusement as he turned back towards Macca. But once the girls had gone his roar switched to a nervous chuckle before he said, 'Fuckin' hell! Did you hear that?'

'Shush,' said Macca, who had seen Mike Finch and his mates heading towards them.

Despite being wary of the group of lads, Macca couldn't help but stare as he noticed the bloody mess that was Mike Finch's face.

'What the fuck are you gawping at?' demanded Finch.

For a moment, Macca continued looking with his mouth agape as the blood poured from Mike Finch's left ear. He then turned his back swiftly away from the group of lads. Despite his handiness, he and Spinxy stood no chance against them. Spinxy wasn't a fighter and Macca wouldn't take on the three bully boys on his own.

It usually rankled him but not today. He knew that Mike Finch was only reacting angrily because of his humiliation at being beaten. Finch didn't want people like Macca to know his opponent had won. And even though Macca wasn't prepared to take Finch on, he had the satisfaction of knowing somebody else had put him in his place. Not only that, but Mike Finch would be reminded of it every time he looked in the mirror and saw the missing chunk in his left ear.

'What the fuck?' said Spinxy once Finch and his mates were out of hearing range. Macca nodded but didn't say anything, so Spinxy carried on, 'We'd better watch out for this new guy. If he can do that to Mike Finch, then fuck knows what he'd do to us if we wound him up.'

'I know. I think he lives over the main road from me. I saw him the other day. I heard he was hard. He goes around with another lad called Shay who's pretty handy too. But I've never had anything to do with them.'

'Fuckin hell! I'm glad I don't live near him.'

'It's alright. They've lived on the estate for a few years, and they never bother me. We only really see people from the other side of Stockport Road when we're on the precinct. It's a big estate so they don't really hang out near us.'

'Thank fuck for that,' said Spinxy before they heard the

bell signalling the end of lunch break and picked up their backpacks ready to return to class.

That evening Macca was on the way to the chippy when he bumped into his mate Leroy Young, a mixed-race lad who was fifteen, the same age as Macca, and who lived on the next road to him although he went to a different school. Macca's grandma had sent him to get some tea.

'Hey, Lee, fancy coming to the chippy?' he asked.

Leroy, who had been kicking a stone against the pavement, paused and looked up. 'Yeah sure.'

He drew up close to Macca and asked, 'How much have you got?'

Macca knew straightaway what Leroy was after, and he was swift to react. 'Eh, don't even fuckin' think about it. It's my gran's money. She knows exactly how much everything costs and she'll be counting her change when I get back. If owt's missing, she'll have all of our fuckin' balls on a plate.'

Leroy laughed. 'Might taste better than the shite we get from that chippy.'

Macca joined in his laughter. He got along with Leroy who was good fun and always up to mischief. Macca wasn't aware of it yet, but they might have gravitated towards each other because of what they had in common. They both had fathers who had walked out of the family home years prior and left their mothers to bring them up single-handed.

Macca was glad to be going to the chippy. Although his grandma could be a bit of a battleaxe, he liked her visits because she often helped him and his mother out financially. Sometimes she'd treat them to a chippy tea, other times she'd give him a couple of quid, and some days she brought food with her and gave it to his mum.

He knew his mum struggled to make ends meet. It had been years ago when his father, Vernon, had deserted them. Since then, Macca hadn't seen him, and from what his mother had said, she'd never received a penny from his dad.

Macca's mum was on benefits and never had any spare cash. His grandma was always moaning that her own money 'didn't grow on trees' either but Macca knew she was better off than them because she'd been receiving a private pension since his grandad died as well as her own state pension.

Macca and Leroy were in the chippy queue when two other lads walked in. The sound of their laughter drew his eyes towards them, but he wished he hadn't looked when he caught the gaze of Todd Brown at the same time as he heard him say, 'He's a fuckin' pussy, mate. He just thinks he's hard 'cos he has his mates around him all the time.'

Macca assumed he was referring to his fight with Mike Finch and he smiled in acknowledgement, hoping to get on the right side of Todd and his mate.

'You're from our school, aren't you?' asked Todd, flicking his head back as though demanding a response.

'Yeah. I think you're in the year above me.'

Macca knew what year Todd was in, but he was attempting to appear casual.

'Did you see the scrap today?' asked Todd's mate, laughing.

Macca smiled. 'Yeah, he pasted him.'

Leroy, who had heard all about the fight from Macca on the way to the chippy, had a look of concern on his face.

Macca had picked up on it and was a bit wary too. But he admired Todd's victory and saw no harm in trying to endear himself to these two. The last thing he and Lee needed was to have to go up against them. He needn't have worried as Todd's mate was already warming to him.

'I wish I'd have fuckin' been there,' he said. 'I'd have loved to have seen Finch's face when Todd bit his fuckin' ear off. Our team have played football against him and his mates. They're a bunch of twats.'

'He screamed like a girl,' said Macca, smiling again.

'Fuckin' hell, did you see what it looked like?'

'Yeah, him and his mates walked past me. There was a piece of his ear missing, and it was pumping blood.'

'Nice one!' yelled Todd's mate, giving Todd a celebratory slap on the back as a woman in the queue gave him a scornful look and shuffled a few paces away from the boys.

'Turn it in, Shay,' said Todd, looking uncomfortable rather than proud. 'He fuckin' asked for it. He shouldn't have thought he could slap me around just 'cos I'm the new kid.'

'He's like that,' said Macca. 'He's always having a go at kids in my year. Mostly he picks on the soft ones, but I've heard he's after me.' He shrugged then, afraid he might have said too much. Not wanting to reveal his own reputation as someone who could handle himself, he added, 'I don't know why. I ain't done owt to him. He's just a dick who thinks he's hard.'

Macca was rewarded with a grin from Todd before the man behind the counter shouted, 'Next please,' and Macca turned to give his order.

Once Macca had been handed his chips, he turned to go.

He and Leroy were on their way out of the door when Todd said, 'Wait for us.'

'Alright,' said Macca, too cautious to refuse but worried about what Todd Brown could want with him.

He looked at his mate Leroy and could tell he was worried too.

2

June 1986

Although Macca was nervous about what Todd might have to say, he was a little reassured by the fact that Shay had been so friendly. Todd had seemed less amicable, but maybe that was just the way he was. He had one of those stern-looking faces with a square jawline and rigid features as though he was perpetually angry. But he had grinned at Macca.

While they waited, Macca and Leroy didn't speak but Macca could see that his friend looked uncomfortable. He thought that perhaps, like him, Leroy was wary of being overheard by the older boys. The few minutes while they were waiting seemed to last forever but at last Todd and Shay came out of the chippy.

Straightaway, Todd looked at Macca and asked, 'What's your name?'

'Mark McNeil, but my mates call me Macca.'

Todd seemed pensive for a moment before saying,

'I think I might have heard of you. Have you got any older brothers?'

'No, just me.'

'Who do you hang around with at school?'

'Chris Spinx, Spinxy, mostly but sometimes a couple of others too.'

Macca reeled off the names of a couple of the other lads in his class, but Todd shook his head. 'Nah, I've not heard of any of them.' Then he asked, 'Is Mike Finch the cock of my year?'

'Yeah, that's what everyone says. Well, they did but it'll be you now.'

Todd didn't smile as Macca would have expected. Instead, he looked serious when he said, 'The trouble is, that'll mean every fucker will want to have a go. I wanted to keep my head down in this school. I've already been expelled from my other school for scrapping, but Finch wouldn't leave me alone. I tried warning him, but he just took the piss. And then when he started prodding me and trying to trip me up in the yard, I just fuckin' lost it.'

'I don't blame you,' said Macca.

Shay laughed. 'You didn't need to bite his fuckin' ear off though.'

Macca could tell his words weren't reproachful. Instead, he appeared amused and impressed by what Todd had done. Todd, however, looked shamefaced.

'I didn't mean to go that far. I was just fuckin' angry. And at least now he'll think twice before he has a go in the future.'

'No worries,' said Macca. 'I bet everyone else will think twice before they have a go too.'

'I hope so. I get sick of the hassle. It was like that in my old school, always someone wanting to have a go. And I don't take shit from anyone. I get enough of that from my stepdad.' Then he spat before adding, 'Wanker.'

It was obviously a sore point, so Macca didn't ask about it. But there was something else he was curious about. 'Did you get done at school?'

'Nah, no one grassed.'

'Finch wouldn't. He'd be too scared of losing face by crying to the teachers. Good job really.'

'Yeah, I'm glad no one else did either.'

'They were probably scared too.'

Macca saw that look of shame on Todd's face again and it became evident to him that he wasn't a bully. He didn't even like what he had done. But he did it because he couldn't help himself. Macca guessed he had a temper and that made him lash out in defence. He didn't seem a bad lad though and Macca thought he was probably the type who was alright with you as long as you were alright with him.

His thoughts were validated when Todd asked, 'Do you two wanna hang out tomorrow night?'

Macca looked across at Leroy whose eyebrows rose in surprise and Macca said, 'Yeah, sure.'

'OK, we'll meet you here about seven.'

Macca agreed before they all parted company. Leroy, who had remained quiet throughout the exchange, waited until the two older lads were some distance away before he said, 'Fuckin' hell, I can't believe we're gonna hang out with Todd Brown and Seamus O'Reilly. That's well cool.'

Macca smiled but didn't respond. He had mixed feelings. On the one hand, he was chuffed that they wanted to hang out with him and Leroy but, on the other hand, he was apprehensive and kept asking himself why? Maybe, because Todd was new to the school, he wanted an ally.

But, at the moment, he was more concerned with getting back home before his chips went cold. 'Come on, I'd better get back or Two Chins will be on my fuckin' case,' Macca said to Leroy.

Two Chins was the nickname he used to refer to his overweight grandmother, although both she and Macca's mother were unaware of it. Whenever she laughed, her chins would wobble, to Macca's amusement. He'd hate her to find out about the nickname though; she might have wound him up at times, but he loved her really.

Macca walked into the flat to find Grandma Doris sitting on his mother's sofa with a plate on her knee, a fork in her hand and a glum expression on her face. The lounge doubled up as a dining room with a tiny, mostly unused Formica table pushed against the far wall and two teak, uncushioned dining chairs tucked underneath. There was a small kitchen further along the hall, as well as the two bedrooms occupied by Macca and his mother, and the bathroom.

His mother kept the lounge tidy, but the furniture was old and jaded. The sofa sagged under his grandma's weight. It was an odd design with leaves and flowers in shades of brown, cream, vanilla and rust, and was supported by wooden legs, a style more suited to the Seventies than the Eighties.

His mother had bought it in a second-hand shop a couple of years ago at a bargain price. To make it more appealing, there was a scattering of cushions with covers crocheted by his grandma in bright complementary colours, the largest of which was currently being used to pad out the saggy bit under her sizeable backside.

Macca's mother normally used one of the matching armchairs. The legs had gone on the other one, so it was no longer used to sit on. Instead, Macca's mother had adopted it as somewhere to stack the clean washing ready to sort and put away.

'Jesus Christ!' his grandma yelled as soon as she saw him. 'Where the bloody hell have you been, lad? Peeling the bleedin' spuds?'

He smirked. 'Nah. Lee was peeling and chopping. I was working the fryer.'

She raised her hand threateningly in mock irritation then chuckled. 'You cheeky little sod. Ger over here with 'em. Me bleedin' stomach thinks me throat's been cut.'

Macca walked over to his grandma, but he couldn't resist taunting her a little. 'You can have 'em but only if you're nice to me, and tell me I'm the best-looking, most wonderful and brilliant person you've ever laid eyes on.'

At that moment his mother, Debbie, walked through the door carrying plates and forks for herself and Macca. 'Give over taunting your grandma before she gives you a clip round the earhole.'

'He'll get more than a bleedin' clip if he doesn't watch himself,' said Doris.

'I was only messing,' he said.

Macca had already decided not to carry on the wind-up. He could tell his grandma was salivating and he knew her bonhomie wouldn't last much longer now she'd smelt the chips.'

They were tucking into their chippy tea when Macca smiled and said, 'Anyway, I don't need to blackmail my grandma, she already knows I'm the best-looking, most brilliant lad she's ever met.'

'Give over,' said his gran, laughing. 'Your bleedin' head's that big, it's a wonder you can get through the door. You're a looker alright but so was your father and look what a shit he turned out to be.'

'Mum!' Debbie complained. 'Don't say that to him.'

'Why not? It's true, isn't it?'

Debbie sniffed. 'Well, I suppose he was a bit full of himself.'

'A bit?' Doris scoffed. 'Y'know your trouble, Debbie, you never could resist a handsome face.'

'Oh, give over, Mum. Not that again.'

Macca could see his mum was getting irritated with his grandma, but she did have a point. His mother might be short of cash, but it didn't stop her going out in search of her elusive perfect man. Debbie was still young at thirty-eight and had kept her figure. She enjoyed her nights out and had hooked up with a few boyfriends in the years since his dad had left them. But none of her relationships lasted.

The shortage of cash hadn't curtailed her smoking habit

either. But Macca didn't blame her really. She had to have some pleasures in life. After all, she had worked hard to look after him and she had done a sight more for him than his absent father ever had.

3

June 1986

'Aw, you lucky bastard,' said Spinxy. No one will mess with you now you're a friend of Todd Brown's. What's he like anyway?'

It was the next day at school and Macca had just told Spinxy what had taken place at the chip shop the previous evening.

'He's alright,' he replied. 'I thought he'd be bragging about what had happened, but he wasn't. I still wouldn't get on the wrong side of him though. He was expelled from his last school for fighting.'

'Fuck!'

'I know but at least he's alright with me.'

'Can you two be quiet please while I'm taking the register?' said their form teacher, Mr Taylor, curtailing any further discussion about Todd Brown.

By the time the class were on the way to their first lesson, the conversation between the two boys had switched to other subjects. They were walking along the corridor when

Macca spotted Todd walking towards him. He wondered whether he would acknowledge him, but he needn't have been concerned.

'Hiya, mate, you alright?' asked Todd, giving Macca a friendly pat on the back. 'I'm looking for the science labs. Do you know where they are?'

Macca gave him directions, aware as he did so that they were attracting a lot of curious stares. Macca was glad people would soon become aware of his connection to Todd Brown. Perhaps Mike Finch and his mates would change their minds about having a go at him once word got round.

'Cheers, mate,' said Todd as he made his way to the biology labs. 'See you tonight.'

Macca turned and watched him walk away, noticing as he did so that Todd was on his own. He had been correct in his assumption that Todd wanted an ally. It must be hard starting a new school and not knowing anyone, especially when you already had a bad reputation.

'I wish I could hang around with Todd Brown,' said Spinxy who was full of admiration for anyone who could fight.

'You can,' said Macca. 'Come round to ours tonight and you can come with me and Lee to meet him.'

Macca knew Spinxy lived a bus ride away but, despite that, he often came to visit Macca and spend time with him and Leroy.

'Aw, great,' said Spinxy with a huge grin lighting up his face.

When Macca walked over to the precinct that evening,

accompanied by Leroy and Spinxy, Todd and Shay were already there.

'Alright, mate,' said Todd, stepping forward.

'Yeah,' said Macca who then introduced his two friends after having been prompted by Spinxy.

'Yeah, I saw you last night,' Todd said to Leroy. Then he turned to Spinxy. 'I don't know you though, do I? You from our school?'

Macca almost laughed when he saw Spinxy's look of horror but instead he helped him out, saying, 'Yeah, he's my mate from school. Remember, I told you about him last night. He was with me today too when I saw you in the corridor.'

'Oh yeah, I thought his face looked familiar.'

Spinxy's horrified expression was replaced by one of relief. Then Shay asked. 'So, what should we do?'

'Dunno,' said Todd. 'We can't fuckin' do the offie again, not after that twat nearly caught you last night.' As he spoke, he nodded towards the off-licence, which was a few shops along from the chippy. Then he turned to Macca and his friends. 'What do you lot do for fun round here?'

Macca laughed. 'Same as you. There's a shop near us, under the flats. We've nicked some stuff from there a few times. One of us usually buys summat while the other two sneak behind the shelves at the back of the shop. You have to watch out for Aggie behind the counter though. She caught me once and went bloody mad.'

'Come on then,' said Shay. 'What are we waiting for?'

'Are you coming out, Mandy?' asked Joanne as she stood

at the mirror of the bedroom they shared, layering mascara onto her lashes.

Joanne was a pretty girl of average height with hair a lovely shade of chestnut brown, which she wore in the 'big Eighties' hairstyle that was popular. Her sister, Mandy, was taller and not quite as pretty. Her hair, a shade darker than Joanne's, wasn't as big either but she was still an attractive girl.

Mandy shut her exercise book. 'Yeah, why not? I've finished all my homework and I'm not seeing Pete tonight.'

'Why, what's he up to?'

'Nowt much. He just said he's got loads of studying to do.'

'He's always studying.'

'I know, well, he is doing his A levels, isn't he?'

Joanne was a year younger than Mandy who was in the last year of school before sixth form. Mandy had hooked up with Pete at school when they had both been in the same drama group. But Joanne couldn't see the appeal. She thought he seemed a bit boring.

'Come on, hurry up,' said Joanne, putting a long-tail comb back on the dressing table. She had just finished backcombing her hair so that it was bigger than ever, and she was now watching her sister putting some books back onto the shelf of the bedroom they shared.

'Alright, let's go. But you'd better watch out that Dad doesn't see you wearing mascara. He'll go mad.'

Mandy didn't bother backcombing her hair, preferring to let her permed curls hang loosely. Nor did she put on any makeup; unlike her sister, she wasn't interested in any of the local boys because she had Pete.

'Right, I'll go first then.'

Joanne led the way, walking down the hall while Mandy stuck her head inside the living room and announced to her parents that they were both going out for a bit.

Joanne heard her dad shout back, 'Alright, but make sure you're in by ten, both of you.'

Joanne pulled a face and dashed out through the front door with Mandy following behind. When they reached the end of their avenue, they saw two of the girls from the estate sitting on a wall chatting, so Mandy and Joanne went to join them.

The wall stood at the end of a row of houses but the people who lived at the last house didn't seem to mind who sat on it. Joanne knew that the adults in the house spent most of their time at the pub and didn't lavish much attention on their home or garden, which was full of weeds and strewn with litter. The corners of the wall were chipped and some of the cheap bricks were full of mould like many of the houses, which were already showing signs of decay even though the estate had been built only ten years before.

In the street a handful of small children were playing on a battered old scooter with one of them pedalling away while the others shouted at him to let them have a go. Joanne recognised some of them who lived at the end house. A girl of around five sat on the pavement and cried, complaining that her older brothers always left her out of things. Joanne knew she shouldn't have been out at this time of night as it was already past nine, but it was nothing new.

There were a few vehicles lining the streets, which were a mix. The battered family cars were driven by those who could scarcely afford it but there was also a couple of flash, nearly new motors. The latter were owned by the criminal fraternity and even the youngest kids knew not to damage them.

Joanne and her sister had only been there a few minutes when they saw a group of lads in the distance. Joanne felt a surge of excitement, wondering if Macca would be with them. She'd had a crush on Macca for as far back as she could remember. He'd always been one of the cool kids even though he looked angelic as a young child with his blond hair and beautiful eyes.

She watched them approach and was pleased to spot Macca's unmistakable hair colour. As he was still some distance away, her imagination filled in the rest of the details: penetrating blue eyes, a confident gait and a mischievous smile that always made her heart race.

The lads were drawing nearer, and Joanne felt herself blush as Macca locked eyes with her. She smiled and was rewarded with a cheeky grin in return. Then the lads stopped in front of them.

'Hi, girls, it's your lucky night,' Leroy said.

'Who's yer mates?' asked Trisha, a plain-looking but forward girl who lived on the next street to Joanne and Mandy.

'Todd and Shay,' said Leroy proudly. 'They live on the other side of Stockport Road.'

'Oh, yeah,' said Trisha, preening herself as she eyed up Todd. 'I've heard of you before.'

Shay managed a smile, but Todd just looked warily at the girls. Joanne wasn't interested in their exchange; she was too busy smiling at Macca who nodded and asked her and Mandy if they were alright.

'Yeah,' they both answered, and Joanne thought he was going to say something more until Todd spoke.

'Come on, lads, we've got stuff to do.'

He began to move away, and the rest of the boys followed suit. Joanne was left gazing after them, her eyes on one boy in particular. She was disappointed. She'd gone to all that trouble, wearing her new top and putting on makeup to impress Macca. And all she'd got in return was a couple of words.

4

July 1986

It was two weeks later and the boys were walking along Hyde Road; Macca, Todd, Leroy and Shay puffing on cigarettes while Spinxy chomped on his second chocolate bar. Shoplifting was becoming a regular pastime for the four of them and they were in high spirits having succeeded in lifting a lot of confectionery from the estate shop as well as two packets of cigarettes.

As they walked, Macca and Todd chatted. Macca found he was warming to his new friend more and more. Todd told him in a straightforward, almost apologetic way about the reason he was expelled from his previous school and the trouble he'd had there.

'I used to go around with a couple of lads. They were both handy but then I found them picking on wimpy little kids. I don't like that. No one should pick on someone smaller and weaker than themselves. I wouldn't join in but then they started giving me shit, telling me I was a killjoy and that I was scared.

'That just fuckin' annoyed me so I ended up telling them to fuck right off. I didn't bother with them after that. I started knocking about with another lad, Greg, who was alright but them two didn't like that. So, they started having a go, not just at me but at Greg too.

'They knew I wasn't scared of them, so they didn't push it too far with me. But then I found out off Greg that they'd jumped him one night after school when he was on his own. I fuckin' lost it big time and had a go at both of them at break time. It turned into a scrap between them two and me and Greg. They were winning because Greg isn't really hard. But I wasn't gonna let them beat me.'

Then he lowered his voice as he said, 'So that was why I poked one of them in the eye.'

'You did what?' asked Macca, incredulous.

'I heard it somewhere about self-defence. If they can't see you, they can't fuckin' beat you. I'd completely lost it by then so I just fuckin' went for it.'

'How bad was it?' asked Macca, dreading the answer.

Todd had the grace to look ashamed. 'Well, he didn't go blind but, well, he did have to go to hospital. They operated on him and managed to save his sight.'

Macca gulped. 'Shit!'

'Yeah, I know. I didn't mean to go that far but, like I said, I just fuckin' lost it. I can't stand bullies.'

The lads went silent for a moment. Macca knew that Todd was aware of his discomfort at what he had just told him. He didn't hold it against Todd. He could understand it in a way. From what he had said the lad deserved it, and Todd did seem OK with him and his mates. Macca wanted to let Todd know that he was still alright with him, but he couldn't quite find the words. It was Todd who broke the silence with a complete change of subject.

'Hey, that Joanne's fit, isn't she?'

Macca smiled. 'Yeah, she's dead fit. Her sister's nice as well.'

'She's got her fuckin' eye on you, mate.'

'D'you reckon?'

Macca knew Todd was right, but he was wary of appearing too cocky.

'Why don't you ask her out?' said Todd.

'Might do.'

Macca had already thought about asking Joanne out. He could tell she liked him, and he liked her too. But where would he take her? She was a nice girl from a good family, and he felt sure she'd want more from him than spending her nights hanging about on the streets. But he didn't have the money to take her to the pictures or a youth club.

He'd considered inviting her round to his house when his mum was out, but he didn't want to scare her off. Nice girls didn't go round to the houses of lads they'd only just met. But Todd had made him think twice. If even he'd detected her interest, then maybe he should do something about it.

It wasn't long before the lads became bored and in need of further adventure. Macca had noticed that while he was becoming more acquainted with Todd, Leroy and Shay were also getting to know each other. Spinxy, meanwhile, had hovered next to Macca, taking in everything that Todd had been telling them but not saying anything.

'What d'you wanna do now?' Todd asked the group.

'The mineral factory's not far off,' said Leroy, glancing across at his new mate Shay and smiling broadly before looking at Macca. 'There's beer there as well. We got a few bottles last time, didn't we?'

'Yeah,' said Macca. 'But it's hard to get a whole crate over the wall.'

'It'll be easier with five of us,' said Todd, grinning.

'How d'you mean?'

'I'll show you. Which way is it, Lee?'

Leroy pointed the way and now they had a new sense of purpose, it wasn't long before they reached the factory. They walked round to the wall that bordered the other side of the yard. 'We cut a piece out of the barbed wire. It was about here,' said Macca. 'You can't see it till you're up there but it's easy to pull it apart so you can get over. If someone gives me a leg up, I'll show you.'

Spinxy gave him a leg up and Macca examined the barbed wire until he found two endings that had been shoved together. He pulled them apart while the other lads watched as a gap appeared between them.

'OK, I'll tell you what we'll do,' instructed Todd. 'Two of us will go over then pass the crates to those on the other side.'

'I'll do it,' said Leroy and Spinxy at the same time, and Macca was amused at his friends' eagerness to impress their new, older mates.

'OK, come on then,' said Todd, forming a cradle with his hands. 'Spinxy, you go first. You can sit on top of the wall, Macca, while they give you the crates and you pass them to us on the other side.'

Then Spinxy thought of something. 'But how will I get back over the wall?'

'Easy,' said Macca. 'It's not as high on the other side. You can easily climb back up.'

Spinxy seemed happy with that, and he and Leroy were soon in the yard with Macca sitting on top of the wall.

Macca had no sooner grabbed a hefty crate from Leroy and passed it to Todd and Shay than he saw Spinxy approaching with another crate. 'Take some out,' he whispered. 'It'll be too heavy.'

Spinxy did as he asked with some help from Leroy, but Macca heard the loud clinking of bottles as they rushed to remove them. 'That's enough,' he said. 'Pass it to me.'

Spinxy reached up with the crate while Leroy went in search of another one. Macca had it on the top of the wall, ready to pass to Todd and Shay when he saw Leroy dash back towards him yelling, 'Fuckin' hell! There's someone coming.'

Leroy leapt at the wall, digging the toes of his shoes into the mortar to gain purchase while he scrambled up. Spinxy tried to follow suit, but he was heavier than the other lads and it was obvious to Macca that he was struggling.

The sound of someone approaching carried to Macca now and he and Leroy sat on the top of the wall whispering words of encouragement to Spinxy as he tried to join them. Todd and Shay were still on the outside. Todd was demanding to know what was going on, but Macca was too focused on his friend, Spinxy, to acknowledge him.

'Run at it!' Leroy encouraged. 'We'll grab your hands.'

Macca saw the look of desperation on Spinxy's face as he took two steps back, preparing to run at the wall. Then he became aware of more noises, chains rattling and bolts sliding till the back door was open. Out stepped a man, middle-aged with a bald head and poor fashion sense.

'What the bloody hell?' he yelled. 'Come here, you robbin' little get.' Then he stepped out of the door and raced towards Spinxy.

5

July 1986

Joanne was hanging out on the street again. She'd caught a glimpse of Macca earlier making his way out of the estate with his mates. She hoped he would come back but now she was becoming bored with waiting for Macca to reappear. After the disappointment of their previous encounter two weeks ago, she had hoped the boys would come back this way when they'd finished doing whatever it was that they were doing.

She'd tried to persuade Mandy to stay out with her while she waited for Macca to return but Mandy had insisted on going back home. 'You should too,' she had said to Joanne. 'You know what Dad's like if we get in late.'

'We're OK for a bit,' Joanne had said but Mandy wouldn't be persuaded, which left Joanne with Trisha and the other girl, Shell.

Joanne wasn't that keen on either girl. Trisha was a bit too forward for her liking. She had a reputation for sleeping around and Joanne was afraid that she'd get a bad name too if she hung around with her too much. And Shell could be spiteful, always having little digs at Joanne and Mandy as though she was jealous of them. Joanne would have preferred not to be in their company, but she wasn't prepared to stay outside alone.

After chatting for a while, Shell said, 'I'm going home.'

'Me too,' said Trisha, looking at Joanne.

'What time is it?' asked Joanne, realising she had lost track of time.

'Twenty past ten,' said Trisha.

'Shit! See you.'

Joanne left the girls, eager to get home as quickly as possible. But really there was no point in her rushing. She was already late and knew she'd be in trouble.

When she reached home, she placed her key in the lock, trying to be as quiet as possible as she opened the door. She was glad to hear the TV, which would hopefully drown out the sound of her arrival. Then she turned and pushed the front door to, holding her breath as the latch clicked into place.

If she could just get upstairs without her dad noticing, she could at least get rid of her makeup so he didn't see it. She'd also check with Mandy whether he'd been on the hunt for her. If not, she could pretend she'd been home for a while.

She trod lightly on the stairs, stopping to recover every time she heard the slightest creak. When she reached the top, she was relieved to step onto the landing and head towards the bedroom she shared with Mandy. But then she heard the bathroom door opening. She hoped it was her sister or younger brother. But she was out of luck.

'And what time do you call this?' demanded her father, Alan.

Joanne was about to make her excuses when her father did a double take and asked, 'What the bloody hell have you got on your face?'

'It's only a bit of makeup.'

'A bit? You're bloody covered in the stuff! Where have you been anyway?'

'Just out, talking.'

'Talking? Talking to who?'

'Trisha and Shell.'

'Jesus Christ! Not that pair.' Joanne could almost visualise the cogs turning over in his brain as he tried to make connections: the makeup, hanging out with Trisha and Shell, getting in late.

'And why didn't you come home when your sister did?' he asked.

Joanne shrugged. 'Dunno.'

'I hope you've not been bloody chasing lads with that pair of tarts. You'll end up as bad as them.'

Joanne felt herself flush, and her dad was quick to react. 'Oh my God! That's it, isn't it? You've been bloody ladding it with them two tarts. Jesus Christ, Joanne! You're not even sixteen yet. You should be studying like your sister, not out chasing after lads. That won't get you anywhere in life. All that will get you is a bellyful of trouble.'

Her blush intensified. She hated it when her dad spoke like this. He prided himself on being an upstanding citizen. He was a factory manager and stood as the local councillor. Joanne knew he thought that placed him above everyone else on the estate and he was overprotective. She was offended that he thought she behaved like Trisha but was too embarrassed to defend herself.

'Your bloody face says it all,' he continued. 'You've got guilt written all over you. Right, that's it now. You're staying in for a week, and I want you to stay away from them two tarts.'

Joanne was devastated. She knew there was little chance of seeing Macca now. Her sister rarely went out and there was no way she was going to tell Trisha and Shell that she was banned from hanging around with them. That would only cause a load of trouble. But she knew from experience that arguing with her dad would get her nowhere. Once he had set the rules, he never backed down.

'Come on, quick!' Macca yelled to Spinxy. 'Hurry up!'

He clocked the look of desperation from Spinxy who was searching around him trying to decide what to do.

'Fuckin' run at it!' yelled Leroy.

To Macca's relief, Spinxy ran at the wall, lifting one foot and trying to grip it into the mortar as he had seen Leroy do. Then he scrambled up the wall clutching it with his hands. But he was struggling so Macca reached down quickly and locked his fingers round Spinxy's wrist.

'Come on! I've got you. Lift your other hand.'

Spinxy did as he was told, taking another unsteady step up the wall and reaching up with his other hand. Macca was relieved when Leroy grabbed it, but he didn't know how long he and Leroy could take Spinxy's weight before they toppled over the wall and into the yard.

He and Leroy yelled instructions at Spinxy as the man

drew closer. Then the man was on Spinxy, clutching at the bottom of his legs and trying to yank him down from the wall. Macca and Leroy clung on tightly, but Macca could feel Spinxy slipping from his hands. He was torn about what to do. Keep holding on and risk falling over? Or let go and make a run for it? He flashed a look at Leroy and could tell he was thinking the same.

Fortunately, just when Macca was about to give up, he felt a strong hand on his leg, gripping him tightly. He turned momentarily, curious, and saw Todd's head looking back at him, one hand clutching his leg and the other on Leroy's. He assumed Shay must have given him a leg up so he could reach them.

'Quick, pull him!' he said to Leroy.

They heaved simultaneously and were relieved to see Spinxy's head appear above the wall. Then Todd let go of their legs, and while Spinxy scrambled over the wall, Macca and Leroy slid to the ground and made a run for it.

As he fled, Macca could hear the man opening the gate. He looked round to see Spinxy a few feet behind. And then the man was hot on his tail.

'Quick, Spinxy, run!' he yelled.

For several minutes Macca and the other lads kept running. Intent on getting away, Macca didn't turn back but he hoped Spinxy wasn't far behind and had managed to get away from the man. After a while Todd and Shay stopped running and Macca, noticing that he could no longer hear running feet behind him, did the same.

He turned to see Spinxy some distance behind but, thankfully, the man had stopped running. He was bending forward and panting as though struggling to get his breath back. Focusing on the man, Macca could tell from his sagging paunch that he was unfit.

His friends had obviously spotted it too because Leroy then shouted, 'Ha ha, come and get us, you old bastard.'

The man stretched upright and shouted, 'Don't you worry, you won't bloody well get away with this. I know who you are, and I'll be round to your houses in the morning.'

But Macca knew it was just bravado. They didn't recognise him so there was little chance of him knowing who they were. Sensing this, the lads taunted the man.

'Decrepit old bastard. You can't even run!' shouted Shay.

'You won't find us. You've got no fuckin' chance,' Leroy said with a laugh.

A few seconds later, Spinxy drew up alongside his friends, clutching his side and breathing heavily. 'I've got a stitch,' he complained.

'You're so fuckin' unfit,' Leroy teased. 'Even that old bastard nearly caught you.'

Spinxy rushed to defend himself. 'No, he didn't. Anyway, I made it, didn't I?'

Shay laughed. 'You'll have to get fit if you're gonna go out on the rob with us.'

'Course I will,' said Spinxy, standing up tall and trying to pretend that the pain in his side had gone.

Todd then held up the two bottles of beer that he had managed to run off with. Macca smiled in amusement noticing that Shay had managed to run off with two bottles as well.

'Come on,' said Todd. 'Let's go somewhere where we can drink these.'

'Yeah, and you're on rations,' said Shay, laughing again at Spinxy.

They walked for a while, ensuring they were a good distance away from the mineral factory. Eventually they reached a green area with a copse, one of a few planted by the council to lend a rural feel to the urban sprawl. The lads sat down on the grass and opened the bottles, passing them around to each other.

Macca felt a contented glow. He was still buzzing from the thrill of the chase and had a sense of satisfaction from enjoying their spoils. But he was also loving the camaraderie with the other boys.

Then a thought occurred to him. Todd and Shay had stood by them. They could have run off with the crates of mineral and left them to face the consequences. But they didn't; they stayed with them and even helped them to escape. Not only had he and his friends had fun in Todd and Shay's company but they had also earned their loyalty. And that gave Macca the biggest buzz of all.

6

July 1986

As Todd trudged home he had the same dejected feeling he always had when he had to return to the house he shared with his mother, stepfather and two younger brothers. He put his key in the lock and stepped inside to be greeted by the familiar unwashed smell that permeated the carpets and furnishings. Todd was so familiar with it that he barely noticed.

From the hallway he could hear petrified screams coming from the living room and assumed that his mother, Sandra, and stepdad, Kev, were watching yet another horror film. As he opened the living room door, the stale odour of filth combined with that of booze and cigs. His mother and stepdad sat gulping extra-strong lager from cans, their attention never drifting from the large TV screen despite his presence. The can-sized ring marks on the coffee table spoke of many evenings spent in a similar way.

'What you watching?' he asked for the sake of something to say.

'Shush,' warned Kev.

Sandra, who had been about to respond, stayed silent but she glanced briefly across at Todd and flashed an apologetic smile. Her cheeks were flushed from the booze, lending some colour to her otherwise pallid complexion. She was thin and appeared dowdier every time Todd saw her, her outdated clothes swamping her skinny frame.

Kev was slim too apart from his huge beer belly, but he was also muscular, a result of his days spent labouring on various building sites. A self-professed man's man, he often went for a drink with the lads straight from work. But sometimes he stayed in, choosing to drink at home instead and encouraging Sandra to join him.

'Can I have a packet of crisps?' Todd asked.

'There's none left,' grumbled Kev. 'Those two greedy little bastards have eaten them all. Now shut up and let me watch this.'

Todd tutted. He hated it when his stepdad referred to his brothers like that and had told him so but each time he did, he received a slap for his cheek. So, most times he let it pass without comment.

'Is there owt else I can have?' asked Todd who had rushed out that evening without his tea, eager to get out of the house before his detestable stepdad was due home.

'I'll have a look,' said Sandra.

She was getting out of her seat when Kev stopped her. 'No you fuckin' won't! If he wanted summat to eat, then he should have been here for his fuckin' tea.'

His attention switched back to the TV screen. 'Look, you've made me miss what's happened now.'

He got up and angrily pressed at the buttons of the video

player, rewinding the film so he could recapture the parts he'd missed.

'Please, Mam, can I have summat to eat?' Todd pleaded.

'You've already been told no!' yelled Kev. 'Jesus Christ! Can I get no peace in this house? I'm trying to fuckin' watch this. I've already had to smack that pair of little bastards for making a racket and now I've got you at it.'

Todd didn't argue any further. He knew he was wasting his time, so he decided he'd sneak some food out of the kitchen while his stepdad was absorbed in the film. But his first concern was for his younger brothers, Ryan and Dylan. Aged nine and ten, they were younger than Todd and had been born to a different father than him.

After her two marriages had failed, Sandra had chosen not to marry again or to have any more children. Todd was glad because he didn't want to be officially related to Kev although he was still expected to refer to him as his stepdad. It also meant there wouldn't be any kids with Kev's blood running through their veins.

Todd got on with his half-brothers even though they could be a menace at times. They were the only siblings he had and he felt protective of them. Knowing how nasty his stepdad could be, Todd rushed upstairs to see if his brothers were alright.

He pushed open the door to the room his brothers shared. Todd spotted Dylan first who was lying on the bottom bunk reading a comic, a look of sadness clouding his boyish features. Todd looked up to the top bunk to find Ryan lying on his bed with his head buried in his pillow and the sound of sobbing coming from him.

'Ryan, are you alright?' asked Todd, striding over and laying a comforting hand on Ryan's back.

Ryan looked up, his face smeared by tears and mucus. 'He hit me,' he said in a small voice.

'Why?' asked Todd.

As Ryan swallowed back a sob, Dylan answered his question. 'He hit us both for making a noise while they were watching telly, but he hit Ryan the hardest.'

'What, with his hand?'

'No. He used his belt.'

'Show me,' Todd said to Ryan.

Ryan shook his head, so Todd addressed his brother. 'Where did he hit him?'

'On his legs. Show him, Ryan.'

With his bottom lip trembling, Ryan lowered his trousers. Already annoyed, Todd held his breath in apprehension. But it was just as bad as he had anticipated. Ryan winced as the material of his trousers brushed against the backs of his legs and, once he had pulled his trousers down sufficiently, Todd could see why. There were a series of red welts along the backs of his thighs.

A surge of anger shot through Todd till his limbs were rigid with tension. He felt a burning hatred so intense that it seemed as though his head was about to burst into flames.

'The fuckin' twat!' he yelled, turning to exit the room.

'No don't!' yelled Ryan. 'Don't say anything to him or he'll hit you too.'

'I don't give a shit!' said Todd. 'He's not fuckin' getting away with that. You two stay here.'

He stormed out of the room and raced downstairs, shoving the living room door open.

'You fuckin' bastard!' he bawled at his stepfather. Then his eyes flitted to his mother. 'Have you seen what he's done?'

Sandra, suddenly appearing defensive, said, 'They were misbehaving so he gave them a smack.'

'Gave them a smack? He took the fuckin' belt to them! I can't believe you're defending him. That's well out of order.'

His mother looked shamefaced and was struggling to support her bullying partner till Kev stepped in. 'Don't you fuckin' talk to your mother like that! I was giving them some discipline, that's all. And I'll do what the fuck I like in my own home.'

'You're disgusting!' shouted Todd. 'You're just a fuckin' bully. You should try picking on someone your own size instead of little kids.'

'If you don't shut your fuckin' mouth, you'll get some too.'

'Make me, you sick bastard.'

Kev turned to Sandra. 'Have you heard how your fuckin' son speaks to me? Are you going to let him get away with that?'

'Todd, don't antagonise him, love,' she pleaded.

Her compliancy angered Todd further. 'You're pathetic! Why don't you stand up to him for once?'

'You're pushing your fuckin' luck!' shouted Kev, getting up from his chair.

'No, you are. Just because she lets you do what you want, you think you can get away with...'

Before he had chance to say anything further, Kev had sped across the room and was gripping him by the throat. 'You cheeky little bastard. Just who the fuckin' hell do you think you're speaking to? I'll teach you not to fuckin' backchat me.'

Todd could feel the strength of his stepfather's grip forcing his windpipe inwards till he struggled to get his breath. Unwilling to give in without a fight, he clawed at Kev's hands, digging his nails in till he broke the skin. In the background he could hear his mother pleading with Kev.

'Let go of him, Kev love. He's learnt his lesson now. Kev! Kev, you're gonna kill him.'

She must have got through to Kev because he eventually released his hold. Todd gasped for air while his stepdad walked away with a smirk on his face muttering, 'That'll fuckin' teach the little cunt.'

Todd still hadn't recovered from his ordeal, but he felt so irate by his stepdad's words that he charged him from behind, aiming wild punches at his back and satisfied when one connected with the back of his head.

As Kev turned round to retaliate, Sandra leapt between them. 'Don't, Kev, please. He's learnt his lesson. Let me deal with him.'

But Kev wasn't pacified so easily. He pushed against Sandra, trying to get to her son.

'Please, Kev. Calm down,' she pleaded. 'I'll deal with him. Then we can sit and finish the film off.'

Kev pushed her to one side and began aiming a series of powerful punches at Todd's head and torso while Todd held up his hands to try to defend himself. Sandra stepped in again and was rewarded with a sharp blow to her nose, which burst into a crimson spray.

She held her hands up to her face and shrieked with pain. 'Kev, no! Please.'

The sight of the blood brought Kev to his senses and for a moment he stood spellbound, taking in the sight of Sandra's damaged face. 'You shouldn't have got in between us, you silly cow.'

He retreated to his armchair and Sandra dragged Todd off into the kitchen. Defeated, Todd complied with her wishes. The shock of the blood had unsettled him as well. He cared too much for his mother to see her hurt and felt partly responsible. But he also hated the way she was so complicit in Kev's bullying behaviour.

'Sit down there,' she said to Todd, leading him to a kitchen chair. Then, noticing that Todd's face was also now bleeding, she said, 'Let me get a wet cloth to clean you up. It'll be alright in a minute once he's calmed down.'

'It's not alright though, is it, Mum? He shouldn't be allowed to get away with it. Why do you let him treat your kids like that?'

'Shush,' she cajoled, bringing a damp flannel over to him.

Todd angrily pushed her hand away. 'No! You haven't answered me. Why do you fuckin' let him get away with it?'

'Don't, Todd. You know how it is,' she said docilely. He's not that bad really, y'know. If it wasn't for him, we'd be out on the streets. It's his wages that keep a roof over our heads. And if it wasn't for him, then you and your brothers wouldn't have half the things you have.'

'What things? He spends most of his money on booze and cigs.'

'Eh, now you know that's not true. Look...' Then she swung open the cupboard door and, as if to illustrate her point, she withdrew a packet of cakes. 'Here, have one of these,' she said, tearing the packet open. 'But don't let him know.'

Todd stared at her, incredulous. He knew he was wasting his time pleading with her to leave his abusive stepdad. He'd tried so many times before but all to no avail.

As if interpreting his silence as acquiescence, she added, 'He's not so bad really, y'know. It's just that temper of his. But you can make it easier on yourself by not upsetting him.'

'What? And just put up with it like you do, d'you mean?'

Sandra didn't reply. Instead, she withdrew two of the cakes and placed them on a plate, which she then put in front of him. Todd didn't see the point in arguing any further with her. And besides, he was starving. So, he took one of the cakes and rammed it into his mouth while his mother wiped the blood from her own face.

He was still fuming about the situation but currently there was nothing he could do. It wouldn't stop him trying in the future though. He harboured a festering resentment against his stepdad and knew he couldn't just stand by like his mother and watch him abuse his two brothers. And one day, when he was big enough and strong enough, he'd make sure he got his own back on the nasty bastard.

7

Sept 1986

It was a couple of months later. Macca hadn't seen anything of Joanne in that time except when she was with her parents, but he'd been too busy with his friends to let it worry him. He, Leroy and Spinxy were spending increasing amounts of time in the company of Todd and Shay, and Macca was enjoying it.

The gang had fallen into a natural hierarchy with Todd as their leader. Macca was the person Todd had taken to the most, even though he had known Shay longer. Macca presumed it was because he and Todd were usually the ones with the ideas whereas Shay, like Leroy, was a bit haphazard. It didn't seem to trouble Shay though as he had hit it off with Leroy.

Spinxy was the odd one out. Macca knew it was because he was a bit slower than the others, less cool, less streetwise and always desperate to impress. But Macca knew he was a good mate who would always have his back.

After school, Macca found Todd on the estate., aimlessly

wandering around with his head bent forward. 'Alright, mate?' he asked.

Todd looked up and Macca was surprised to see that he was wearing a polo neck top, which wasn't his usual style. It reminded Macca of the time at school when Todd had turned up with his collar buttoned all the way up and his tie fastened tightly. Macca had thought it strange at the time but he hadn't known Todd well enough to probe. It made him wonder what Todd was hiding.

'Why are you wearing that?' 'Eh, you've not got a hickey, have you?' he teased.

Todd heaved and let out a puff of air. Then, after checking nobody could see, he pulled down his collar saying, 'It's to hide this.'

Macca stared aghast when he saw the heavy bruising to Todd's throat. 'Fuckin' hell! Has someone jumped you?'

'You could say that,' Todd muttered.

'Who? Was it on the way home last night?'

He was already thinking of ways that their gang of five could exact their revenge on whoever had attacked Todd, but his friend silenced him when he heaved another sigh and said, 'It was my stepdad. And it's not the first time he's done it. He fuckin' loves strangling me.'

Todd was shocked. 'Your stepdad? Fuckin' hell! Why would he do that?'

'Because he's a cunt. He's always having a go at me. And my brothers. You should have seen our Ryan's legs a couple of months ago where he'd took the belt to him just because he wouldn't shut up while him and my mum were watching the telly and getting pissed.'

'But why? Why did he do that to you?'

Todd nodded. 'Because I had a go back at him. I'm not having him talking to me like I'm a piece of shit. He's strangled me before. It's his favourite punishment, but this time was worse. Every time he does it, he goes a bit further then lets go just in time. I swear, mate, he'll fuckin' kill me one of these days.'

'Was your mum there? Couldn't she have stopped him or is she too scared of him?'

'I dunno. She does try to stop him but he just goes fuckin' apeshit. She still stays with him though no matter what he does. I've told her to get rid, but she won't.'

'Why not?'

''Cos she says we need the money. My mum doesn't work and they're both pissheads. She likes having a drink with him and he's not that bad to her. It's me and my brothers that cop for it. I don't think he wants us. He just wants her all to himself and he can't stand the fact that she's got kids.'

'If your mum won't do owt then why don't you?'

'I did. Why d'you think he fuckin' did this to me?'

'No, I don't mean that. I mean, why don't you report him? Y'know, tell the cops or summat.'

'Oh yeah, like they'd be bothered about anything I've got to say. They'll think I'm just a kid. Besides, with a family like mine, I've got no fuckin' chance.

'Anyway, suppose they did take notice of me. What would they do? Put him inside and put us kids into care. My mum would go fuckin' mad. She'd blame me for splitting the family up and for him being sent down. Believe it or not, she loves the jerk and she'd probably never forgive me.

'And what would I do then? I know I hate living with

that bastard, but I don't wanna end up in care. I wouldn't be able to see my brothers or my mates. Ryan and Dylan would be taken somewhere for younger kids and fuck knows where I'd end up. So, I've got no fuckin' choice. I've just got to put up with it, haven't I?'

Later that evening Macca was home alone. His mother had gone out and told him to stay in. Often, he'd sneak out and make sure he was back before the pubs shut. But tonight, it was pouring down with rain, so he decided he'd prefer to stay in and watch TV.

He'd finished *The Bill* and by the time his mother returned home, he was viewing an X-rated film on the video recorder she had acquired. From what he could hear, she wasn't alone. He quickly switched over the TV so his mother wouldn't know what he'd been watching.

When she walked into the living room, she was upbeat, smiling as she said, 'Hiya, son, are you still up?'

Macca could tell by the slight slurring of her words that she'd had a few drinks. He nodded in response and his mother's eyes strayed to the TV screen. 'What's this you're watching?'

Macca shrugged as she took in the late-night music show, knowing it wasn't his type of thing. 'Nowt really,' he replied. 'I was just gonna go to bed 'cos there's nowt on.'

His mother gave him a knowing look then said, 'This is Bernie.' A man in his early forties stumbled into the room. 'Bernie, this is my lad, Mark.'

The man sized him up through bleary eyes then slurred, 'Hello, son, pleased to meet you.'

He walked over to Macca and shook his hand in an exaggerated gesture then stepped back towards Debbie, his stray hand eventually finding her waist. 'He's a fine-looking lad,' he said. Then, giving her waist a squeeze, he added, 'Takes after his mum.'

Debbie giggled coquettishly. 'Go on with yer.' Then she addressed Macca. 'Eeh, we've had a lovely night. Bernie took me for a meal, didn't you, Bernie?'

'Only the best for you, love,' he said patting her on the backside.

Debbie squealed in delight then said, 'Behave yerself. My son's sat over there.'

'Oops, sorry,' said Bernie. Then he eyed Debbie's backside appreciatively and added, 'Can't help myself when I'm around you.'

Debbie grinned then said to Macca, 'It was a lovely Chinese restaurant in the city centre called the Kwok Man. I had chicken and sweetcorn soup for starters, and the sweet and sour pork for the main course was gorgeous. Wasn't it, Bernie?'

She looked at Bernie who was now leaning against her with his arm draped across her shoulders. 'What? Oh yeah. It was bloody gorgeous.'

'We'll have to take you and my mum one night, won't we, Bernie?'

'Yeah sure,' he replied but his response was lacklustre, and Macca knew straightaway that it would never happen.

Macca had seen enough. He hated it when his mum got a new fella and started acting all girly. It was pathetic in a woman of her age. And this guy was a total jerk, all lechy and smarmy.

He got up off the chair, switched off the TV and announced, 'I'm going to bed.'

'Oh, alright, love. See you in the morning,' said Debbie.

As Macca made his way upstairs, he heard Bernie say, 'Are you putting some music on, Debbie?'

'I can't, the hi-fi's broken,' his mum replied.

Macca felt a moment's pity for his mum. She'd been going to get the hi-fi fixed for months but never seemed to find the money for it. And she loved her music.

His feelings of pity were soon surpassed by other thoughts. He knew his mother was secretly pleased to see him leave the room. It was obvious from the way she and this guy were acting that they wanted to get it on with each other. He felt irritated at the thought and a bit disgusted. How could she, with a creep like that?

He stamped his way up the hall deliberately making as much noise as he could to convey his distaste. Then he made sure he slammed the bathroom and bedroom doors before he finally settled into bed.

But when he tried to go to sleep he could still hear his mother and the man called Bernie who said, 'Come on, Debs, are we putting the TV back on, or what?'

'Shush,' Debbie replied then she giggled again before saying, 'Alright then but keep it low. Mark's trying to sleep.'

The TV drowned out the sound of their voices apart from the occasional giggle and Macca recoiled, imagining what that seedy man could be doing to his mum. He was still feeling irritated. Why couldn't his mum and dad have stayed together then she wouldn't have to carry on like that? But his parents would never have stayed together if what his grandma said was anything to go by. According to her his dad was a heavy drinker who had never been any good.

He still saw his dad sometimes and got on with him alright. He always asked Macca how he was getting on and gave him a treat when he saw him. But his visits had become less and less frequent over the years. Now they had reached the point where the atmosphere between them was awkward because it was like talking to a stranger.

Macca knew his mum was getting a name for herself. He'd overheard the gossips in the estate shop. At the time he'd felt like contradicting them, but he didn't because he had no defence. They were right. His mother carried on like an old slapper.

Despite all that, Macca loved his mum to bits. She might have had her faults, but she had always been there for him, unlike his dad. Macca knew deep down that the only reason his mother entertained so many men was because she struggled with being on her own and would have liked to find someone decent to settle with. But for some reason she always attracted the dregs and they never hung around for long.

He wished, not for the first time, that there was a way he could earn some money. Then his mother wouldn't have to keep bringing these creepy men back home and he wouldn't have to listen to the gossip about her.

8

Oct 1986

Macca and his friends were in the company of Shell and Trisha. Leroy was larking around trying to impress them and Macca could tell by the look on Shay's face that he was also keen. But Macca had no interest in the two girls. He didn't fancy Trisha. Shell was quite pretty, but she had been around.

In fact, Shell was the girl that Macca had lost his virginity to a couple of months prior. At the time, he'd not seen Joanne for a while and when Shell had come on strong, his friends had encouraged him to go for it. Eager to pop his cherry because most of his mates had, and curious to know what it was like, he'd gone along with it.

But he'd known as soon as Shell had given in to him on that first night that she wasn't the girl for him. She'd become clingy afterwards, expecting to see him again, but Macca didn't want to carry on. Girls like her were only good for one thing and, once he'd found out about her reputation, he didn't want to be with her.

'Eh, remember that night when we broke into the school, Macca?' asked Leroy, looking at the girls for a reaction. 'It was fuckin' ace, wannit? I'd have loved to have seen Robinson's face when he found his Bunsen burners were missing and then saw them all over the school field.'

'Turn it in, Lee. That was two years ago.'

'So? It was still ace.'

Macca was embarrassed. He didn't want to be reminded of the stupid things he'd done when he was younger. It wasn't as if they'd gained anything from it. Leroy had wanted to get at his schoolteachers, and Macca had gone along with it.

'What the fuck did you do that for?' asked Todd who was obviously unimpressed.

'Teach them a lesson,' said Leroy, proudly. 'Ha ha, teach them a lesson, makes a change from them thinking they can teach us summat.'

Todd shook his head. 'Come on, we're going.'

He moved away, and Macca and Shay fell into step with him, followed by Spinxy. Leroy whispered something to Shell before breaking away from the girls and joining his friends.

'Why are we going?' he asked. 'That fuckin' Shell was well gagging for it.'

'Why don't you keep your fuckin' gob shut?' said Todd.

'What d'you mean?'

'Telling them you broke into the school. How d'you know you can trust 'em?'

'They're not gonna grass us up. That fuckin' Shell fancies

me. Anyway, it was two years ago. The police aren't gonna do owt now.'

'And how do you know that?'

Leroy shrugged and, as if he knew he wouldn't get anywhere arguing with Todd, he turned to his friend, Shay. 'Eh, have you ever hotwired a car?'

'Yeah, course I have,' said Shay.

'It's dead fuckin' easy, innit? Me and Macca got a Sierra one night. It was well smart.'

Todd looked at him, but this time there was no scorn in his eyes. 'That's good to know,' he said. 'It might come in handy sometime.'

'How do you mean?' asked Leroy eagerly.

'Well, you won't be robbing no fuckin' schools with us. It's a waste of time if you're getting fuck all out of it. We need to do stuff that pays.'

'Like what?' asked Shay.

'Well, I've been doing a bit of thinking. We've been together for a couple of months now and we need to step things up. With five of us, there's all kinds we could do. This isn't about pissing about like kids. We need to do things that will pay, and I don't mean drugs either. I'm not having anything to do with fuckin' drugs. It causes too many problems. Druggies and alkies, I can't be doing with 'em.'

'Sounds good to me,' said Macca who was learning to trust Todd more and more since he had got to know him.

'OK, well I've had an idea,' Todd continued. 'And I need to know you're all up for it. Don't be agreeing with it and then backing out. We all need to stick together.'

'Alright. Tell us what it is, and we'll tell you whether we're up for it.'

'OK, but if you're not up for it, you've gotta leave the gang and you can't tell anyone else what we get up to.'

'What about a gang name?' asked Leroy.

'No, we're not bothering with that. Names are for druggie gangs and, like I said, I don't want any part of that.'

He had stopped walking by this time, and he looked at each of the lads in turn who were standing around their self-appointed leader. He waited until each of them had indicated their agreement. Then he took a deep breath and outlined exactly what he wanted them to do.

Joanne was sitting in the living room at home watching *Wogan* with her parents. It was a while since her father had admonished her for wearing makeup and hanging about the streets with Trisha and Shell. After that, her father had voiced his opinion many times, convincing her that if she carried on going about with those two girls, she would get a name for herself. It had worked because she no longer hung about the streets. But life had become boring.

Nowadays, her only form of entertainment was the occasional cinema visit with her sister or a visit to the home of one of her school friends. In the case of the latter, it was mainly on the odd weekend because they didn't live close by. Her father wouldn't let her come home alone on the bus late at night but also refused to pick her up.

Joanne was now in the last year of school and her sister,

Mandy, was in the sixth form studying for A levels. This wasn't the life Joanne wanted but she'd decided to put up with it for now until she was old enough to do something about it. She wanted glamour and excitement with a boyfriend and an active social life. Instead, she had rare nights out and a monthly meal out with her parents, sister and younger brother.

The programme ended and Joanne's father glared across at her before saying, 'How come you're not upstairs studying like your sister?'

Here we go again, thought Joanne who was sick of being compared unfavourably with Mandy.

'I've finished my homework. It only took me half an hour.'

'Are you sure?'

'Yeah, it doesn't take me long. I'm not doing A levels, am I?'

'No, and you won't be doing well in your O levels either if you don't put the work in.'

'I don't need to do well. I won't need them for a job.'

'It depends on the job,' said her mother, Gillian, who often backed her husband up.

'Are you still going on about working in a bloody shop?' asked Alan with a look of scorn.

'Yeah, why not?' said Joanne, sulkily.

'Because there's no bloody prospects, that's why not. You'd be better off staying on at school and getting some Alevels, then you'll be able to get a good job.'

'But I don't want to,' Joanne complained. 'I want to leave at the end of this year. I hate studying.'

Her mother frowned before saying, 'Well, Alan, I suppose not everybody's academic like Mandy.'

Alan turned his glare onto her and fumed. 'She's not working in a bloody shop. Over my dead body. What sort of prospects will that give her?'

Gillian turned to her daughter. 'Have you thought about any other options?'

'Yeah,' said Joanne. 'I want to work in a fashion shop or go into hairdressing.'

Alan scowled at his daughter. 'Oh, hairdressing now, is it? Washing people's greasy heads and sweeping up? Is that how you want to spend your days?'

'But I wouldn't be doing that forever. Only while I'm training.'

Joanne was surprised when her mother defended her again. 'Well, I suppose it has better prospects than working in a shop. There's a woman at work called Freda whose daughter is running her own hairdressing shop, and she's doing well out of it from what Freda tells me. In fact, Freda's always complaining that her daughter earns more than she does working in the office.'

'Yeah, but from what you've told me, Freda's never going to be more than a filing clerk,' her father countered.

'Well, yes, there is that. But you'd have to climb quite a way up the ladder at our place to be earning more than Freda's daughter. And our Joanne might not be cut out for working in an office.'

Alan sighed and flicked the channel over, indicating that it was the end of the conversation, but Joanne could tell he wasn't happy. She, on the other hand, smiled inwardly, grateful to her mother for sticking up for her for once, and content that she had won a battle in the war against her dad's imposing standards.

9

Oct 1986

'House break-ins,' said Todd matter-of-factly.

Macca heard Spinxy's audible intake of breath as Todd looked around the group, gauging their reactions. Shay's expression was impassive while Leroy had a look of excitement and Spinxy one of shock. Macca was just as shocked as his friend, but he had a lot of respect for Todd, so he decided to listen to what he had to say.

Todd's words seemed to have silenced them and they all stared wide-eyed as he continued.

'This is a bit different from grabbing a few cigs and toffees from the shop or breaking into a fuckin' school, so if any of you are worried about it, best say so now.'

Nobody spoke as Todd continued to look at each of them in turn. His gaze settled on Spinxy who twitched nervously.

'Spinxy?' asked Todd.

'What?' As he spoke, Spinxy flashed a questioning look at Macca as if seeking his approval.

'It's up to you,' said Macca.

'Are *you* up for it?' Spinxy asked tentatively.

'Might be. Let's see what he has to say.'

'OK,' said Todd. 'But if I tell you stuff you've got to promise not to tell anyone else what we're up to. If we get caught, I'll know who's fuckin' ratted on us and we'll get you.'

'Alright,' said Spinxy, and the other lads nodded.

Once he'd gained their agreement, Todd continued. 'OK. Well, for a kick-off, we won't be doing them round here. There's too much chance of us being recognised and, besides, nobody's got fuck all worth nicking. So, I think we should go somewhere where they've got money.'

'Where?' asked Shay.

'Stockport.'

'Stockport?' asked Macca with disdain, thinking of journeys there on the bus with his mum and grandma.

'Yeah, my aunty used to live in Adswood. My uncle used to take us there in his car and there's some fuckin' well smart areas round there with massive houses.'

Shay had a puzzled frown. 'What, in Adswood?'

Macca could understand his bewilderment. Adswood wasn't exactly one of the better areas in Stockport.

'No, near there,' replied Todd. 'Erm, Cheadle I think was one of the areas and Bramhall. My uncle used to take us all over the place.'

'Do they still live there?' asked Macca.

'No, do they fuck. I'm not shittin' on my own doorstep. I told you; we're going where no one knows us.'

'I don't know,' said Spinxy who had finally plucked up the courage to speak out. 'I mean, it's not like doing a bit of shoplifting, is it? These are people's houses.'

'So what? They can well afford it. You should see the size of the fuckin' houses near Stockport. They'd hardly miss a bit of stuff. Anyway, they've got it all insured so they'll soon get it back.'

'How will we get there?' Leroy chipped in.

Todd smiled. 'That's where you come in. You and Shay. You said you're good at hotwiring cars, didn't you?'

'Yeah but, some of 'em can be a twat to start up.'

'That's why the two of you can do it together. You should be able to pull it off between you. And I want you to get motors that can shift in case the police are after us.'

Macca felt a rumble of fear in his tummy at the mention of the police, but Todd was so animated that what he had to say also excited him. The questions continued to come from the rest of the gang, and it wasn't long before Todd had fully outlined his plan.

Leroy and Shay would steal a car on the same night that they were to do the job. Todd had insisted that only the two of them went for the car as a large group of lads would arouse more suspicion. Leroy and Shay would pick the other lads up at one central location and go straight to the job.

The car wouldn't be targeted at random. They would choose a location where the owners left their cars unattended for some time as this would also mean that it would be a while before the car was reported as stolen. One of the ideas Todd had put forward was cinemas at the start of a late-night film but he was open to other suggestions as they fleshed out their plans.

When it came to targeting properties, this would also be planned in advance. Todd suggested they do a recce in a specific area a few days beforehand and choose the house based on ease of access, quick getaway, location et cetera.

Todd had even decided the type of objects they would go for: electricals that were high value but easy to shift as well as jewellery and cash. When asked where they would sell the goods without arousing suspicion, he revealed that the same uncle who had taken Todd around well-to-do areas had also told him about a second-hand shop that fenced stolen goods.

With this revelation, it was obvious to Macca where Todd had got the idea from in the first place, but it was also obvious that Todd had put a lot of thought into their proposed criminal venture. Unlike Leroy, Todd wasn't just doing this for kicks. He wanted to make money from it. And, the way he was talking, Macca was so confident they could pull it off that he agreed to go in on it.

The other lads were all of a like mind even though Spinxy had seemed reluctant at first. Macca wasn't sure whether he had agreed just to be a part of the gang, and he promised himself that he would have a quiet word with Spinxy when he got him alone at school. He didn't want to drag Spinxy into something he might regret but he also didn't want Spinxy bottling it and letting them all down.

Once he had gained all their agreement, Todd said, 'This is just the start, guys. If you can pull this off then there's all sorts we can do in the future. We'll just use the stolen cars for house jobs at the moment but we could even look into selling them on when we find someone who buys stolen cars. Then there's post offices, late-night petrol stations, all sorts. I tell you, we're gonna be fuckin' rich!'

'Ace!' said Leroy, and Shay was wearing a smile too.

Macca was busy thinking about the implications, but he liked the idea of having money in his pocket.

'So,' continued Todd. 'If everyone's up for it, we need to lay down some rules. Firstly, if summat goes down we all need to back each other up.'

'How d'you mean?' asked Spinxy.

'Well, if the cops come after us, we need to back each other's stories. And if there's any trouble from anyone we deal with, then we're all in it together. Oh, and, like I said before, no fuckin' drugs. Is everyone alright with that?'

'Sure,' said Macca while the other lads muttered their assent.

Macca was liking the sound of this more and more. Not only was he now the member of a gang, but he also liked Todd as a leader especially because he was loyal and seemed trustworthy.

When he went home at the end of the night, Macca's feelings had shifted from nervousness and excitement to contentedness. It might be crime, but it was also an opportunity. He was sick of having no money. Sick of going without. And sick of seeing his mother prostitute herself to a load of lowlife scum. Now Macca was going to earn his own money. And that would change his and his mum's lives for the better.

10

Nov 1986

'Are you sure you're OK with this?' Macca asked Spinxy for the umpteenth time.

'Yeah,' snapped Spinxy before he tried to soften his tone by adding, 'It'll be a fuckin' buzz, mate.'

'OK, see you later then.'

It was the night of their planned house break-in and they had just left school for the evening. Macca watched his friend walk away in the direction of his own home. He'd quizzed him about his motives for wanting to take part in the burglary several times until Spinxy had eventually grown tired of it.

Spinxy kept insisting he was fine, but Macca knew him of old. He tried to mask his unease by acting casual, but Macca could see right through it in the way he snapped at him and the way he seemed to drift off into a world of his own as though things were preying on his mind.

Macca could understand it; he was uneasy himself. He'd never done anything like this before, but Todd made it sound so inviting: the prospect of easy money. And that was something that both Macca and Spinxy craved. It was fortunate that Macca had a good relationship with Todd who understood his qualms and had agreed for him and Spinxy to play a lesser role in the burglary.

Macca made the rest of the way home alone. He was now in his last school year, and he no longer saw Todd there as Todd had left in the summer. Throughout the journey home thoughts ran through his mind about the forthcoming evening. They were to meet at five near Macca's home, because Todd wanted to go through the final arrangements again.

It wasn't long before that time arrived. 'Right, don't forget,' Todd said, turning to Leroy and Shay, 'you need to be outside the social club by eight o'clock. You already know the cars to go for. Out of the three cars we sussed, at least one of them should be there. It's got to be one of them three though. All of 'em are fast cars, and the owners all stay in the club getting pissed till at least twelve. That gives us four hours till they'll notice their car's missing.'

None of them passed comment about the drink-driving. To them it was normal for some adults to behave in that way, at least those who could afford a car anyway.

'I know,' said Shay. 'We've already been over this.'

'Well now we're fuckin' going over it again. If we want this to work, then it's all got to be right. Trust me, I know what I'm fuckin' talking about.'

Macca picked up on Todd's irritability. He seemed on edge and Macca guessed it was because he didn't want to risk anything going wrong. Macca thought again about how Todd's uncle had influenced his friend's life. He was starting to realise by now that Todd's uncle must have spent a lot of time on the wrong side of the law.

'Right,' Todd continued, turning to Macca and Spinxy this time. 'Meet me here at ten to eight. Then we'll go to Byson Street, round the corner from the club, and wait for Shay and Lee to pick us up once they've got the car. And don't be fuckin' late any of you or…'

But Macca missed the rest of what Todd was saying because at that moment he spotted his grandma heading towards them on the way to visit his mother.

'Fuck, it's Two Chins,' he whispered. 'My gran.'

Todd looked up and nodded and all the lads went quiet as they watched Macca's grandma waddle up the street.

'Hello, Mrs McNeil,' said Todd as Macca's grandma drew closer.

Macca was surprised that Todd knew his grandma, but he followed suit. 'Hiya, Gran.'

He received a scowl in response as his grandma eyed Todd and Shay warily before her eyes settled back on him. 'Come on, I've got some pies for your tea. You don't want them to go cold.'

Macca looked at his friends, shrugged then fell in step with his grandma.

'What the bloody hell's going on?' she asked as soon as they drew away from the boys.

'What d'you mean?'

'You!' she said. 'Hanging about with the likes of them. Don't you know that bleedin' Todd's a villain, and the other one's not much better either?'

Suddenly Macca realised how Todd knew his grandma. Macca had overlooked the fact that she lived on the same side of the estate as Todd and Shay. And, judging by what she had just said, she also knew them.

'None of his bloody family are any good,' she continued. 'A whole family of bleedin' villains. But what I want to know is, what are you doing hanging about with them?'

'Todd's alright. Shay is as well. We have a good laugh.'

'Aye, I bet you do, getting up to no bleedin' good. And what was that about not being late?'

A feeling of trepidation gripped Macca and he felt his stomach growl. This was all he needed, for his grandma to go poking her nose in. 'Nowt,' he lied. 'It was just about meeting up later.'

'Oh no, you don't,' she said. 'Not if I've got anything to do with it.'

'It's up to my mum, not you,' he said, incensed now by her heavy-handedness.

'Oh, is it?' she asked. 'Well, we'll see what your mum's got to say when she finds out who you've been hanging about with.'

Indoors the complaints continued. 'Do you realise who he's been knocking about with?' Doris said to Macca's mum. 'Only that bleedin' Todd Brown.'

'Who's that?' asked Debbie, nonplussed.

'Todd Brown. The Browns!' Doris stressed. 'Haven't you heard of the Browns? A right bunch of villains, they are. They live a couple of streets from me. I've told you about them before. His uncle's a bloody thief, always up to all kinds. They used to live round here till they did a moonlight flit and moved to Stockport. I was bleedin' glad when they did. I was sick of the washing going missing off the line. And now *he's* knocking around with them.'

Debbie turned to Macca, and he saw the shocked expression on her face.

'Todd's alright, Mum, honest,' Macca offered before she had chance to speak.

'Oh no he isn't,' said Doris. 'He's always up to no good. I've heard about him bloody fighting and him and that other one, Shay, getting banned from the shop near me because they were always pinching from it. And now our Mark's planning on going out with them later. I've told you before, Debbie, you need to keep your eye on him, or he'll be up to all sorts.'

Debbie was by now recovering from the initial shock and she too rounded on Macca. 'You're not going out,' she said. 'You can stay in, then I know where you are. And in future, stay away from them.'

'Aw, Mum,' Macca complained. 'I haven't even done owt.'

'No but it's what you're gonna do that I'm worried about,' his grandma chipped in.

Debbie also levelled her next comment at Macca. 'You heard what your grandma said. You're not going about with lads like them. They'll be getting you into all kinds of trouble. And I've got enough on my plate.'

Macca, knowing he had no chance of winning an argument against both women, blew out his cheeks. His grandma took the moment's lull to hand him the bag of pies, saying, 'Right, now go and put them on a plate and bring me the brown sauce.'

Macca grabbed the bag and stormed out of the room, annoyed that his plans had been foiled but also concerned.

If his mother had stopped him going out, then how the hell was he going to take part in the house break-in? And how was he going to get word to his mates that he wouldn't be joining them?

11

Nov 1986

Macca had been in his room since not long after tea. He didn't fancy hanging around while Two Chins was in that mood. She'd only carry on having a go at him. Besides, he needed to think about how he was going to get out of the house now that he'd been grounded.

He couldn't let the lads down, not when Todd had put so much thought into the job. And they'd all been involved in the preparation. Macca was also conscious of the fact that if he let the lads down on their first ever proper job, they might never trust him again.

Macca didn't have a TV in his room as his mother couldn't afford it. Nor was there a clock in his bedroom, so for the last hour he had been pacing between his and his mother's bedroom, checking her bedside clock to see what time it was. In between he felt bored as he made feeble attempts at school homework that didn't interest him at the best of times, let alone when he had so much else on his mind.

His plan was to sneak out of the house once his grandma had gone. There was no point doing it while she was here because she'd be listening out for him and would soon put a stop to it. Then he'd get nothing but earache from her for days after.

His mother, on the other hand, was much easier to deal with. If it hadn't been for his grandma, she probably wouldn't even have grounded him, and even if she found out that he'd sneaked out, she probably wouldn't do much about it.

He was surprised that his grandma was still here as she usually complained that she didn't like to stay out till late with all the thugs hanging about the streets. Finally, at seven o'clock, just as he was beginning to despair, he heard the living room door open and, as he listened, he caught the conversation taking place in the hallway between his grandma and mother although it was his grandma who was doing most of the talking.

'Now, don't forget what I've told you, Debbie, keep your eye on him.'

It was obvious to Macca who the 'him' referred to. Then he heard her say, 'Right, I'll be off. Time's getting on.'

His mother shouted, 'Mark, your grandma's going now.'

Macca came to meet them in the hallway, knowing that he would be expected to say goodbye to his grandma before she went, same as he did every time.'

Doris grabbed him and planted a sloppy kiss on his cheek. 'Right, I'm off,' she repeated. 'Now you behave yourself for your mother.'

'Course I will,' said Macca, feeling a flood of guilt as he tasted the lie on his tongue.

He gave it a few minutes before he chanced coming out of his room again. When he reached the hallway, he could hear dishes clanging about in the sink. That meant his mother was doing the washing up from teatime. A quick glance told him that the kitchen door was open, but he knew that if she was washing up, she would have her back to the door. He needed to make his escape now.

Macca tiptoed along the hallway, catching a glimpse of his mother's back as he passed the kitchen. He carried on stealthily making his way towards the front door, which he opened as quietly as possible then quickly shut it again. He thought he heard his mother calling out, so he raced along the landing of the flats till he reached the stairs, which he took two at a time.

Macca knew he was early for his meeting with Todd and Spinxy, but he'd wanted to make his getaway as soon as he could. He felt relieved just knowing that he'd got out of the flat but now he needed to get away from his home on the off-chance that his mother might come looking for him.

He decided to call at Todd's house and let him know that he was no longer able to meet near his home. But, at the same time, he'd keep an eye out for his grandma just in case she had got waylaid on her way home, and he'd make sure he took a route that didn't pass her house.

Todd was still on edge, the buzz of adrenalin making him fractious. It was so important to him that tonight should go well. He had put a good crew together and was already planning a long-term future for them. Although he got along well with all the lads, who regarded him as their natural leader, he knew that tonight would be a test for them. If they weren't up to doing the job, then he'd have to rethink his plans.

He was particularly fond of Macca who, like him, was bright and full of ideas whereas Shay, although a good friend, was more of a follower than a leader. Leroy was good fun but could be a bit reckless unless he was kept in line. But the biggest worry for Todd was Spinxy. He was well aware that Spinxy was shitting himself about tonight, and he just hoped that he didn't bottle out.

For the whole evening Todd had tried not to get on the wrong side of his stepdad because he didn't need the extra hassle. Not tonight. He was sitting watching TV in the lounge with Kev, his mum and younger brothers when there was a knock at the door.

Todd's eyes shot to the clock. Ten past seven. Who could it be? Kev's words echoed Todd's thoughts when he said, 'Who the fuck's that at this time?'

'I'll get it,' said Todd, an inner instinct telling him that this was somehow connected with him.

He was proved right when he opened the door to find Macca standing there. 'Macca, what the fuck?' he whispered.

'It's OK, I just can't meet near mine. My mum's grounded me, and I've had to sneak out. I don't know how we're gonna tell Spinxy though. Have you got a phone?'

Kev, who must have realised from the voices that the caller was somebody for Todd rather than himself or Sandra, shouted, 'Will you shut the fuckin' door? We're getting a draught in here.'

Todd turned back, hesitated for a moment then focused back on Macca. 'Wait out here. I won't be a minute.'

He grabbed his shoes, a few coins from a pile of change on the kitchen top and a key to his stepdad's garage then dashed from the house without saying goodbye. He'd face the consequences later.

Once outside, he said to Macca, 'Come on, I've got some money for a call box. We'll ring him and get him to go straight to Byson Street. I just hope he's not set off yet.'

12

Nov 1986

Macca and Todd stopped at the first phone box they came across and Todd handed Macca some coins to ring Spinxy. Unfortunately, Spinxy's mum told them he wasn't in.

'Shit,' said Macca. 'He must have set off.'

'OK, well, with a bit of luck he'll go straight to Byson Street.'

The lads took their time heading to Byson Street, taking a circuitous route, so they wouldn't arrive too early. They had just reached the main road when Macca spotted Joanne standing at the bus stop. She was with her parents and sister, Mandy.

As the lads drew nearer, Macca realised that Joanne and her family were all dressed up and he presumed they were going out somewhere. She was wearing a smart leather jacket. Her hair was backcombed and looked freshly styled, which enhanced her pretty features.

He tried to make eye contact as he passed her by.

Despite the scornful look from her father, Macca flashed a full-on grin in Joanne's direction. He was rewarded by a subconscious smile before she let her head drop and looked away. When he and Todd drew further from Joanne and her family, he could hear her father complaining about something and guessed from the way he had eyed him that it was about him and Todd.

'How come you never went out with her?' asked Todd. 'It's obvious she fancies you. She went dead fuckin' red as soon as she saw you.'

'Are you joking?' said Macca. 'Did you see the way her dad looked at me? He's dead fuckin' stuck-up, and her mum too. I wouldn't get near her.'

Todd shrugged. 'It wouldn't fuckin' stop *me*.'

Macca didn't want to continue the conversation. Seeing Joanne and her family all dressed up like that made him realise how different they were from his family. His mum and grandma never took him out in the evening. He wondered for a moment where they might be going dressed like that: the pictures perhaps or maybe for a meal. This realisation, together with the way Joanne's dad had looked at him, brought home to Macca how unattainable she was to him. But he tried to shrug it off. He was too busy at the moment for girls anyway.

By the time they arrived at Byson Street it was ten to eight, so they knew they'd have a wait till Shay and Leroy arrived with the car. What was more concerning was the fact that Spinxy might not arrive in time if at all as he'd still be waiting near to Macca's home.

Todd glanced at his watch. 'Y'know what, I should have waited for him on my own but it's too fuckin' late now. I don't know if he'll get here in time, so we'll have to change the plan a bit just in case.'

The original plan was for Todd and Shay to enter the property while Macca and Spinxy waited outside in the garden and Leroy stayed in the car ready for a quick getaway. They had chosen a house with a tall hedge bordering the road so that they couldn't be spotted by passers-by.

This meant that once Todd and Shay had passed the goods through the window to Macca and Spinxy, they would take them to the front of the garden and put them behind the bushes ready to load the car. When Todd and Shay had finished, they would join Macca and Spinxy and between the four of them they would be able to quickly load the car up, minimising the time that they were in view of the public.

The house was detached and situated on a corner so there was less chance of people from neighbouring houses spotting what they were up to. Another bonus was that, despite the size of the house, it wasn't alarmed.

'You'll have to shift the stuff to the front of the garden yourself if Spinxy doesn't get here in time,' said Todd to Macca. 'But, don't worry, any you can't manage on your own, just put them down under the window. I'll send Shay out just before we've finished so he can help you. Then, once I'm out, we can all load the car.'

'OK,' said Macca, feeling a tremor of trepidation.

Fifteen minutes later and they spotted a flash car approaching them and Macca and Todd were pleased to see Leroy behind the wheel with Shay beside him. Spinxy still hadn't arrived, and Macca glanced nervously around him.

'We'll have to go without him,' snapped Todd.

Macca nodded solemnly and they set off up the street.

They had just turned the corner when Macca spotted Spinxy dashing towards them.

'That's Spinxy!' he yelled. 'Pull over.'

Leroy did as he asked and Spinxy joined them in the car. He plonked himself on the back seat next to Macca, panting with exertion. 'Fuckin' hell, where were you?' he asked.

'We couldn't wait near mine,' Macca replied before explaining what had happened. 'We did try to ring you, but you'd already gone out.'

'Ah, yeah. I called round to a mate's before I came to meet you.'

'Why the fuck would you do that?' demanded Todd.

'Just to see him, that's all.'

'I hope you didn't tell him where you were going.'

'No, did I fuck! I wouldn't do that.'

The lads fell silent, and Macca could sense the tension in the car. He glanced at Spinxy who had beads of sweat on his forehead and Macca guessed that it wasn't just from running to meet them.

Eventually they arrived in Cheadle and parked up outside the house they had earmarked. Macca could feel his heart hammering in his chest, he was so nervous, but he was also excited. He was about to do his first job.

13

Nov 1986

Everything had been going well. They had several items lined up behind the bushes including a games console, two portable TVs, a boom box, a video recorder, a camera and two kids' money boxes. Spinxy had grabbed the video recorder and was carrying it out to the car. He had reached the end of the drive when Macca saw him rush back in a panic.

'Get down,' he whispered. 'There's a fuckin' guy walking his dog.'

Macca quickly ducked down behind the bushes and turned to look at Todd and Shay who were making their way towards him carrying a large TV. 'Quick,' he whispered. 'Get down here.'

Todd and Shay rushed towards him as fast as they could considering the size of the TV. Macca helped them to place the TV down on the ground, ensuring they didn't make too much noise.

'What the fuck?' asked Shay.

'Shush!' Macca whispered. 'There's a guy coming.'

Macca could feel his adrenalin levels skyrocketing again. He'd been worried that the guy would spot Todd and Shay before they had chance to hide, and he'd wondered how Todd would react. He dreaded the thought of him doing something rash to silence the man. Macca peeped through a gap in the bushes and saw that the man was almost level with them. Thank God they'd hidden in time!

They were all so silent now that Macca could hear the man's footsteps and the pitter-patter of the dog's paws along with the sound of the dog's panting. It was accompanied by the throbbing beat of his own heart as he waited for the man to pass.

Macca thought he'd collapse with shock when the dog started growling in their direction and the man stopped, level with them. 'What, Barney? What is it?'

Please don't look, please don't look, Macca kept repeating to himself as the man peered down at his dog. Macca glanced across at Spinxy who seemed even more tense than *he* felt, his shoulders raised so high they looked as though they had been locked in position.

The man stayed there for an age. Meanwhile the dog was still growling at them. Macca hoped the man wouldn't bend over to see what had disturbed the dog because he'd be sure to spot them through the branches.

Then the man stepped forward so that he was one pace ahead of his dog. 'Come on, Barney. Let's get going,' he said.

Just then the dog locked eyes with Macca who took a sharp intake of breath. He was clammy with perspiration and felt a bead of sweat dribble down his forehead. The dog's growling changed to an insistent bark and Macca willed it to go away. 'It's probably just a squirrel,' said the man. 'Come on.'

Macca saw the dog's head move forwards as the man dragged on its leash. But the dog was persistent and for a few seconds it fought against its owner. Then Macca saw the man bend over to the dog and for a moment he thought he might spot them. But he didn't look their way. Instead, he picked the dog up and carried on walking with it, muttering, 'Oh, you are a silly boy, Barney. Come on, let's get you home.'

As soon as the dog walker had passed, Macca and the others let out a collective breath. 'Thank fuck for that!' whispered Todd. 'Give it a couple of minutes till they're well out of the way and then we'll load the car.'

As they waited, Macca turned to Spinxy. 'Well spotted.'

Macca was pleased when Todd repeated his praise. Macca had known how nervous Spinxy had been and, even though Macca had been nervous himself, he'd known that he wouldn't bottle it. On the other hand, he had doubted Spinxy's resilience. Thankfully he'd come good in the end. And he'd also saved the day by alerting them about the man and his dog.

As they loaded the car, Macca kept watching for signs of other people around. Fortunately, there was no one and it didn't take long until the last of the goods was inside the car and Leroy was starting the engine.

'Yay!' shouted Shay as they set off down the road.

Macca saw him fumble inside his pockets and was amazed when he pulled out a wad of cash and some jewellery. Todd then matched him by pulling out some banknotes, a gold chain and several expensive-looking pendants.

'Wow!' said Spinxy. 'I bet they're worth a bomb.'

Todd laughed. 'We'll find out tomorrow when I try to flog them.'

'What should we do next?' asked Leroy.

'We'll go down the offie and get some cans. We need to fuckin' celebrate,' said Todd.

'Alright,' said Spinxy. 'As long as we're not out too late. I don't want my mum and dad giving me earache.'

The rest of the lads groaned. 'We've just pulled off our first job. We've made a fuckin' mint, and all he's bothered about is getting home so he doesn't get grief off his fuckin' parents,' said Shay, laughing.

The rest of the lads, including Macca, joined in his laughter. They were on a high. It was a good feeling. And, at that present moment in time, he felt invincible.

It was late when Todd arrived home. Once they'd stashed the goods away in a corner of the garage his stepdad rented, he'd gone to the local park with the rest of the lads, and they'd celebrated on cheap cans of lager and cider. The garage was situated in a block that was at the other end of the street from his home, and his stepdad used it for tinkering with old cars. He knew his stepdad wouldn't come in there at this time of night.

Unfortunately for Todd, his stepdad and mum were still up when he got home. And, judging by the look on his stepdad's face, he had been waiting for him.

'Ah, here he is!' he announced as Todd walked through the front door.

Kev was sitting in his armchair ironically drinking the same brand of cheap lager as Todd had just been drinking in the park. The living room door was wide open, so he had a full view of Todd arriving home.

'What fuckin' time do you call this?' he demanded.

Todd shrugged. 'Dunno.'

'Oh, I bet you do. What the fuck have you been up to till this time?'

'Just hanging out with the lads.'

Todd was trying his best to appear sober, but he was conscious of the slight slurring of his words as he spoke.

'Have you been fuckin' drinking?' shouted Kev.

'Only a bit,' said Todd.

Kev got up out of his chair. 'And I suppose you paid for that with the fuckin' money you stole from me, didn't you?'

There was no mention of the garage keys and Todd was relieved that Kev didn't seem to know they were missing. 'Nah, that was only a few pence,' he answered. 'And I borrowed it. My mate needed it for the phone. I was gonna give it back. You can have it now if you want.'

He reached inside his pocket, feeling for the money, but wasn't daft enough to pull out the whole wad, or the garage keys. Instead he separated a single note and looked at it in his hand, relieved that it was only a fiver. He put out his hand, offering it to Kev.

'Where the fuck have you got that from?'

In his drunken state, Todd had overlooked the fact

that his possession of a fiver might make Kev suspicious. But he soon thought up something. 'I did a job for a mate,' he said.

'What kind of fuckin' job? And who is this mate?'

'He's called Rob. He lives over Stockport Road. He needed some help fixing his car.'

'A likely fuckin' story. What do you know about cars anyway?'

'Nowt much. But he's been teaching me a few things.'

There was some element of truth in the tale. Rob did exist but he wasn't a friend of Todd's; he was a friend of Shay's. Rob and Shay had been to secondary school together and Rob had been lucky enough to get a job at a garage helping to repair cars, unlike Todd and Shay who had signed on the dole.

As they spoke, Kev made his way over to Todd and snatched the money from him. Then he lifted his hand and swiped Todd across the head. 'That's for fuckin' thieving from me.'

Todd hardly felt the blow; his feelings were numbed by the drink but then Kev followed it up with another one. 'And that's for fuckin' lying. Did you honestly think I'd believe that bag of shite you've just told me? Now get to fuckin' bed!'

Todd turned and walked away, too tired to retaliate. During the exchange his mother had sat watching and hadn't muttered a word. Suddenly, Todd found the situation funny. What a dickhead his stepdad was! If he'd had even an inkling of what Todd had been up to tonight, he'd have gone apeshit.

That thought amused Todd and, as he climbed the stairs, he giggled to himself. He'd had a brilliant time with the lads, he was still merry from the booze, and tomorrow he was going to cash in from tonight's adventure.

14

Nov 1986

Macca was impressed when he saw Shay and Todd pull up in a nearly new Vauxhall Cavalier, with Shay at the wheel.

'Wow! Nice motor. Where did you get it?' he asked.

'It's not nicked,' said Shay. 'My mate let me borrow it. His boss is off, so he's let us have one of the cars they're working on for a couple of hours.'

'He must be mad. He'll get sacked if his boss finds out.'

'He won't find out,' chipped in Todd. 'And don't worry about Rob. He's a handy lad to know. Shay gives him a few quid for his trouble. His boss is under the hospital, so Rob lets us know whenever he's not in work. Then, if we need to use a car for a bit, we know where to get it.'

'But why do that when you could easily nick one?'

'Because we don't need anything fast or fancy. We just need something to put the goods in so we can go and sell them. There's no point taking too many risks if you don't have to, and it would be daft to get nicked for driving a stolen car just when we're about to offload the goods.'

Macca nodded. Again, he was impressed by how switched on Todd was. He had thought of everything.

They quickly loaded the car boot up and ten minutes later Shay pulled up outside a shop on the main road in Levenshulme. The three of them got out of the car and Todd led the way inside.

From the outside the shop looked run-down. It had one large window with the words *Sullivan's Stores* engraved in rounded gold lettering so that the two words formed a circle. The gold was faded, and the windows were of opaque glass, making it difficult to see what was inside.

'You hang back,' Todd said to Macca as they went through the door, so Macca wandered around the shop while Todd and Shay approached the counter.

Macca was fascinated by the interior of the shop, which seemed to stock a vast array of goods including electricals, small items of furniture, clocks and musical instruments. There was a display cabinet with a glass top like those in jeweller's stores. It contained watches and large items of expensive-looking jewellery. Macca guessed from the prices of some of the items that they were solid gold. He also surmised that they were priced more competitively than those sold from new.

As he walked around Macca came across a boom box that took cassettes. He was fascinated by the assortment of buttons that it housed, and he spent some time fiddling about with them while he waited for Todd to speak to the owner.

He looked up when he heard Todd say, 'Right, we're on. Let's go and get the stuff from the car.'

When they brought the items into the store, Todd spent some time negotiating a deal with the owner. Eventually, happy with the deal he had struck, Todd exited the shop with Shay and Macca following behind.

'Let's split it now,' said Shay when they got back to the car.

'No, drive round the corner. You never know if this place might get fuckin' raided.'

Shay did as instructed and pulled up in a back street. Todd then took the money out of his pocket. Added to it was what remained of the cash from the previous evening once they had taken out money for drink. He added the whole lot together and then split it five ways.

'Here you go,' he said to Macca, handing him a wad.

'Wow!' said Macca, gazing at the pile of cash in his hand. He'd never seen so much cash.

Todd then said to Shay, 'Come on, let's get back.'

But a thought had just occurred to Macca. 'Hang on a minute. I saw summat I wanted in the shop. Can I go and get it?'

'Go on then but hurry up. Me and Shay want to go and spend our spoils.'

A few minutes later Macca got back into the car, proudly carrying the boom box he'd spotted earlier.

'What the fuck do you want that for?' asked Shay.

'It's for my mum. Her hi-fi's broken.'

'You should have got one that plays CDs. They're all the rage now.'

But Macca had spent the bulk of the money and knew he couldn't have afforded a more expensive one.

Todd's next comment surprised him. 'You should have told me. We've just let a brilliant one go. It played CDs and cassettes. I would have let you have it cheap if I'd have known.'

Macca hadn't even thought to ask about the other boom box. He hadn't wanted to cut into everyone else's profits. But he was more well thought of by Todd than he realised. He wasn't too bothered though. Even the cassette player was better than what he and his mum had at the moment.

Macca couldn't wait to show his mum the boom box when he got in. Checking first that his grandma wasn't around, he entered the flat where he found his mother at the kitchen sink washing the dishes.

'Look what I've got you, Mum,' he said.

He proudly held out the boom box in front of him with a wide smile.

'What the bloody hell's that?' she asked.

'It's a boom box.'

'I know what it is but where the bloody hell have you got the money from for it.'

Macca was halfway through telling the story he had fabricated on his way home about doing a bit of work for a friend who let him have the boom box in payment. He knew his friends used similar stories on their parents. But she stopped him before he had finished.

'Never mind. I'd rather not bloody know,' she said. 'But if it's what I think it is then you'd better get rid of it before your grandma comes round and I don't want you bringing anything else like that home.'

'But, Mum. I haven't nicked it.'

She cast a sideways glance. 'Do you think I was bloody born yesterday? I know who you've been knocking about with and your grandma's right – you'll get into no end of trouble if you carry on like that.'

Then she wiped her hand on the towel and walked over to him. He knew the boom box had caught her interest despite her harsh words. She sniffed. 'It doesn't bloody play records anyway.'

'I know but they're going out. They're being replaced by CDs, didn't you know? I couldn't get you one that plays CDs, so I got this instead. It plays cassettes.'

'Well, like I said, it's no use to me if I can't play my favourite records on it, and I haven't got many cassettes.'

'You can soon get some though. Here, the guy that I got it from threw a few in with it.'

He pulled out one of several cassettes that he was carrying in his pockets and, placing the machine on the table, he loaded it up and pressed play. The sound of Stevie Wonder filled the room. He was one of Debbie's favourite artistes. Macca had known that when he'd grabbed it along with a few others from the shop while Todd and Shay had been busy negotiating with the shop owner.

He could see his mother was coming round to the idea of the boom box and her interest was heightened when he pulled the rest of the cassettes from his pockets. Knowing she was tempted, he read out the names of the artistes: Whitney Houston, Diana Ross and Elton John.

'You sure it's not nicked?' asked Debbie.

'Sure,' said Macca, telling her what she wanted to hear.

'OK, take it in the living room. But if your grandma starts asking questions, be careful what you say.'

Macca smiled. 'There's nowt to tell, Mum. I told you; it's not nicked. I got it from a guy for doing some work for him.'

He could tell from the look on her face that she wasn't buying his tale. But he also knew she was happy to receive the boom box. And Macca was happy too. He knew how much she missed her old hi-fi and there was no way she'd have been able to afford to have it fixed let alone buy a new one.

But the other reason he was happy was because he knew that if he kept his mother supplied with goods, she'd turn a blind eye to what he was up to and maybe she'd stop relying on creepy men to provide her with a few quid here and there.

15

Dec 1986

It was a big night for the gang. With the money they had been earning from house break-ins they had decided to go uptown to celebrate, at Todd's suggestion. Spinxy called to the flat for Macca and they made their way through the estate where they had agreed to meet the other lads.

As they walked along, Macca couldn't help but notice his mate's smart new footwear. 'Jesus, Spinxy, them are a well smart pair of trainers you're wearing, aren't they?'

Spinxy beamed. 'Yeah. I got 'em yesterday. Latest design. Seventy quid they set me back.'

'Fuckin' hell, that's a lot of dosh for trainers.'

'Yeah, they're worth it though.'

They found the other lads on the street talking to Shell and Trish, and went over to join them.

Shay spotted Spinxy's trainers straightaway. 'Fuckin' hell. They're well smart. Where did you get 'em?'

Macca could see Spinxy swell with pride, especially when the others showed their admiration too. Now Macca realised why his friend had spent so much money on a pair of trainers. He had always wanted to be one of the cool kids, which meant wearing the right gear. And now that they were all earning plenty, it gave him the chance to do that.

'I might get myself some of those,' said Leroy, talking a fistful of cash out of his pocket and casually flashing it.

Macca could see Shell was impressed and he knew that had been Leroy's intention. He'd been wanting to impress her for a while.

'Anyway,' Todd interrupted. 'We're off out now. See you again, girls.'

He walked away with the others following. 'Hey, why did you do that?' Leroy complained. 'They might have come with us.'

'No, they wouldn't,' said Todd. 'Tonight's for us lot. I don't want any girls in the way.'

An hour later they were entering one of Manchester's finest Italian restaurants. As they walked through the door, the maître d' eyed them warily.

'Yes, gentlemen. What can I do for you?'

Macca noticed the stress he placed on the word 'gentlemen' and he had no doubt that Todd had noticed it too.

'We wanna table for five,' said Todd.

The maître d' made a pretence of looking through his bookings before declaring, 'I'm afraid that won't be possible. We're full this evening.'

Todd scanned the restaurant where there were a few unoccupied tables. 'You don't look full to me.'

'Oh, those tables are booked, with the exception of the smaller tables, that is.'

'Right, well you can get a couple of smaller tables and push them together then,' Todd insisted.

'I'm afraid that won't be possible. But there are other restaurants in the locality, and some of them are more budget-friendly.'

'I don't want to eat at any other restaurants,' said Todd. 'My uncle recommended this one.' He flashed a wad of cash, adding, 'Money's no object.'

The maître d's eyes lit up at the sight of the cash, but he was still cautious. 'To be honest, gentlemen. We don't usually admit all-male parties. This is a peaceful restaurant, and we'd like to keep it that way.'

'We're not here for trouble,' said Todd. 'We just want a nice meal in a nice restaurant. Now, are you gonna serve us or do I have to tell my uncle and all his business associates to give this place a miss in future?'

'Oh, well, I erm, I suppose we could accommodate you. Give me a moment.'

He wondered away and Todd smiled at the other lads as they waited. Two minutes later he was back.

'This way, gentlemen, please,' he instructed.

The lads followed him to another area of the restaurant where there were a few booths, which were currently unoccupied. He sat them in the one at the furthest side of the room before saying, 'A waiter will be over shortly with your drinks order.'

'Tosser!' said Todd once he had left them. 'He did have free tables after all. Anyway, fuck him! Let's have a fuckin' good time.'

This area of the restaurant didn't look quite as upmarket as the area visible from the entrance, but it was still luxurious. The table was highly polished and set out with a number of silver knives and forks and expensive-looking glasses. Their seats were plush and covered in quality leather and the décor was tasteful and set off nicely by sophisticated lighting.

'Wow! This is fuckin' ace,' said Spinxy gazing around at their surroundings.

They leafed through the menu. At first Macca was shocked by the prices but then he realised that they could easily afford them. For the next three hours he tucked in, as did the rest of the gang, ordering a starter, main course of fillet steak, a side dish and a sweet.

When they ordered wine, the young lad serving them looked concerned. But he didn't question their ages, and Macca guessed he was wary of starting anything with them. It was a brilliant night, and all the lads left the restaurant feeling replete and upbeat. It felt so good to be eating and drinking in one of Manchester's best restaurants, somewhere Macca could never have dreamt of eating only a few months previously.

16

May 1987

When Joanne came in from school that afternoon there was a letter waiting on the mat for her. She picked it up, suspecting it was in connection with a job and hoping it was good news. Her parents were still at work and Mandy wasn't home from college yet. After a few moments' deliberation, she decided to open it once everyone was home. It was probably bad news anyway.

Later, when the family were seated in the lounge, Joanne took out the letter. She slipped her fingers under the seal and opened the envelope, pulling out the folded paper and opening it up. As soon as she read the words 'We are pleased to inform you…' she knew it was good news.

Joanne quickly scanned the rest of the contents then beamed a smile at her sister and mother. 'I've got it!' she yelled, waving the letter in the air. 'I've got a job!'

'Which? Which one?' asked Mandy.

Joanne studied the letter again so that she could quote

the full name of the firm that headed the fancy paper. 'Guy Campbell Hair Salons,' she quoted. 'It's on Deansgate.'

'Oh my God!' squealed Mandy. 'I've seen it. It's really posh and expensive. Me and my friend looked in the window when we were in town one day. We couldn't believe how much they charge. Are they paying well?'

'Yeah,' said Joanne, quoting the starting salary. 'It's more than most of those that turned me down.'

Mandy threw her arms around her younger sister. 'Then that's because it was meant to be.'

Joanne passed the letter to her father who studied it intently. Finally, he looked up from the letter saying, 'Well, I suppose it will keep you off the streets, won't it?'

Mandy explained all about how it was a more upmarket salon than those based locally. 'Joanne will do well there,' she added.

'And that's a good starting salary for a school leaver,' Gillian chipped in.

Outnumbered by the rest of his family, Alan finally conceded, 'Good, well I suppose congratulations are in order. Well done. If you work hard, you could make something of it. And let's hope the other girls at the salon are from good families unlike those you hung about with in the past.'

Joanne smiled but she knew his good wishes had been given grudgingly. Although the job at Guy Campbell was a good opportunity, her father had really wanted better for her. He'd wanted her to go into further education.

But Joanne wasn't interested in what her father wanted. She had a mind of her own and she'd socialise with whoever she liked. And that didn't mean on the streets either. Once

Joanne had a bit of money in her purse, she intended to start going out to pubs regardless of the fact that she was still underage. Other kids on the estate did it so why shouldn't she?

It was unusual for Macca to be home at seven thirty, but he hadn't felt like hanging out with his mates that evening. It was raining outside, and he fancied a bit of time chilling in front of the TV or playing games on the new console he had recently bought.

He'd been on a couple of jobs lately and it was good to have money. The most recent job had been last night. Todd had been to sell the goods that day while Macca had been at school and Macca had just met up with him to receive his share of the pay-out.

His mother wasn't in the living room or kitchen where he had expected her to be, so he'd walked further down the hall where he'd found her bedroom door open. Looking inside and seeing his mother sitting at her dressing table with her back to him, he asked, 'What are you doing?' even though it was obvious she was getting ready to go out.

'Oh, hiya, love,' said Debbie, glancing over her shoulder. 'I'm going for a few drinks with a friend of mine. I was going to leave you a note.'

'Is your friend a man?' asked Macca, his tone becoming hostile.

'Well, yeah, but he is only a friend.'

'You're not gonna bring him home, are you?'

His mother turned fully now. 'What is this?' she asked.

'If I want to bring him home, I will, and I don't have to ask permission from you or anybody else.'

Macca dropped his head and muttered, 'I don't like some of the men you bring home.'

Debbie looked shocked. 'Why? What's wrong with them?'

They're leches, drunks, bores and most of them are only after one thing, thought Macca. But he didn't know how to put his thoughts into words without offending his mother.

Without waiting for Macca to reply, Debbie continued, 'Jimmy's alright. And it's not like that with me and Jimmy. He's really old, y'know. He's just a friend, like I said.'

But Macca knew that no matter how his mother might dress it up or even if she actually believed it was just a harmless few drinks with a friend, Jimmy would have other ideas. They always did. And it pissed Macca off. He didn't like his mother giving it away for a few drinks and maybe a few backhanders now and again.

Still stuck for words, he reached into his pocket and withdrew a fistful of fivers. 'Here, you can have this.'

At first his mum looked shocked but then her shock was replaced with another expression: one of relief, and it struck Macca that she wasn't going out because she wanted to but because she saw it as a way to make some money.

Hesitantly she reached out and took the proffered money, saying, 'Thanks, love, I won't have to go out after all. I didn't fancy missing *Bread* anyway.'

Macca smiled. 'Good. I'll watch it with you.'

Then his mother became pensive, and he had a feeling he

knew what was coming even before she said, 'You will be careful, won't you, love?'

'Course I will, Mum. I always am.'

'OK, we'll leave it at that but for God's sake, don't let your grandma know.'

17

June 1987

Joanne had finished school that day and was looking forward to starting work at Guy Campbell's salon the following Monday. She and her school pals had wanted to do something to mark the occasion even though two of them were staying on to the sixth form.

For days they'd discussed how drunk they were going to get as soon as school was over. But the pubs didn't open till 5.30pm so Joanne had persuaded them that they should all go home and get ready, then go to her local, The Grey Goose. Her reasoning was that Shell and Trisha had told her how good it was when she'd seen them on her way to the shops.

Secretly she longed to bump into Macca. Every time she pictured him with his lovely blue eyes and mischievous smile her insides turned to mush. Lately, she'd only seen him from a distance walking through the estate with his mates. She hadn't had any opportunity to talk to him, but she still hadn't got him out of her system.

As she got ready to go out, backcombing her hair then fluffing it up to its full volume with a pintail comb, she was on a high. She sipped on the can of lager she had sneaked into her room then put down the comb and began to apply her makeup.

They arrived early and Joanne and two of her pals found a table while the other two went to the bar. Although they were in rounds, Joanne was determined not to get drunk because she knew that if she did there'd be hell to pay with her dad when she got home. He thought she was at one of her friend's houses and she'd convinced him that her friend's dad would bring her home.

But there was no harm in having a couple of drinks, and she'd have a few mints before she got home to disguise the smell of booze. Her pals returned from the bar and Joanne grabbed her half of lager and lime and tucked in. She was soon enjoying the atmosphere, laughing and joking with the other girls as they gossiped about school and boys.

She had been in the pub for around half an hour when she saw Macca walk in with one of his mates. She'd wondered where he was as she'd already seen three of his usual crowd sitting at a corner table downing pints and smoking cigarettes. Their eyes locked as he strolled to the bar and Macca gave her a confident smile, which made her blush.

'Ooh, they look alright,' said her friend Lisa. 'Well, one of them does anyway. I think he likes you as well judging by the way he just smiled.'

'I know him off our estate,' said Joanne.

The other girls looked towards the bar where Macca and Spinxy were queuing to be served. By now the lads had their backs to them but the girls carried on watching until they were served, and both lads turned around, each carrying a pint of beer.

Suddenly, Joanne felt as though all eyes were on her. Macca was looking over again and smiling, and everyone was staring at her, awaiting her reaction. Joanne felt self-conscious but she smiled back anyway, pleased that he'd noticed her.

Macca, Spinxy and Leroy had been hanging around with Todd and Shay and getting up to mischief for almost a year by the time Macca left school. When Macca and Spinxy heard the final bell ring for the end of day, a gigantic roar went up among the school leavers. They dashed from the classroom without waiting to be told and made their way home.

At last, they were free to start the celebrations although Macca and Spinxy didn't have much to rejoice about as neither of them had a job to go to. It did mean they had more time to do what they wanted, though, without the worry of the authorities taking action for absenteeism.

That evening Macca and Spinxy went to The Grey Goose. Through the haze of cigarette and cigar smoke Macca found Todd, Shay and Leroy sitting on a table in the corner and as he looked across at them his eyes settled on Joanne who was seated with a bunch of girls he'd never seen before.

Macca flashed her a smile and she was obviously embarrassed. Suddenly it occurred to him what a fool he'd been to have never asked her out. Fuck what her dad thought! He still liked her, and he could tell she liked him by the way she blushed when he smiled at her.

Once they had got their drinks, he decided to stop over at Joanne's table, passing his pint to Spinxy and telling him he'd join him later. 'Hi, how are you?' he asked Joanne. 'I've not seen you for ages.'

'I'm good thanks,' said Joanne.

Her friends were watching but that didn't bother Macca. 'Eh, how about me and you meeting up one night? I'll take you for a drink or even a meal if you fancy,' he said.

Now it was Joanne's turn to smile. 'Yeah, OK.'

He passed her a pen. 'Here, I managed to get hold of this. Can you write your number on a beermat for me?'

She wrote the number down then stood up and stepped away from the table. He presumed it was so she could talk to him without the other girls overhearing. 'Can you do me a favour?' she asked. 'When you ring my house, if my mum or dad asks your name, can you tell them it's Mark, not Macca?'

Macca smiled and nodded knowingly. He understood her reasoning. If he said Macca, her parents would know straightaway who he was, and they would disapprove. But she obviously didn't intend for them to know. A part of him felt put out but he tried not to let it show. It would have been nice to have gained her parents' approval.

Having got her number, Macca strutted across the pub until he reached his mates. A roar went up as soon as they spotted him.

'Yay!' yelled Shay. 'What does it feel like to be a free man?'

'Fuckin' great,' said Macca. 'No more having to put up with dickhead teachers.'

Macca was enjoying being in the pub. There was a

party-like atmosphere as numerous underage drinkers celebrated the last day of school. As he took up the seat his friends had saved for him, all thoughts of Joanne were now on hold while he joined in the banter with his friends.

'What will we do if the landlord comes over and asks us our age?' said Spinxy with a worried look on his face.

Todd and Shay laughed. 'Fuckin' lie,' said Shay. 'Like everyone does.'

'He won't ask,' said Todd. 'He doesn't give a shit how old the customers are as long as they're spending plenty of dosh. I mean, look around the place; hardly anybody's fuckin' legal.'

'Yeah,' said Shay. 'We've been coming in here ages, and no one's said fuck all.'

'But what if there's a raid?'

Shay shrugged and it was Leroy who responded. 'We're sat near the fuckin' fire exit. I don't know about you but the minute I spot a copper coming through the door, I'm gonna fuckin' leg it.'

'I doubt whether much will happen to us,' added Todd. 'They'd have to arrest nearly all the customers and I can't see them doing that. It'd probably be the landlord who'd cop for it.'

Macca had been thinking along the same lines as Spinxy although he wasn't as worried as his friend. Even though he was two years underage, for him the fact that he had left school felt like a coming of age and what better way to celebrate than by coming to the pub for the first time?

After a few minutes, a dark-haired lad of about seventeen or eighteen came over to them carrying a pint. Shay stood up to acknowledge him. 'Alright, mate, how you doing?' He gave his mate a hearty slap on the back then turned to the others. 'This is my mate Rob. The one I told you about who works in a garage and lends me and Todd cars.'

'Alright, mate?' said Todd. 'Why don't you grab a chair and join us?'

Rob did as Todd suggested and as soon as he was sat with them, Leroy said, 'I fuckin' love cars, me. You should have seen the one I nicked the other day.'

Todd gave him a warning glance, which Shay responded to by saying, 'It's OK, Rob won't say owt.'

'Nah, will I heck,' said Rob. 'I don't give a shit. Even my fuckin' boss sells ringers.'

'You're joking?' said Todd, sitting up straighter in his seat. 'I didn't know that.'

'How can you tell?' asked Leroy.

'Well, we had this car brought in and I noticed the plates had changed. I asked the boss why and he got all fuckin' snappy with me. But I'm not daft, I know what was going on, so I kept my eyes peeled and saw it happen with another one. When I asked him about that one, he gave me a backhander to keep my gob shut.'

'What does he do that for?' asked Spinxy.

'Do you not know what a ringer is?' asked Shay, causing Spinxy to squirm with embarrassment.

But Macca didn't know what one was either, so he was glad when Rob explained. 'They get a nicked car and swap the plates. Most times it will be for plates from a car that's been written off and they'll swap the chassis plate under the bonnet too. And if they do a respray as well, no one will have a fuckin' clue that it was the same car.'

Macca took in how intently Todd was listening to

everything Rob had to say so he wasn't surprised when he said, 'I need to arrange a meeting with your boss.'

'Why?' asked Rob.

Todd smiled. 'I think we could do a bit of business with him.'

18

June 1987

When Macca walked through the doors of the unemployment benefit office the first thing that hit him was the smoke-filled atmosphere as bored, unemployed adults stood in line. The fuggy environment reminded him of his first experience of the pub. And, judging by the smell of weed, over-the-counter cigarettes weren't the only thing people were smoking.

Macca made his way through the crowds and joined the shortest of three queues. He stood behind a much older man who looked shabby and smelled putrid. The man's hair was matted, and his clothes were bedraggled, and Macca wondered what sort of job would suit somebody like him if he was lucky enough to gain employment. He was glad when he made it to the front of the queue, but it had taken an hour and three-quarters. He knew how long it had been because he kept checking the time on the calculator watch he'd bought with the spoils from his latest job.

One of the battle-weary clerks looked at him then waited.

He didn't speak and Macca wondered what he was waiting for. He was about to ask when he saw someone in the queue next to him slide a card across the counter.

'I haven't got one of them,' Macca said to the clerk who was still staring at him expectantly.

'Why? What have you done with it?'

'Nothing. I never got one. It's my first time here.'

'Right. Well, in that case, you'll need to be interviewed. Walk to the end of the counter and you'll find a door in the corner. That takes you through to the interview suite.'

'What? You mean I've got to queue up again?'

'Not necessarily. It depends if there's anybody else waiting to be interviewed. There are a few booths though so you might be in luck.'

Macca walked through the door in the corner and found himself in an area with a line of booths across the wall. Thankfully it wasn't crowded like the other room. The booths were separated at the sides by screens but open at the back.

He walked past the first one where a woman was sitting on a chair with a baby on her knee, a pram pulled up close to her and two toddlers pulling at her clothing as they vied for her attention. At the back of the booth was a glass partition separating the woman from a clerk who was attempting to interview her.

In the next booth sat a woman who was waiting for a clerk to appear. She stared vacantly at him as he passed and then grinned as she pushed her hand under the waistband of her skirt then forced it down. He could tell straightaway that there was something not right with her and he guessed she was mentally disabled.

The next booth was vacant, so Macca took a seat and waited for somebody to appear at the other side of the glass. Meanwhile, he could hear moaning sounds coming from the next booth and it was obvious to him that the woman was pleasuring herself.

When the clerk arrived, she was a burly middle-aged woman with a scowl on her face. She sat down and took out some forms from underneath the counter then started asking Macca questions such as his name, address and date of birth. During this time the moaning continued.

The clerk, suddenly realising that something was amiss, put down her pen and tutted. Then she stood up and shouted to someone in the back office. 'Andy! Will you come and sort Brenda out? She's at it again.'

Macca stifled a grin as the clerk took up her seat again and picked up her pen. Noticing Macca's amusement, she glared at him then carried on with the form as though nothing had happened. The woman's tone was patronising and when the form-filling was finally over, she sent him to another area where he had to queue again so that a more senior member of staff could check through the form before he was allowed to sign on.

All in all, the procedure took over four hours and Macca was glad to get it done with. He walked outside into the fresh air with his grandma's often-used words ringing in his ears: *You don't get owt for nowt in this life.*

Despite it all, he preferred to be in the position he was in rather than working for peanuts in a factory or shop. The dole was just a little add-on to the money he was making with Todd and the rest of the lads. The stuck-up staff might look down their noses at him, but Macca knew that he could earn more money in a week than they could earn in a month.

Aug 1987

'So, how's the new job going?' asked Macca.

He was sitting on his bed with Joanne, chatting. They had been together for two months now and were enjoying getting to know each other.

'Good. I mean, I spend most of the day washing hair and sweeping up, but I love it there.'

'What is it you love about it?'

'It's, I dunno, you're gonna laugh, but it's glamorous. Y'know, everybody dresses really nice and wears makeup and trendy hairstyles.'

'Bit different than round here then?' he asked.

'I suppose it is really although, to hear my dad talk, you'd think I'd committed a cardinal sin by going to work in a hairdresser's.'

'What's so bad about a hairdresser's?'

'Nothing. He wanted me to stay on at school, didn't he? Like my sister. He's always going on at me telling me I could get a really good job like Mandy. He's always praising her too but never me.'

'God, I bet you hate your sister, don't you?'

'No, just the opposite. I love her to bits. Mandy is the best sister in the world. She studies really hard and deserves to do well but my dad needs to understand that we're both different. University isn't for everybody. He's been a bit better since I started work though. Maybe he realises that no amount of nagging will change my mind now.'

'Hairdressing's not a bad job,' said Macca, thinking that at least she had a job, unlike him.

'No, I don't think so. Once I'm trained up, I could go mobile or get my own shop.'

Macca smiled. He loved listening to Joanne. Her life was so different from his and those of his mates. Like him, they were mostly from broken homes or had fathers who were a waste of space. Her dad might be a moaner but at least he cared about her future. What job prospects did he have?

He tried not to focus too much on his troubled life. When he was with Joanne, he could switch off from all that and make the most of the time with her. All the girls he'd known up to now were devious, but Joanne was different. She was good and honest and saw things in a different light. Anyone else would have been bitter that their sister was the brainy one but not Joanne. She was positive and made the most of what she had.

They carried on chatting and getting to know each other till it was time for Joanne to go. He offered to walk her home, agreeing to stop at the end of her street so she wouldn't be spotted with him.

When they got there, he didn't want to let her go but he knew he had to as her dad would only give her grief if she got in too late. He gave her a goodbye kiss, which gave him a warm glow inside. Then he gave her another and another before finally letting her go.

As he walked back through the estate towards his own home, he felt like he was walking on air. He passed a bunch of kids aged about thirteen or fourteen. They were larking about just like he and his mates used to do not so long ago.

'Hiya, Macca,' said one of the kids.

One of his friends joined in: 'Alright, Macca. I like your jeans. I bet they cost a bomb, didn't they?'

Macca grinned. 'Yeah, and the rest.'

He carried on his journey home, still smiling. Since he'd been in Todd's gang, he'd grown used to the adulation of the younger kids. He no longer dressed shabbily in whatever clothes his mother could pick up cheap. Nowadays, he could afford designer gear and in the eyes of the younger kids that made him someone who was to be admired and respected.

He'd bunged them a fiver each a couple of times. He'd been in their shoes and knew what it felt like to have nothing. But now things were different. He was earning good money. It made him feel like he was someone. And, better than that, he was dating the most gorgeous girl on the estate. He might not have job prospects like her but the money he earnt meant he could shell out on both of them and give her a really good time.

19

Aug 1987

Todd had asked Macca to go with him to the garage where Rob worked. It wasn't a formal meeting, but Rob had finally been persuaded to tell them when his boss, Clive, would be around. As they stepped inside the shuttered entrance, they reached a small office with a public area outside where two customers were waiting.

Separating the public area from the workshop was a tape with a sign hanging off it, bearing the words 'Staff Only'. They could see Rob working on a car that had been lifted onto a platform. When he caught sight of them, he smiled awkwardly. Macca knew Rob hadn't wanted this meeting and had been stalling them for weeks.

For a few minutes they waited patiently but as soon as they saw someone coming out of the office, Todd stepped in front of the two waiting customers.

'Eh, there's a queue here,' said a woman.

'Tough, this is important,' said Todd as he walked inside the office.

Macca followed Todd's lead and, once inside, he shut the door behind them. He knew that Todd would want this conversation to be private. Behind a counter sat a stocky man in his late forties who Macca guessed was Clive.

'Are you the boss?' asked Todd.

'Yeah. Why? What's it to you?' said Clive, stiffening.

'I think we could do a bit of business.'

'What kind of business?'

'Ringers.'

Clive was becoming defensive now. 'What the fuck are you talking about?' he demanded.

'You heard. Ringers. You know, the knock-off cars that you do up and sell on.'

Macca could feel his heart speeding up at this confrontation, but Todd kept his cool. Clive looked alarmed and for a moment he didn't speak but Todd soon filled the silence.

'Don't pretend you don't know what I'm talking about because I know that you deal in ringers here.'

Clive had now recovered from his initial shock, and he came back at Todd. 'Get out of my fuckin' office! Who the fuck do you think you are coming here and accusing me of selling ringers?'

But Todd wasn't going anywhere. He slammed his hand down on the counter to show Clive he meant business. 'I know for a fuckin' fact you do, so don't try lying.'

Clive's eyes drifted towards the closed door, and Macca guessed at his train of thought. Clive was thinking about his assistant, Rob, the realisation suddenly dawning on him that he had been betrayed by one of his staff. And Rob was the obvious choice as he was in the same age group as Todd and Macca.

'Right,' said Todd. 'Now that I've got your attention, I'm gonna tell you what's gonna happen.'

Macca could see the fear on Clive's face, but he tried to keep his own expression impassive despite his qualms. He didn't want to undermine what Todd was doing by displaying his unease.

'We're gonna let you have a steady supply of knocked-off cars, which you can do the business with and sell on. We want a sixty per cent cut of the profit for every car we bring in.'

'But I-I-I already have a supplier,' said Clive who'd obviously realised the futility of continuing to lie. 'And I have a better deal with him than that. There's a lot of fuckin' work goes into turning a car around you know. We have to find new plates, do a respray, fix any dents that might…'

Todd cut him off. 'Yeah. We already know about all that. And we know how much it costs to turn a car around. So don't think you can get away with thinking we're stupid.'

Clive then stood up, straightening himself to his full height of around five five. Macca was surprised how small he was, which looked odd given his broad frame. 'Get out!' Clive repeated. 'You can't fuckin' come in here telling me what to do.'

Todd surprised both Clive and Macca by clutching Clive around his throat. 'Watch the door,' he ordered Macca.

Striding across the office, Macca reached the door and stood with his back to it so nobody could come inside. By the time he had turned around, Clive was gasping for breath as Todd squeezed tight on his windpipe. Macca felt ill at ease but at the same time he was confident that Todd wasn't daft enough to go too far.

As Macca watched, Todd continued to squeeze until Clive's eyes were bulging and his cheeks were flushed pink. Macca was beginning to have concerns now but just as he was going to say something, Todd released his hold. Clive's shoulders slumped, and he drew his hands up to his throat, gasping for breath and flashing Todd a look of terror mixed with resentment.

'OK are you ready to talk business now?' asked Todd. 'Oh, and by the way, don't forget I've got inside information on your operations so don't even think about pulling a fast one. Rob will stay to oversee things and if I hear that you're giving him a hard time then me and you will need to have another chat.'

'Yeah, yeah, whatever you want,' gushed the terrified man.

'That's more like it,' said Todd with an enormous smile on his face, and Macca felt relieved that Clive was now about to comply with Todd's wishes.

20

Sep 1987

Joanne had been seeing Macca for three months now and they were getting along fine. Tonight, they were going for a night out in Manchester with Macca's friends and Shell and Trish from the estate.

Leroy had finally succeeded in persuading Shell to go out with him but only as part of a group. Joanne knew that Shell was just using him to get what she wanted as she'd said as much but it was nice to have the company of other girls and go out as one big group.

They started off in The Grey Goose where they had a couple of drinks before going on to Manchester. Joanne thought they'd have taken taxis but Todd insisted they get the bus so they could all be together.

She was a bit put out by his bossiness at first, but the other lads went along with his suggestion, including Macca, who seemed to hang on to Todd's every word. She couldn't understand why; it was as though Todd was in charge of them all and they had to comply with his suggestions.

Todd's decision turned out to be a good one as they occupied an area at the back of the bus and began singing songs. She was enjoying the camaraderie as much as anyone as they belted out silly childish tunes and rhymes such as 'We're off in a Motor Car' and various rude versions of 'Mary Had a Little Lamb'.

By the time they reached Manchester, they were all in good spirits. They had more drinks at some of the bars before going to a nightclub. The club was packed and she was looking around for empty seats when Todd said, 'Wait here. Be back in a minute.'

He nodded at Macca and Shay who followed him while Leroy and Spinxy stayed with the girls. It felt a bit awkward as they all stood around waiting for the other lads to come back. Shell and Trish were sharing banter with Leroy, but Joanne decided to watch what was happening with the others.

Led by Todd, they approached a table where two couples were sitting. Todd said something to the couples then passed them something that looked like money. Both couples got up and walked away, and Todd and Shay slid into two of the vacated seats. She saw Macca wave them all over so she told the rest of the group and they all went to join them.

'What happened then?' she whispered to Macca once she was sat next to him.

'Nothing – don't worry about it,' he said dismissively before saying to Todd, 'Are we sorting the drinks out?'

'Yeah, come on,' said Todd.

They walked over to the bar without stopping to ask

everyone what they were having. It wasn't long till they returned, empty-handed.

Joanne was just about to ask Macca what had happened to their drinks when Todd announced, 'The barman will be over in a minute with some champagne.'

Two minutes later Joanne watched in awe as a barman appeared with three bottles of champagne and several glasses on a tray. She hadn't even realised the club offered waiter service. But maybe it was because Todd had paid them off too.

Todd took charge of the drinks and he, Macca and Shay popped the corks and filled everyone's glasses. Then Todd proposed a toast.

'To good friends and having each other's backs,' he said.

They all responded, and Joanne focused on having a good time. There was something niggling her about Todd's behaviour, but she tried not to let it bother her. She was with Macca whom she'd had a crush on for as far back as she could remember. And nothing else really mattered.

Later she was on the dance floor with Macca while Todd and Spinxy danced nearby. The others had chosen to stay at the table where Todd had ordered more drink. She had noticed Shell and Trisha becoming flirtier with the boys as the drink flowed, so she guessed Shay and Leroy were hanging around to see if anything might come of it.

Joanne was having a good time dancing to 'When the Going Gets Tough' when she felt someone grope her backside. Knowing it wasn't Macca, whose hands were in the wrong position, she let out a yell of alarm.

'What's wrong?' demanded Macca.

'Someone's just grabbed my backside,' Joanne complained, turning round to see an ape of a man grinning lecherously at her.

'What the fuck!' yelled Macca, striding over to the man. 'Have you just groped my girlfriend's arse?' he demanded.

'Sorry, mate. I was just having a bit of fun. I didn't realise she was with you.'

Macca stepped further forward. By now his chest was puffed up and his head thrust forward as he pointed at the other guy, his fingers only centimetres away from his face. 'It doesn't matter who she is. You've got no fuckin' right to do that, you cheeky bastard!'

'Get your fuckin' hand out of my face!' the man yelled but Macca persisted.

By this time Todd had sidled over to where Macca was standing. 'He's right,' he said to the man. 'You should fuckin' smack him one for that, Macca. I wouldn't put up with it if she was my girl.'

The man's friend, sensing there was trouble, also stepped forward. The situation escalated so quickly that Joanne didn't know how it happened or who threw the first punch. But, within seconds, there was a full-on fight between Macca and Todd and the other two lads.

Macca was trading blows with ape man while Todd was laying into his friend and Spinxy was shouting at them to leave it. By the time the bouncers saw what was happening, Todd had his opponent on the floor and was kicking viciously at his torso and head.

'Stop!' yelled Joanne when she saw a spray of blood burst from the man's nose.

The bouncers came in force, grabbing the four men and hauling them out of the club with Joanne and Spinxy following close behind. Any worries she had of the situation escalating outdoors were soon allayed as the two men quickly dashed away.

'That'll fuckin' teach 'em,' said Todd.

While Macca and Todd discussed the fight, each trying to justify his actions, Joanne stood shivering. It was cold out by now and she hadn't brought a coat. She wondered where they would go from here and how the rest of the group would react when Spinxy told them what had happened. But there were other more pressing concerns going on in her head. She was troubled by the level of violence, and the unease she had felt all night had now spiralled.

It was the following day. Macca had received a call from Joanne saying she wanted to see him. He knew it was because she was bothered about what had happened the previous night, so he'd asked her round to his mum's flat.

'I just can't understand why you had to get so violent,' she said as they sat on the bed in his room.

Macca furrowed his brow. 'That wasn't violent, Jo. I only threw a few punches. We were just protecting ourselves. They started it.'

'What about Todd?' she asked. 'He was violent. That man was pouring in blood where he'd kicked him.'

'That's just Todd,' he said.

'What d'you mean.'

'Well, he's got a bit of a temper, hasn't he?'

'And doesn't that worry you?'

Macca hadn't thought of it like that. Since he'd been palling around with Todd, he'd seen him as a friend rather than a threat. 'No,' he said. 'Todd's alright really. He's a good mate.'

'He's bossy!'

Where the hell had that come from? 'Bossy?'

'Yeah. He likes to be in charge, doesn't he? Making us all get the bus, deciding what we had to drink.'

'He just wanted us all to have a good night, that's all. Why are you complaining? It was champagne for fuck's sake.'

'Don't swear at me, Macca.'

'Sorry,' said Macca with a smile on his face. It was easy to forget she wasn't like the other girls on the estate. Shell and Trisha wouldn't have batted an eyelid if he'd used language in front of them.

'Where does he get his money from anyway? In fact, where do you get your money?'

'I told you, I do a bit of work for a mate. Keep it to yourself though 'cos it's on the side.'

Joanne nodded but he knew she was still concerned. He could see he was going to have to tread carefully with her. It was best not to let her know what he got up to. He decided to deflect, hoping her could win her round.

'Anyway,' he said. 'I don't want you worrying. I was trying to protect you after all. D'you think I'm gonna let some lech grab your arse and do nothing?'

She was mellowing a little so he flashed his eyes, put his arm around her and drew her to him. 'You're special, Jo, and I won't let anyone have a go at you. I wanna look after you.'

He gazed into her eyes and slowly drew his face towards hers. Then he silenced her concerns with a passionate kiss.

21

May 1988

Joanne loved it at Guy Campbell's where she had been for nearly a year now. All the staff worked five days a week, one of which had to be a Saturday as it was their busiest period. She was also allowed day release to attend college.

Her boss was great and, even though she hadn't been there long, she felt as though she was already progressing. Most of her tasks involved sweeping and tidying up as well as reception duties and washing the clients' hair. But she had also recently been allowed to stand and watch while some of the more senior stylists carried out cuts, colouring and perms, providing the customers were happy with it.

Sometimes she had to work late but she always got early finishes on other days to compensate. It didn't bother her too much; she was just happy to be working in that environment. It was so glamorous. All the stylists wore trendy clothes and turned up to work with a full face of makeup, so she did the same.

They were a friendly bunch, and often went out after

work on a Saturday. Most of the older staff only had a couple of drinks before they returned home to their families, but the younger ones stayed out later. Sometimes they went for something to eat and then on to other bars and nightclubs. Joanne had been so eager to fit in that she was usually one of the last to go home and she was enjoying the social life.

Her father didn't seem to mind either. She had overheard him telling her mother that he was just glad she'd stopped going about with the local girls who had a bad reputation. By that she knew he meant Trisha and Shell. But Joanne did still see Trish and Shell as well as Macca; she just hadn't told her father that because she knew he wouldn't approve.

Watching Leroy break into a car was like poetry in motion to Macca. For each different make and model, he employed a slightly different method of entry and he'd bragged to Macca that there wasn't any car he couldn't get into anymore. What amazed Macca was the speed in which he did it.

Macca was still a learner though and tonight Leroy was giving him lessons. He'd already broken into one car just to show Macca how it was done and now it was Macca's turn. They were inside a shopping centre car park, on the top level where fewer people would be milling about. Leroy pointed to a Toyota Celica, which was parked nearby.

'Right, your turn. You're gonna do that one.'

Checking there was no one about, Macca walked over to the car. Leroy passed him the long piece of metal with a hook on the end, which he had tucked inside his long, hooded coat. It was called a Slim Jim, Leroy had explained, and it was one of his favourite tools of the job.

Macca took the tool and slid it down between the window of the car and the rubber seal surrounding it.

'That's it,' Leroy encouraged. 'Now, feel around. You should feel the bars that connect to the lock. You need to catch them with the hook.'

Macca tried for a while, but he was having no joy. 'Give it here,' Leroy instructed. 'I'll show you where it is.'

He took the tool from Macca and deftly manoeuvred it into position. 'There,' he said, encouraging Macca to grab hold of it. 'Can you feel it now?'

Macca swapped places with Leroy again, amazed when he felt the tool connect. He levered it as Leroy had shown him and was chuffed when the door gave way. 'Shit,' he said, once the door was open. 'There's a fuckin' steering lock.'

'No probs,' said Leroy, producing a crowbar from inside his coat then pushing Macca to one side.

He soon smashed the lock, to Macca's amazement, then said, 'Get in, we're having this one.'

He passed Macca a screwdriver and showed him how to start the car.

'Fuckin' hell,' said Macca. 'Where do you manage to fit all those tools?'

'Ha ha, I've got pockets specially sewn in. My sister did it for me.'

Macca laughed, feeling the thrill of adventure as he managed to start the car and they set off for the exit of the multi-storey car park. It was great knowing he was playing his part in their latest illegal venture.

They hadn't gone far when they heard a police siren coming from somewhere behind them. Leroy turned and looked out of the rear windscreen.

'Fuckin' hell, they're behind us,' he yelled. 'Put your foot down.'

For a moment Macca felt a rising sense of panic. But then realisation dawned on him, and he ignored Leroy's instructions. 'What the fuck?' shouted Leroy. 'You're going too fuckin' slow. Do you want us to get caught or what?'

'They're not after us,' said Macca, coolly.

'What? How do you know?'

'Because the owner probably won't have reported the car stolen yet. We've only just got it, and no one saw us. And even if the owner came back to his car and reported it straightaway, there's no way the police would be on it that quickly.'

Macca flashed a grin at Leroy whose expression changed once he understood what Macca had told him.

'They'll be after someone else,' Macca added.

Sure enough, after a couple of minutes, the police car left the main stretch and took a road to the left.

Leroy slapped the dashboard and squealed in delight. 'You're fuckin' on it, aren't you, man?'

Macca smiled back. Although he was outwardly calm, he was hyped up with adrenalin, his senses on high alert throughout the journey. He was glad when, fifteen minutes later, they ran the car into Clive's garage using the spare keys Rob had loaned them, and then locked up.

Macca was satisfied with his evening's work. He was learning fast, and he knew that the stolen cars were a good earner.

*

Shay was enjoying having cash in his pocket. He'd been earning good money for a while now from the house break-ins as well as his share from any cars he stole for Clive to modify and sell on. But, despite his joy at being better off than he had ever been in his life, he also felt pushed out.

He had been aware for some time that Todd was beginning to favour Macca over him like the time a few months ago when he had taken him to cut a deal with Clive over the stolen cars. Since then, Todd and Macca seemed to be getting even closer and Shay didn't like it. He'd been mates with Todd for years and wasn't happy with being usurped.

But in a way it was good to distance himself from Todd. He was a good mate, but he was also controlling and unpredictable. That temper of his had got them into a lot of trouble in the past. So, Shay was content to do his own thing from time to time. And he also had other mates to help him do that.

Today he was going to a pub called The George. Unlike The Grey Goose, The George wasn't a place where underage youngsters hung out having a good time. It was more the kind of establishment where people met to cut illegal deals or where alkies and druggies went to get totally wasted.

The booze was really cheap and that was reflected in the clientele. As Shay walked inside, he noticed the rank odour of unwashed bodies along with tobacco smoke and cannabis. It didn't make a pleasant mix especially when teamed with the manky, beer-stained carpet, torn upholstery and jaded décor. But none of that bothered Shay; he was here for one reason only and once he'd got what he wanted he'd be off.

Shay went straight to the bar and ordered a beer. Standing next to him was a man who he'd known off the estate for years. Pemby, as he was known, was a heavy drinker who dabbled in other things from time to time. He was also the sort of person who would be able to point Shay in the right direction to obtain what he wanted. Shay bought him a drink too then struck up conversation.

Within five minutes Shay had steered the discussion to the reason for his rare visit to the George. Pemby pointed out a middle-aged man on the other side of the pub. He was a big guy with an equally large presence. His group of cronies were the loudest in the pub and as Shay drew near, he picked up on the crude and mocking language as well as their jeers and exaggerated laughter.

Shay locked eyes with the man and asked for a quiet word. He led him to inner hallway of the pub, which had several doors leading off from it: the toilets and two others marked 'Private'. Without preamble, Shay told him what he wanted, they cut the deal and Shay strode out of the pub, leaving the man to resume his raucous banter with his mates.

22

June 1988

Macca was feeling good. Between the house break-ins and the car thefts, he'd been doing well these past few months. Occasionally he had a pang of guilt about what he was doing but then he thought about the reassurances Todd had given him.

All the houses they targeted were those of well-off people with plenty of money. They were usually insured anyway so they wouldn't miss a few things. The same went for the cars. When Macca thought about it that way, what he was doing felt justified. Why should some people have plenty while the likes of him and his mother struggled?

But what made him feel really good was the change in his mother. Since he'd been providing her with a regular income together with other treats from his illegal gains, she had stopped bringing strange men round to the house. She still went out every now and again but with her friends rather than men. And that, to Macca, was well worth the risk he took every time he broke into a house or stole a car.

Today he was feeling particularly happy with himself. He'd just had the pay-out from his last job and it felt great to have money in his pockets. He decided to treat his mum and had called at the off-licence for a bottle of that cava she liked and a box of chocolates. He had also decided to grab a few cans for himself; his mum didn't usually mind him having a couple as long as he kept her sweet.

He walked inside the house whistling as he looked forward to watching a film on the TV with his mum while they scoffed on takeout. But, as soon as he got in the door, he was alerted to his grandma's presence when he heard the words 'That's him now' – and the tone in which they were uttered didn't sound at all friendly.

Macca was surprised to find his grandma there on a Saturday evening. She didn't usually come round at that time, and he wished she hadn't bothered. Although he thought a lot of his grandma, he had a feeling this wasn't a social visit.

He found his mother and grandma in the lounge, each seated on an armchair, his grandma staring daggers at him while his mother looked troubled. 'What's wrong?' he asked.

'You might well bleedin' ask?' said his grandma. 'What were you doing last night?'

A memory of the last car he'd stolen with Leroy flashed back to him. Unlike the previous one, this one was too close to home. He'd told Leroy that, but his friend had gone for it anyway. Despite his protests, Macca had got inside the car and sat in the front passenger seat while Leroy sped away. They passed an old biddy, her face vaguely familiar, and Macca had clocked her shocked expression but then thought no more of it. Until now.

Determined to bluff it out, he said, 'Nowt. I was just hanging out with my mates. Why?'

'Why?' came the outraged cry from his grandma. 'I'll bloody well tell you why. Because Gladys Thompson saw you driving off in a flash car. That's why.'

'I don't know what you're talking about.'

'Oh, I think you bloody well do. You were with that dark-skinned lad, and he was driving it.'

'Oh that. Yeah, it was Leroy. He borrowed it off a mate.'

'Give over. It must have been some mate to be driving a car like that. How the bloody hell does he afford it at his age?'

'He's older than Leroy, and he works.'

'OK, so tell me what he does.'

Macca shrugged. 'Dunno.'

'I thought as much. And what's the name of this mate.'

There was no mistaking the emphasis that Doris placed on the word 'mate', implying that he was fictitious. 'Dunno,' Macca persisted. 'Leroy just said a mate let him borrow it.'

'Oh, pull the other one. Some bloody mate he must be to lend a good car like that to a pair of scallywags like you!'

'Mum!' Debbie protested. 'Leave him alone. He's told you he's done nowt wrong so why are you accusing him of lying?'

'Jesus Christ! Wise up, Debbie. It's bleedin' obvious he's up to tricks. He's as bad as his father.'

'Oh no he isn't! And you leave Vernon out of this. Mark's not a bit like him. You're just assuming Mark's up to no good because of that interfering old busybody Gladys. Has it not occurred to you that she might have got it wrong?'

Macca knew his grandma's thoughts on Gladys

REDEMPTION

Thompson. He'd heard her talk about the woman often enough. His mother had apparently hit a raw nerve as his grandma didn't say anything further. She just grunted, tossing her head back and heaving her massive bosom under her hands like a Les Dawson character.

Knowing he had an ally, Macca said, 'Yeah, leave it out, Gran. It's Saturday night. I've come with some stuff so me and my mum can have a nice night in watching TV, and all I've had from you is grief.'

He pulled the bottle of cava from the carrier bag he was holding and handed it to his mum. 'I got you your favourite.'

Debbie smiled and took the gift. 'Aw, thanks, love.'

Next, he took out the chocolates and scoffed one. 'Do you want one, Grandma?' he asked with his mouth full as he held the box out to her.

Doris swiped the box away and Macca only just managed to keep a grip on it and stop the chocolates from falling all over the floor. 'No, I bleedin' don't,' she yelled.

'OK, suit yourself.' Macca took out another chocolate and placed it in his mouth, chewing on it tauntingly, knowing how much his grandma liked chocolates. Then he turned to his mum. 'I'll just go and put my beers in the fridge then I'll get us a takeout.'

He turned towards the door but was stopped by his grandma, her tone indignant as she said, 'Hang on a minute! Where the bleedin' hell have you got this lot from?'

'I bought them.'

'Oh no you didn't. I wasn't bleedin' born yesterday. You might get away with soft-soaping your mother, but it doesn't wash with me. How the bleedin' hell could you afford that lot on the dole?'

'Mum!' yelled Debbie. 'Will you leave him alone for Christ's sake.'

Doris stood up. 'No, I bleedin' won't.' She pointed around the room to the boom box, the new curtains, expensive vase and various other items Macca had helped his mother acquire over the past few months and said, 'I suppose they came from the same place as this bleedin' lot, did they? Fell off the back of a lorry, no doubt. It's about time you got wise, Debbie. Or maybe you let him get away with it so you can have all your new stuff. Is that it?'

When Debbie didn't say anything in her own defence, Doris said, 'Aye, I thought as much. You're as bad as him. The pair of you are a bleedin' disgrace.' She picked up her handbag and put on her coat. 'I'm not staying in this bleedin' thieves' den for a minute longer.'

Before Doris left, she turned her attention to Macca, leaving him a parting shot, 'I suppose you think you're bleedin' clever, don't you? Well, it might seem like fun now while you've got a few quid in your pockets, but there's only one place you'll end up if you carry on down that road, and you won't be acting so cocky then.'

She stormed out of the house ranting as she went. Macca caught a few of the words: 'I told you not to marry the bastard, but you wouldn't listen. Like father like bleedin' son.'

Then she was gone.

23

Sept 1988

It took Doris two months before she came back to see Macca and his mother. He'd got used to not having her around but, in a way, he missed her – and he knew his mother did. He'd come downstairs one day and there she was, sitting in the sagging armchair scowling at him.

It was difficult after that. Every time she visited, she ignored him, as though he didn't exist, while she chatted away to his mother. Macca had just accepted it up to now. She'd calm down eventually and at least she was talking to his mother now. He was glad of that at least because his mum had looked much happier having Doris around.

Today Doris had decided to break her silence. She surveyed him as he was putting on his shoes. 'And where are you off to? Going somewhere with those deadbeat mates of yours and getting up to no good, are you?'

But Macca refused to take it from her. She wasn't his mother after all. 'If you must know, I'm meeting Todd at the gym.'

His story was true. He *was* going to the gym although he and Todd also had plans to meet the rest of the lads later at The Grey Goose.

'A likely bloody story,' his grandma said.

'No, he does go to the gym,' chipped in Debbie in his defence.

'Aye, that's as may be but we both know that's not all he gets up to.'

She glared at him, awaiting his response, but Macca wasn't going to be intimidated. 'What I get up to is my own business.'

'Not when you're bloody thieving, it isn't,' said Doris who was now becoming irate.

Macca had had enough. He stood up and walked up to his grandma, hovering over her to let her know that he wasn't threatened by her words. 'What do you expect me to do when I can't get a fuckin' job? And the only jobs I could get are for shit pay? Do you think I enjoy seeing my mum having to entertain a load of scum, so they'll spend money on her?'

'Eh, that's enough,' said Debbie. 'Don't speak to your grandma like that.' But a look of shame coloured her features.

'I always helped you out when I could,' his grandma said, her demeanour now contrite.

'Yeah, well I don't need your money anymore. Me and my mum do alright, and we don't need handouts from you. Or maybe that's what's wrong with you; you can't stand it because you don't rule the roost anymore.'

This time it was Macca's turn to storm out. As he made

for the door, he didn't hear any response. He knew that by the time his grandma recovered from the shock of his verbal onslaught he would be out of there.

Todd was already at the gym when Macca got there. It was something they had been doing for the past few months at Todd's suggestion. He had reasoned that it didn't do any harm to be carrying a bit of muscle and it would help them to be able to handle themselves if anything went down.

Already a big lad, Todd was rapidly gaining muscle, and, at almost nineteen years of age, he looked every bit the hardman that he was. Macca was pleased to find that he was also gaining muscle and it suited him well. At first Shay had been happy to go to the gym with them but he didn't have the discipline of Todd and Macca, so he soon grew tired of it while Macca and Todd had remained gym buddies.

When Todd had suggested joining the gym, Macca hadn't been sure what 'if anything went down' referred to. Having seen how Todd had handled Rob's boss, Clive, when they first started supplying him with stolen cars more than a year ago, he assumed it was something to do with that. Maybe Todd wanted to ensure that they kept him in line.

But he should have known that Todd wouldn't settle for house break-ins and car thefts. He was ambitious and always on the lookout for money-making opportunities. Now it seemed he had thought of something. Macca listened while he outlined his proposition.

'There's this mate of my uncle who does a bit of dealing,' he began.

'What, drugs you mean?'

'Yeah, drugs. Anyway, he has a bit of trouble sometimes with druggies who won't pay up. He lets them have the drugs on the agreement that they fetch him the money when they get it. Most times it works out. They know they have to keep him sweet if they want to carry on getting their supplies. But a few of them are taking the piss.'

'Right,' said Macca, wondering where this was leading.

'Well, he needs a bit of help collecting. Y'know, someone to slap 'em around a bit till they cough up. I thought we'd be perfect for the job.'

Macca was shocked. 'But you always said drugs were a mug's game and you'd never have anything to do with them.'

'I still think that. They are a mug's game and I'd never fuckin' take 'em. But that doesn't mean we can't earn a bit of money from the idiots that do. Fuckin' hell, Macca, these people are lowlife scum. Not only are they shoving all kinds of shite in their gobs or in their arms, but they're also expecting it for free. That's taking the piss if you ask me. Anyway, it's a good earner.'

'But the house jobs and cars are good earners, and we don't get any hassle from them.'

'We wouldn't get any hassle from this. In fact, it'll be easier than the house and car jobs. All we need to do is smack them around a bit. Have you ever known a fuckin' junkie put up a good fight? Most of them don't even know what fuckin' day it is. Anyway, I can't stand those losers. It wouldn't bother me to give one or two of them a good slap.'

But Macca still wasn't sure.

'Listen,' Todd continued. 'We can earn money a lot quicker doing this than we can robbing cars and houses. And there's less risk. I mean, a smackhead isn't gonna call the cops on us, is he?'

'How much does it pay?' asked Macca.

'We get a twenty per cent cut from each one.' That didn't really mean much to Macca and when he flashed a puzzled look, Todd explained, 'Some of these dickheads owe him hundreds.'

'How? Surely, he doesn't let them have that much?'

'Well yeah. A lot of them sell the drugs on then give him what they owe once the drugs are sold. The problem is though, they don't always stick to the arrangement. And that's where we come in.'

Macca was beginning to realise that this friend of Todd's uncle was doing more than a bit of dealing. It sounded as though he was a main dealer with several minions selling drugs on his behalf.

'How many of them owe him?' asked Macca.

'At the moment, fifteen. Imagine it, if every one of them owes him five hundred, we get fifteen lots of a hundred quid. That's fifteen hundred quid just for smacking a few junkies around.'

'But what if they haven't got the money?'

'Then they should have thought of that before they took the piss, shouldn't they? Besides, junkies will always find a way to make money. Once they're hooked on summat, they'll do anything to get their next fix. Some of these bastards would sell their grandma if they thought it would stop their cravings. We just need to make sure that the money comes to us before it goes on more fuckin' drugs.'

Macca felt a flash of guilt. The word 'grandma' reminded him of the set-to he had with Doris earlier. But he soon dismissed his guilt pangs. He needed to focus on what his mate was telling him. Todd was offering him an easy way to make money and he was seriously considering it.

'What will we do about the house break-ins?' he asked.

'The other lads can still do them. It doesn't take five of us.'

'And the cars?'

'We'll do a few but we'll still get a cut of any the others do because it's us that have got the arrangement with Clive. I'll sort it out with the other lads. They can do most of them.'

'What about Shay?'

'What about him?'

'Doesn't he wanna do this with you?'

'I dunno. I haven't asked him. I think you'll be better at it. You're tougher than Shay. Besides, there's something not right with him lately. He's always been a bit ropey but he's all over the place at the moment. I don't know why.'

'What d'you mean?'

'I dunno. I can't put my finger on it. But he's not right somehow. Anyway, I'm asking you first. If you're not up for it, then I'll see what Shay thinks.'

Macca didn't bother asking whether Todd had asked Spinxy and Leroy. He knew that Todd didn't have as much respect for them as he did for him and Shay.

'We'll be quids in, Macca.' Todd assured him. 'Less hassle, more money. What do you say?'

Macca grinned. 'OK. I'll come to the first one with you, see what I think.'

24

Oct 1988

Macca accompanied Todd to the address they had been given. It was in the same block of flats where Macca lived but at the opposite end of the sprawling development. They made their way up the stairs, which had landings after every two fights bordered by a concrete slab that only reached waist height. From that point upwards the landings were open to the elements. Macca noticed the smell of urine and the rotting debris among the dust and leaves that had blown in.

A large balcony ran the length of the flats and again it was bordered by a pebble-dash concrete slab that only reached waist height. Macca knew of people who had thrown themselves off the balcony and onto the pavement below. It didn't surprise him. Living in a place like this could easily drive you to suicide.

Going to a different part of the development made Macca view it with fresh eyes. Each individual flat had a tacky plastic front door and windows surrounded by flimsy-looking panels. The panels were dirty and stained, and many of the windows had discoloured lace curtains behind them with the odd piece of hardboard where the windows had been smashed in. Was it really that bad in his part of the flats?

Todd soon found the address they were looking for and hammered on the front door. It was answered by a youth who didn't look much older than them, and Macca took in the strong smell of weed that met them. The youth was skinny, of average height and had one of those aggressive faces with hard lines that made him look as though he'd had a troubled upbringing. When he caught sight of them, he grimaced and demanded, 'What the fuck do you want?'

'We've come to collect for Billy McGregor,' said Todd.

The youth tried to shut the door, but Todd had preempted him. He blocked it with his foot then shoved the youth back and stepped inside. Macca followed him and shut the door behind them.

They stumbled into the first door they came to, which appeared to be the lounge, although Macca had never known a lounge like it. There was no furniture as such, just beanbags, cushions and upturned crates with planks of wood on them. One of the makeshift tables was full of drug paraphernalia and empty beer cans and another contained takeout trays with the remnants still stuck to them. Here there were other smells mixed in with the weed, the overall tone one of dirt and decay.

'I ain't got it,' said the youth, stepping away and bouncing on the balls of his feet.

Todd nodded at Macca who began to ransack the room. He found a few large plastic boxes dotted around. Macca turned them all out, tipping their contents onto the floor in search of money. There was clothing, a watch, a few photos and various other personal items.

'Leave them alone, you bastard!' shouted the youth.

Todd gripped the youth and pushed him up against the wall, his hands around his throat while an emaciated mongrel barked at him but didn't dare to step forward.

'Then tell us where the fuckin' money is then. Seven hundred and sixty fuckin' quid you owe.'

'I ain't got it!' the youth yelled.

'Right, then we'll take the drugs.'

'I ain't got any.'

'Well, what the fuck have you done with 'em then? You must have sold them on in which case you'll be quids in.'

'Get your fuckin' hands off me,' the youth whined and was rewarded with a few smacks around the head.

Todd caught the lad hard on the nose and it burst into a flurry of blood and mucus, which ran down the lad's face. He squealed and raised his hands to cover his nose. Todd gave him a few seconds to recover while Macca continued ransacking the room, pulling up rancid, stained cushions and looking under them for drugs or cash.

'That was just a taster. Now, tell us where the money is, or you'll get some more.'

The lad was about to plead again that he didn't have it when Todd punched him hard in the gut.

'Alright, alright!' panted the youth, now clutching his throbbing midriff. 'I-I've only got two hundred,' he managed to say between sucking in air.

'You sure?' asked Todd, grabbing him by his hair and pulling his head up.

'Alright, I can let you have three but, I swear, that'll leave me with no food, and the fuckin' rent's overdue as well.'

'If you're expecting pity then you won't fuckin' get it,' said Todd. 'Now show me where the money is.'

'OK, wait here.'

He stumbled from the room and Todd flashed Macca a look. Macca knew he wouldn't settle for that and as Todd set off after the lad, he followed behind. They found him in the bedroom, reaching underneath a grubby mattress. He pulled a wad of notes out and began counting them out. But Todd didn't want whatever the lad could spare or thought he could spare. He wanted it all. Todd upended the mattress and flung it against the far wall. He told Macca to pick up the remaining cash while he grabbed the wad from the lad's hand.

'No, no, don't clean me out, please. I swear, I ain't got no more,' pleaded the lad.

Todd began to count the notes and asked Macca to do the same. 'How much?' he asked once they'd both finished counting.

'One eighty,' said Macca.

'And I've got two forty here. That makes four twenty.' Then he turned to the youth. 'That means you still owe three hundred and forty.'

The youth, no longer cocky, shrank back, expecting another hiding. But Todd surprised Macca when he peeled of a couple of tens and threw them to the ground. 'Make it three sixty. You can take the twenty. Get yourself summat to eat. You look like you could do with a fuckin' good feed. We'll be back next week for the rest.'

The lad was grovelling on the floor for the twenty before they'd even left the flat.

'How come you let him have twenty back?' asked Macca. 'I thought you wanted the lot.'

Todd shrugged. 'I dunno.' Then he laughed. 'But don't tell anyone or they'll think I've gone fuckin' soft.'

It was moments like this that made Macca realise Todd wasn't all bad. Neither was he but, like Todd had reasoned, these people owed money and they were just there to see to it that they paid up.

He'd been doing the collections with Todd for weeks now. There wasn't much to it really. Todd carried out most of the punishments and he was there just for backup. He got the feeling Todd enjoyed it and he didn't want to spoil his fun, so he only joined in when necessary, like the times when there was more than one person at the property or when they had a druggie who was a bit handy with his fists.

There were often times like today where Todd had done something that seemed a bit odd, and Macca wondered whether he had a softer side. Then again, it might have been just another way to demonstrate his control over the people who owed money, gaining satisfaction as he saw them grovel for a few crumbs.

Occasionally Shay came with them if there was a perceived threat, and they needed more manpower, but mostly it was just Macca and Todd. Macca was still involved in the house break-ins and car robberies too but out of all his jobs, the collections were by far the easiest. Todd had been right; they were onto a nice little earner.

25

Dec 1988

Macca and Spinxy were walking through the estate on their way to meet Todd. He hadn't mentioned where Shay and Leroy were tonight but Macca presumed they were on a job.

They were approaching the end of a narrow street that led onto a busier road. When they turned the corner, they could see Todd in the distance but ahead of him were three other youths.

'Shit,' whispered Spinxy. 'It's the MPG.'

The MPG were a local gang whose initials represented the words 'money, power and girls'.

'It's OK,' said Macca. 'They've got no problem with us. I often see them round here and they're alright.'

But as the youths drew nearer, Macca could tell from the expressions on their faces that the vibe was anything but alright.

'Are you Todd Brown's gang?' asked the gang leader, a handy-looking lad with acne scars.

'Yeah, that's right,' said Macca, wondering what they wanted.

'I heard you'd been dealing on our territory,' said the lad.

'No, not us,' said Macca. 'We're anti-drugs.'

'That's not what I heard.'

Without saying anything further, the lad drew out a small utility knife and rushed him. Acting on instinct, Macca side-stepped the lad just as he was about to thrust the blade. The momentum caused the lad to topple over, and Macca jumped on his back, wrestling him for the blade.

He couldn't see what was going on around him, but he could hear scuffling and groaning. He presumed the other two MPG members were setting about Spinxy. Eventually he took command of the knife and jumped to his feet.

His intention had been to fend the gang off while he tried to convince them that he was telling the truth. But he could see that the other MPG members had Spinxy on the ground and were kicking him viciously, their feet clad in sturdy boots.

'Fuckin' get off him!' Macca yelled, holding out the knife in as menacing a fashion as possible. 'Or you'll get some of this.'

One of the lads turned away from Spinxy, and pulled out his own blade. He charged at Macca, surprising him with his speed and ferocity. Macca was quick to react, and he swerved to avoid being cut. But he wasn't quite quick enough. He didn't feel anything at first, but the lad's proximity told Macca that the blade had caught him. A quick glance at the blood on his arm confirmed it.

In the intensity of battle, Macca didn't notice Todd's approach till he heard him let out a loud tribal yell as he swiped at the blade-wielding youth with a knife so large it made the MPG's blades look like toys. His first swipe missed so he came down with the knife again, partially severing two of the youth's fingers. The youth screamed and grabbed at his damaged hand, temporarily letting down his guard.

By now the gang leader, minus his weapon, was on his feet. Spinxy's attacker had joined him, waving his own utility knife. The three of them grouped together, trying to prepare for another attack from Todd. The leader grabbed the blade from his injured friend and stepped to the fore.

For a moment there was a stand-off. Todd looked shaken by what he had done but then Macca noticed a swift change in him. Todd tried to cover his shock with an immense show of bravado, as though he chopped people's fingers off every day of the week.

'Who else fuckin' wants some?' he yelled, slicing the large hunting knife through the air to show he meant business.

It missed the MPG's leader by mere centimetres, and he held up his hands in a placatory gesture. 'Not me, mate. I was just asking why you've been dealing on our patch. But it's OK. We can come to an arrangement if you want, share the territory.'

'I'm not interested in no fuckin' territory!' Todd screamed at them. 'You bunch of drugged-up dickheads. Fuckin' do one before I cut you up good and proper.'

The three lads didn't wait to be told twice. Stepping away backwards in case Todd came at them from behind, they waited until they were some distance before they turned around and ran.

'Fuck!' shouted Todd, putting down his weapon. Then he

took hold of Macca's arm and examined it. 'We need to get you to the hospital, mate.'

Macca looked down at the cut on his arm, which he had been clutching to stem the blood. 'We can't. They'll be there.'

'Shit, yeah. OK, they'll probably go to the infirmary so let's get you to Stepping Hill Hospital instead. We're not far from the garage. Clive will lend us a car.'

'What the hell just happened?' said Macca. 'I don't even know what they were on about, summat about us dealing on their turf.'

'I bet word's got back to them about the collections,' said Todd. 'Well, they can fuckin' do one. We're not dealing, we're just collecting, and the collections are a nice little earner, so we'll carry on with them. We'll just have to be careful in case them bastards want to start summat again.'

As Todd spoke, Macca noticed that Spinxy was now up off the ground. 'How are you, Spinxy?' he asked.

Spinxy was looking dazed. 'It fuckin' hurts,' he complained.

'What does? Your head?'

'Nah. Nah, I fuckin' curled up, didn't I? But the bastards kept booting me in my back and legs.' He rubbed his back to demonstrate his point.

'OK, you'd better come to the hospital as well,' said Todd.

'Nah, my mum'll fuckin' kill me if she knows I've been scrapping.'

Todd let out a sigh of exasperation. 'OK, we'll drop you off later.'

Then he picked up his knife, wiped it on some grass and led the way to Clive's garage.

REDEMPTION

*

The following day Joanne had just come in from work when there was a knock at the door. She opened it to find Shell standing on the doorstep. It was the first time she had ever known Shell to call at her house and she surmised straightaway that something wasn't right.

'Oh. Hi, Shell,' she said with a note of alarm in her tone.

'I need to have a word,' said Shell, urgently.

Joanne guessed that this might be something she didn't want her family to overhear so she grabbed her keys and walked down the garden path with Shell.

'What is it?'

'It's Macca. He's been injured. 'They were in a fight with another gang, and this guy pulled a knife on him.'

'Shit! You're joking. When did this happen?'

'Last night.'

'Is he alright?'

'Dunno. I heard Todd had taken him to the hospital pouring in blood.'

'Oh my God!' said Joanne.

For a moment she stood in shock, Shell watching her with what appeared to be a grimace on her face.

Eventually Joanne spoke. 'I'm sorry, Shell. I need to go back in,' she said. 'I need to phone Macca.'

She rushed back indoors. She was relieved that her father wasn't home yet, and her mother was in the kitchen preparing their evening meal while Mandy was upstairs. Taking advantage of their absence, Joanne rang Macca from the phone in the hall.

'Macca! How are you? Shell told me you'd been injured. Are you alright?'

'Yeah, course I am. It's just a bit of a cut, that's all.'

'But Shell said you'd been to the hospital.'

'Yeah, I did, but it's no big deal. It just needed a couple of stitches.'

'What happened? Shell said a gang attacked you, and that you're in a gang.'

She sensed a moment's hesitation before he replied. 'No, she's getting it confused. We were attacked by a gang, but I was just with my mates – Spinxy and Todd.'

'Well why did they attack you?'

'Because they're nutcases. It's that MPG lot. They love having a go at people.'

'Oh my God. You're lucky it wasn't worse if they were carrying knives. Were your friends stabbed as well? Are they OK?'

'They're fine. It was only me.'

Joanne couldn't help thinking that that sounded a bit strange but then he said, 'I think the guy that did it shit himself when he saw the blood. It was probably the first time he'd used a knife. Anyway, Todd walloped his mate and then they scarpered.'

'Thank God for that,' she said.

Joanne was still confused as to why the gang had picked on them. She had a feeling it was something to do with Todd, who she felt was a bad influence on Macca. She was about to pursue the matter when she heard a key in the front door lock so she rushed to finish the call. Her father was home.

26

Jan 1989

'How's your arm now?' asked Joanne two weeks later.

'Fine, it was nowt.'

'Well, it didn't look like nowt to me. Let me have a look how it's healing.'

'No, stop fussing. I've told you it's fine.'

He smiled to lessen the harshness of his words and for a moment he gazed at her with those ravishing blue eyes. When he leant in for a kiss, Joanne responded. She felt his hand graze her nipple and immediately became aroused. Macca slipped his hand down her top and then underneath her bra.

It took all her willpower to break the kiss and pull away. 'Not now, your mum's downstairs. We'll have to wait till she's out again.'

'But it's been a week since she left us alone in the house and I want you, Jo.' He looked at her again. 'I can't get enough of you.'

Joanne felt her heart flutter under his intense gaze. Even

though they'd been together for a year and a half, he still had this effect on her. Every time she saw him, she was filled with desire and just a glance from him in a certain way sent ripples of pleasure tingling down her spine.

She loved being with Macca and was always excited at the prospect of seeing him. He had a cheeky charm that she loved, and she enjoyed their banter. Apart from that, he was very loving and affectionate.

But the only drawback with Macca was that her parents wouldn't approve. She'd met his mum a while ago and she seemed really nice. And they spent a lot of time at his home when he wasn't taking her out up town and splashing the cash. But she never took him to her home.

As far as her parents were aware she was seeing someone called Mark who she had met on a night out in Manchester with her friends from work. And she daren't tell them any more than that. Macca didn't seem to mind. He understood how she felt and said he'd rather see her on the sly than have her parents trying to break them up.

Joanne knew there were things he kept hidden from her. He'd told her he was on the dole but that he did bits of work for Todd's uncle. Apart from always having lots of money on him, he was constantly having to meet up with Todd, and she wondered exactly what sort of work he was involved in.

Since she'd been seeing Macca, she had been treading a thin line. She wanted the thrill and excitement of being with him but didn't want to get in too deep because instinct told her he was involved in something bad, and she didn't want any part of that.

'Come on,' he said. 'Let's go out.'

'Where?'

'Anywhere you like. We can go to town if you like, hit the shops and maybe a few bars later, have summat to eat, whatever you fancy. It'll give you a chance to show me off.'

'Me show you off?'

He laughed teasingly. 'Yeah, you can show everyone what it's like to have such a cool, gorgeous boyfriend. Let 'em see how lucky you are.'

Joanne smiled and tapped him playfully on the arm. 'Cheeky sod.'

They made their way downstairs and hadn't quite reached the bottom when they heard the front doorbell. Macca answered it. 'Oh, hiya Gran.'

She bustled past him and then eyed Joanne before saying. 'Well, aren't you gonna introduce me then?'

Macca smiled. 'Yeah, this is Joanne.' Then he turned to Joanne, saying, 'And this is my gran.'

'Joanne who?' asked Doris.

'What do you wanna know that for?'

'It's Walker,' said Joanne.

'Oh yeah. You're not Alan Walker's girl by any chance, are you?'

Joanne smiled. 'Yeah, that's right.'

Doris held her hand out. 'Well, I'm very pleased to meet you.'

'Thanks,' said Joanne. 'Me too.'

'We're just going out,' said Macca. Then he addressed Joanne. 'Let's just say tarrah to my mum and then we'll be off.'

Joanne did as he suggested and then they made their way out of the house as Doris made her way in.

*

'Bloody hell, that's a turn-up for the books, isn't it?' Doris said to Debbie once Macca and Joanne had gone out. 'You never told me he was seeing Alan Walker's girl.'

Debbie wasn't sure what her mother was getting at. 'Yeah, he's been seeing her for ages now; it must be about eighteen months,' she replied. 'I told you he had a girlfriend, didn't I? I'm surprised you've not seen him with her up till now.'

'I knew he had a girlfriend, but you didn't tell me who she was.'

'That's because I didn't know. All I knew was that she's called Joanne and lives somewhere round here. Who's Alan Walker anyway?'

'Bloody hell, Debbie, you're hopeless. He's the local councillor. He's got a decent job as well. Factory manager or summat. I know his mother.'

Debbie laughed. 'Well, I don't know everyone like you, do I, Mum? I'm not as nosy.'

'Eh, less of your bloody cheek,' said Doris. 'Anyway, my point is, she's from a decent family.'

'Good, I'm glad.'

'Is it serious?'

'I dunno. He really likes her though – I can tell. She comes round here quite a lot.'

'Good. Well, let's hope she can keep him on the straight and narrow and away from all those deadbeats he keeps knocking about with.'

'Oh, he still sees them as well,' said Debbie, but she wished she hadn't spoken when she saw the anguished expression on her mother's face.

Debbie knew there was little chance of him giving up his mates or his way of life. It was something she'd grown to accept and, if she was honest with herself, she'd got used to having extra money in the house.

She had expressed her concerns to him over what he got up to, but he always assured her that everything was fine, and he wouldn't do anything that could get him into trouble. She only wished she could believe it. But for now, she'd keep her thoughts to herself. There was no point upsetting her mother.

27

Feb 1989

Billy McGregor was a man in his mid-forties. He was what Macca's grandma would have called a bit of a character. Always joking, Billy had a crude humour, but could be serious when needed. He stood at over six feet and always wore a T-shirt even when it wasn't hot. Macca wondered whether that was to demonstrate his manliness or to show off his huge, tattooed arms. Unfortunately, the tight-fitting T-shirts also showed his enormous beer belly.

Billy lived in a big, detached house in Heaton Moor, a middle-class area full of professional types. But, from what Todd had told Macca, he used to live on the estate near to Macca and still frequented some of the pubs there. Macca supposed that was why a lot of the people owing Billy money lived nearer to them than they did to him.

Macca had got used to going to the house. Often Billy's wife or one of his kids would answer the door and would lead them through to what Billy liked to call his office. It wasn't an office as such. There was a table there with chairs around it and a filing cabinet but there wasn't a desk. This was as far as Macca got inside Billy's home, but Macca could tell it was a smart gaff from the exterior and the way the hall was decorated. Even the room Billy called his office had a plush carpet and expensive-looking pictures on the walls.

Today Macca and Todd were visiting Billy to hand over money from collections. Since their set-to with the MPG there hadn't been any repercussions. Macca hoped Todd's recklessness had scared them off, and Todd had suggested it wasn't worth mentioning the fight to Billy. He didn't want him thinking they weren't up to the job.

They found Billy sitting at the table waiting for them with a satisfied smile on his face. 'Has the bint gone?' he asked, referring to his young, attractive wife.

'Yeah, she's just walked down the hall.'

'Good. That means we can get on with things without her poking her nose in. She does my fuckin' head in at times.' Then he grinned lecherously. 'Still, she has her uses, I suppose.'

Macca humoured him by returning a smile but Todd's only response was to pull out a chair and sit himself on the other side of the table to Billy. Macca followed suit.

'You two been behaving yourselves?' asked Billy.

'Course we have,' said Todd.

'How did you go on with that last lot?'

'Great!' Todd enthused, passing him a wad of cash. 'We got most of them. There's only two of 'em still owing but even they've paid some off. We'll make sure we get the rest though. We're going round to see one of 'em after this.'

'Who are they?' asked Billy. Todd passed him a sheet of paper containing the details and Billy said, 'I might have fuckin' known those two would be trouble. Don't take any shit from them. Do whatever it takes but make sure you get my money.'

'Don't worry,' said Todd, 'we will.'

Billy got up from his seat and opened the filing cabinet from which he pulled a file and extracted a sheet of paper off the top. As per usual there was a list of names and addresses, which Billy had written together with details of how much they owed.

He passed it to Todd. 'Here's the next lot. See how you get on with them.'

Todd nodded. Billy then grabbed a calculator and returned to the previous list. He added up the figures Todd had marked next to each name and calculated the share due to Todd and Macca.

Billy grinned as he handled the wad of cash. 'I reckon there should be five thousand one hundred and twenty here, which means I owe you two lads one thousand and twenty-four quid. Let's have a look, shall we?'

Macca hated it when Billy counted the cash. He always had a dread that it wouldn't all be there. It had only been short once due to Todd's miscalculation and only by eighty pounds. Billy had gone apeshit and told them in detail what would happen if he thought they were trying to put one over on him.

Surprisingly, Todd had kept his cool rather than retaliating and Macca had presumed it was out of fear of losing further jobs from Billy rather than fear of Billy himself. Macca had learnt by now that nobody scared Todd. In the end Billy had solved the issue by taking what was due to him anyway and deducting the loss from their cut.

Since then, Todd had been obsessive about checking the

figures then getting Macca to do the same and checking them once again himself. Fortunately, due to Todd's diligence they had never been short again.

Billy finished counting the money and smiled. 'Nice job, lads.'

Then he separated the amount they were owed and passed it over to Todd, who tucked it into his pocket ready to split with Macca later.

'Give us a ring when you've got the next lot,' said Billy. 'Here's the other list back too. Make sure you sort them two out.'

'Don't worry, we will,' said Todd.

Billy then led them out of the house and, as usual, they heard him locking up and sliding a heavy bolt across the front door.

'You getting behind the wheel?' asked Todd, referring to their trip back in the car they had borrowed from Rob.

'Yeah, sure,' Macca replied.

'Great, I'll give this lot a scan.'

They got inside the car and Macca took off down the road. 'There's only six this time,' Todd commented, as he glanced at the list of names.

'And them other two,' Macca responded.

'Yeah, don't worry about them. We'll make sure we get it. Don't forget to stop off on the way home.'

Macca was about to reply when he was stopped by a yell from Todd.

'Fuckin' hell! I don't fuckin' believe it.'

'What? What's the problem?'

'The fuckin' tosser! No wonder he never wanted to come to Billy's with us.'

'What? What are you on about?' asked Macca.

'It's Shay. He's on the fuckin' list. And he owes Billy three hundred and ten quid.'

28

Feb 1989

Although Macca had tried to avoid stealing cars locally, he couldn't detract from the fact that Clive's garage wasn't a million miles away from home. Therefore, there was always the risk of being spotted by someone he knew.

Today he was driving a nearly new Merc to the garage and was only two streets away. He was sitting at traffic lights waiting for them to change when someone approached from the passenger side. Curious, Macca glanced across to find Gladys Thompson who was now knocking on the window to attract his attention.

That bloody woman! Why was she always around when he was inside a nicked car? It was as though she was spying on him. He knew she wouldn't be able to resist telling his grandma and he really could have done without getting any more stick from Two Chins, especially after he had won her round again by introducing her to Joanne. He drove on without speaking to Gladys.

Macca decided that the way round it would be either to

tell his gran that he was helping a friend who worked at a garage by test-driving the cars or, alternatively, he'd deny it altogether. Hopefully that would keep his gran off his back.

Once he'd delivered the car, Macca met up with Todd. 'Have you seen Shay yet?' asked Macca.

'No, I've been busy with a few other things. Besides, I think it's better that you come with me. Come on, we'll go round there now.'

Macca felt a bit uneasy about being involved but he knew that by now Todd regarded him as his right-hand man. Therefore, it was only fitting that he helped Todd sort out any problems even if those problems happened to involve other members of their gang.

'I'm still fuckin' fuming,' Todd complained as they made their way round to Shay's house. 'I can't believe Shay could be such a fuckin' knobhead. He knows how I feel about drugs. I knew he hadn't been right lately, but I feel such a dick now for not knowing why. It's because he's been drugged out of his fuckin' head half the time. I can't believe it. Why didn't I see it?'

'Probably because you weren't looking for it.'

Todd glanced back at Macca then stayed quiet for a few moments, but it was obvious that he was still troubled by Shay's behaviour as he then said, 'He might be in deeper than we think, y'know.'

'What do you mean?'

'I think he's been on them a while judging by how he's been acting. He's been like that for at least a few weeks. And how the fuckin' hell has he clocked up three hundred and ten quid of debt with Billy? That's a lot of fuckin' drugs. I've got a feeling he's been dealing. There was me thinking the

MPG were pissed off about the collections, but it might have nowt to do with that. It might be because they know Shay's been dealing on their turf.'

'Well, we'll soon find out,' said Macca as they turned into the road where Shay lived.

It was Shay's mum who answered the door and it took Shay a while before he responded to her shouts and came downstairs. As soon as he spotted Shay, Macca knew he'd taken something recently, which was probably why he'd taken so long to appear. His pupils were huge and his eyes bloodshot but, aside from this, there was something about his behaviour. He was happy and animated as though something exciting was about to happen.

'Hi, lads, everything alright?' he asked. 'What's happening? Are we going on a job? I'll be up for it? Not done a house for a while.'

His voice was too loud, and he didn't seem to care who could hear him; again, it was probably an effect of his recent drug use.

'We'll tell you outside,' said Todd.

'OK give us a sec. I just need to get summat from my room. I'll be down in a minute. Do you wanna wait inside?'

'No, it's OK. We'll wait out here.'

Todd didn't speak much while they waited for Shay, but Macca could tell by his body language that he was seriously pissed off. It was a couple of minutes before Shay came out of his house and fell into step with them as they walked down the street.

'So, what's going on?' asked Shay.

'We need to talk,' said Todd. 'Let's go to the park.'

It was getting late by now and Macca knew the

playground would be almost deserted. It would therefore give Todd the chance to speak to Shay in private and do anything else he might have in mind.

'Fuckin' hell, this is like secret service,' said Shay when they arrived at the park.

Todd still hadn't told Shay why he wanted to talk but now he led them to a deserted corner. As they walked, Macca looked around him. There were no longer any young children in the park, just some youths on a bench who were smoking and drinking cans of cheap lager. They were far enough away not to hear what was being said though.

Eventually Todd stopped walking and turned to face Shay, who almost bumped into him. 'Right, now I'll tell you what I want to talk about,' said Todd. His tone was hostile, and Shay stepped back slightly while Todd continued. 'I wanna talk about you and the fuckin' debt you've clocked up with Billy McGregor.'

'Billy McGregor? I don't know no Billy McGregor.'

Todd's hands shot out as rapidly as a supersonic jet and he gripped Shay by the throat. 'Don't fuckin' lie to me! It's bad enough that a mate of mine is taking drugs without you lying about it. How do you think I felt when I saw your name on the fuckin' list?'

Macca could detect a tremor in Todd's voice, which gave away his shock and emotion at finding this out about his long-time friend Shay.

'What list?' Shay struggled to ask.

'Bill McGregor's fuckin' list. The list of lowlife druggies who owe him money.'

Shay looked shocked, as though he had suddenly realised that he couldn't lie his way out of this anymore, and Todd eased his grip to enable him to respond. 'I-I didn't know you were collecting for Billy.'

Todd let go of Shay, pushing him away as he did so. 'Oh, so if you'd have known who we did the collections for, you'd have used a different supplier, would you?'

'It's OK,' said Shay. 'I'll get the money to him.'

'Are you fuckin' serious? This is about more than collecting the cash, Shay. You've let me down big time. How many fuckin' drugs have you been taking to rack up three hundred and ten quid of debt? And what are you on?'

'Just a bit of weed, that's all. And it wasn't all for me.'

'Oh, you've been selling it on, is that it? Is that why Macca got sliced by the fuckin' MPG? Well, in that case, you won't need any cash from working with us, will you? So, you can fuckin' do one. I need lads I can depend on, not fuckin' druggies.'

'It's not that bad, Todd, I swear. I don't take that much and I ain't been selling it on. I've been getting it for mates.'

'What fuckin' mates?'

'Just mates.'

'Tell me!' Todd yelled, grabbing Shay by the throat again. 'What fuckin' mates?'

When Shay shook his head, Todd responded by pummelling him with his fists. Macca stood back, watching. He felt bad for Shay but, at the same time, he understood where Todd was coming from. He was distraught that his mate was on drugs and was reacting in the only way Todd knew how. And he wasn't about to stop him; Shay had to learn.

After a while Todd took a break and stood back to assess the damage to Shay's face, which was already beginning to swell. 'Right, are you gonna tell me now who these mates are?'

'Why do you wanna know?'

'Because I wanna know what I'm fuckin' dealing with here, Shay. And because I don't believe you. I think you're fuckin' dealing as well as taking drugs yourself and you know how that makes me fuckin' feel. Now, are you gonna tell me?'

This went on for two more rounds of pummelling before Shay finally gave in, his face now bloody as well as swollen. 'They're your mates too!' he yelled, spitting out a tooth.

'What?'

'Leroy and Spinxy. They've been on it too.'

Macca's feeling of shock mirrored the expression on Todd's face. 'Fuckin' idiots!' he spat, in tandem with the intense disappointment that Todd was exhibiting.

29

Feb 1989

'You're a bunch of fuckin' knobheads!' Todd yelled to Shay. 'How the fuck can we run an operation with you lot drugged out of your fuckin' heads half the time? What have they been taking? Same as you?'

'Suppose,' muttered Shay.

'Suppose? What the fuck does that mean? You must know what they've been taking seeing as how you're the one that was supplying them. And how the fuck did they know about the drugs?'

'I might have mentioned it to them.'

'You must think I'm fuckin' stupid!' screamed Todd. 'You've obviously told them about the drugs hoping you can sell them on.'

When Shay didn't respond, Todd paused for a moment, deep in thought again before he said, 'Right, turn your pockets out.'

Shay did as he asked. But he was too willing. The few

coins and packet of chewing gum fooled neither Macca nor Todd, who stepped forward. 'Now let's do it properly.'

He pulled a few reefers, a packet of pills and a fistful of notes out of Shay's pockets. 'This isn't just a bit of weed. What is it? Ecstasy?' Without giving Shay chance to reply he yelled, 'You fuckin' cunt!' kicking him hard in the shin before he pocketed the drugs. 'Right, these are going back to Billy, and I'll have the fuckin' money you owe too.'

'I ain't got it all,' pleaded Shay. 'But I'll get it to you, I promise.'

'Too fuckin' right you will,' said Todd, counting out the notes he had taken. 'Right, there's one hundred and sixty here so that means you still owe a hundred and fifty.'

'I'll let you have it; I promise I will, but I'll need to get some work first. It'd be easier if I was working with you. I could let you have it out of my next job.'

'Don't push your fuckin' luck!' snapped Todd. 'I've told you, I don't have druggies working for me.'

'I'll ditch 'em, I swear. I wasn't doing that many anyway. Leroy does tons more than me.'

Todd flicked a glance at Macca who quickly chipped in, 'I'll talk to Leroy. And Spinxy. I'll make sure they know the score.'

'Make sure you fuckin' do!' said Todd to Macca's relief. Then a thought occurred him. 'You're not taking owt are you?'

'Am I fuck! I feel the same as you, Todd, about drugs. It's a mug's game.'

Macca didn't want his friends to get a taste of the same treatment Todd had dished out to Shay whose face was now tinged purple and daubed with blood. He hoped he could talk some sense into them once they knew how Todd felt. Besides, he wasn't that happy with the situation himself. Drugs were for losers, and he was surprised that two of his long-standing mates could be so stupid.

'Let me know how you go on though,' said Todd. 'If they're gonna be a problem, I wanna fuckin' know about it and I'll be keeping my eye on all of 'em.'

'Does that mean we'll still be working with you?' begged Shay.

Todd was obviously having a good think about the situation. He knew as well as Macca did that an operation with only two of them wouldn't be as effective as one with five. And Macca knew that Todd had high ambitions for them all.

'Right, this is how it's gonna be,' said Todd. He turned to Macca. 'Me and you will have a word with Leroy and Spinxy together,' he said, in a change of heart. 'I'll ring you tomorrow to arrange a meet-up. There's no way they're getting off fuckin' lightly with this.'

Macca didn't argue with him. He was beginning to accept that Todd was right. They might have been his friends but why should they get off lightly when Shay had got a good beating? 'OK,' he said, tremulously. 'But can I ask the questions? I need to know what the fuck's been going on.'

Todd nodded then addressed Shay. 'And you can carry on working with us providing you give up the drugs.' Shay was about to respond but Todd cut in, 'And I want no fuckin' bullshit. I'll be watching you. And if I find you're still dealing then I want fuck all to do with you. And no tipping off Leroy and Spinxy that we're onto them either. Me and Macca will deal with it.'

'Sure,' said Shay. 'Whatever you say, boss. I promise, no lies.'

Macca wondered if he detected a note of sarcasm in the word 'boss'. But, no, surely he wouldn't dare.

Todd didn't seem to have picked up on it as he responded, 'There'd better fuckin' not be. There's no second chances.'

Then Todd walked away without saying another word to either of them. Shay cast a glance at Macca, his expression beseeching. But Macca was disgusted with him as well and there was no way he was going to say anything to soften the impact of Todd's words. So, he walked away too, choosing to go home alone.

Tonight had troubled him. All the lads were aware of how he and Todd felt about drugs. He remembered the time when they first set up the gang and all swore that they would avoid the stuff because it always led to problems, and they were going to be better than that.

At the time they'd all shared Todd's belief that they were going to do great things. But now, both Macca and Todd felt deceived. Then it occurred to Macca that maybe the fact that he and Todd had been collecting for a supplier had made the other lads think it was suddenly OK to do drugs.

But it wasn't OK. As Todd had said, there was a difference between doing the collections and getting directly involved in dealing themselves. Or perhaps the difference wasn't so apparent. Macca refused to think about it any more tonight. He'd follow Todd's lead and see where it took them, and he'd hope that the other lads would see sense, and that everything could go back to how it was.

*

Five minutes later he was almost home. He'd had enough for one night and as he walked along the landing to the flats, he decided that what he needed was a few cans in front of the TV before turning in. He hoped he could persuade his mum to watch something decent for a change instead of the usual crap she watched like *Last of the Summer Wine* or *The Flying Doctors*.

He put his key in the lock and stepped into the hallway. There was the sound of voices coming from the lounge. It was a man's voice, and he hoped his mum hadn't brought one of her men back home. But then he realised the time. She normally brought them back after the pub and it wasn't late enough for that.

Macca pushed open the lounge door, surprised to find two policemen sitting on the sofa. All conversation stopped as three faces peered up at him, his mother's etched with worry.

'Mark McNeil?' asked one of the policemen and Macca nodded. The policeman stood up and took a step towards him, then the other one did the same. 'We're arresting you in connection with the theft of a vehicle.'

The police then quoted the vehicle registration and read him his rights. Macca flicked his eyelids shut and exhaled slowly, the stress of the moment getting to him. As if things weren't already bad enough, it looked as though this night had just become a lot worse.

30

Feb 1989

Joanne and her sister were in their bedroom sitting on the bed and listening to music. As Kylie Minogue sang, *I Should Be So Lucky*, Mandy asked, 'Are you not seeing Macca tonight?'

'No. Shush, don't let them hear you,' whispered Joanne.

Mandy smiled. 'You can't keep it from them forever y'know. They're bound to find out sooner or later who Mark is. And you *have* been seeing him for ages.'

'Over eighteen months,' said Joanne, proudly. 'Mum keeps trying to get me to bring him round to introduce him to them but there's no way. As far as she's concerned, he's someone called Mark who I met on a night out in Manchester but imagine what her and Dad would be like if they knew it was Macca? You know what Dad's like, he'd only give me a load of grief.'

'Yeah, I know. He might even make you finish with him.'

'No way! I'm nearly eighteen now. I can see who I like.'

'Try telling *him* that.'

'I will if he starts. He's not gonna stop me. I love Macca.'

Mandy fell silent for a moment then she looked a bit awkward before she finally took a deep breath and asked, 'Is he the one you want to settle down with though?'

'What do you mean? What's wrong with him?'

'Nothing. Well, I mean, Dad will want you to be with someone who's got prospects, won't he? And Macca, well, what does he do exactly?'

Joanne became defensive. 'This and that.'

'What's this and that?'

'Just stuff. He helps his mate's uncle with things. Anyway, it's not his fault he couldn't get a permanent job. And he does alright. He's always taking me out to nice places. And he treats me well. I don't know why people have a downer on him. He's really nice. And he's funny. We're always having a laugh.'

'Are you sure all his money comes from doing jobs for his mate's uncle?'

'Yeah, course it does.'

'What kind of jobs are they though, Jo?'

'What d'you mean?'

'You know, are they all legal and above board?'

'Yeah, course they are. Macca's not like that.'

'Um, well, it's up to you but I wouldn't want to be in your shoes when Dad finds out.'

Macca was feeling troubled when he woke up in his own bedroom and glanced at the flashy digital alarm clock he had bought. When he realised the time was 13.17, he sat up in the bed and cursed. 'Fuck!'

He couldn't believe he'd lain in that late but, then again, the police had kept him in the station for most of the night while they fired questions at him. Fuck Gladys Thompson! Not only had she dobbed him in to the police, but she'd also given them the registration number of the car he was driving. And a quick check on their system had verified that the car was stolen.

Although the police had released him without charge, Macca knew they'd be trying to gather other evidence such as the location of the vehicle. They'd also be checking out the alibi he had given for his whereabouts at the time of the incident.

Now he was panicking because the car was still at Clive's garage. He had been only two streets away from the garage when Gladys spotted him, and he was worried that the police might make the connection. They could be searching the garage now for all he knew.

Macca went downstairs to find his mum lethargically putting some shopping away. She looked up at him as he walked into the kitchen, and he could tell she was troubled.

'What time did you get back last night?' she asked.

'About five in the morning.'

'Bloody hell. That was late. No wonder I didn't hear you come in. What have they said?'

'Not much. They're trying to nab me for a stolen car. Some old biddy told them she saw me at the wheel.'

'And were you?'

'No, course not.'

Her expression told him she didn't believe him, but she didn't push the matter. Instead, she asked, 'Have they charged you?'

'No, they've got nowt on me, only the word of an old biddy.'

'Your friend Todd rang,' she said, changing the subject.

Suddenly Macca recalled that he was supposed to be going with Todd today to speak to Leroy and Spinxy about the drugs. 'Shit!' he said. 'Why didn't you tell me?'

Without waiting for an answer, he went through to the living room and shut the door behind him. Then he picked up the phone, another item his illicit earnings had bought, and dialled Todd's number.

'Hi, mate, you alright?' he asked.

'Where the fuck have you been?' asked Todd. 'I've rung you three times.'

Macca realised Todd had probably made the other two calls while his mother had been at the shops.

'I've only just got up,' he replied. 'I was at the fuckin' cop shop till five this morning. Some old biddy saw me driving that Merc I nicked, and she's told the cops. She's even given them the reg, so they know it's nicked. I need to get to the garage to sort things with Clive before the cops get onto it.'

'Have they charged you?'

'No, I've denied it and told them I was with Joanne.'

'Right. Is she OK with that?'

'Dunno, I haven't spoken to her yet. That's summat else I need to sort.'

'Shit! OK, tell you what, you get on to Joanne now. The cops are more likely to visit her before they twig about the garage. You can go to the garage after that. Oh, and don't worry about Leroy and Spinxy. I've already called a fuckin' meeting with them and Shay for later. I'll talk to them on my own if you can't make it. Ring me when you're done and let me know how you've got on.'

'Cheers, mate. Will do.'

Macca put the phone down. For a moment he thought about the situation with Todd. He had hoped to be there so he could act as buffer but without him there he worried about how the meeting might go. Then it dawned on him that if Todd was meeting Shay, Leroy and Spinxy on his own, he wasn't likely to get physical as he'd be outnumbered. He just hoped Todd handled it right.

But he couldn't afford to dwell on that now. He needed to speak to Joanne as soon as possible. He felt bad for putting this on her but when the police had asked where he was on the night in question, she was the person he thought of. He couldn't ask his mum because she'd already told the police he'd been out but she didn't know where. And somehow, he felt that the police wouldn't take his mates seriously.

Joanne, on the other hand, came from a nice family. Her dad was a councillor for fuck's sake! Surely that would carry some weight. Aside from that, he knew she was mad about him so hopefully she'd do all she could to make sure he stayed out of prison.

Turning to make sure his mother hadn't quietly slipped inside the room while he had been talking to Todd, he lifted the phone receiver again and dialled Joanne's number.

31

Feb 1989

'Joanne!' she heard her mother shout. 'There's a call for you. It's Mark.'

Joanne flashed her sister a smile then bounced down the stairs.

When she reached the bottom, she found her mother waiting in the hall with the telephone receiver in her hand. Although wall phones were now fashionable and even cordless for some people, Joanne's parents still insisted on having the phone on a table in the hall so that whoever was on it didn't disturb anyone else.

'It's about time we met this Mark,' commented Gillian as she handed the phone receiver to her daughter.

'You will soon,' said Joanne.

She put the phone to her ear, and was thrilled to hear Macca's voice on the other end of the line. 'Hiya, babe, you alright?'

'Yeah, yeah, I'm good,' she said, at the same time listening for her mother's fading footsteps so she was sure she'd have some privacy. 'What have you been up to?'

Despite his enthusiastic greeting, as soon as she heard him speak again, she had an inkling that he was troubled. 'I need a favour, Jo,' he stated.

'Depends what it is,' she teased.

He emitted an audible breath down the line and then the tone of his voice changed. 'I'm in a spot of bother.'

'What?'

'The police are trying to pin a stolen car on me.'

'What do you mean "pin" it on you?' she whispered so her parents couldn't overhear. 'What happened?'

'It's this old biddy. Someone my gran knows. She's saying she saw me driving a stolen car. She's a right old cow. My gran can't stand her.'

'Never mind the old biddy, did you do it or not?'

Joanne could sense a moment's hesitation then he said, 'No, course I didn't. But the thing is, unless I give the police an alibi for yesterday, they'll charge me with it and then I'll be well in the shit.'

Joanne knew what was coming so she wasn't surprised when he said, 'If they think I was with you then I'll be in the clear.'

'Oh no,' she said. 'You're not getting me involved.'

'Right, so what are you gonna do, Jo? See me go down for something I didn't do?'

His voice had taken on a note of desperation by now and she felt obliged to offer something to help. She did love him after all. 'What about your mum or your mates? Can't they give you an alibi?'

'No. My mum was in the house when the cops came

round. She told them she didn't know where I'd been all day. And there's no way the police would believe any of my mates.'

'Why not?' she asked, putting him on the spot.

He hesitated again before saying, 'Well, they're not like you are they, Jo? Your family's a bit, you know, posh.'

Joanne laughed. 'I'm a junior hairdresser, Macca. That's not posh. I'm not bloody Vidal Sassoon.'

'No, but your dad's a councillor, isn't he? The cops would believe you.'

'No, I'm not doing it. Anyway, I was out with Sonia last night,' she said, referring to one of her work colleagues.

'So, the cops aren't gonna know that, are they? You can easily tell them you were with me.'

'I don't know.'

'Jo, please, I'm begging you. You don't want me to end up inside, do you? If I get time, we'll never see each other.'

'Why would you end up inside if you're innocent?'

'I told you, they're trying to pin it on me. I need proof that I didn't do it.'

Joanne hesitated for a moment as she mulled things over. If he was innocent, then she really couldn't see there being a problem.

'I'd come and visit you,' she said flippantly, hoping it was the end of the discussion.

'No, Jo. I wouldn't want you in a place like that full of hardened criminals. It wouldn't be fair on you. So that means we wouldn't see each other for months, maybe longer. Maybe I'd get a few years.'

Joanne was weakening. The thought of not seeing Macca for years was unbearable. 'What would I have to do?'

'Just tell them you were with me in the evening from about six, six thirty. Tell 'em we went round a few pubs. Throw in a couple of names, *The Town Hall Tavern*, *The City Arms* and *The Vine*, but tell 'em you can't remember what the rest were called.'

'But what if they find out I'm lying?'

'They're not gonna do.'

'They could. They could show the pub staff photos of us and see if they remember us.'

'Jo, you've been watching too many episodes of *The Bill*. Do you really think they'd go to all that trouble for a car? They're far too busy with bigger crimes. Besides, the cops know the staff wouldn't remember us. The pubs are mobbed on a Saturday.'

The more he tried to convince her, the more she was inclined to provide him with an alibi. She had a niggling doubt that he was lying but her worry about not seeing him for a lengthy period was foremost in her mind. She didn't know how she'd cope; she was mad about Macca and couldn't imagine a life without him. And what harm could it do? After all, it was only a tiny lie, which would make sure they stayed together.

Finally, she conceded, 'OK, I'll do it. But I don't want anything like this to happen in the future, so you'd better make sure you stay out of trouble.'

'Babe, I haven't been in trouble. I told you, it's that old biddy trying to stir things up. She's probably done it on purpose 'cos her and my gran have...'

But Joanne didn't want to hear any more. 'Right, I'm going,' she said as her mother walked back through the hall and up the stairs.

Without any closing endearments, Joanne put the phone down. She resented Macca for putting her through this. Fair enough, there was little chance of her being caught out according to what he had said but it was still wrong to lie. And then there was an even bigger problem: how were her parents going to react when they found out?

Macca heaved a sigh of relief when he came off the phone. Thank God Jo had come through for him. He fuckin' loved that girl! He still felt bad for asking her and for lying but what choice did he have? He didn't want to risk being sent down.

He knew he'd been a bit out of order telling her he could get years when it was more likely to be a few months. He might even just get community service. But he didn't want to take that chance. The other thing he hadn't told her was that he had already given her name as an alibi down at the station, so it was an even bigger relief that she had come through for him.

Now that he'd sorted things out with Joanne, his next priority was to speak to Clive about the car. But he was disheartened to find that despite ringing his number several times, there was no reply. He called the garage but was rewarded with a recorded message telling him the opening hours. Fuck! What was he gonna do?

Finally, deciding he had no other option, he walked round to the garage. The shutters were down but Macca knew there was a door at the side. He walked round and tried the handle. It was locked so he knocked heavily until Clive came to answer it.

'Fuck's sake!' said Clive. 'What the fuck's got into you.'

'I've been trying to ring you. How come you didn't answer the phone?'

'Oh, that was you, was it? It's a Sunday for fuck's sake. I don't answer the garage phone on a Sunday. We're shut, aren't we?'

'The Merc,' said Macca. 'We need to get rid of it. The cops are on to me.'

'Chill, mate. It's already being dealt with.'

'But we can't keep it here. They might come and raid the place. They know I was driving it two streets away.'

'How?'

'I was seen, and the cops had it down as stolen. I was at the station all night last night being questioned.'

'Have they charged you?'

'No. I gave them an alibi.'

'Right. Well, I was just working on it when you nearly hammered my fuckin' door down. I don't normally keep hold of 'em for too long when they're hot. Besides which, I've already got a buyer for it. A guy I know has been looking for a good Merc like this, so it'll be going to him as soon as it's ready. I've filed the numbers off and changed the plate. I'm just about to do the respray. Trust me, mate, if the cops come round here, they won't fuckin' recognise it as the same car.'

'Thank God for that!'

'OK, well the sooner I can get rid of you, the sooner I can get the job done, so fuckin' do one, will you?'

Macca smiled at Clive's abrasive manner, relief now flooding his body. It was good to hear that things were in hand with the car. Hopefully he'd walk away from this no problems. Now the only other thing he had to worry about was his mates' involvement with drugs and fear over how Todd would handle it.

32

Feb 1989

By the time Macca arrived at the pub for the meeting with Todd and the rest of the lads, he was almost half an hour late. He found them in a small side room, which they occupied alone. Macca guessed that whatever had taken place earlier would have put other customers off sitting anywhere near to the gang and even the staff would be keeping their distance.

This didn't surprise Macca when he set eyes on Leroy's face, which was swollen and smeared with blood. He had hoped to act as a buffer so that Todd wouldn't go too hard on his mates, but it looked as though he was too late for that.

'Glad you could make it,' said Todd, smiling. 'Have you managed to sort everything out?'

Macca walked over and took up the seat that Todd had saved for him. Then, lowering his voice, he gave the lads a brief rundown of what had happened so far that day.

'Aw, that's great,' said Todd. 'Clive will soon have rid of

the car, no worries.' Macca nodded in response and Todd continued. 'Go and grab yourself a drink and I'll fill you in on what me and the lads have been discussing.'

Macca could tell by the emphasis Todd placed on the word 'discussing', as well as the state of Leroy's damaged face, that it hadn't been a friendly conversation. When he came back from the bar, Todd didn't waste any time on bringing Macca into the meeting.

'Right,' he began, 'me and the lads have had a chat, and they've agreed to avoid drugs in the future. Unfortunately, Leroy took a bit more persuasion, but we got there in the end.'

Macca examined the reactions of his friends: Leroy and Spinxy. Leroy appeared slighted, his expression stony, whereas Spinxy looked terrified, and Macca knew at once that Spinxy would have caved in as soon as Todd confronted them.

But Macca's sympathy for both of them was limited. He was as anti-drugs as Todd and couldn't believe his old mates had fallen into that trap. In a way it was best that Todd had dealt with them because his heavy-handed approach would have been more effective than anything he would have said to them.

For a while Macca and Todd stayed in the pub with the rest of the gang. During that time the atmosphere between the group was stilted with Spinxy trying to ingratiate himself with Macca and Todd, while Leroy and Shay talked among themselves.

Once Macca had drained the last of his pint, Todd stood up and announced, 'Right, come on. We need to see Billy again.' Then he turned to the rest of the lads, adding, 'And don't fuckin' forget what I've told you.'

Shay and Spinxy answered in the affirmative while Leroy nodded, his facial expression still sombre. Spinxy quickly stood up, saying, 'I need to go too.'

Macca knew Spinxy had been to the bar for another drink and now he eyed the pint glass, which was still half full.

'What about your pint?' asked Leroy.

'Oh, it's alright,' he answered nervously. 'I er – I've just remembered I need to go somewhere.'

Macca resisted a smile. He knew that Spinxy didn't want to be regarded as colluding with Shay and Leroy and was grateful that he at least had his loyalty. Or perhaps it was the threat of further violence from Todd that had prompted his hasty exit.

Leroy watched the three of them leave the pub before he turned to his mate Shay and asked, 'Why the fuck didn't you back me up? We could have fuckin' took Todd on if we'd all stuck together. Instead, Spinxy started wailing like a fuckin' baby and you just sat there and watched me get a pasting. We should have fuckin' told him to do one and gone out on our own.'

'He did the same to me,' said Shay, defensively.

'Well, I still think we should have took him on.'

'No, we fuckin' shouldn't! What we got off him was nowt. I tell ya, I've known Todd for years and he's a fuckin' head the ball. He was expelled from school loads of times for beating people up. He nearly blinded one lad.'

'So, we're just supposed to put up with it, are we?'

'No, we're fuckin' not. We just have to be a bit smarter, that's all.'

'What do you mean?'

'I mean, we can carry on doing drugs without him knowing about it. We just have to be careful he doesn't find out.'

'But it's got fuck all to do with him anyway. If we leave the gang, we can do what the fuck we want,' Leroy argued.

'Do you really think he'd let us get off scot-free if we walked away? Anyway, we do alright with him, don't we? And Todd's got big plans: warehouse robberies and stuff like that. It pays a lot. We could stick with him and still do the drugs on the side. Best of both worlds, innit?'

Leroy smiled. 'OK, yeah. I didn't think of it like that.'

'That's 'cos you're still pissed off 'cos he beat you up. Are you up for it then?'

'Yeah, sure.'

'Right, well tell your fuckin' face that. I know you're pissed off, but don't let the other lads know how you feel. We've gotta play it cool, Lee. If Todd and Macca can do their own fuckin' side-line, then they're not the only ones. We just need to make sure they don't find out about it, that's all.'

33

Feb 1989

Joanne was in her bedroom playing music and trying out some new makeup while Mandy was out at her boyfriend's house. When her dad shouted up the stairs for her, she tutted and looked at her reflection in the mirror, which showed one eye in a shade of blue and the other one bare.

'In a minute,' she shouted, grabbing at a tissue and attempting to remove the eyeshadow.

'No, now! You need to come now,' her dad shouted, and she could tell by his tone of voice that he wasn't happy.

Joanne trudged down the stairs expecting to find him waiting at the bottom for her. But he wasn't there. He was sitting in the lounge and there were two police officers there too, both young men in uniforms.

'Sit down!' ordered her father. 'These officers want to speak to you.'

The sofa was taken by the officers but, fortunately, her mother got up and said, 'Here, have my seat. I'm going to put the kettle on. Would any of you officers like a drink?'

Joanne waited while her mother took details of the drinks everyone wanted and then left the room. While she waited, she could feel her heart racing. She already knew why the police were here. She had been expecting them ever since Macca's call, but it didn't make her any less nervous that she might slip up and say the wrong thing.

After verifying her name, one of the officers, a red-headed man with a round face, began by saying, 'We'd like to ask you a few questions, Joanne. We're here in connection with a crime that's been committed.'

The officer noticed Alan's jaw drop at the same time as Joanne did. 'Oh, don't worry, Mr Walker, the officer was quick to assure him. Your daughter isn't being accused of anything. We're simply here to ask her a few questions.'

Alan's expression turned to one of relief, which was soon replaced by an accusatory glare in Joanne's direction before the officer continued speaking to her.

'Can you tell me please, Joanne, who you were with yesterday between the hours of six thirty and eight o'clock in the evening?'

'Yeah, I was with Macca,' said Joanne, trying to disguise the slight tremble in her voice. 'I mean, Mark; Mark McNeil.'

She was aware of her father's glare intensifying when he recognised the name.

'OK, and where were you both during that time?' asked the police officer.

'Town. We went to some pubs.'

'And which pubs were they?'

Joanne found in her panic that she couldn't remember

them all and she desperately searched her memory for the names Macca had given her. 'Er, erm, the *Town Hall Tavern*,' she said.

'And were you in there during all that time?'

'No, we went to a couple of others too. We were doing a pub crawl. Erm, one was the *Vine*,' she added, suddenly remembering one of the other names. 'And there was another one, next to it.'

'OK, so what time did you arrive in the *Town Hall Tavern*?'

'About six o'clock, maybe six thirty.'

'That was a bit early to go out drinking on a Saturday night, wasn't it?'

'He met me straight from work.'

'OK, and which pub did you go to next, after you left the *Town Hall Tavern*?'

Joanne hesitated. She was afraid to give the names of the pubs in a different order to what Macca had done and hoped she hadn't already slipped up by telling them they'd gone to the *Town Hall Tavern* first. 'I can't remember,' she said. 'But they were all around that area where all the banks and insurance companies are.'

The questioning continued for some minutes and Joanne was glad when the officers finally stopped quizzing her. She watched as they finished their drinks and made polite conversation with her parents before finally getting up from the sofa and allowing Alan to show them to the door.

Heaving a sigh of relief, Joanne stood up too and entered the hallway. She was about to dash up the stairs when her father, having shut the door on the officers, turned to her and said, 'Hey, not so bloody fast.' Then he pointed to the lounge.

'You can go and sit back down in there. I want a word with you.'

When Macca and Todd arrived at Billy McGregor's house, Macca was surprised to see that it was Billy himself who answered the door. He leant back and took a drag of a giant cigar, puffing his chest out as though he was quite proud of himself. Macca couldn't help thinking what a fuckin' cliché the man was.

'Come in, lads,' he said, swaggering down the hall to his office.

As he reached the door his wife appeared, and Billy addressed her. 'It's alright, I've answered it. You can take your pretty arse back to whatever you were doing.'

He patted her dismissively on the backside then his hand slid under her buttock, giving it a squeeze until she squealed with embarrassment and dashed away. Billy stared after her lasciviously before he turned back to Macca and Todd.

Licking his lips, he said, 'I'll be having some of that later. But first we've got things to see to. Come on, lads.'

He walked into his office with Macca and Todd following behind. Billy then followed the usual procedure, puffing on his cigar while Todd passed him the details of customer payments along with the cash. Then Billy set his cigar down while he counted the money, making sure it was all there before handing Todd their share.

Billy smiled smugly. 'Good, you've done well this time. Here's your next lot. Make sure they all cough up too. I want no shit off 'em.'

He reached for another list of names, which was lying

on the table, but, standing up, Todd stopped him before he could hand it over.

'No, that's the last,' he said. 'We're sacking it off.'

Billy looked as shocked as Macca was and he scratched at his crotch as he asked, 'Why? What's the problem?'

'No problem. We just don't wanna do it anymore.'

Billy looked put out. 'Well, there must be a problem. It's a good earner, this. You must be fuckin' mad to turn it down.'

Todd snarled back at him. 'I don't give a shit what you think, and we don't owe you an explanation.'

'What about you?' Billy asked Macca.

'Same as him,' said Macca, deciding that if Todd was turning down further work with Billy, then he must have a good reason for it.

Billy got out of his chair and walked across to Todd. Then he squared up to him, flexing his huge muscles as he asked, 'You sure you don't wanna change your mind?'

His face was mere centimetres from Todd's and his attitude must have angered Todd because he didn't wait for Billy to take things further. He gave him a swift uppercut and Billy's head bounced back. Quickly recovering, he launched himself at Todd until the two of them were engaged in a full-on fist fight.

By the time Macca got up out of his seat they had already taken several swipes at each other. Macca was undecided about what to do. Should he leave them to get on with it? But what if Billy got the upper hand? Watching them, he surmised that they were evenly matched, and blood was already gushing from Billy's nose and Todd's mouth.

Then Macca heard a piercing shriek, and he looked up to

see Billy's wife standing at the door, her hand held up to her mouth as she shrieked then shouted, 'Get off him!'

That made up Macca's mind for him. He couldn't risk her calling for backup, so he tried to get between the men and prise them apart. Then he was shouting too, 'Come on, Todd. Leave it!'

But Todd was too engrossed in the fight and by now he was getting the better of Billy who was panting heavily, his arms now cumbersome as he fired tired punches at Todd. Macca could see the determination in Todd's expression and was worried he would go too far. By this time Billy's wife had left the room but he could still hear the faint sound of a woman's voice. He had to get Todd out of there.

'Todd, stop! She's calling for backup. Todd!' he shouted repeatedly.

Eventually Todd seemed to come to his senses. He paused from thumping Billy who was now backing off and looked dazed. Macca locked eyes with his friend and felt a shiver as he detected the madness there. Trying to calm the situation, he talked more slowly.

'Come on, Todd. He's learnt his lesson. Let's go.'

As though in a daze, Todd nodded and backed away from Billy who waited till they were in the hallway before shouting, 'Right, go on then, fuck off, the pair of you. There's plenty more where you came from, and they'll be only too glad of the money.'

Macca was surprised at Billy's nerve considering the hiding Todd had already given him. He looked at his friend who glared, and Macca could see the tension in the tendons around his neck and shoulders. 'It's OK, let's go,' Macca encouraged before shouting to Billy, 'Don't worry, we're fuckin' going. I wouldn't wanna hang around an old lech like you for a minute longer.'

That seemed to defuse Todd's anger and he grinned at Macca as they continued towards the front door. Then he yelled, 'Yeah, you fuckin' old pervert.'

Macca was glad to get Todd away from the house. 'Shit! I thought you were gonna do him in there for a minute,' he said once they were outside. 'Aren't you worried about repercussions?'

'From who?'

'The big boys. Whoever Billy buys his supplies from.'

'Nah, Billy wouldn't dare tell them. He'd be too scared of losing face 'cos he got a hiding from a youngster.'

Todd didn't say anything more, but Macca knew it was a good job he had been there because if he hadn't stopped Todd then he was certain that his friend would have killed Billy McGregor.

34

Feb 1989

Alan gave Joanne a look of contempt as he asked, 'So that's who Mark is, is it? That bloody lowlife scum who lives on the estate? Is that who you're seeing?'

'He isn't lowlife, and he isn't scum.'

'Don't bloody bandy words with me. I know exactly what he is. What I want to know is why you're covering for him.'

Joanne could feel a flush creep across her cheeks as she lied. 'I *was* with him.'

'Well how come you told us you were going out with Sonia from work?' Gillian chipped in.

'Because I knew *he'd* go mad,' Joanne replied, placing emphasis on the word he as she referred to her father.

'Don't you dare take that tone when referring to me!' blasted Alan. 'Do you bloody wonder why I'm angry? Not only have you chosen to knock about with one of the estate's criminals, you're also lying to the police. And it was bloody obvious you were lying. It wouldn't surprise me if you end up getting into trouble over this especially when the police find out that he wasn't with you at all.'

His words struck fear into Joanne and for a moment she didn't say anything. She loved Macca to bits, but she didn't want to risk getting into trouble for him. Her father took her silence as a sign of compliance, so he continued to chastise her.

'I want you to finish with him,' he demanded.

Despite her fear of repercussions for what she had done, Joanne couldn't bear the thought of losing Macca, so she snapped back at him. 'No, no chance. I'm not finishing with Macca. You don't even know him. He's really nice. You won't even give him a chance, just because his family aren't well off.'

'It's got sod all to do with that! I know exactly what he is. I've seen him and the band of thieves he hangs around with. The bloody lot of them are jailbait and I won't have you hanging around with the likes of them.'

'You can't stop me. I'm nearly eighteen.'

'Oh yes, I bloody well can. While you're living under my roof, you'll do as I say. I don't care how old you are. I can't have my reputation tarnished because of who you choose to hang about with, not to mention the trouble you might get into.'

'Right,' said Joanne. 'Well, in that case, I'm leaving.'

She stormed out of the room and dashed up the stairs to her bedroom, dragging a suitcase off the top of the wardrobe and throwing clothes into it haphazardly. She was sick to death of her father telling her what to do. She was almost an adult now and it was about time she was treated like one. Besides, he had no right to judge Macca, who had always been good to her and never done her any harm.

In her heart of hearts though she knew that the amount of money Macca flashed about was more than he could earn from doing a few odd jobs for friends. She'd long had suspicions that he operated on the wrong side of the law, but she'd chosen to ignore it up to now.

Joanne was too in love with Macca to want to face the truth. And she didn't want to lose him despite what he got up to. Naively she decided to speak to him and try to persuade him to adopt a different lifestyle. Surely, if he loved her enough, he'd do that for her.

As Macca and Todd walked away from Billy McGregor's house, Macca asked, 'What's wrong anyway? Why are we packing it in?'

'Because I've had enough of the old cunt.'

Seeing that Todd was still angry, Macca trod carefully. 'Right. I didn't know that.'

'Neither did I till I saw his smug fuckin' face when he was counting the money out. It made me realise that twats like him are profiting from the misery of others. I suppose it was finding out that the lads were taking that did it. That and the way he treats that young, good-looking wife all his fuckin' drug money has bought.'

The thought occurred to Macca that they too had been profiting from the misery of others, but he wasn't foolhardy enough to comment. Instead, he remained silent for several seconds until Todd spoke again.

'Anyway, I've got other plans. A real money maker.'

'What's that?' asked Macca.

'Armed robbery. It's a good earner. My uncle's putting a team together so we'll want a driver and a couple of other guys who will be tooled up. It doesn't matter if you haven't used a gun before. I can soon teach you. I know a secluded spot where we can go to practise. You won't need to use it anyway. Once they see you're tooled up, they'll shit themselves and hand over the cash straightaway.'

At the mention of guns, Macca tensed. House break-ins, car theft and collections he could deal with, but this was a different proposition altogether. Macca liked the feel of money and the risks he took to get it gave him a buzz, but he had no intention of hurting innocent people.

He knew, however, that despite what Todd might say about the guns just being used as a deterrent, there was always a chance that he might come up against a have-a-go hero. Then he might be pushed into a situation where he had to use his weapon. And once that trigger had been pulled, there was no going back. He shuddered at the thought, knowing it was a step too far for him but he was wary of saying no to Todd.

'I erm, no, s-sorry Todd. That's not my thing.'

'What d'you mean?'

'It's too dangerous. Someone could get killed.'

Todd stared at him for a moment, his expression intense, and Macca could feel his heartbeat speeding up as he awaited his response. But Todd surprised him for the second time when he said, 'Fair enough. It's not everyone's bag. If your heart's not in it, you're not gonna be able to pull it off. It takes a lot of bottle.'

Macca wondered if he was trying to lure him in with

the suggestion that he didn't have the guts for it, but he wouldn't be drawn in. Instead, he asked, 'What would you be robbing?'

'Can't tell you that. If you're not gonna be part of it, then it's best you don't know. Anyway, my uncle knows some guys he can put me in touch with so it's not a problem. I just would have liked some of my own onside, that's all. I was gonna ask Shay but since the drugs I'm not sure. Lee's a fuckin' loose cannon and as for Spinxy...'

He didn't finish the sentence, but he didn't need to; they both knew that Spinxy would never have the guts to get involved with anything like that.

'Are you sure there aren't other ways you could make plenty of dosh?' Macca asked, hoping to dissuade his friend from such a reckless course of action.

Todd sniggered. 'Nah, the higher the risk, the bigger the reward. Sometimes, you've just gotta go for it, mate. Anyway, it's your loss. You're missing out on a brilliant opportunity.'

But Macca's mind was made up. There was no way he was getting involved in anything like that. He wished Todd wasn't either but knew that it was a waste of time trying to dissuade him. He only hoped that for Todd it wasn't a step too far.

35

Feb 1989

Joanne struggled off the bus carrying her overstuffed suitcase in one hand and a carrier bag in the other. It was fortunate she had been here before, so she knew the way. But it felt a long way from the bus stop even though it was only a ten-minute walk. Today the walk took longer, and she kept swapping the case and carrier bag from one hand to the other to give her arms a break.

She'd left home in a rush, ignoring her mother's pleas to stay and her assurances that she would be able to resolve things with her father once they had both calmed down. Instead, she'd trundled down the stairs, not even stopping to say goodbye to her father who was still in the living room. Joanne had been saving for a while for her own property, but she didn't have enough for a deposit yet. She just hoped her friend, Sonia, would be happy to put her up.

Eventually she arrived at her friend's home, a two-bedroomed flat in Fallowfield. She approached the front door and gave it a tentative knock. The door was answered by Sonia, an attractive mixed-race girl and Joanne's work colleague. She eyed Joanne and her suitcase inquisitively.

'Joanne, what are you doing here?'

Joanne burst into tears as she explained to Sonia that she had fallen out with her father over her seeing Macca, omitting to mention anything about the police involvement.

'Would you mind if I stayed here for a while?' she pleaded.

'Yeah, sure. I mean, I'll have to shuffle things around a bit, but we could make it work.'

Then Joanne caught sight of Sonia's three-year-old son, Brandon, playing with a wooden train set on the living room floor, and she felt bad. 'Where will we all sleep?' she asked.

'Oh, don't worry. You can sleep in Brandon's room. He can share mine.'

'Are you sure? I don't like turfing him out of his room.'

'Don't worry about Brandon, he'll get in bed with me, won't you, cheeky?' she said to her son who had come to stand next to her, curious about the presence of her friend. 'He'll love it. He's always trying to get in my bed anyway. Aren't you, cheeky monkey?'

Joanne knew the situation wasn't ideal, but it was all she had at the moment. 'Thank you so much,' she said to Sonia. 'It's only till I've saved enough for a deposit on my own flat and I swear I'll make it up to you one day.'

As soon as she had settled in, Joanne asked Sonia if she could use her phone so that she could ring Macca. She wanted to let him know where she was before he tried phoning her at home and got an earbashing from her father.

She'd give it a couple of days before she rang home as

she didn't feel like dealing with the situation at the moment. Joanne knew her mother would try to persuade her to come back but she didn't want to. Although she loved her father, she was sick of him dictating to her and now that she had made the break, she knew there was no going back.

When Macca answered the phone, he sounded cheerful, but he picked up on her worried tone of voice straightaway. 'What's wrong, babe?'

In between sobs, Joanne explained about her leaving home.

'Shit, I'm so sorry. I didn't know it would cause trouble between you and your family,' said Macca.

Joanne felt a moment's irritation. What did he expect would happen when the police came calling? 'Well, it has,' she said. 'And all because of you getting up to no good.'

'What do you mean? I ain't done owt. I told you. It was that old biddy trying to stitch me up.'

'Don't lie, Macca! Do you think I'm fuckin' stupid?!'

At that moment Sonia came into the hall and flashed her a warning look. Joanne realised she'd sworn loud enough for Brandon to hear, and she covered the mouthpiece while she apologised to her friend. By the time she went back to her call, Macca was ready for her.

'You worry too much, babe. I'm sorry you've had a fallout with your parents. I tell you what, I'll make it up to you. Why don't I get us some tickets to the VIP lounge at that new club in town?'

'You think that'll make it alright, do you?' Then she lowered her voice. 'Sonia's had to turf her little boy out of his own room so I can stay here. But I've got nowhere else to go until I finish saving for the deposit on my own flat.'

'Aw, I'm sorry, babe. You could come to ours, but my gran would go ape if she found out we were sleeping together. She's so fuckin' old-fashioned. Anyway, how much are you short?'

'About two hundred quid.'

'No probs. I can help you with that. We'll soon have the deposit between us. I'll have you moving in in no time. It'll be a proper little love nest for us.'

Joanne was so relieved at not having to inconvenience Sonia for too long, that her annoyance at Macca was soon forgotten. Instead, she became excited at the prospect of having her own flat; a place where she and Macca could be together without anyone interfering. She'd become so carried away by the prospect that she completely overlooked the fact that Macca had skilfully diverted her from discussing his nefarious activities once again.

36

March 1989

Macca lifted the champagne bottle and asked Joanne, 'You want a top-up?'

'Why not?' she said, watching as he filled her glass.

They were having a meal at one of Manchester's best restaurants to celebrate her moving into her new apartment in Didsbury. It wasn't too far from her friend Sonia. But, unlike Sonia's place, Joanne's wasn't a council flat. It was a private one-bedroomed apartment in a converted Victorian house. The rooms were massive, and Joanne was enjoying making it her own.

The past few weeks had been stressful since she had moved out of the home she had shared with her parents, sister and brother since her childhood. Thankfully, things were back on track with her mum, and she and Mandy had even been to visit Joanne in her new apartment. But things were still difficult with her father. Whenever Joanne went round to the house, he hardly spoke to her, choosing instead to become engrossed in the TV or newspaper when he wasn't outside in his garden or shed tending to some job or other.

Since then, Macca had gone out of his way to make it up to her, knowing that her current problems had stemmed from providing him with an alibi. She had accepted his help with the deposit, because she wanted to stay with him, and the apartment gave her the perfect opportunity to do that. But it didn't take away the festering resentment that had been building within her. Joanne had been so busy since moving that she hadn't had chance to challenge Macca about his lifestyle, but now she was ready to tackle him.

'Where do you get the money for all this?' she asked, pointing to the opulent surroundings.

'Aw, come on, Jo, not that again. We're having a nice time, aren't we?'

'Don't try to skirt round it like you usually do. I've ended up in the shit with my dad because of what you get up to, so the least you can do is be straight with me.'

Macca took a mouthful of his champagne then sighed. 'Look, Jo, as long as we have a good time, what does it matter where the money comes from?'

'It matters to me!' she screeched.

'Shush,' said Macca. 'You've got everyone looking at us. We can talk about this later.'

'No we can't, Macca, because you'll change the subject like you always do. I want to talk about it now.'

Macca blew out a puff of air then, after a pause, he lowered his voice and said, 'OK, maybe I don't have a run-of-the-mill job like most people but I'm not into anything heavy. It's all low risk and I promise I'll never ask you to provide an alibi for me again.'

Joanne looked at him, stony-faced. 'What sort of things are you into, Macca?'

'I can't tell you.'

'Yes, you fuckin' can!' she hissed. 'If the man I'm with is breaking the law, then I need to fuckin' know about it.'

'No, listen, babe. This is all on a need-to-know basis. If I start telling you stuff then it could incriminate you, couldn't it? So, it's best that you don't know. But I promise you, it's nothing too heavy.'

'Why do you have to do it, Macca?'

'I've got no fuckin' choice, have I? There's not exactly tons of jobs out there for someone like me with no qualifications. And even the ones that are there are shit. Do you really think we could afford to go to places like this if I was stuck in some dead-end job earning crap money?'

'You could work your way up or go to college or summat.'

'No, I fuckin' couldn't. I've never been a one for studying and who's gonna give me a job with prospects at my age when there are plenty of kids straight from school they can choose from? I do what I do because I don't have a choice, Jo.'

'I still think there must be another way. How are we gonna have a future if you get sent down?'

Macca put his hand on hers. 'I promise I'll be careful.'

Joanne gazed at him and shook her head. She still wasn't happy with the situation, but she'd run out of things to say. Anything she did say he only countered so it seemed a waste of time. He must have picked up on her ill feeling because he then spoke.

'There's another reason I do what I do.' She raised her head inquisitively, encouraging him to continue. 'If I didn't bring money in then my mum would have to, and I don't like the way she used to get her money.'

'What do you mean?'

'I'm talking men, Jo. Fuckin' seedy, horrible men that she used to bring round the house, fuckin' touching her up in front of me and making dirty comments to her. I don't want her doing that no more and the only way I can stop it is by making sure I give her plenty of money, so she doesn't go out looking for it somewhere else.'

Joanne could see how worked up he was getting. She was shocked. She'd had no idea. Macca's mum had always seemed such a nice lady but then, she supposed, Macca and his mum had lived a different life from her. It didn't mean Debbie was a bad person, it just meant that, like Macca, she was making the most of the only opportunities on offer to her.

Suddenly, Joanne felt bad. The atmosphere had turned sour between them. She wished she hadn't put Macca on the spot like that. It all made sense now. She understood why he did what he did. The trouble was, now that she finally knew, she wasn't sure whether she could handle it.

37

April 1989

It was a week later, and Macca and Todd were sitting upstairs on the 192 bus, chatting as they made their way into Manchester to meet the other lads. They were having a rare night out on the town and Macca was looking forward to it.

'How come Leroy and Shay didn't come with us?' asked Macca.

'They went out earlier. I was busy meeting someone, so I just said we'd see them at the club.'

'Right, OK. Spinxy is at some family do so he said he'll meet us inside later. What was your meeting about? Was it the armed robberies?' asked Macca.

'Shut the fuck up!' said Todd, looking around the bus to make sure no one had overheard. 'I don't want anyone to know about that stuff so stop fuckin' asking, OK?'

'Sorry,' said Macca. He felt a bit stupid for asking. If he was involved in that stuff, he'd keep it to himself as well, in the same way that he didn't like telling Joanne what *he* got up to.

'No worries. Just be fuckin' careful in future. All you need to know is that it's happening and it's a good earner.' Then Todd changed the subject. 'I'm having a few doubts about those two you know.'

'Who? Leroy and Shay?'

'Yeah.'

'Why?'

'They're always going off on their own for some reason. It wouldn't surprise me if they were still doing fuckin' drugs. They could be scoring from Billy for all I know but there's no way of finding out 'cos I don't have owt to do with him anymore.'

'Fuck! Come to think of it, Leroy has been a bit of a loose cannon.'

'How d'you mean?'

'When we went for that car the other night, he was a bit out of it. I didn't think anything of it at the time but, now I come to think, he might have been high on summat.'

'Fuckin' tosser! I swear, if I find out they're dealing or even taking drugs again, I'll fuckin' have 'em.'

When Macca and Todd arrived at 21 Piccadilly nightclub it was packed. They queued at the bar and got themselves a drink before going in search of Leroy and Shay. As they made their way through the crowds on the ground floor there was no sign of their friends.

'They said they'd save us some seats,' said Todd. 'Come on, let's try upstairs.'

The upstairs area wasn't as packed, but it was dark. It was

known as the place where couples went if they wanted to have some alone time together. As Macca passed the sofas that abounded on the first floor, he could see why. Some of the couples were taking full advantage of the dimness and were getting carried away as they indulged in some heavy petting.

Eventually they found Shay and Leroy ensconced on one of the sofas and deep in conversation. But when they went to join them, Shay and Leroy fell silent. After what Todd had told him on the bus, Macca immediately became suspicious. He tried to act normal as he greeted his friends, but Todd's expression was steely.

The four lads chatted and had a couple more drinks till Spinxy arrived and came to join them. Macca saw that his appearance was in complete contrast to Leroy and Shay. Spinxy was sober whereas the other two were high on something. Macca couldn't determine whether it was just drink or whether they had taken something else too, but he suspected the latter.

'I'm gonna see if I can get us in the VIP lounge,' said Todd.

'Nah,' said Leroy. 'There's not as much talent in there. I'm going down.'

'Me too,' said Shay. 'See you in a bit.'

'Hang on, wait for me,' said Spinxy who trailed after them.

Macca watched them walk away then stop. Shay and Leroy were deep in discussion again. Spinxy said something to them and got a reply from Leroy. Macca couldn't hear what was being said from here, but it was clear that Shay and Leroy weren't going downstairs. Spinxy shrugged and went without them.

'Those two fuckers are up to summat,' said Todd who had also been watching them.

'Yeah, but what?'

'Dunno but I'm gonna find out. They're already fuckin' high but they might be dealing as well.' As Leroy and Shay set off walking again, Todd said, 'Let's follow them. Hang back though. Don't let them know we're watching.'

As Macca and Todd trailed them, the two lads split up and went in opposite directions, Leroy down the stairs, and Shay further along the upstairs area.

'You follow Leroy; I'll take Shay,' said Todd.

Leroy was in a rush, and it took Macca all his efforts to keep him in sight. He saw him turn off to the right but by the time he'd got to the bottom of the stairs he'd lost him. He saw Spinxy on the dance floor and hoped he'd help him find Leroy, but he was too far away and Macca didn't want to lose Leroy altogether.

The club was even more packed than earlier. Surrounding the dance floor were throngs of clubgoers chatting and flirting. The room felt hot and fuggy as they puffed on cigarettes while downing cheap booze.

Macca negotiated the crowds, searching avidly for signs of Leroy. It took him a while before he set eyes on him tucked away in a corner of the club. But he wasn't alone. He was talking to another guy. It was someone Macca didn't recognise, and he wondered what the conversation was about.

He snuck behind a group of girls who stood between him

and Leroy. When they eyed him warily, he said, 'Sorry, just waiting for my mate,' nodding his head in Leroy's direction and hoping the dance music had muted his voice enough for Leroy not to hear him.

Through a small gap between two of the girls Macca had a limited view of Leroy although he couldn't hear what was being said. The girls glared at him. He knew they were uncomfortable at his proximity but when he smiled and shrugged his shoulders, they carried on talking among themselves.

Macca could just see the top half of Leroy's body and that of the other guy. And as he watched, he saw something change hands. He couldn't tell what Leroy had passed to the other guy but then he saw quite clearly that what was passed back to Leroy was money.

'Shit!' cursed Macca, realising that Leroy must be dealing.

Leroy's customer walked away, and Macca was about to challenge Leroy when he realised he wasn't the only person watching him. To one side of Leroy was a bank of seats at which sat a group of lads. They didn't look friendly. There was something not right about them. And they were fully engaged in observing Leroy.

One of them whispered something to another who responded with a frown.

'Shit!' cursed Macca again.

He had a bad feeling about this. Were they after drugs too? Or were they up to something else? If they had also seen the exchange, then they would know Leroy was loaded up with drugs, cash, or both. Leroy was now walking away, and Macca tried to skirt round the group of girls so that he could follow him. He had to warn his friend. But before he had chance to get to him, the four lads were up out of their seats and in pursuit.

38

April 1989

Todd found Shay in the seated area around the other side. He must have been even more high than Todd had realised because he was approaching random strangers. By the time Todd had made his way to the same side of the club as Shay, he had already spoken to two people, and he was now on his third. It was a guy who was seated on one of the sofas with a girl. Todd saw the lad reply to something Shay said and just as Todd drew nearer, Shay withdrew something from his pocket and held it out in his hand for the couple to examine.

Todd caught up with Shay and what he saw confirmed his suspicions. Shay was holding out a handful of small, coloured pills. The lad had taken some notes out of his pocket and was making a grab for the pills when Todd strode up and swiped the pills from Shay's hand.

'I fuckin' knew it!' he yelled. 'You fuckin' moron. What did I tell you about taking shit? And now you're fuckin' dealing it!'

He didn't give Shay chance to respond as he pinned his arm behind his back and marched him to a quieter corner of the club before setting about him with fierce punches. Todd was aware of the girl screaming somewhere in the background and someone speaking, possibly the lad who had been buying drugs from Shay. But Todd's anger overrode everything else.

He hated that Shay was not only taking drugs but dealing them as well. So, his old mate wasn't just wrecking his own life, he was wrecking other people's too. Todd detested drugs, which had already caused him enough suffering. And now Shay was going to pay the price for what drugs had put Todd through.

It took him a while before he had calmed down enough to stop hitting Shay. He replaced his punches with yells as he demanded to know if Leroy was dealing too.

'Y-yeah,' said Shay and Todd could tell he was too afraid to even bother trying to lie.

'Where is he now?'

'Dunno, downstairs.'

'Right,' said Todd, grabbing Shay by the arm. 'You're coming with me. We're gonna fuckin' find the little scrote.'

'If he's still here,' muttered Shay.

'What d'you mean?'

'He might have gone home. He said he was only staying till he'd got rid of the last of his gear.'

'Sold up already? For fuck's sake! How long have you two been in the club?'

'About an hour, maybe an hour and a half, before you two got here.'

'And you were dealing all that time?'

Shay looked at the ground as he replied, 'Most of it.'

Todd swiped him across the head, which sent him reeling. 'You pair of fuckin' idiots!' he shrieked. 'Right, let's go. I wanna find him before he fucks off.'

Despite Macca's feelings about drugs, he wasn't about to see one of his mates robbed because of them. He rushed to catch up with Leroy and warn him he was being followed but it was difficult to keep him in sight through the denseness of the crowd.

Leroy flicked in and out of view and Macca managed to keep tabs on him before he realised that Leroy was heading for the exit. Oh no! That meant he was in big trouble. Once they were outside the club and away from the bouncers, there was no telling what the other lads might do.

And Macca knew that he and Leroy couldn't handle four of them, especially when they already had an advantage over Leroy who was clueless as to their existence. He really needed Todd and the other lads but where were they? If Todd was still upstairs, there was no way Macca could get to him in time and then back to Leroy.

His eyes searched frantically around the club and then settled on Spinxy who was unaware of the current problems. He was dancing near a group of young women and Macca had no doubt he was trying to impress them with his moves. Macca raced to the dance floor and shouted over the sound of the music.

'Spinxy! Spinxy!'

But Spinxy was oblivious.

Macca carried on making his way towards him as fast

as he could through the dense crowd, shouting his name and attracting curious stares from the clubgoers. Eventually he was rewarded with the sight of Spinxy turning his head towards him, his expression one of confusion.

Spinxy left the dance floor and headed towards Macca. As soon as he was in hearing range, Macca said, 'Go and find Todd. He might be still upstairs. Tell him we've got a problem with Leroy and a gang of lads. Once you find him, fetch him outside.'

Macca didn't want to give all the details in front of the listening hordes, but he hoped that he had managed to convey a sense of urgency to Spinxy. And he knew Todd would understand the gravity of the situation.

He sped away from Spinxy, turning his head to see him dashing towards the stairs. As Macca got nearer to the club doorway, he felt his heartbeat speeding up. He no longer had eyes on Leroy or the lads who had followed him. But he knew they'd be outside by now and he felt the adrenalin coursing around his body knowing that something bad was going down. And until help arrived from his mates, he would have to handle this alone.

39

April 1989

Macca dashed out into the night air and felt the chill of it on his skin, making him shiver. Neon strobes highlighted a gruesome scene. The four lads were surrounding Leroy who was slashing a knife through the air to fend them off. Then they were on him. One of them gave Leroy a swift kick to the torso, striking him so hard that the knife catapulted through the air and clattered to the ground metres away.

The youths felled Leroy and launched a savage attack. Their feet struck his torso, his limbs, his head. Leroy shrieked in pain. Then the yelling stopped. Leroy was now curled up, his arms over his head for protection. But the kicking continued.

A visceral impulse kicked in and Macca grabbed the knife. Then he charged at the gang, sinking it in to the first one he reached. The youth recoiled in shock as the blade sunk into his flesh, piercing his insides. Fuelled with testosterone and adrenalin, Macca withdrew the knife and plunged it again and again. Meanwhile, a skinny one of the lads scoured Leroy's pockets regardless of his friend's plight.

The other two were trying to drag Macca off while the skinny one was now some distance away holding a fistful of cash. Then Macca felt movement from behind. It was Todd, Shay and Spinxy who rushed at the two lads. Skinny lad was running away with Leroy's money. The other two, realising they were outnumbered, also bolted.

The only remaining member of the gang lay bloody and lifeless next to Leroy. And as Macca stood and stared at the two bodies, he was dumbstruck.

'Fuck!' yelled Todd, dropping to the ground and feeling Leroy's wrist for a pulse. 'The bastards have killed him! Fuck.'

Then Shay examined the other body and looked up at Macca, his expression grave. 'This one's a goner too.'

For a moment there was silence. Macca felt the air close in around him, heavy with tragedy and devastation. Then the silence was broken by the sound of sirens and the clamour of an avid crowd that had begun to gather.

'Quick! Let's go,' yelled Todd, attempting to drag Macca away from the bodies.

But Macca refused to go. He stood dazed and the knife tumbled from his hand as he stared in shock at his old friend Leroy. His eyes then shifted to the other body, crimson as his life's blood oozed from him. And for Macca it was all too much. He felt tears flood his eyes at the knowledge of what he had done.

The sound of sirens intensified, and Todd pulled hard at him. 'Come on, Macca.'

'No! No! I'm not leaving Leroy,' Macca shrieked.

Then Todd broke away, running after Shay and Spinxy who had already fled the scene. But Macca remained. Alone and bereft.

It was the first time Macca had been confronted by death let alone been responsible for it. The police had found him kneeling on the ground and sobbing over Leroy's body. What happened after that was all a blur for Macca who was led away by the police and bundled into a police car while the swelling crowd of onlookers watched.

Looking back, there were certain periods of that night that he had blocked from his mind. He couldn't remember the precise moment when he had plunged the knife. He had told the police as much, but they wouldn't believe him.

The parts that he could recall were the fact that his friends had been with him before running off although he hadn't told the police that. It was bad enough that he was in deep shit without landing his mates in it too. The police knew from witnesses that other lads had come out of the club, but they couldn't prove who they were.

Macca also remembered the relentless questioning and the cold hard cell. His time spent at the station seemed to last indefinitely before he was eventually charged with the death of Gary Crompton and released on bail pending trial. His grandma had put up the surety to secure his release, but according to his mum, Doris hadn't been very happy about it.

But the clearest memories were of the distressed look on his mother's face when he had told her the sorry news, and his grandma's angry reaction. Other recollections, the most painful ones, were yet to surface.

'You bleedin' idiot!' Doris had screeched. 'I told you no good would come of you hanging about with that lot, but you wouldn't bloody listen.' Then she'd turned aggressively to his mum. 'None of you would listen. You should have stopped him hanging around with them like I told you. And now look what's happened. He's ruined his bleedin' life as well as ruining someone else's.'

She had then stormed out of the house leaving his mum in tears and Macca with an unbearable burden of guilt hanging over him.

It was now two days later. Macca had spent most of the time since then ensconced in his room, refusing to deal with the outside world. His muscles were perpetually tense, his appetite lost and his bowels on fire as his stomach reacted to his vague recollections of that fateful night. He didn't think he could face his grandma's angry accusations again. He knew he was fucked and didn't need anyone else ramming that message home to him.

He found his mother in the kitchen preparing food. 'I thought I'd make you something to eat,' she said.

Her voice had no warmth to it. She might as well have been talking to a stranger. Her manner was uncomfortable, jumpy, and she couldn't meet his eyes.

'You need to get summat down you,' she continued, her mothering instincts overriding everything else.

'I've told you, I'm not hungry.'

'OK, well I'll put it on the table when it's ready. Eat what you can,' she said, turning towards the work surface. She went quiet for a moment, continuing to slather butter onto a sandwich before turning back to face him and saying, 'Joanne's rung again. You're going to have to tell her, y'know. I've told her you're not well and can't take visitors but it's not fair to leave her hanging on like that.'

'I know, I know,' he snapped. Then, realising he shouldn't be taking it out on his mother, he softened his tone, adding, 'I'll ring her later.'

He could have done without the reminder. But he knew it had to be done. It was a moment he had been dreading but he'd already made his mind up. He'd ring her this evening and deal with the consequences.

40

April 1989

When Joanne answered Macca's call, she felt a thrill of excitement. 'At last,' she said. 'I thought I was never gonna get to speak to you.'

But then she remembered that he'd been ill, too ill to get to the phone, and a momentary feeling of guilt took hold. 'Sorry. How are you?' she asked.

'Not brilliant,' was the terse reply.

'What was it? Some sort of bug or summat? Your mum didn't really say.'

'No, I haven't been ill, Jo.'

She noticed that his tone of voice was subdued and immediately sensed there was something not right. 'Why did your mum tell me you were then?'

His sigh was audible from the other end of the phone. 'Because I told her to. I'm sorry, Jo. I couldn't face you. I couldn't face anyone.'

'What is it, Macca? You're scaring me now.'

Another sigh, and then he said, 'There was some trouble a

couple of days ago, outside 21s. A gang of lads had gone after Leroy, and I went to help him. And, well… the police are saying I stabbed a lad. Well, I did stab him. I just don't remember doing it.'

'But how do they know you did it?' she interrupted. 'If you can't remember doing it, then it might not have been you.'

'It was, Jo. There were witnesses and…'

She heard his voice break, but she needed to know the rest. She was gripped by panic now, her heart thudding in her chest, and she was finding it difficult to keep calm. 'And what, Macca? What the fuck's happened?'

'He's dead, Jo.'

'What? No! You can't be fuckin' serious. Are you telling me you've killed someone?'

She heard a choking sound before Macca replied, 'I didn't mean to. I don't know what came over me. I think I just fuckin' lost it.'

For a moment she was silent, desperately trying to take it all in. But she was struggling to process it and the phone hung limply in her hand as she tried to digest his words.

'Talk to me, Jo,' he cried.

'What the fuck do you want me to say?' she yelled. 'What can I say after what you've just told me? I can hardly fuckin' believe it. Why would you do something like that?'

'I didn't mean to,' he repeated. 'I swear. And now I'm scared that I've cocked everything up. I don't know what to do. I can hardly believe it myself.'

'Don't give me that,' she bit back. 'Don't play the fuckin' victim, Macca. You know exactly what you've done. How could you? How fuckin' could you?'

'Jo, please, you've gotta believe me. I didn't mean to do something like that. Please, I need you, Jo. I fuckin' need you,' he sobbed.

'Well I don't fuckin' need *you*. It was bad enough having to cover for you when you nicked that car, leaving me in the shit with my dad. Oh, and by the way, he still hasn't forgiven me for that. And now you tell me you've killed somebody and have the fuckin' cheek to expect me to stand by you. No way! No fuckin' way. We're history.'

Joanne slammed the receiver back in its cradle, her hands shaking. She was shocked to hear that the man she loved could do something like that. He was a killer! It was the worst crime imaginable. And he was guilty of it. Macca. *Her* Macca. Only, he wasn't *her* Macca anymore. She couldn't be with someone like that. She just couldn't.

She didn't often drink at home but now Joanne reached for a bottle of vodka, which she knew was in the cupboard. It had been a birthday present from a friend; a present that she hadn't even opened. But she opened it now and took a swig of it neat. It made her cough but, regardless, she poured some into a glass and took sips from it until her hands were steadier.

Thoughts were racing around inside her head. She was repulsed to think that she had been so close to a killer and was afraid of how this would affect her. This led to thoughts about her family and how they would react to the news. Then she considered the victim's family who had been left without a son because of Macca's actions.

And the more she reflected on the situation, the more upset she became until she had cried out all her anguish.

*

It was that night when Macca's memories fully resurfaced. He woke up in a sweat, screaming and having palpitations with the nightmare still clear in his mind.

Leroy surrounded and being kicked to death. His screams. Then his silence. The sight of his battered, lifeless body on the ground. Then that of the other lad. The gore. His blood-soaked clothing. And the knife with its crimson-streaked blade, which Macca plunged into the lad repeatedly.

Once the memories had returned, Macca couldn't get them out of his mind. He carried on yelling, his hands covering the front of his head as though trying to quell the pain. Hearing his screams, his mother dashed into the room and ran up to him.

'What is it, love?' she asked, concerned.

'Make it go away, Mum,' he yelled, peering between his arms as his hands still covered his head.

Debbie crossed the room and sat on his bed. 'I'm sorry, love, I can't make it go away,' she said with a catch in her voice.

'No!' Macca yelled. 'No-o-o-o-o.'

For a moment Debbie stood there looking helpless. Then, using her mother's instincts, she gently pulled his hands away and took him in her arms. Debbie drew his head to her chest in that way she had always done when he was a child. He clung to her, his hands now gripping her arms as he sobbed into her chest.

'I killed him, Mum. I killed him!'

'Shush,' said Debbie as she held him close and rocked him

like a baby, stroking his hair, and whispering comforting words.

Macca needed this. Joanne had rejected him. His grandma had castigated him. And he had to know that at least his mother was there. He couldn't face this alone. It was too much. Now that he could remember it all, the repercussions rippled through his mind and body like a raging storm. And it was hell to deal with.

41

April 1989

The day after next Joanne went to see her family. She'd needed some time to process what Macca had told her before confronting them with it. Ideally, she'd have liked more time, but she realised that the rumours of what had happened would soon be spreading around the estate and she felt she owed it to her family for them to hear it from her first.

Since his first call Macca had rung again begging her to hear him out but she'd told him bluntly that she didn't want to talk. Then she'd put down the phone. He'd rung another two times but each time she had slammed down the receiver as soon as she heard his voice. She thought about unplugging the phone but then nobody else would be able to contact her.

It was Mandy who answered the door and she greeted her in her usual loving way before dashing upstairs, saying, 'I'll be back in a minute.'

Joanne walked into the living room to find her parents

watching TV. She assumed her younger brother was in his room either watching TV or playing on his games console.

'Oh, hello, love. We didn't expect you tonight,' said her mother but she didn't get up to hug her like she would have done if her father hadn't been there.

'Hi, Mum. Hi, Dad,' said Joanne and her father nodded.

His lacklustre response made her realise that this was going to be even more difficult than she had anticipated. Looking away from the TV momentarily, he spoke.

'Well, aren't you going to sit down, for heaven's sake? You know we don't stand on ceremony in this house.'

Joanne took a seat on the sofa and for a moment she stayed silent, trying to pluck up the courage to say what she had to say. But her mouth went dry at the thought of it and her heart was beating frantically.

At that moment, Mandy walked into the room. 'Sorry about that,' she announced cheerily. 'I didn't mean to ignore you. It's just that I had to finish something I was working on. How are you anyway?'

Maybe it was the affectionate vibes from her sister or maybe it was the fact that Joanne had got herself so worked up but as soon as her sister had finished speaking, Joanne burst into tears.

'Hey, what's up?' said Mandy and Gillian simultaneously, and Mandy put a comforting arm around Joanne's shoulders.

Once she had calmed down a little, Joanne said, 'I need to tell you something. And it's not very nice.'

Even Alan broke off from watching TV on hearing her words and Gillian turned to him and said, 'Can you turn it off for a bit?'

He did as requested and the family sat observing Joanne

as they waited for her to speak. Mandy gave her an encouraging squeeze and Joanne began. 'It's about Macca.'

She tried to ignore the automatic scowl on her father's face, determined to get this over with. 'I'm not seeing him anymore, if that makes you feel better,' she snapped at him.

'Well, thank God for that! I was wondering when you were going to see sense.'

'Shush,' said Gillian. 'Let her speak.'

Joanne swallowed before adding, 'He's done something bad, and I can't be with him anymore.'

'How bad?' asked Mandy who had pulled away from her now with a look of alarm on her face as she examined her sister's features.

'Very bad. The worst.' Joanne could hear the tremble in her own voice when she said, 'He's killed someone.'

'Oh my God!' said Gillian while Alan and Mandy stared at her with their mouths agape.

'What happened?' Mandy asked.

Joanne slowly went over the details of what Macca had told her before she burst into renewed tears, saying, 'He keeps phoning me, but I don't want to talk to him.'

'I should bloody well think not. You've done the right thing,' said Alan.

But Gillian's reaction was more sympathetic. 'Oh, you poor love,' she said, crossing the room and plonking herself next to her on the sofa so that Joanne was sandwiched between her mother and sister. Then Joanne felt the comfort of her mother's embrace while Mandy stroked her arm.

'You must stay here for a bit. He won't ring you here. And even if he does, you don't have to answer the phone. *We'll* speak to him, won't we, Alan?'

'Course we will,' said her father. 'Stay as long as you want.'

And in that moment, despite the heartbreak of losing Macca and the dreadful knowledge of why, she knew that at least she had the support of her family. And it was a comfort to know that things were back on course with her father.

Macca held the phone in his hand, listening to the number of rings – eighteen, nineteen. When he got to the twentieth, he put the phone back on its cradle, feeling dejected. If only he could talk to Joanne, he'd be able to explain things. Then maybe he could talk her round, make her understand that he'd done what he'd done out of panic when he'd seen Leroy being kicked to death.

But ever since he'd told her what had happened, she'd refused to speak to him. At first, she'd slammed down the phone as soon as she heard his voice but for the past two days, she hadn't even bothered answering it. She'd have to answer eventually, surely. How else would other people be able to get hold of her?

It was now four days since he had been arrested and he still wasn't eating properly. In fact, he had already dropped a couple of pounds due to his loss of appetite and the stress-induced stomach cramps that frequently had him running to the lavatory.

In all that time he hadn't spoken to anyone apart from his mother, not even Todd or Spinxy. And when he had heard his grandma calling for a visit yesterday, he had stayed in his room out of her way. He dreaded going outside and seeing the reactions of people once they knew what he had done, especially Joanne's family. So, he stayed indoors watching TV to try to take his mind off things. But it wasn't working.

'You can't go on like this, y'know,' said Debbie, surprising him.

Since that night when she had comforted him, his mother had stayed silent. It was as though she didn't know how to deal with the situation either. But now she was obviously ready to face things.

'You need to stay strong, Mark. Anything could happen. It might not be as bad as you think. You need to get out and take your mind off things while you're waiting for your court case. Wallowing around this place isn't doing you any good. Look at you. You're starting to look ill.'

'I can't, Mum. I can't face it.'

'You'll have to face it sometime. As long as you stay local and don't go anywhere near that nightclub, you'll be OK.'

'I know. Just leave me alone, will you? I can't fuckin' deal with it.'

Then he fled upstairs, immediately feeling bad for snapping at his mother. But what he had said was right. He wasn't ready to face things yet. He preferred not to think about it although he knew that at some point he would have to.

And it wouldn't just be the people on the street he would have to face. It was life in prison too. Once the court case was over, there was no doubt in his mind that he would be sent down for a long time. And the thought of that terrified him.

42

May 1989

Todd answered his front door, surprised to find Macca standing outside. 'Hi, mate, you alright?' he asked. Then, taking a swift glance inside to make sure his stepdad wasn't watching, he turned back to Macca and said, 'Hang on. I'll be out in a minute.'

True to his word, Todd soon appeared on the other side of the door. 'Fuckin' hell, Macca. I was beginning to think I'd never see you again. I've rung loads of times.'

'I know – my mum told me. I'm sorry. I just couldn't face talking to anyone after what's happened.'

'Fuckin' hell,' he repeated. 'You look shit, mate. How much weight have you lost?'

Macca shrugged. 'Dunno.'

'It's a lot though, innit?' said Todd, concerned. 'And it's only been a few weeks.'

'Six.'

'Six weeks? And you ain't been out in all that time? Not even to the gym?'

'No. I told you. I couldn't face it.'

'You could do with getting back to it, mate, get a bit of muscle back on you.'

Todd realised they had been walking aimlessly. Or rather, *he* had. Perhaps Macca had a sense of purpose because Todd knew that the direction they were taking was away from the part of the estate where Macca lived.

'Do you wanna go to the pub?' Todd asked.

'Yeah, but not the estate one. Can we go to one of the others on the main road?'

Todd assumed Macca wasn't talking about Stockport Road, which divided Todd's part of the estate from the part where Macca lived. Instead, they were heading in the direction of Plymouth Grove. There weren't so many pubs there and he wasn't very familiar with them. The nearest one was full of old men, so he didn't go in there much, but he didn't mind a change if that was what Macca wanted.

'Sure. I take it you've not seen anyone yet then?' he asked, aware that Macca was unlikely to know anyone in the pub where they were going.

'No, only my mum and gran.'

'What about Jo?'

He spotted the quiver on his friend's lips. It was obviously a sore point. Macca shook his head and Todd wondered if that was because he couldn't trust his voice to remain steady when he talked about her.

Todd had felt put out at not hearing from Macca but now he understood how painful all this was for him and his irritation turned to sympathy. Swinging his arm around his mate's shoulder, he said, 'Don't worry, mate. I've still got your back.'

He felt a relaxing of Macca's shoulders, but it was only slight. Macca was still very tense.

They soon arrived at the pub.

'How have things been with you?' asked Macca once they were sitting in a quiet area of the pub away from the guys playing pool and darts.

'OK, same as usual.' Todd realised his faux pas straightaway. How could things be the same as usual when Leroy was no longer with them? 'Well, y'know,' he backtracked. Obviously, there's only been the three of us, but we've still been doing the cars and Shay and Spinxy have done the odd house, but I've been busy with the other stuff.'

He didn't want to go into too much detail in case someone heard them, but Macca would know he was talking about the armed robberies.

'How has Shay been?' asked Macca.

'How d'you mean?'

'Has he been behaving himself?' asked Macca and Todd knew he was referring to the drugs.

Todd sighed. 'Dunno. I think he might still be at it. I've not seen him doing owt but he's not always easy to get hold of. He spends a lot of time out and about, and he doesn't tell me and Spinxy where he's been.'

'Have you said owt?'

'Yeah, I've asked him where he's been a few times but he just fuckin' comes out with shite. I've warned him as well that he'd better not be dealing shit. But how can I prove it? You wouldn't have thought he'd have needed any more warnings or pastings from me after what happened to Leroy.'

It was the first time either of them had mentioned Leroy by name and he could see the shift in Macca's features. He was obviously struggling with the whole situation. Todd quickly shifted the emphasis, asking, 'Are you looking for any work yet?'

'Yeah. That's why I wanted to see you. I could do with the cash. My mam's got fuck all food in the house. She'd have been out by now trying to latch on to some bloke, but I don't think she's had the cash to even do that.'

'It'll do you good to keep busy,' said Todd. 'Do you fancy going back on the cars? I think Clive could do with a few more.'

'Yeah, why not? What have I got to lose? I might as well make some cash while I can 'cos it won't be long before I'm behind bars.'

Todd high-fived him. 'Good on yer, mate. Like you say, might as well get on with it while you can.'

After a daytime session in the pub with Todd, Macca was feeling more upbeat than he had been for weeks. He couldn't wait to get back to work on the cars. Like Todd had said, it would take his mind off things, but it would also give him some much-needed cash. He knew he'd been a pain for his mum to live with over the past six weeks and he wanted to make it up to her by bringing some money into the house.

Splitting from his friend, he carried on home, crossing Stockport Road and making his way through the estate. His mind was so focused on everything he and Todd had discussed that he had temporarily forgotten his desire to avoid anyone he knew in case they brought up what had happened.

As he walked, Macca wasn't bothering looking ahead of him. He supposed the beer had made him a bit inattentive because it wasn't until he was a few metres away that he saw her. Joanne. With her parents. She must have come to visit, or she might even be staying with them. He didn't think she'd moved back in with them because he'd rung her recently at the flat and she had put the phone down as soon as she heard his voice.

But now she was in front of him. It was a chance to talk. A chance to explain. Surprised at setting eyes on her, he didn't pay heed as he rushed up and said, 'Jo! Jo. It's great to see you.'

He saw her visibly flinch but, emboldened by the beer, he was undeterred.

'Jo, please, hear me out at least.'

She turned her head to one side to avoid making eye contact with him and it was her father who spoke. 'She doesn't want to speak to you so bugger off and leave her alone! My daughter doesn't want to be with a cold-blooded killer. She's from a decent family, which is something you wouldn't know about. I'm surprised you've got the bloody nerve to keep pestering her after what you've done.'

'Let her speak for herself!' cried Macca, enraged by his attitude. 'Jo, listen to me. I need to talk to you. I need to explain what happened.'

Joanne's mother spoke next, her tone nervy: 'We don't want to hear about things like that. Please, go away, and leave my daughter alone.'

Macca was now standing in front of the three of them

and facing Joanne, who was sandwiched between her parents. Realising it would do him no favours if he lost it, he tried to ignore the animosity from Alan and Gillian as he pleaded with her. 'Jo, will you at least give me a minute? I'm not gonna do you any harm. You know me, Jo. I'd never hurt you. I love you!'

'Huh! You don't even know the meaning of the bloody word. Yobs like you aren't capable of love,' said her father.

Then, Alan took Joanne's arm and side-stepped Macca, dragging his daughter away. 'I suggest you keep well away from Joanne in the future and stop bloody ringing her, otherwise I'll report you to the police for harassment.'

Macca watched in awe as the family walked away, leaving him staring after them. 'Let me hear it from Joanne!' he shouted. 'Let me hear Jo say that she doesn't wanna talk to me.'

Joanne turned around briefly and gave him a beseeching look. What did it mean? Was she asking him to keep away? Or was she telling him that she couldn't talk to him while her parents were there?

Then, her father dragged her by the arm again till she faced forward and they carried on walking. Encouraged by the shred of attention from Joanne, Macca continued shouting until eventually, separated by distance, he realised that she could no longer hear him. He was wasting his time and any feeling of positivity from his meeting with Todd had now vanished.

43

Sept 1989

Macca didn't want to work today, but he was done with hanging about the house. It was five months since his arrest and his court date was looming closer. He wanted a final chance of liberty and an opportunity to behave like a lad of nineteen because the likelihood was that he was going to prison and once he was released, he would no longer be a teenager.

He'd chosen to spend some time with Spinxy because he couldn't think of anyone better to have fun with apart from Leroy, who was no longer with them. The thought of his dead friend saddened him, but he didn't want to dwell on it. He was trying to be positive. Spinxy was always up for a laugh, and Macca was determined to make the most of today while he still had the freedom to do so.

They started off by lifting some sweets, cigarettes and a few cans of beer from the estate shop just like they used to do before they'd got into more serious crime. It made Macca reflect on the old days with nostalgia; the days before he had become involved with Todd and Shay, and everything had started to go wrong.

Alternately puffing on the cigarettes and chewing the sweets, they made their way to the park. There they binged on the cans of beer, sharing some banter as well as memories of their schooldays. It felt so good to be transported back to that time that when Spinxy started pratting about on the swings and roundabout, Macca joined in, laughing as though he didn't have a care.

When they had tired of that, they made their way towards Hyde Road, the other main road that bordered their part of the estate. Macca wasn't sure what they were going to do when they got there but for him, today was all about spontaneity.

As though mirroring Macca's thoughts, Spinxy asked, 'What do you wanna do now?'

Macca shrugged, searching around for some inspiration. Then he spotted the railway depot, a busy place where engines were taken in for maintenance and stored overnight. There were often trains running in and out of the place and, as Macca eyed the carriages standing in the sheds, a thought occurred to him.

'Come on, we're going in there,' he said.

'What for?'

'Just for a laugh. Come on.'

They scaled the wall and, taking care that they weren't seen by any of the engineers and maintenance crew, they dropped down on the other side.

'Wow!' whispered Spinxy. 'Look at all those trains.'

Macca laughed; giddy from the beers they had consumed. 'Haven't you ever seen a train before?'

'Yeah, but I've never been on this side of the wall. There's fuckin' loads of them, isn't there?'

Macca grinned and surveyed the place. The sheds were in rows, many of them containing carriages but some of them empty. There was a train sticking out of the shed. Two members of staff were stood by the side of it deep in conversation. Then another two men approached them.

Macca could tell by the uniforms of the two new men that they were the driver and guard. They spoke for some time then the other two men broke away and the driver walked toward the front of the train.

'He's gonna drive it out,' murmured Macca. 'Come on, we're gonna sneak on it.'

'What for?'

'For a laugh, what d'you fuckin' think?'

They crept towards the train, taking care not to be spotted. Macca was the first one to board, climbing onto the coupling between carriages and using the various parts of the mechanism to manoeuvre his way to the top. He heard the unmistakable sound of the engine starting up and looked down to see Spinxy still standing on the ground.

'Hurry up,' he urged, before it sets off.

Spinxy mounted the coupling then struggled to climb up the front end of the carriage. 'Hurry up,' Macca urged again, holding out his hands and giving him a final tug until they were both on board. 'Right, let's lie down on top of here while it sets off,' he encouraged.

They were about to lie down when one of the workmen ran out of the shed. Spotting them on top, he shouted, 'Eh, what the bloody hell do you think you're playing at?'

For a moment Macca was alarmed. But then he realised

that the train had already set off and was picking up speed. There was no way the workman would get to them in time, and neither would he reach the guard or driver to warn them to stop the engine.

He looked at the man and gave him the V sign, satisfied as he saw him becoming increasingly annoyed and yelling at the top of his voice in a futile attempt to put a stop to their antics. Spinxy joined in with Macca, giving the man crude hand signals and laughing at his reaction.

Once they were well away from the depot and the workman had become nothing more than a dot on the horizon, the buzz wore off. They'd done it. They'd got on top of the train without being caught. But what now?

With the thrill of adventure, Macca got up unsteadily onto his feet. He could see Spinxy watching him ardently, curious at this latest level of daring. That gave Macca an even bigger feeling of satisfaction. He steadied his feet, holding his arms out at either side.

Macca took it all in, enjoying the feel of the wind caressing his skin and ruffling through his hair. And the tickle in his tummy as the train throbbed beneath him, zooming through miles of open space. For the first time in ages, he felt free.

'This is fuckin' ace!' he yelled, giggling.

Then he ran along the train as if to prove he could and felt it bounce with each wanton step. He reached the end of the carriage, exhilarated, then turned and ran back to Spinxy. For a moment Macca worried that the guard might hear him. But even if he did, he couldn't do anything to stop them while the train was moving.

When Macca rejoined Spinxy, he could tell from the

eager expression on his face that he wanted to join in, so he encouraged him. 'It's brill, honest. You'll love it.'

Spinxy got up but his footing was more unsteady than Macca's had been.

'Put your arms out,' instructed Macca. 'It'll steady you.'

He watched Spinxy do as he told him, noticing how stiff he now seemed. But as Spinxy grew steadier, he also became more relaxed. Macca could tell from his body posture as well as the smile that appeared on his face.

'You ready?' asked Macca, and Spinxy nodded.

Macca set off again, this time with Spinxy running behind. Macca reached the end of the carriage first and turned around to find Spinxy some distance behind. For a few fun-filled seconds they stood facing each other, both with their arms held out for balance.

'This is well fuckin' cool!' said Spinxy.

Macca laughed and they continued to stand there for some moments while he decided what to do next. Jump across to the next carriage? Or just lie down and enjoy the view of people and houses whizzing by? Then they could end their adventure at the next station and climb back down.

Macca and Spinxy were still laughing, and Macca was so exhilarated that he didn't notice the bridge at first. It wasn't until they were close to it that he realised how low it was.

'Fuck!' he shouted.

Macca instinctively squatted then tried to straighten his knees and push his legs out till he was in a prone position. It was happening so quickly, and he suddenly realised that Spinxy wouldn't have seen the bridge because he had his back to it. His friend's expression was one of confusion at Macca's sudden urge to lie down.

'Quick. Get the fuck down!' yelled Macca.

But Spinxy's perplexed expression remained. Hadn't he heard him above the sound of the engine? Or was he still puzzled about Macca's actions?

'There's a bridge,' shrieked Macca. 'There's a fuckin' bridge! You need to get down.'

A look of recognition crossed Spinxy's features. *Thank God!* But then he turned, wanting to see it for himself. Macca's brain screamed, *No! There isn't time*. But he didn't have chance to do anything. At last, Spinxy bent his knees. It was a panicked effort to make himself small. But he was too late. He hadn't quite managed it.

His head took the full impact of the bridge. Smack! And then he was gone. And Macca stared in despair at the empty space where Spinxy had stood grinning only moments before.

44

Sept 1989

'He looks a bit bloody shifty if you ask me,' said Doris. 'Well, even more shifty than usual I mean, and that's saying summat.'

The front door slammed shut and Macca heard his mother's footsteps coming back down the hall. Then she appeared in the living room.

'You'd think she'd at least talk quieter if she's gonna slag me off on her way out,' Macca said sulkily.

His mother smiled wryly. 'She has got a point, you know. Well, not that I'm saying you're shifty but there's summat not right. What is it, love? Is it the court case?'

She took a seat next to him on the sofa and put her arm around him. But Macca flinched and moved away. He couldn't deal with her pity, not at the moment. It was too much. Memories of first Spinxy and then Leroy flitted through his mind and his eyes filled with tears. He struggled to hide them, but it was useless.

'Bloody hell! You are upset, aren't you?'

She tried to move close to him. Through his peripheral vision Macca saw the concern in her face. He turned his head away. If he couldn't see her then he wouldn't have to react. But she persisted.

'It might not turn out that bad, love. Try doing something to take your mind off it. You're hanging about the house again like you were before. It's not good for yer, y'know.'

Macca couldn't take it anymore. He got up off the sofa and stormed out of the room. 'Just let it go, will yer? You're not fuckin' helping, going on at me all the time!'

By the time he reached his bedroom, Macca was already regretting taking it out on her. She was only trying to help, after all. But how could she help? She didn't even know what the problem was. She'd assumed it was his imminent court appearance but that was only part of what was going on in his head.

In fact, for the past day he'd pushed all worries about his court case to the back of his mind. At the forefront of his thoughts was Spinxy and what had happened yesterday on the train. Macca threw himself on the bed and let the tears fall as he cast his mind back yet again to what had happened.

Soon after Spinxy had been swept from the carriage by the collision with the bridge, the train pulled in at a station. Waiting until the passengers had climbed aboard and the guard had gone back inside, Macca then slid down from the carriage and ran. He didn't look back. His priority was to get away from there as quickly as he could.

Since then, he had been in a state of trauma. He couldn't eat or sleep properly, and he was terrified to go out in case somebody connected him with what had happened to

Spinxy. If somebody mentioned his friend's name, he didn't know how he would deal with it.

Macca had been watching the regional news and he'd scanned the local paper. But up to now he'd found out nothing. The only person Macca had confided in was Todd, who had promised to keep him up to date if he heard anything in relation to Spinxy.

Macca had only been in his room for a few minutes when he heard the phone ring. He sat up. What if it was Todd? Trying to tell himself it was probably someone for his mum, he listened carefully till he heard footsteps padding down the hall again and then a knock on his bedroom door.

'Macca, there's someone on the phone for you.'

He wiped his eyes and swung the door open. 'Who is it?'

'Don't know. Some woman.' His eyes opened wide in expectation till she added, 'It's not Joanne.'

Macca furrowed his brow. He was tempted to tell his mum to get rid of whoever it was, but curiosity got the better of him. 'OK, I'll take it in here,' he said.

Then he picked up the bedroom extension and waited for his mum to put down the phone in the living room. He didn't want her listening in.

'Hello,' he said, his tone inquisitive.

'Hello, is that Mark?' said a woman's voice, which sounded older than his mother but not as old as his grandma.

'Yeah, that's right.'

'Oh hello,' she said, and he could tell from her tone that she was bothered about something. Her next words told him what it was. 'My name's Viv Spinx. I'm Chris's mum. I was wondering if you might know where he is. You see, he didn't come home yesterday and I'm worried sick.'

Fuck! Spinxy's mum. That was the last thing he had expected. In all his panic about yesterday, he hadn't considered the possibility that she might ring him to find out what had happened to her son.

'I erm, no, I haven't seen him. I mean, erm, I saw him yesterday but then he said he was going home.'

'Oh, and what time was that? Do you know?'

'Er, late afternoon I think… yeah, it was 'cos he said he was going home for his tea.'

'Oh, that's strange because he never made it here. I wonder what's happened to him. Where did you leave him?'

'On Hyde Road. Then I came home, and I thought he'd carried on to his house.'

'Oh my God! That means something must have happened to him on the way here then.' Macca heard a choking sound and knew she was trying to fight back tears. Then she seemed to steady herself as she said, 'OK, thanks. I'm going to have to ring the police. Bye.'

Macca stared at the receiver for a moment then quickly pressed it back onto the cradle as though it was contaminated. He felt the thumping of his heart, the shaking of his hands and the shallowness of his breath. Then he heard a knock on his bedroom door again.

'What?' he shouted, and his mother let herself in without waiting for an invitation.

'Who was it?'

'No one important.'

'Are you sure? What's going on, Mark?'

'Nowt,' he snapped. 'Leave me alone, will yer? Can't I have any privacy?'

His mother shut his bedroom and left him alone with

his thoughts. *The police! Shit.* That meant they would be coming to question him. But then, he supposed it was only going to be a matter of time before someone got the police involved. If only he hadn't told Spinxy's mum that he was with Spinxy yesterday.

Macca was panicked now. He didn't know what to do for the best. What should he say to the police? Finally, he decided he'd have a chat with Todd and see what he suggested. He rang his number, but Todd's mum told him he wasn't at home.

It was the next day when Todd rang back. In the meantime, Macca had become increasingly worked up, going over everything in his head and dreading a visit from the police at any minute. But before he had chance to ask Todd's advice, his friend hit him with some news.

'Have you heard? It's been on the radio.'

'What?' asked Macca, his stomach churning as a feeling of dread gripped him.

'They've found Spinxy's body, but the head wasn't attached. They found that separately, about two hundred metres away.'

'Fuckin' hell! No way.'

'Yeah sorry, mate, but I told you he wouldn't survive that.'

In his heart Macca had known that too but to hear it for real was another matter. And the fact that Spinxy had been decapitated by the impact with the bridge gave him a cold chill.

'Fuckin' hell!' he repeated, lost for words.

He reflected on the call with Spinxy's mother the previous day. How the hell would she take the news? Did she even know yet? He felt beset by guilt but knew that he couldn't be the one to tell her. He wouldn't be able to handle it, especially knowing that it was his fault.

'You alright, mate?'

'No, I-I've got to go.'

As soon as he was off the phone Macca ran to the bathroom. The churning in his stomach had risen up his oesophagus and now he had that unmistakable feeling of his mouth filling with saliva. He was going to vomit.

Macca only just made it to the bathroom and afterwards he stood at the sink tidying himself up. His pallid reflection stared back at him in the bathroom mirror, worry and guilt reflected on his face. He couldn't fuckin' handle this!

He opened the bathroom door ready to head back to his room again. At the moment, he just wanted to be alone. To deal with the intractable thoughts that were gushing through his mind. The sight of his mother met him and as she cast an anxious glance in Macca's direction, his eyes flitted to the two other people behind her. It was the police.

45

Sept 1989

'Come on, Mark, I'm your mother. You might not have been able to tell the police, but you can tell me. What's happened? How did your friend end up dead like that? I mean, he was decapitated, for God's sake! Who would do a thing like that? Is it that other gang again, the ones who killed Leroy? Is it a revenge attack?'

The police had just left the flat. They'd spent half an hour with him asking questions, many of them similar to the ones Spinxy's mother had asked the day before. Macca had kept to the same story; he had spent time with Spinxy, then they had both departed for their respective homes and he didn't know what had happened to Spinxy after that.

The police didn't mention a train, just that there was a heavy blow to Spinxy's head and that he had been decapitated. When they described what had happened, Macca had to fight the urge to vomit again.

He was lucky in a way because they didn't regard him as a suspect so he decided he would keep to the same story and hope this wouldn't come back on him. But no number of lies could change what had happened to his friend and the overwhelming feelings of hurt and guilt that assailed him.

'No, Mum. I've already said, he was OK when I left him,' he replied with a tremble in his voice.

'Well, I don't bloody well believe you. I knew there was summat wrong. I could tell by the way you've been acting for the last couple of days, holed up in your room, not eating, frightened to go out.'

'I'm not frightened to go out.'

'Oh yes you bloody are. And I tell you summat else, I'm frightened too. I'm scared to bloody death, Mark! Just what the hell are you involved with?' Then she flung her arms around him and burst into tears. 'I don't wanna lose you, love. Could you not have just kept your nose clean? It's only a few days till your court case. I'm worried sick about that as it is and now you have to spring this on me.'

Macca was finding it difficult to deal with his mother like this. In the past she'd turned a blind eye to most of his misdemeanours. But then it had just involved money. Now it was different. Now people were dying.

For a while she'd even accepted what had happened to Leroy and the fact that her son had killed someone in revenge. She'd even comforted him when he had found it difficult to deal with. But she'd understood that he had acted on impulse in the heat of the moment. And he'd been straight with her about it, unlike now when he couldn't bring himself to tell her the truth. Because Macca knew that what had happened this time had been because of his own recklessness. And even his mother would find it difficult to forgive that.

Eventually she gave up and left him alone in his room, but he knew that this wasn't the end of it. His mother wanted answers and she'd probably rope in his grandma to help ensure she would get them. But he was determined not to crack. He couldn't let them know what had happened. The only other person who knew was Todd, and he had sworn to keep it to himself.

With Todd it was different. He understood. Maybe it was because he'd done bad things himself. Thinking of Todd, and how he was, made Macca realise how much his life had changed. That he could now entrust his secret to someone he hadn't known till three years ago when he couldn't even tell his own mother.

That was how low he'd sunk. Like Todd, he was a violent man. Reckless. Foolish. A wanton criminal. His girlfriend didn't want to know him. Two of his best friends were dead. And all he had to look forward to now was a long stretch behind bars when the court decided his sentence in a few days' time.

46

Oct 1989

Joanne walked into her old bedroom at her parents' house to find Mandy studying. For a moment she was torn between disturbing her for a natter or leaving her in peace. But Joanne didn't want to be downstairs. She was upset with her father who was relishing the fact that it was the first day of Macca's trial.

Joanne wished she hadn't decided to visit her family today of all days but maybe subconsciously she hadn't wanted to be alone. Heedless of her feelings, Alan had spent most of the time going around the house whistling. Then, although he hadn't said anything to Joanne, she'd interrupted a heavy discussion between her parents when she had walked into the kitchen. As soon as she appeared, the conversation had stopped abruptly, making it obvious to her what they had been talking about.

Nodding at Mandy who smiled back, Joanne plonked herself on the bed that was still earmarked for her and stared at the ceiling for some time, deep in thought. She turned to watch Mandy scribbling away in an exercise book, her face full of concentration.

Eventually, Mandy put down her pen and looked across at Joanne. 'You look miserable. What is it? Is it the trial?'

To Joanne's surprise, her sister's understanding touched her, and she found her eyes filling with tears. 'Yeah. I can't stop thinking about it. He'll probably end up inside for a long time, won't he?'

Mandy frowned and walked over to her, taking a seat next to her on the bed and taking hold of her hand. 'We don't know yet, Jo. Until all the evidence is given, nobody knows.'

'I can't see him getting away with killing a man though, no matter what the circumstances were. Can you?'

There was a sympathetic edge to Mandy's voice as she said, 'No. I can't. I think he'll definitely end up in prison. It's just a matter of how long he'll be there.' Then she paused a moment before adding, 'But y'know, it shouldn't make any difference to you how long he's behind bars unless you're thinking of getting back with him.'

'No, am I 'eck,' said Joanne, her tone of denial a little too strident.

Mandy began stroking Joanne's hand as she said, 'I know it's hard. I know how much you think of him but you're no longer together, Jo, and you need to put it behind you. Forget Macca and get on with your life. You're still young and you're really pretty. You'll easily meet someone.'

Joanne forced a smile as she said, 'Thanks.'

But although Mandy was very compassionate towards her, she didn't really understand, not deep down. Because for Joanne there would never be anyone like Macca. It wasn't just about his good looks; Macca was the typical loveable rogue. He had a mischievous way about him that always made her want to laugh, and he was confident and charismatic with his cheeky smile and sense of adventure. That's why she'd always been drawn to him and probably always would.

Even though she'd ended the relationship with Macca, Joanne still cared. She wished she didn't because love like this hurt too much, and it was impossible to let go. And Joanne knew that whoever she met in the future, she would always compare them to Macca because he would never be fully obliterated from her thoughts.

It was now the fourth day of Macca's trial. Since the police had visited him about Spinxy's death there had been no comeback. At least that was one less thing to worry about, although he'd still carry the burden of guilt with him for the rest of his life. He tried not to dwell too much on Spinxy's death to avoid becoming overwhelmed with grief. Right now, he had other matters to worry about.

When the trial began, he had been full of nerves, but he'd tried to hide it behind a show of nonchalance. His mum and grandma had sat in the public gallery every day and he didn't want them to know how much it had got to him. Todd also put in an occasional appearance although he wasn't there all the time. As the trial had progressed Macca's nerves had gradually dissipated.

Playing down the gravity of the situation in his mind, he likened the trial to having a vaccination at school when he'd been a young kid. The day you've been dreading finally arrives, but you try to put on a brave face in front of your mates, claiming that needles don't bother you. Then you find out it isn't going to take place till the afternoon, so you relax for a while until it draws nearer.

By the time you're standing in the queue you're in such a state that you're finding it difficult to disguise your inner turmoil. You're expecting to be taunted by your mates only to find that they've gone into a state of tense silence too. Being the accused in a trial meant that the nervous anticipation was on a much bigger scale.

For three days he had been listening to all the evidence from both sides. It had given him something to focus on till he found his attention wavering as the evidence was repeatedly read out, discussed and argued over. Occasionally his eyes flitted to the public gallery, but he soon glanced away when the anguish on his mother's face became too much. He was touched by his grandmother's loyalty considering how scathing she had been about his lifestyle, and the sight of her also affected him as he thought about how much he had let them both down.

Now it was becoming clear that the trial was winding down and just like on school vaccination day, his anxiety was growing. As the prosecution and defence did the summing up, he could feel his hands become clammy. After a particularly damning summing up by the defence, a trickle of sweat ran down his spine and he felt physically sick.

Next it was over to the judge who went over the main points again. As his summing up drew to a close, Macca became aware of how rapidly his heart was beating. The judge then deferred to the jury for their verdict and the spokesman didn't hesitate in getting to his feet and responding with the word 'guilty'.

There was a murmur of voices in the public gallery and Macca thought he heard a distressed cry, but he couldn't look. He was desperately trying to hold it together. The judge asked for hush and the place became silent once more so that the judge could decide on the sentence. Macca had been told that the sentencing decision might be deferred but this judge had already decided. The words 'ten years' came through loud and clear. Macca didn't realise he'd been holding his breath till he heard the sentence and let this breath go in a desperate sigh.

As he was led away from the court, he risked a glance over at the public gallery. He knew his mother would be upset but curiosity got the better of him. In the few seconds it took to vacate the court he caught sight of both his mother's and grandma's distressed faces as well as Todd's glum expression.

But then he spotted someone else. She was sitting right at the back and must have slipped in unnoticed because he hadn't seen her there before. It was Joanne. Her head was bent down as though to hide her sadness. He kept his eyes fixed on her for as long as he could, but she didn't meet his gaze. The last sorry sight he had was of Joanne standing up and dashing from the courtroom without speaking to anyone.

47

Oct 1989

Macca walked into his cell carrying his pizza and chips. He'd been in Strangeways for a week now and was still adapting to prison life. The food portions were measly, and he guessed that a lot of the meals were made from cheap ingredients as they tasted foul.

The food was the least of his concerns. Being on lockdown for twenty-two or twenty-three hours a day took some getting used to especially when he had to spend that time with a bucket in the room, which sufficed as a toilet. The stench could be unbearable at times as the bucket was only emptied once a day. Added to that was the odour of unwashed flesh as showers took place once a week.

The sounds of prison life were something else that took some getting used to. Macca would often hear footsteps and the jangling of keys as the guards marched along the landings. Prisoners would also make conversation by shouting from cell to cell. Added to all of that were the screams and cries of some prisoners, which made it loud and unsettling.

Ten years was a long time to be in prison, but he supposed he had been lucky in a way. After all, he had killed a man. But the judge had taken account of the circumstances and sentenced him for manslaughter. With a bit of luck, he hoped to get time off for good behaviour and serve substantially less than that.

This was one of the better meals he'd had. But because the portions were small, he'd been so hungry since arriving at prison that he ate anything he was given.

He tucked into the meal, trying to quickly ram as many chips into his mouth as he could while he had the chance. But he wasn't quick enough. From where he sat on the top bunk, he looked across to the cell door to find his cellmate Kenny standing there. He was holding his tray with a wide grin on his face. As Macca watched, Kenny slammed the cell door shut then made his way over to him.

Kenny was six foot three and about twenty-five stone. He had what Macca would describe as mad eyes and was also one of the prison bullies. Macca knew he was no match for him despite the gym training he had done, and he was ashamed to admit to himself that he was afraid of the guy.

Without Todd to look out for him, in here he was nothing. Being new inside and unaware of the prison hierarchy, Macca had taken a lot of hassle from Kenny in the past week. He'd helped himself to anything he fancied while Macca had stood back helplessly, frightened of getting on the wrong side of him.

Kenny chuckled. 'Ha, I bet you thought you'd get it down you before I got back, didn't you?' He paused before adding, 'Wrong!' in a singsong voice. Then he reached up and grabbed the pizza from Macca's plate. 'I'll have that for a start.'

'Aw, come on, Kenny, I'm starving. You had most of my dinner yesterday.'

Kenny laughed and patted his rotund stomach. 'I'm a big lad, aren't I? I take a lot of fuckin' feeding whereas a little wimp like you can make do with a lot less.'

The insult annoyed Macca. He was average height and toned rather than skinny but was diminished by Kenny's huge bulk.

Kenny rammed the pizza into his mouth, tearing off a large portion with his teeth. The sight of the tomato sauce smeared across his big ugly face irritated Macca. It was bad enough having your food stolen but even worse having to watch it being devoured by someone with the eating habits of a pig.

Macca focused on his chips, hoping Kenny would now eat his own meal and leave Macca to at least finish his. But Kenny's hand came up again and he grabbed a fistful from Macca's plate. His hands were so huge that only half of the chips remained.

Something in Macca snapped. 'Fuck off!' he shouted, instinctively covering the rest of his meal with his palm. Noticing the anger on Kenny's face, Macca quickly backpedalled. 'Aw, Kenny, mate, come on. You've already got my pizza.'

As soon as he had pleaded with Kenny, Macca grabbed most of the remaining chips on his plate and shoved them into his mouth. It was so full that he was having trouble chewing them, but he persisted knowing it might be the only food he got that day.

Kenny dropped his own tray onto his bed and his arm shot out. He snatched the last of Macca's chips. This time, he didn't eat them though. Instead, he forced them into Macca's mouth so hard that Macca felt like he would choke.

'Think you can tell me to fuck off, do you? Well, you can have your fuckin' chips now. Go on, eat them, you twat!'

He continued to push the food into Macca's mouth and down his throat till he was coughing and spluttering. Macca wrestled with Kenny's arm, trying to pull it away so he could spit the chips out, but Kenny carried on relentlessly till Macca was fighting for breath.

Macca had visions of himself being asphyxiated. He knew the guy was capable of it. After all, Kenny was in prison for killing someone in a pub brawl and according to rumour he'd already served time for GBH.

In a panic, Macca lashed out at Kenny and jabbed his fingers in his eyes, a trick he'd learnt from Todd. Kenny's yell was excruciating. 'Aah, you little fucker!' he yelled, yanking Macca's arms away then covering his damaged eyes with his hands. 'You're gonna fuckin' die for this!'

Without waiting for him to recover, Macca spat the chips out then jumped down from his bunk and launched himself at Kenny. They both landed on the cell floor. For a moment Macca had the advantage. He had landed on top and while Kenny squinted and tried to focus on him, Macca landed a few rapid punches around his head and face.

Kenny's eyes weren't too badly damaged, just bloodshot, and he soon recovered. It didn't take him long to gain the upper hand. Macca continued to rain punches down on him, so Kenny went straight for the throat, holding it in a savage grip that had Macca fighting for breath once more.

While still clenching Macca's throat in his meaty palms, Kenny flung him off, and spun him round till Macca felt the impact of the hard cell floor on his buttocks and back. Then Kenny was on top, and he continued to strangle the life out of him.

'You little cunt!' he yelled. 'Don't ever try to take the fuckin' piss out of me again.'

He carried on squeezing Macca's throat, shouting and cursing at him. Macca was terrified. He could see the anger on Kenny's face, which was now scarlet and sweaty. There was nothing he could do to stop him. He couldn't even plead as Kenny was crushing his windpipe and making speech impossible.

Macca waved his arms about and tried to pull Kenny's hands away. But it was futile. Kenny's hold was becoming stronger. The harder he pressed, the more Macca despaired. Macca was vaguely aware of a stream of expletives spewing from Kenny's mouth. But he couldn't make out the words. And then his vision was fading. He could no longer pick out Kenny's features. The face of his nemesis was now just a large angry red blob.

Then the sound of Kenny's yells was met by other sounds. Shouting. A door slamming. Then heavy feet. It was a couple of seconds before Macca realised what was happening. He could just about make out the uniforms of a number of guards who were battling to wrench Kenny away while Kenny grappled and turned his vitriol onto them.

'Get the fuck off me! Bastard screws,' he yelled.

Once he felt the release of Kenny's weight being hefted from him, Macca shot up, panting, aware by now of his shaking hands and thundering heartbeat.

'You alright, son?' asked one of the friendlier guards as four others dragged Kenny out of the cell.

'You'll fuckin' pay for this, you little twat!' Kenny yelled, and Macca felt a shudder of fear.

To Macca's surprise the friendly officer let him remain in the cell. 'You'll both be up before the governor,' he said. 'He's gonna want answers. But I'll leave you for now to get on with your dinner.'

Once the door was locked and Macca was on his own, he inhaled deeply a few times and tried to recover himself. Then his mind switched back to what had prompted the fight. Becoming aware that his stomach hadn't stopped growling, he attacked the remaining food on Kenny's plate and scoffed it. Then, still hungry, he picked up the chips he had spat on the floor and devoured them too.

48

Oct 1989

Joanne read through the letter for the umpteenth time. It was the second one she had received since Macca had been banged up, but this one was far more worrying. In it he described how another prisoner had attacked him and tried to strangle him to death.

She knew she should ignore the letters and chuck them in the bin, yet she couldn't help but read them. The problem was that Joanne still cared, and she found the letter upsetting. Poor Macca. He might have done something bad, but did he deserve to be locked away with an animal like this?

She read through the final paragraphs again.

I got loss of privileges, but they've shipped Kenny out to another prison so at least I don't have to worry about him anymore. Strangely, the other prisoners are showing me more respect since they found out how I stood up to him so I'm gonna make sure I stick up for myself in future. It might lead to a few more scraps though.

It's been so peaceful in the cell since they got rid of Kenny but lonely too. I don't half miss you, babe. I'm sorry about what I did but, I swear, I didn't mean to kill the guy. I just lost it when I saw what they were doing to Leroy. It was like I knew they'd kill him, and I was right because they did.

One of the guards has told me I'll be getting a new cellmate soon. I just hope he'll be alright. I can't tell you how good it is to be rid of Kenny. Apart from being a nasty bastard, he snored like a pig and kept me awake half the night.

Anyway, how are you? I hope your job's going well and that you're enjoying life in your new flat. I wish I was there with you. Maybe one day, eh, if you'll ever forgive me? Take care.

Love you always,
Macca x

Joanne put the letter to one side, her eyes steamy. For someone who had spent the past few years indulging in a life of crime, Macca wrote a good letter. She could almost hear him speaking to her and describing everything he was experiencing. The most touching part was his words of love. She knew he still loved her. She felt the same. But she knew he was no good for her. Macca might be fun, loving and attentive, but he was still a criminal who had committed a heinous crime.

For two days Macca had enjoyed the solace of having the cell to himself. But now it was wearing off. Being locked up on your own for most of the day could do strange things to you, and Macca sensed that he was hitting a slump, the despair eating at him like hungry maggots.

When the cell door opened he watched the man walk inside then heard the door slam and the sound of the key turning as the guard locked up. During this task, the guard hadn't uttered a word. The inmate placed most of his possessions on the bottom bunk apart from his ghetto blaster, which took pride of place on top of the small table.

Once all that was taken care of, he held out his hand to Macca who was stretched out on the top bunk. 'Name's Jojo,' he said, his accent part Mancunian, part West Indian.

Macca had been eying up the man, initially disappointed at having to share his cell again after his experience with Kenny. But now he was surprised at Jojo's friendly manner, and as he watched him, he noticed his wide smile displaying perfect white teeth. He was a slim man with pleasant features framed by a raft of grey-tinged dreadlocks. From the few lines on his face Macca would have placed him at around fifty; old enough to display an air of wisdom but young enough to still be full of vitality.

Macca was so busy studying him that he forgot to return the greeting until Jojo's intent gaze reminded him. He stuck out his hand and allowed Jojo to shake it vigorously. 'I'm Mark but my mates call me Macca.'

Jojo smiled. 'Right, Macca it is then.'

Macca couldn't remember whether he'd seen him around the prison, so he asked if he was new in.

'No, I've been here a while, but the governor likes to shift us around now and again. Good job really because we were three to a cell. I can't tell you how unpleasant that was.'

'Three? Fuckin' hell! I thought two was bad enough.'

'It is when you're stuck with Kenny.'

'Do you know him then?'

'Oh yeah, he's got a bit of a name as a hardman. Doesn't bother me though. I know too many people. How was it with him?'

Macca was wary of saying too much in case of repercussions. Some of Kenny's mates were still in the prison and he didn't know whether they had found out the full details of his fight with Kenny yet. He also wasn't aware of how much Jojo already knew or whether he was someone he could trust.

'Oh, don't worry about me,' said Jojo. 'I'm not a fan. Got no time for scrotes like him.'

His words together with his affable manner put Macca at ease and he said, 'It wasn't brilliant to be honest. He tried to strangle me. I think he'd have done it too if the screws hadn't walked in.'

'Ah, so that's why they shifted him. Well, no need to worry about him now. He won't be coming back.'

Then Jojo smiled again before flicking a switch on his ghetto blaster till the sound of reggae music filled the small cell. It was a sure sign that Macca's two days of peace and quiet were up. He just hoped he wouldn't have any problems with his new cellmate.

49

Oct 1989

Macca's worries about Jojo proved unfounded. He had a friendly, outgoing and upbeat manner about him, and Macca took to him straightaway. Jojo played reggae and soul music on his ghetto blaster throughout the day. At first it irritated Macca but as the days wore on, he found it strangely uplifting especially as Jojo's favourite track was 'Don't Worry be Happy'.

Jojo didn't seem to see the irony of a tune like that in a place like this. Or perhaps he did, and that's why he played it. Repeatedly. Whatever the reason, it did the trick, because Macca had found himself in a better place mentally since Jojo had entered his life. The music also drowned out some of the less pleasant sounds of the prison.

It was a few days later when Macca asked, 'What are you in for?'

'Huh, breaking the law, same as everybody else in this place. Well, except for the screws, that is. But then, I ain't so sure about some of them. What about you? Let me guess, you robbed a shop or broke into someone's home?'

Macca felt a touch vexed that Jojo had underestimated him. 'Manslaughter,' he said, puffing his chest out.

Jojo nodded sagely and Macca realised he had been tricked into disclosing his crime when Jojo still hadn't given details of his.

'Suppose you got a few years for that one,' said Jojo.

'Ten.'

'Sounds about right.'

His blasé response to Macca's crime made Macca realise he had been foolish in thinking his hardman act would impress Jojo. He'd never known a man so laid-back and Macca was beginning to realise that Jojo had probably heard it all before especially if, as he had said, he'd been inside for a while.

'What did you do?' Macca asked.

'Me? Oh, bad things. Too many bad things.' Then he sighed but Macca detected a slight grin as he said, 'I'm what they like to call a career criminal. But they're gonna be surprised because them things are gonna change.'

'What do you mean?'

'Oh, I've got a new life waiting for me on the outside.'

Then Jojo tapped the side of his nose, a habit Macca was learning to associate with the older man. It was an indication that Jojo had had enough of this conversation for now.

Todd felt a surge of adrenalin coursing through his body. He was excited but also a little apprehensive. Today was the big one. They were going to rob a security van at gunpoint and if they managed to pull it off, he would be quids in.

His uncle Rod had put together a team of five. Todd hadn't been able to recruit anyone but nevertheless he was thrilled to be entrusted as part of the team. They were going to use three cars: two men in two of them and one in the other. Ideally, Rod would have liked two men in each car, but they couldn't find anyone else.

The only member of Todd's gang still around was Shay, and he didn't feel that he could trust him anymore. Shay was still taking drugs no matter how many times Todd had tried to persuade him against them, and the more drugs he took, the less Todd trusted him. They still did the odd job together, but those jobs were rare and Todd guessed Shay had found other ways to make money.

Uncle Rod had worked out the route that the vehicle would follow once the security guards had collected from the big high street banks, and he'd pinpointed a quiet spot where the heist would take place. Using the three cars, they planned to block in the van when it stopped at the lights then make their move.

Todd had done armed robberies before but nothing on this scale; usually using a knife or a replica gun at a petrol station or post office. Aware of this, Rod had paired him up with an experienced getaway driver, Colin, but all of them would be carrying sawn-off shotguns. Rod would be travelling with one of the other drivers.

By the time they were on their way, Todd was buzzing with excitement. He tried to make conversation with the driver, but Colin was too focused. 'We're nearly there now. Keep your eye out for a security van,' Colin instructed before he checked his rear-view mirror to make sure the other two cars were still with them.

It was Colin who saw the van first. 'There it is,' he announced.

Todd stared through the windscreen, and eventually spotted it some distance away. He was impressed at Colin's sharp powers of observation. He wouldn't have seen it for ages if Colin hadn't told him.

Colin pulled out, overtaking other vehicles in his haste to catch up with the van. Peering through the rear windscreen, Todd noticed that the car containing his uncle was with them, but he couldn't see the other. Assuming it was just beyond view, he turned his head and concentrated on what was happening in front. Colin had now bridged the gap between them and the van.

'We need to wait till it stops at some lights,' said Colin. 'But we can't wait too long, or they'll know we're onto them.'

He shot forward rapidly till there was only a blue Merc separating them from the van. They were approaching a set of lights, which were on green. And Todd watched Colin start to move into the outside lane, preparing to overtake the Merc. That way he'd be nicely placed to take the van once it stopped.

'Come on, go to red, go to red,' murmured Colin, willing the lights to change.

Todd glanced through the rear windscreen again. Still one car behind them. But where was the other? He faced forward again just as Colin slammed on the brakes. The driver of the Merc had rapidly switched lanes and edged in front once more.

'Shit!' hissed Colin.

They were almost at the lights now and they were still green. Colin slipped in behind the van with the rogue Merc to the right of it.

'We can still take it,' he said. 'Come on, go to red, go to red.'

Then the lights changed but to Todd's consternation the van slipped through while they were on amber.

'Fuck!' cursed Todd.

'It's OK,' assured Colin. 'There's some more lights coming up.'

The road became single lane and the Merc slipped ahead of them again. They weren't far off the next set of lights and Todd saw them change to red.

'We'll make it,' said Colin. 'The lights have only just changed. He won't fuckin' get through this time. When we stop, run straight out. I'll tackle the driver. You take care of whoever's driving that fuckin' Mercedes.'

Todd's heart was beating rapidly now. They were almost at the lights. Then he heard the vehicle come to a skidding halt as Colin slammed the brakes on and ran out. Todd was just behind him. He watched Colin run at the van. The car containing Rod pulled out and sped up the wrong side of the road till it was in front of the van, effectively blocking it in.

Todd concentrated on the Merc behind the van as Colin had instructed. But he hesitated, too absorbed by what was going on around him. The driver got out. He was running at Colin. Then he lunged, trying to wrestle the shotgun from Colin.

'Get the fuck off him!' yelled Todd.

The man was big as well as fast. Before Colin was aware of what was happening, the man had pinned him to the ground and was fighting him for the shotgun. Todd aimed his gun at the man. 'Get the fuck off him!' he yelled again. 'Or I'll shoot.'

But, at the moment, he was afraid to shoot. Even if he shot the man, he might risk hitting Colin as well. It was all happening too fast. As Todd watched in horror, the driver's door of the van opened, and two security guards jumped out. While the driver of the Merc grabbed the shotgun and aimed it ahead of him, the two guards kept a hold of Colin.

Todd realised that the man must have been aiming the gun at his uncle and whoever was with him. But the van was blocking his view of them, so he didn't know how they were reacting. Were they still inside the car taking cover or were they a standing target? Shit! This guy looked as though he meant business.

'Put the fuckin' gun down!' yelled Todd. 'Or I'll shoot.'

'No!' the man shouted back. 'You put yours down or, I swear, if you try owt, these two will fuckin' cop for it.'

Todd couldn't risk having his uncle shot. He was amazed at the man's courage. Who was this have-a-go hero? He might have been a cop for all Todd knew. Or maybe ex-military. He panicked. He didn't know what to do. Then the man lifted the gun slightly, adjusting it to his target and barked, 'Keep fuckin' still!'

He swung the gun back, pointing it at Todd momentarily, shouting, 'You put *your* fuckin' gun down,' before swiftly swinging it back again. Todd sensed that the man was going to shoot. He was outnumbered. He would have no choice.

But Todd couldn't take that chance. So, he pulled the trigger, beating him to it.

A loud gun blast filled the air and the man dropped to the ground, a spray of scarlet staining his shirt. Then Todd saw his uncle and driver appear carrying their shotguns. They advanced on the two guards and ordered them to open the back of the van while Colin got up off the ground and reclaimed his gun.

Todd was immobile with shock. 'Come on!' yelled Colin. 'We need to help.'

Coming to his senses, Todd ran to the van, taking bundles of cash from the other men and stashing them into the boot of the car. By this time, their fifth man had arrived. He was providing cover in case any other members of the public decided to get involved. But Todd was like an automaton, going through the motions but not feeling it.

When Rod shouted the order, they all got back into their vehicles and made a rapid getaway. Todd slumped back into the passenger seat while Colin floored the accelerator and shot down the road.

Colin was ecstatic. 'We've done it. We've fuckin' done it!'

But Todd couldn't join in his elation. He was too stunned by what had just happened and was staring back at the blood-soaked man who lay on the ground. Todd was convinced he was dead, and the stark reality overwhelmed him. He had just committed his first murder.

50

Nov 1989

Macca had now been sharing a cell with Jojo for several weeks and had grown to respect his wisdom and opinions. Jojo had a great sense of humour and they often shared banter together. Their growing friendship brought out Macca's cheeky side as he teased his friend.

'Ha ha don't tell me,' Macca laughed. 'When you get out, you're gonna make something of your life. How many times have you said that and ended up back in here?'

They were lying on their bunks chatting while Jojo's music played in the background. Today they had enjoyed a range of soul and reggae tunes including some by Bob Marley and Eddy Grant and others Macca had never heard of but found he enjoyed. Currently Jojo's favourite tune 'Don't Worry, Be Happy' was playing.

Macca smiled. He now realised why Jojo played the song so much. It summed up his personality as Jojo always managed to stay positive and upbeat despite the conditions inside the prison.

'Ah, you might mock but this time it's for real. All them times before, well, they were before I found the Lord,' Jojo replied.

Macca spluttered. 'It's a pity he didn't find you first, then you might not have ended up in here.'

Macca had been surprised to find out that Jojo was a Christian. With his dreadlocks and love of Bob Marley, he'd had him pegged as a Rastafarian. Jojo always took Macca's teasing well. In fact, he often had a go back, pouring scorn on the younger generation who thought they knew all the answers but still had a lot to learn.

But now his voice took on a serious note. 'Take it from me, Macca, there's more to life than being banged up twenty-three hours a day. And me, well, I've got a plan.'

He tapped the side of his nose conspiratorially. 'Between the two of us, I've got some money put away from a few jobs and this time I'm gonna put it to good use. Maybe get me a shop or café. I could even do Caribbean food. A jerk shop. That would go down well in the Moss,' he said, referring to the local nickname for the district of Moss Side. 'Or maybe even in the city centre,' he added.

'I can't see much call for it in Town,' said Macca.

'Why on earth not? Times are changing, boy. It's not all Berni Inns now, ya know. We've already got Chinatown and The Curry Mile. Why not Caribbean food? People want a bit of spice in their lives.'

Macca laughed at the cheeky grin on Jojo's face when he said the word 'spice'. 'Oh yeah, and you're gonna give it to them, are you?'

'Eh, I get all the spice I need from my good lady. And now it's time to do her proud. She's stood by me all these years knowing I was up to no good. So, I'm gonna put things right. She's done well by my kids too. Put all the money I gave her to good use, sending them to private schools.'

'Really?' asked Macca. 'What do they do now then?'

Sometimes he was fascinated listening to Jojo. He seemed so different to what he had expected from a career criminal, and he often surprised him.

'My boy, he's a doctor; and my daughter, she's a solicitor.'

Macca sensed the note of sadness in his tone, and he wondered why. 'Fuckin' hell, I thought you'd be chuffed that they've both got good jobs.'

'Oh yeah, I'm proud of them. But it's down to my good lady, not me. I was too busy getting up to no good. And now, I never see them. They're too ashamed to spend time with their old man. I tell you, Macca, being in here gives you plenty of time to think. And I've been doing a lot of that lately.'

Macca was taken aback, not really knowing what to say but he was saved from having to respond when a guard entered the cell. 'Governor wants to see you, McNeil. Now.'

Ten minutes later Macca was back in the cell. He could hardly believe what he had just heard. His grandma. A fatal heart attack. Last time he saw her was the day of the trial as she never came to visit him with his mum. But she had seemed fine then, albeit upset, and he couldn't help wondering whether it was that upset that had brought on the heart attack. Again, he was riddled with guilt, just like he had been when Spinxy died.

Without asking any questions but sensing bad news

through the tears that clouded Macca's eyes, Jojo threw his arms around him.

'Come on, let's get you sat down,' he said.

He led Macca to the bottom bunk and, once he had got him sat down, he took the space beside him, pulling Macca's head into his chest and holding him tightly. 'Come on, boy, let it all out,' he said.

Macca let his tears flow, any attempts at bravado now abandoned as he gave release to his heartbreak and explained to Jojo what had happened.

'I'm not even allowed to go to the funeral,' he muttered. 'They said it was next of kin only. My mum would have wanted me there. I know she would. That's why she rang the prison to report it. And now she's got to go on her own.'

Macca's last words were choked on a sob as the reality of it hit him. His grandma was gone. He couldn't believe it. She'd been such a part of his life. And although they hadn't always got along, she had tried her best for him, providing goodies when his mother couldn't afford them and trying to keep him on the right path.

His mind flashed back to the disapproving words she had used: *I told you no good would come of you hanging about with that lot, but you wouldn't bloody listen.* Maybe she had been right because here he was stuck in a cell for the next few years, not even allowed to attend her funeral to show his respects. And he had respected her even if he didn't always show it. But he had done what he wanted to do anyway because it had been a route to easy money.

He had enjoyed the money and the freedom it gave him, but the best part of the money was how it had changed his mum. And he'd do it all again if it meant stopping her from selling herself to the highest bidder. But how could he have explained all that to his grandma?

Macca didn't know how long he'd stayed like that, crying in the arms of this man who he hadn't even known a few weeks ago. But it felt right and reminded him of that other time when his mother had held him like that. It had been two days after his arrest and just after Leroy had been savagely beaten to death.

During the time he had known Jojo, he was learning to trust as well as respect him. He had helped Macca through many dark days inside, protected him and taught him to keep the faith. And for Macca, it was the first time he had known what it was like to have a father figure in his life. It had been natural for his mother to comfort him whenever he was upset. But never his father.

51

Feb 1990

Macca's mourning period was one of the most difficult times of his life. Not only was he grieving the death of his grandma but also of his two old friends, Leroy and Spinxy. Being stuck in such a confined environment also made the grieving process tougher.

If Macca had been on the outside, he could have done things to take his mind off his grief. Having a mate like Todd would have helped because, although he had known Leroy and Spinxy for longer, he had actually become closer to Todd. He was the one who had supported him when Leroy had died, returning the sympathy Macca had shown him when hearing about his abusive stepfather.

Macca also missed his mum. If he had been at home now, they would have been grieving together. Instead, his mother would be alone, and he worried about how she would cope without him and his grandma around. Not for the first time, the guilt ate away at him.

As time wore on, he was finding ways to cope. He went

to the gym whenever he could. It helped to alleviate the stress and boredom. But this option wasn't always open to prisoners who often faced lengthy periods on lockdown with little recreation. He'd heard about Strangeways' reputation for poor standards of care, hygiene and food, much of it due to a lack of staffing and resources. But nothing could have prepared him for the reality.

Sometimes he was snappy with Jojo, and he instantly felt bad. He was just hitting out at the only person around, even though Jojo hadn't done anything to deserve it. In fact, Jojo was the one who kept him going, his positivity helping to lift Macca whenever he hit a low. Macca sometimes wondered how a nice guy like Jojo could end up a criminal.

Today they were being allowed an hour's recreation and Macca was glad the weather was dry as he looked forward to his walk around the yard. It might not sound like a lot of fun for most people, but this was often the nearest the inmates of Strangeways got to some kind of social life.

Macca had recognised a couple of lads who lived on his estate called Daz and Luke. Although he hadn't known them well before he was inside, he soon got to know them once he was locked up. Because they lived near him, they were eager to find out about life on the estate, and as they shared news and details of their criminal activities, he soon struck up a friendship with them. Daz and Luke were two years older than Macca and were both serving time for robbing a local convenience store.

Jojo usually hung out with his own group of friends and Macca stuck with Daz and Luke as they walked around the prison yard. This didn't bother Macca as he and Jojo both benefited from a change of company now and again.

This day Macca was deep in conversation with Luke. Daz was only half-listening while looking across to the other side of the yard where the inmates were walking in the opposite direction as they completed the circuit.

'Stop fuckin' lookin',' warned Luke. 'Do you wanna get on the wrong side of the scousers or what?'

'I'm not looking at them. There's a guy off our estate. I know him,' said Daz.

'Who?'

'Dunno. I can't remember his name.'

'Which one?' asked Luke.

'You can't see him now. You'll have to wait till he's opposite us again.'

Curious, Luke and Macca both waited. But Macca didn't have to wait till the prisoner was opposite them. He recognised him from some way off. With his big muscular frame and stern features, he was unmistakable.

'Todd!' shouted Macca, smiling when his friend looked across and locked eyes with him.

Without thinking, Macca crossed the yard and ran to join his friend.

'Keep in line!' shouted a guard.

By that time Macca had already made it to the other side. For a moment he tensed, expecting the guards to haul him out. But he quickly fell in step with Todd, hoping they wouldn't bother now he was back in line even if he was on the opposite side. As they walked, Macca gave his mate a friendly slap on the back.

'Fuckin' hell, fancy seeing you here.' He laughed.

He listened in astonishment while Todd told him all about the armed robbery, which had led to him being inside.

Although he had known Todd was involved in this type of illegal activity, it was the first time he had opened up about it. Perhaps because Todd no longer had anything to lose by sharing details of his crimes.

By the time Macca got back to the cell, he was buzzing with excitement. 'Fuckin' hell, do you remember me telling you about my mate, Todd?' he asked Jojo. Without waiting for Jojo's reply, he added, 'He's only gone and got himself banged up in here, hasn't he? That's who I was talking to in the yard just now.'

'Is he the one that's an armed robber?' asked Jojo.

'Yeah,' said Macca, picking up on Jojo's disparaging tone. 'Is that what he's in for?'

'Yeah. They did a security van. Todd shot this guy that got involved. Turns out he was an ex-soldier.'

'And you think that's a good thing?'

'No,' said Macca, defensively. 'I didn't say that. He didn't mean to harm him, but he thought the guy was going to shoot his uncle, so he panicked and pulled the trigger first. Anyway, he didn't kill him. The guy survived.'

'Right, I suppose that makes it alright then,' said Jojo dryly.

Macca couldn't understand what was wrong with him. Macca had been so excited to meet his old mate that he hadn't thought about the downside of things: the fact that Todd had shot someone and the fact that he was now banged up for God knew how long.

Jojo had made him think about the implications till he didn't feel excited anymore. Instead he was busy wondering what had got into Jojo. Was he jealous? Macca didn't know but he chose not to go into it, jumping up onto his bunk and spending some time reflecting while Reggae music played on in the background.

Jojo had difficulty sleeping that night. Macca might have been overjoyed that Todd had entered the prison, but he wasn't. Jojo already knew a lot about Todd and what he'd heard he didn't like. Prison had given him and Macca plenty of time to talk and they'd both confided in each other about their lives. Jojo had therefore learnt all about Todd's influence on Macca and it seemed to him that the lad was partly responsible for the escalation of Macca's crimes from petty to more serious.

Was he being judgemental for seeing things that way? He didn't think so. He merely wanted better for the lad. Jojo thought a lot of Macca. He could see why he'd gone astray. Because of his own background, Jojo was quick to spot the same pattern of behaviour. He'd made many mistakes in his life and missed out on the important things like being there for his kids instead of banged up in prison half the time.

Since he'd taken to religion, Jojo had changed. He was determined to make it up to his family before it was too late. And someone like Macca still had plenty of time to turn his life around. The lad had become something of a pet project for Jojo, who wanted to convert him to religion too. To make him see that there was more out there for him.

Jojo hadn't had much trouble persuading Macca to attend chapel. It was the focus of the week for many prisoners even though the majority of them weren't religious. Rather than a chance to worship God, it was an opportunity to escape from the monotony of prison life for a while. In Macca's case, Jojo hoped that some of the sermons might have got through to him.

At times Jojo wondered whether he was right to have got so attached to the lad. Some might ask what right he had to dictate, given his own past. But he knew deep inside that for him it was a chance to influence a young life for the better. He wanted to make up for the fact that he had been such a bad father to his own kids, so for him Macca was like a surrogate son. And there was no way he was going to let Todd ruin all his hard work.

52

March 1990

It was a particularly noisy night. There were lots of cell-to-cell conversations taking place in a language Macca couldn't decipher. Apparently, it was called back slang and Jojo didn't understand it either. Back slang was a way for the inmates to have discussions without the screws knowing what they were talking about.

'There's something going down,' said Jojo echoing Macca's thoughts. 'I've never known it so noisy. Pity we don't know what the hell they're saying.'

Jojo walked across to the barred window and looked outside. 'Yeah, I thought so,' he announced. 'They're swinging a line out there. Summat's definitely going down.'

Macca looked out of the window and saw that there was a piece of string swinging from cell window to cell window. It had some sort of plastic container attached to the end of it, to weight it down, maybe a shampoo bottle or something similar. As he watched, an inmate caught the string and grabbed the container.

A few seconds later, the inmate reattached the container, presumably with a piece of paper inside containing a message. It struck Macca as curious that there should suddenly be such a flurry of activity and he thought that Jojo was probably right. He decided to ask Todd about it at recreation tomorrow.

In the few weeks that Todd had been in the prison he had become ingrained into prison culture. He had soon got to know the prison's leading inmates and although he had started out by exercising with Macca, Daz and Luke, he no longer always joined them at recreation. Tomorrow though, Macca would make a point of calling him over for a chat.

'What's going down?' Macca asked Todd the next day.

'Shush,' said Todd, looking at Daz and Luke and then scanning the yard for prison officers. 'Can I trust you guys?' he asked.

'Course,' said Daz. 'We'd never grass to a screw.'

Todd lowered his voice before continuing, 'People are pissed off. The conditions in this place are shit. There's no point complaining 'cos the governor does fuck all about it. No man should be forced to live like a fuckin' animal, so we're taking matters into our own hands.'

'How?' asked Macca. 'What's happening?'

'We ain't finalised the details yet but it's gonna go down big time. Are you guys in?'

'What do we have to do?' asked Daz.

'I'll let you know but there's gonna be an uprising. People won't put up with that shit anymore. I need to have a few more conversations but I'll come back to you.'

Then he left their company and headed towards a group of men, one of whom had a reputation for being a prison top dog.

When he got back to the cell, Macca deliberated over whether to tell Jojo about the conversation with Todd. In the end, he decided that out of all the people he had met inside, Jojo was the person he could trust the most, so he told him what had taken place.

'Oh my God!' said Jojo. 'I thought as much.'

'What do you mean?' asked Macca.

'I mean there's gonna be a full-scale riot. One of my friends mentioned the disquiet among inmates. I can understand it. But believe you me, no good's gonna come of it.'

'Why?' asked Macca.

'You can't change the system from in here. Conditions have been bad for a long, long time and nothing ever changes. Don't forget, we're the underdogs in here. Nobody's gonna take any notice of a bunch of criminals, are they?'

'How do we know if we don't try?' asked Macca.

'Well, that seems to be the view of a lot of them in here. But if they go about it the wrong way, they're only gonna extend their sentences. I've only got a few months to serve and I ain't gonna do anything to jeopardise my freedom. I told you, I've got big plans for when I get on the outside.'

Macca resisted the urge to yawn as Jojo continued with his rant. 'I for one won't be getting involved and if you've got any sense, you'll stay the hell out of it too.'

Macca didn't say anything. He was conflicted. He could understand the views of Todd and most of the other inmates.

It was inhumane to have to live the way they did, and he'd love to be part of something that might change the system. He also felt a degree of loyalty towards Todd.

But, like Jojo, he was looking forward to being on the outside again and didn't want to do anything to increase his sentence. He also wondered about the futility of it all. In the end he decided to sleep on it. Then, once he'd found out from Todd what would be required from him, he'd decide whether he was in or out.

53

March 1990

Joanne was having a night out with her work colleagues, and she was looking forward to it. Currently she was in her living room sipping a glass of wine and listening to a CD, which played a mix of pop music from artists including Bros, Madonna, Erasure and Kylie Minogue.

When the doorbell rang, she jumped up from her seat and ran to the door. There she found Sonia holding a bottle of wine and grinning widely. She was wearing a short black dress and had her hair braided.

'You look great,' said Joanne. 'Come in.'

'So do you,' Sonia responded as she followed Joanne through to the kitchen. 'I love that outfit.'

Joanne smiled, pleased with her choice of matching short skirt and cropped top in a fetching shade of mid blue. 'I got it last week from a little shop in the Arndale.'

'Suits you.'

'Thanks. How was Brandon?'

'Oh, he was fine. He loves staying at my mum's. He gets spoilt rotten.'

'Are you OK to stay here then?'

'Sure. I'll pick him up in the morning.' Then Sonia grinned again. 'Don't let me get too bloody drunk though. I don't want to crash the car on the way there.'

Once they were in the kitchen, Joanne poured Sonia a glass of wine and they went through to the lounge.

'It's coming on nicely, isn't it?' commented Sonia, looking around at Joanne's new décor. Before Joanne had chance to respond, Sonia spotted something on the coffee table. 'Are you still getting the letters?'

Joanne nodded. 'Not as often. That one just came this morning.'

'What's he saying?' asked Sonia.

'Nothing much. Just the usual about life inside and how fed up he is.'

Joanne reached for the letter then tucked it away in the drawer of a cabinet that stood against the back wall of the room. She preferred not to go into all the details about his life inside and the way his remorse shone through in his words. It would also have felt uncomfortable to mention that Macca was still saying he loved her.

'You'd think he'd have got bored of it by now, wouldn't you?' said Sonia. 'You don't send letters back, do you?'

'No, course I don't,' Joanne replied, neglecting to mention that she had been tempted a few times.

'Why do you still read them?' Sonia persisted. 'Why don't you just bin them? You deserve better than him.'

'You don't even know him!' Joanne snapped before she could help herself.

Sonia softened her tone. 'No, but I know what he did. Sorry but if he's done it once, he could do it again. Do yourself a favour, Joanne, and forget about him.'

'I have. Well, not forgotten about him exactly but... you know what I mean. I'm not gonna go back to him.'

'Then why keep torturing yourself by reading the letters?'

'It's not torture. I'm not going back to him, but I can't switch off just like that.' She clicked her fingers to emphasise her point. 'Anyway, change the subject, Sonia. I don't wanna think about Macca. We're gonna have a brilliant night out, aren't we?'

She raised her glass and clinked Sonia's, then her friend chatted about something else as they finished their wine ready for their big night out.

An hour later Joanne and Sonia were with their work crowd in a popular Manchester nightclub. They found a quiet area where they sat, chatting and laughing with their colleagues.

As the night progressed, members of their group drifted off and Joanne and Sonia decided to go for a dance. Feeling quite merry by now, they immersed themselves into the nightclub atmosphere, dancing and singing along to 'Love Shack' by the B-52s.

It wasn't long until a group of lads joined them, two of them choosing to pair up with Joanne and Sonia. One of the lads attempted to make conversation with Joanne as they danced but he was struggling to be heard above the music. After a few dances, he offered to buy Joanne a drink and she and Sonia left the dance floor with him and his mate.

'They're really nice,' Sonia whispered as they waited for them to come back from the bar.

'Yours is,' Joanne replied.

'Yours too. They're both fit.'

Joanne knew Sonia was right, but her mind was still occupied by Macca. She decided there was no harm in having a drink with the lads so she humoured Sonia because she could see she was excited to spend some time in their company.

Once the lads had come back from the bar, they suggested they should go somewhere quieter to chat. Joanne soon found herself in the same room she and her work crowd had occupied earlier. They sat down, Sonia next to the guy she had been dancing with and Joanne with the other one.

'I'm Tom,' he said. 'My mate's called Jason.'

Joanne smiled. 'I'm Joanne and my friend is Sonia.'

Tom smiled back. 'You look gorgeous,' he said. 'That colour suits you.'

'Thanks,' she said noncommittally, neglecting to return the compliment.

'So, Joanne, where are you from?'

Joanne tried to show some interest as she engaged in small talk with him. Her eyes wandered at intervals to her friend Sonia who seemed happy in Jason's company. When she spotted two girls from work walking to the bar, Joanne was tempted for a moment to make her excuses and join them. But it didn't seem right after Tom had bought her a drink, and she didn't want to spoil things for Sonia by leaving her on her own.

To Joanne's surprise, after a while she found herself enjoying Tom's company. He was interesting to listen to and regaled her with tales of the mischief he and his friends got up to and the holidays he had been on. They chatted for so long that before she knew it the DJ was playing gentler music, indicating that the night was coming to an end.

'Fancy a dance?' asked Tom.

Joanne could see that Sonia and Jason were already on their way to the dance floor, each wearing a wide grin. Seeing no harm in joining them, Joanne said yes to Tom's request. They smooched to three tracks. At first it felt strange to be in the arms of someone other than Macca but by the time the first song had finished Joanne found herself starting to relax.

She enjoyed the feel of being held and the way Tom gazed at her admiringly gave her an odd tingle. But somehow it didn't feel right. When the dancing finished and he asked for her number, she gave it but instantly regretted her actions. What was she doing? She wasn't even looking to meet someone.

Later, as Joanne and Sonia made their way back to Joanne's flat, Sonia said excitedly, 'He took my number.'

'Me too,' said Joanne. 'He wants me to go on a date with him. I wish I hadn't done it now. I'll have to think of an excuse when he rings.'

'Why would you do that? He's gorgeous.'

'I know but I'm not really looking to meet someone. I'm happy on my own for now.'

'Are you fuckin' serious, Jo? Why would you turn him down? He's gorgeous. I knew it. You're still pining after Macca, aren't you?'

'No, I'm not. I just want to be on my own.'

'You turn down this chance, Jo, and you might not get

another. You looked great together and they both seem really nice.'

'I know but…'

'No buts. I tell you what we'll do. I'll arrange a double date. That way you don't have to worry about being nervous. You can just see how it goes. What have you got to lose?'

Joanne smiled back at her friend and capitulated. Sonia could be very persuasive at times.

54

April 1990

It was Sunday. Chapel day. And although it pained Jojo, he had decided not to go. Usually, it was the highlight of his week but today he would not find any solace there. Because today it was going to be carnage.

He cast his mind back to a few days ago when Macca had bounded into the cell after exercise, as excited as a puppy. He'd seen his friend Todd who had told him that the inmates were going to stage a peaceful protest at chapel on Sunday. To choose the holy day on which to act as well as a holy building was sacrilege as far as Jojo was concerned, and he didn't want any part of it. But the prisoners had decided that it would be their best opportunity.

The word 'peaceful' didn't fool Jojo either. He knew what a boiling pot this place was and any attempt at a protest could soon escalate. It wasn't that he disagreed with what the prisoners were trying to achieve. They had every right to feel aggrieved with the dreadful conditions inside the prison.

But there were always a few bad apples who would take the opportunity to wreak havoc and destruction.

He watched Macca stir in his bunk and decided that as soon as he awoke, he was going to have a word with him. Macca had been so full of it for the last few days after he'd told Todd that he wanted to be involved. But Jojo felt sure that the lad didn't know what he was letting himself in for. He wasn't a bad lad really and he still had time to change his path in life. But if he participated in what Todd and his cronies were planning, he'd end up in a whole heap of bother.

'Oh, you're awake, are you?' Jojo said, staring up at Macca who was lying on the top bunk.

'Yeah. Big day today, innit?'

Jojo could tell Macca was still excited. 'You going through with it then?'

'Yeah, why not? It's the only way we're gonna change the system.'

'The system is what it is and it ain't gonna change just because a bunch of prisoners decide to go on the rampage.'

A look of hurt crossed Macca's face and Jojo was glad. He wanted him to see the pointlessness of it all. He reached up and took Macca's hands in his, staring into his eyes as he beseeched him.

'Think carefully about what you're doing, Macca. You need to weigh up the odds: what good it's gonna do you against the damage it could do. I've had a long hard think and that's why I'm not getting involved. I've put up with the conditions for years on and off so I can put up with them a bit longer. It's not worth getting time added to your sentence. You'll be out in a few years if you keep your nose clean.'

'Yeah, but I'll still have to put up with it till I'm released, and what about those that are gonna be stuck here for even longer?'

'Do you think they'd think twice about you and *your* life?'

'Some might. Todd would.'

'Oh, he would, would he? So, how did Todd react when he learnt your grandma had passed away?'

Jojo knew it was a low blow, but he had to get through to the lad. He remembered Macca telling him that Todd hadn't acknowledged the fact that Macca's grandmother had died until Macca had pointed it out himself. Then he'd admitted that he already knew. His only offer of sympathy had been a hearty slap to Macca's back accompanied by the words, 'Oh yeah, I heard. Soz, mate.'

Jojo remembered how hurt Macca had been when he told him that tale and that same hurt was now showing in his strained features. Knowing his words were making an impact, Jojo persisted.

'And what do you think *she'd* have said about you getting involved in a prison takeover? 'Cos from what you've told me, she was dead against you getting into trouble of any kind.'

'It's not a takeover,' said Macca. 'It's a peaceful protest.'

'Oh yeah. And if you believe that then you're even more wet behind the ears than I thought.'

Jojo watched the look of anguish on Macca's face, and he could almost visualise the cogs turning around inside the lad's brain as he digested what he was saying. Adopting as sympathetic a tone as he could muster, Jojo said, 'Todd's probably not even thought about the consequences of staging a protest. He's a rebel and he's been caught up in the excitement of it all. I know he's your mate, but guys like Todd are always going to rebel against authority even if it's a waste of time. He doesn't care about you.'

'Alright, alright!' snapped Macca. 'Turn it in, will you?'

Macca pulled back his hands and turned abruptly so he had his back to him. Jojo knew he'd upset him, and he felt bad for it. But he'd done it for Macca's own good.

Todd was buzzing as he walked through the prison on his way to chapel. Today was the day. They were finally gonna stick it to the man and those fuckin' screws were gonna get what was coming to them.

Telling his mates he'd meet them at chapel, Todd stuck his head inside Macca's cell. He was surprised to find Macca still lying on his bunk. Jojo was sitting on his, and he looked across at Todd as he opened the door. Todd didn't like the expression on his face. It screamed hostility.

'What's going on?' he asked Macca who leant up in the bunk and gazed at him. 'Come on, it's time.' Then he addressed Jojo. 'I thought you'd have been there by now. You usually have a front pew, don't you?'

Jojo smiled wryly. 'Not today. I think I'll do my praying from within my cell.'

Ignoring him, Todd spoke to Macca again. 'You coming or what?'

'Yeah, sure. I just want a word with Jojo. I'll follow you later,' said Macca.

Incredulous, Todd stared at him for a moment. He could hear the nervousness in Macca's voice and, noticing how Macca's eyes flitted from him to Jojo and then back again, he guessed that the old man had been trying to talk him out of it.

'Right, suit yourself,' he said. 'I'll be back later.'

He turned to see a screw approach. As Todd stepped away from the cell door and carried on to the chapel, the screw said something to Macca and Jojo and then locked their cell door.

Todd became aware of the atmosphere within the prison. There was a sense of nervous energy, and he guessed that a lot of the inmates must have been aware of what was about to go down.

When he reached the chapel, he came across some of his mates sitting a few rows from the front. He took up a seat in the same pew and one of the other inmates flashed him a knowing look. A hush descended as a visiting Anglican minister walked to the front and delivered a sermon. Todd and his mate exchanged another glance. Then they waited.

55

April 1990

Todd was already fired up about the way he was treated within the prison. Conditions were bad enough but there were a few nasty screws who were always ready to have a go. One of them had even thumped him and called him a slimy bastard. And he'd got away with it because one of his colleagues had stepped into his defence before Todd had had chance to have a go back.

Macca's refusal to get involved in the protest had only irritated Todd more. He'd thought Macca was a mate, and mates should have each other's backs. Maybe he'd have one last try at recruiting him if he got a chance. He watched while the prison chaplain, Proctor, came to the front of the chapel, thanked the minister for his sermon then started preaching and addressing them all as sinners.

Cheeky bastard, thought Todd. *He's got some fuckin' front! He's got no idea of the shit that people like us have to put up with. I bet he's got a nice cushy home outside this fuckin' place.*

At that moment everything changed. An inmate on the next row from Todd suddenly dashed to the front of the chapel and grabbed the mic from Proctor. He started making a speech about how the prisoners had had enough of the conditions while Proctor tried to wrestle the mic from him. When that was unsuccessful, Proctor tried to disconnect the lead so that the mic wouldn't work.

The inmate's next words were drowned out by a huge roar from the other inmates who were getting to their feet. Proctor was pleading with them to calm down, but it was having no effect. Todd saw a prisoner pull a chair leg out of his jeans and put a balaclava on. He and his mates followed suit by covering their faces and taking up the makeshift weapons that they had secreted in their clothing.

'Right, lads, we've heard enough,' said the inmate with the chair leg.

Then the place erupted. The prisoners were out of their pews wrecking everything in sight and charging at the screws, who backed off. It was mayhem as the prison officers tried to escape while inmates attacked them.

Todd joined in with the crowd. It was payback time. He wanted revenge. To punish those who had punished him. And this was the only way he knew how. He struck a screw on the forehead and felt a glimmer of satisfaction at the sight of the blood. The screws' uniforms were becoming covered in viscous red patches, their agonising screeches competing with the roars of the inmates.

One screw dragged his colleague out of the mêlée and in his haste to get away he dropped his keys. An inmate swiped at them then dashed to the back of the chapel and unlocked the door onto the landing. Todd was tempted to follow but he wasn't finished with the screws yet.

Macca and Jojo heard the disturbance from their cell. 'Oh Lord!' declared Jojo. 'So much for the peaceful protest.'

Macca rushed to the observation window in the door from where he could see hordes of prisoners rampaging. There wasn't a screw in sight but many of the inmates were wielding weapons and tearing up anything they could get their hands on, their angry shouts filling the air. He jumped at the sight of a face on the other side of the window and then realised that it was another prisoner carrying a bunch of keys.

The cell door swung open, and the inmate dashed to the next cell. Macca stepped outside, dumbfounded by the sight that met him. The place was completely out of control. Inmates were tearing doors from cells and dragging tables and chairs out onto the landings then tossing them over the fences and onto the ground below. Further along the landing someone had started a fire.

The thought hit him that Jojo might have been right. This seemed more like a full-scale riot than a peaceful protest. But he couldn't blame the prisoners in a way. Not after how they'd been forced to live.

As he watched, a pack of men, like wild animals, were stampeding through the prison, shouting, 'Beast, beast, beast, beast, beast!'

'Oh shit!' he shouted to Jojo. 'They're going for the nonces.'

'Get in here outta the way,' Jojo shouted back.

But Macca was curious. He trailed the group of men, keeping to a safe distance, as he made his way through the smoky atmosphere, trying to avoid the debris that littered the landings. Macca watched as they burst into a cell and dragged out its screaming occupant. They beat him with chair legs till he was a bloody mess. Then they tossed him, screeching, over the fence.

Macca shuddered, knowing it was a long drop to the ground below. He had no desire to get involved. These prisoners were in such a frenzy that he could see them killing someone and he didn't want any part of that. The death of a man at his hands still weighed heavily on his conscience.

But nor did he do anything to prevent what the prisoners were doing. He didn't like nonces any more than anyone else and there was no way he would risk having the pack turn on him. To his amazement the inmate was still clinging to the railings. Not wanting to be outdone, the crowd whacked at his fingers to loosen them.

Macca couldn't watch anymore. Protesting was one thing, and he couldn't blame anyone for that or for getting a bit carried away, but these guys were going too far. He decided that his part in all of it wouldn't involve attacking nonces and he felt sure Todd's wouldn't either. When Todd came back, he'd follow his friend's lead and do whatever was necessary to draw the attention of the authorities to the terrible conditions the inmates had to put up with.

He made his way back to his cell where he found Jojo pacing up and down with his hands together, beseeching to the Lord.

'Is it as bad as it sounds?' he asked, pausing in his prayers.

'Worse. Jojo, I can't believe it. They're gonna fuckin' kill someone.'

Jojo just looked at him and shook his head from side to side. Macca had been expecting some form of reproach, for Jojo to say, 'I told you so'. Instead, there was nothing. For the first time since he had known him, Jojo was speechless. But he didn't need to speak because Macca could tell by looking at him that he was distressed.

For a while they stayed where they were, both terrified. Macca didn't reveal his thoughts to Jojo for fear of upsetting him, but he guessed that Jojo was probably thinking the same thing. The inmates were completely unruly and if they were attacking the nonces then there was no knowing who they were going to attack next.

What if something should happen to himself or Jojo? Macca may have walked away when he'd seen the sex offender being attacked, but he knew that he couldn't leave Jojo at the mercy of an angry mob.

When the cell door flew open again, Macca felt a shudder of fear. It was Todd. Like many of the other prisoners he was holding what looked like a chair leg. At the sight of his old friend, Macca's fear subsided. There was no reason to fear Todd. He was a good friend and they'd always had each other's backs.

'Come on, you're missing it,' he said to Macca. 'They've thrown one of the nonces over the railings and everyone's chucking stuff at him.'

Macca was about to follow him when he noticed how excited Todd seemed. He was more like a teenager on the last day of the fair rather than a prisoner staging a protest.

Unable to comprehend this behaviour in his friend, Macca gazed back at him in astonishment.

'We're going up on the roof,' said Todd.

'How?' asked Macca.

'One of the guys climbed up the scaffolding to the top of the rotunda and got through the roof space. We're in charge of this fuckin' place now!'

Then, without waiting for a further response, he was off. Macca looked at Jojo, his face a mask of concern and confusion. Jojo was shaking his head as though disgusted at Todd's behaviour. Then he spoke.

'I think it's time we got ourselves out of this place before things get any worse.

For a moment Macca was undecided. He had wanted to take part in the protest despite what Jojo thought. But after what he'd seen, he was no longer sure. And the look on Jojo's face spoke louder than any words. He was terrified and Macca didn't like to think what might happen to Jojo if he left him here alone.

Macca closed his eyes momentarily, took a deep breath, then said, 'OK, you're right. Let's go.'

56

April 1990

Joanne couldn't believe what she was seeing. She'd been watching the news, getting an update on the poll tax protests, when the TV had switched to a scene at Strangeways prison, Manchester. In the onscreen images, inmates were on the roof of the prison, throwing off slates and tearing off coping stones, which they threw down to the ground. There were bare patches of roof where only the rafters remained because all the slates had been lifted.

Some of the inmates were wearing masks and many of them were carrying sticks, scaffolding poles and other weapons. As they tried to shout messages to their families and reporters below, the Home Office drowned out their protests by playing loud music. The inmates responded by waving banners on which they had scrawled their complaints and demands.

The newsreader described how a demonstration against the conditions in the prison had escalated into a full-scale riot. Reports from inside the prison claimed that prisoners were breaking down the walls to get to the sex offenders and tearing up fixtures and fittings. Other accounts revealed that some inmates had been attacked, and prison officers had sustained injuries during the riots.

Then the cameras cut to the scene outside the prison again. On the ground, crowds gathered: anxious relatives of prisoners, members of the press and other onlookers who were enjoying the entertainment. The noise was deafening. As the Home Office played 'Mr Blue Sky' at top volume, it was accompanied by the sound of sirens, people shouting up to the inmates and a helicopter circling overhead.

The news showed a worried woman who was begging for her spouse to get himself off the roof and back to safety. Other onlookers weren't quite so worried. The on-scene reporter stated that it resembled a carnival atmosphere with people eating and drinking while they watched what was taking place. Others were making the most of the occasion by selling beer, T-shirts, burgers and even weed.

Then the camera swivelled up to the roof again where a few prisoners surrounded a fire they had built. While the public watched, they showed off the juicy steaks they had taken from the staff kitchens before throwing them onto the fire to cook. The air filled with smoke as the fires raged.

Joanne searched anxiously for any sign of Macca among the images, but she couldn't spot him. What if he was one of the injured inmates still inside the prison? What if he needed medical attention but no one could get to him?

Below, prison officers with riot shields were gathered, ready to storm the prison. This also caused Joanne anguish. What if Macca was involved in a conflict with the officers? He might get badly injured or maybe even worse.

Then, to her distress, there was footage of the prison doors being opened and an inmate being thrown out onto the stone steps. The camera zoomed in on his badly beaten body. When Joanne saw the profusion of blood, she gasped, and her hand shot to her mouth. Even as he lay there, broken, prisoners on the roof bombarded him with slates and coping stones.

Joanne was still in a state of shock when the doorbell rang, making her jump. She had been so engrossed in the news; she had almost forgotten that Tom was calling round.

She tried to put concerns about Macca out of her mind and plastered on a smile as she went to answer the door. Although she still thought about Macca often, she had to remind herself that she was seeing Tom now so she should focus her attentions on him.

They had been on a couple of dates. To Joanne's surprise, Sonia had only been on one date with Jason because he couldn't cope with her having a young child. Joanne had carried on seeing Tom after she discovered they got along well. And now, she needed to get on with her life.

But despite her resolve, she still couldn't face binning the letters Macca had sent her.

Macca and Jojo weren't the only ones eager to escape the prison. Over a thousand prisoners surrendered on the same day, leaving only the hardcore protestors. As Macca and Jojo made their way outside, they passed packs of men like feral wolves, charging through the prison and inflicting damage on cell furniture.

Macca heard someone say, 'Let's raid the offices,' and he

saw one man laden with food, which he claimed to have lifted from the kitchens. Agonising screams still pierced the air and Macca guessed that the inmates were continuing to inflict their own form of punishment on the sex offenders.

He followed a trail of prisoners who were heading to an outside door. As he made his way along the prison corridors, he kept checking to make sure Jojo was following him. It was one of the smaller doors, which opened out onto some steps, and Macca was glad to be outside.

As soon as they got out of the building, they were met by prison officers with riot shields, and Macca felt a shudder of fear, wondering what lay in store for them. The officers directed them onto a waiting coach. When the coach set off, a cheer went up among the prisoners. Macca wasn't sure what they were cheering for: relief at escaping the marauding men inside or relief at escaping Strangeways itself.

Being aboard the coach was a surreal experience. Some of the prisoners were acting like celebrities, waving at the crowds that surrounded the prison. But Macca and Jojo were just pleased to be away from the riots and out of danger.

Nobody told them where they were heading, and the coach was alive with speculation about possible destinations. Macca was as surprised as everyone else when the coach came to a halt only half an hour later. He looked across to Jojo who was seated next to him, but Jojo was focused on the scene outside the coach.

Macca followed Jojo's eyes to find a group of prison officers in deep discussion. Beyond them he could see a cream-coloured wall that bordered the car park, but it was impossible to see beyond the wall. Then he saw a sign, which read, *Welcome to HMP Risley*. No doubt other prisoners had become aware of it too as another cheer went up.

'It's Cat C,' announced one inmate excitedly.

Jojo turned to Macca. 'That's good. It means we should get a lot more time out of our cells and it's not too far from home either.'

Macca later learnt that the prison was situated in Warrington, just outside Manchester, and he hoped that would mean his mother could visit.

It was another three hours before Macca was allocated a cell, having been searched and gone through the registration process. He found himself in a cell with two other inmates, both young. The most youthful of the two, Sam, was skinny with closely cropped hair and an abundance of tattoos. The other one, Jon, was tall and well-built. He was a good-looking, well-groomed lad, and not what Macca would have thought of as a criminal.

When Sam complained about overcrowding, the prison officer accompanying Macca to his cell explained that they had to take their share of inmates from Strangeways because of the riot. Once the officer was gone, the two lads crowded around Macca, eager to find out more about the riot. Macca told them what he could but when they discovered his involvement was minimal, they lost interest.

'That one's yours,' said Sam, pointing to a narrow bunk. It was a single bunk on the opposite side of the cell to the double bunks where Sam and Jon slept. 'They took the chairs out to make room for it so now we have to sit on our bunks,' Sam continued.

His tone wasn't hostile, more matter-of-fact but Macca could understand them feeling aggrieved. The space between the two bunks and his own was less than a metre. Apart from that, there was a tiny space at the end of the bunks where two cabinets had been placed one on top of the other with a further one on the opposite side of the cell.

A feeling of claustrophobia was beginning to chip away at him and Macca wondered whether Jojo had fared any better. He hoped so. Having to share three to a cell was bad enough at his age but he didn't like to think of Jojo having to repeat the experience. He remembered how unhappy he'd been at having to do it in Strangeways.

Macca put his things in the small cabinet that had been allocated to him, then he sat on his bunk. To his relief, the conversation with Sam and Jon became more general. They explained that, unlike Strangeways, the inmates here spent a lot of time outside their cells. They had been allocated jobs and were given opportunities to learn new skills. Macca was flabbergasted to learn that they also played pool, snooker and table tennis during association, which took place each day, as well as attending the gym.

The two lads, in turn, were shocked to find out about the living conditions in Strangeways, although they admitted that lack of hygiene was the downside to life in Risley. The prison was infested with cockroaches, rats and fleas. Jon also warned Macca about the gangs that controlled the prison and told him it was important to stay on the right side of them.

Macca was glad of the advice offered by both lads about

life in Risley. They didn't seem too bad to get along with and Macca hoped it stayed that way. Living in such close proximity was going to be a challenge but Macca was determined to serve the rest of his sentence in relative peace and hoped that it would pass as quickly as possible.

57

June 1996

Six years and eight months after starting his sentence, Macca emerged from Risley. True to his promise to himself, he'd kept out of trouble and had more than three years deducted from his sentence for good behaviour. Thankfully, he had managed to avoid the prison gangs who controlled the supply and sale of drugs: something Macca still didn't get involved in.

He was carrying a meagre number of possessions as well as a small allowance from the prison intended to tide him over until he could either gain employment or benefits. In reality, Macca knew that by the time he'd paid for his bus and train fare home, as well as a drink and snack along the way, there wouldn't be much of the money left.

Jojo had spent his time at Risley on another wing of the prison, but Macca had managed to chat to him every now and again during association. He had been released several months before Macca, and they had vowed to keep in touch. In fact, he was the only inmate who Macca had decided to keep in touch with; the rest were too ingrained in a life of crime and that wasn't what Macca wanted in the future.

Macca didn't know what had happened to Todd, but he didn't expect him to turn up at Risley. After Todd's involvement in the riots, Macca expected that he would serve more time and be transferred to a category-A prison, as the authorities would see him as a troublemaker.

For the first few weeks after his release, Jojo had kept to his word by sending letters to Macca, but they had eventually tailed off. The letters talked about his plans to open a jerk shop and they detailed how busy he was with the preparation. Macca presumed he must have become so busy that he couldn't find time to write anymore.

Macca had spent his time in Risley productively. He had started off with a cleaning job initially but eventually been upgraded to catering. As his release date approached, he also attended two skills-for-life courses. He hoped this would help him to secure employment now he was a free man.

It was a long journey; first a bus into Warrington, then a train to Manchester and a further bus from the city centre. After two and a half hours he finally reached home. The door was opened by his mum who flashed a broad smile. She flung her arms around Macca and clung on as though she couldn't face letting him go again.

'Jesus, Mum. You're crushing me,' he complained.

She let go and stood back, admiring her only son. 'Bloody hell, you've filled out a bit, haven't you?'

'Yeah, I used the gym a lot. The food was crap, but I bought snacks with my wages.'

'Ooh, you're looking well. I can't tell you how happy I am to have you home.'

Macca felt that if she had bothered to visit him regularly, she wouldn't have noticed such a vast difference in his appearance. But during the time he had been in Risley, she had only visited him twice and that was at the beginning. In fact, she hadn't been to see him for the last four years, claiming that the fares were too expensive.

Full of animation, she bounced along the hall and walked into the lounge. Macca followed her, stopping just inside the door and putting his bag of possessions onto one of the chairs. As his mother watched, he gazed around the room.

It was the same, but it was different. The only item of furniture that had been replaced was the sagging sofa with its autumn-leaf design. However, the matching armchairs remained, as did the Formica dining table and two teak dining chairs, which were still pushed against the far wall. The new sofa was black imitation leather and looked just as shabby as the previous one, but he suspected it was more comfortable to sit on.

The cushions with covers crocheted by his grandma had been transferred to the new sofa. They looked incongruous against the shiny black plastic. For a moment it brought back memories of Doris, and he could feel tears start to well in his eyes. He fought back the surge of emotion, knowing that it would do him no good to indulge in self-pity.

He looked back at his mum. She was different too. Beyond the obvious joy at having him back, she had aged since he had been incarcerated. Her hair was now peppered with grey and there were lines on her face, which he hadn't spotted before. He felt guilty, knowing how much worry he must have caused her.

'I've missed you, love,' she said.

He should have reciprocated. But he didn't. Instead, he walked through to the kitchen and checked out the fridge and cupboards. They were almost empty. Without thinking, he tutted. All the way home, he'd been looking forward to having some decent home cooking. But it was evident by looking at the state of the place and the lack of food that his mother wasn't coping very well.

'Sorry, love, but my benefits aren't due for two days,' she mumbled. 'Actually, I was hoping you'd be able to help me out. Did they give you some money when you left prison?'

Macca tutted again and tipped out his pockets, putting the remaining cash into his mother's waiting hands, apart from a fiver, which he held back for himself. 'That's all that's left,' he said. 'So, you need to make it last until you get your benefits.'

She nodded in gratitude. Macca felt suddenly, inexplicably irritated with her. He'd looked forward to this day for so long. Maybe his memories of life on the outside had been clouded by his experience of prison. Or maybe it just wasn't the same without his grandma. But whatever it was, he felt let down and was already disillusioned by what he had found.

58

June 1996

The following day Macca was feeling more positive. He told himself it wasn't his mum's fault she had been left to cope alone without him or his grandma. As the man of the house, it was his responsibility to put things right. And he'd start by getting a job. The thought of persuading his mother to find work never entered his head. She'd been a stay-at-home mum for so long that it was something he accepted automatically.

Macca recalled the days before he had been sent down. Until he had started earning money, his mother had survived on handouts from his grandma or from one of her boyfriends. The empty cupboards told him that her days of attracting well-to-do men were behind her.

He left the flat, telling his mum he'd be out for most of the day and to have something nice ready for his dinner. His first stop was at the jobcentre in Manchester.

When he arrived, he went around the display boards, selecting cards for various jobs that he thought suited his skills and experience. He queued at one of the desks until a clerk became available, then he took his seat and passed her three cards, two for a chef and one for a cook.

The clerk looked him up and down and said, 'OK, so you're looking for a job as a chef, are you?'

'Yeah, that's right.'

'Have you got any experience in that field?'

'Yeah, four years.'

'OK, let's fill in the form and we'll come to that.'

Macca tried to stifle his boredom while the clerk asked him random questions such as his name, address and date of birth. Then they reached the area of the form where he had to list his experience.

'So, can you tell me the roles you have carried out and the places you have worked starting with the most recent?' asked the clerk.

Macca deliberated at first over what to tell her. He'd never applied for a job before, so he hadn't known what to expect, but he knew that the fact he'd served time was bound to go against him. He was tempted to tell a lie but what if they ran checks? In the end he decided to be honest.

'Four years as a cook when I was inside,' he said.

The clerk gazed at him curiously then asked. 'Inside where?'

But Macca could tell by the way she shuffled uncomfortably that she had already figured it out. 'HMP Risley,' he replied. 'I had some training too, so I know how to cook for a lot of people.'

The clerk hesitated, her pen hovering over the form. 'It might be best to leave that,' she said. 'What about before you were inside? What other jobs have you had?'

Macca shrugged. 'I haven't really. That's why I did some courses while I was inside so I can go on the straight and narrow.'

The clerk put down her pen and fixed her gaze on him rather than the form. 'I'm afraid it's not that easy. With the sort of jobs you're looking for, employers will be looking for relevant experience. Restaurants. Pubs. Business canteens. That sort of thing. You could try going on a college catering course and see if you can gain some experience that way.'

'Why? I've already worked as a cook for four years.'

'Erm, yes but, it's not really the same…'

Macca could see she was struggling to voice the real reason, so he decided to make it easy for her. 'It's because I've been inside, innit?'

She nodded, adopting a sympathetic frown. 'I'm afraid so. Most employers don't look favourably on you if you've been in prison.'

She whispered the last word, as if she was afraid to say it. That annoyed Macca as did the situation he was in. 'Well how the fuck am I supposed to get back on the straight and narrow if no one will give me a chance? I've done my time, now I just want to put it behind me.'

'I'm sorry but…'

Macca had heard enough. Standing up, he pushed his chair back towards the table and stormed out of the building.

By the time he reached the estate, Macca was feeling guilty for taking it out on the clerk. It wasn't her fault the system stank, and he wished he hadn't been so hard on her. But if no one would give him a chance, then how the hell was he supposed to find work?

His next stop was at the unemployment benefit office. It was reminiscent of the previous time he had gone to sign on, although it had now been integrated with the jobcentre. One thing that hadn't changed was the requirement to stand in queues for hours and go through the rigmarole of filling in forms and being interviewed by the snotty staff.

But once he'd finished, he was able to go home feeling that at least he'd achieved something that day. The problem was, he would have to wait for weeks until his benefits came through. And with the meagre amount that his mum received, he didn't know how they would manage in the meantime.

59

June 1996

Despite his knockback at the jobcentre, Macca was still determined to find a job. Since he had been home, Joanne was never far from his mind. He'd stopped writing letters to her while he was in prison because he never heard back. How could he blame her? A nice girl like her didn't want anything to do with a criminal. But perhaps if he could show her that he'd turned his life around, she might reconsider.

He scoured the jobs pages in the newspaper and applied for any chef or cook jobs that he could find. If he managed to get an interview, then he decided he just wouldn't tell them about his life behind bars. Instead, he'd say he worked in a restaurant straight from school, but it had since shut down.

Macca hadn't completed many applications before his money ran out so he couldn't buy any more stamps or envelopes. He managed to scrounge a bit of cash from his mother, but she couldn't spare much. A week later he hadn't heard from any of his applications. Nor had his benefits arrived, and he was becoming desperate for money.

Feeling pressured to earn an income somehow, he decided to visit Shay. Maybe he could put him onto something. But he vowed to himself that it would only be temporary. He hadn't heard anything from Shay during his time inside, although Todd had mentioned him the odd time when he'd seen him in Strangeways. But Shay was the only one of the gang left apart from Todd, and Macca didn't have a clue where *he* was currently residing.

Macca remembered where Shay used to live but when he arrived at the house, Shay's mum told him that he now had his own council flat. She gave him the address. Macca was familiar with this part of the estate and knew that it was where a lot of bad people hung out.

He approached the flat cautiously and was rewarded with the sight of Shay answering the door. His greeting was impassive, just a shake of the head as though he had seen him only yesterday. Then he walked up the hall, leaving Macca to shut the door and catch up with him.

As he followed behind, Macca smelt the strong lingering odour of cannabis. By the time he reached the lounge, Shay was already slouched on a sofa. The living room wasn't the worst he'd seen but it wasn't the best either. Among the dirty pots and general detritus was a two-seater sofa, and Shay was taking up most of that. Alongside Shay was a small table littered with drug paraphernalia.

Shay's clothes were creased and dishevelled, and Macca guessed he must have slept in them.

'Budge up, mate,' he said. 'At least let me fuckin' sit down.'

He joined Shay on the sofa, and it was then that he

picked up on another smell. It was coming from Shay and was a combination of cigarette smoke, booze and stale body odour. Shay reached to the small table and picked up a spliff, which he lit up.

'Want one?' he asked.

Macca realised the reason for Shay's docile manner: he was already stoned.

'No thanks. You know it's not my scene.'

'I thought the nick would have sorted that out.'

It was the first acknowledgement from Shay that Macca had been away. Then, as if his brain was on delay, Shay said, 'When did you get out?'

'Just over a week ago.'

'What you been up to?'

'Nothing much. In fact, I thought you might be able to help me.'

'Oh yeah.'

'Yeah. I'm looking for work.'

Shay blew out a puff of smoke. 'Depends what you want. I'm into the drug scene now, man. You wanna piece of that?'

Macca wondered why Shay was now talking like some New Age hippy, but he bit back his irritation. 'No, I've told you, it's not my scene. Is there owt else you can put me onto?'

'Nowt that pays like this. It's easy money, man. Why the fuck would you wanna do any other stuff?'

Macca realised he was wasting his time but there was one more thing he wanted to ask him. 'Do you know where Todd got transferred to after Strangeways?'

'Yeah. Frankland. He got a six-stretch added on to his sentence 'cos of the riot.'

Macca gave a low whistle. He was familiar with the name, Frankland. Other inmates in Risley had told him it was a category-A prison for those serving sentences of four years or more. It was also nicknamed 'Monster Mansion' because many of its inmates were sex offenders, murderers or terrorists. Macca didn't envy his friend having to serve time in there.

'How long has he got left?' he asked.

'Depends if he gets time off. I reckon he's got at least five years left.'

Macca wasn't convinced his friend would get his sentence reduced due to good behaviour so he might be behind bars for a few years yet. Once they had discussed Todd, an awkward silence descended. Shay didn't ask about his time inside and Macca didn't ask how Shay was. That was obvious from his surroundings and demeanour.

'Right, I'll be off then,' he announced, getting up from the sofa.

'See you around, mate,' said Shay who was still smoking his spliff and hadn't bothered standing up to see him off.

Macca made his own way, glad to get outside and into the relative fresh air of the Manchester suburbs. *Where to now?* he thought, feeling deflated by Shay's apathy. Then he thought of Clive and Rob and wondered if they were still at the garage. He knew Clive could be quite abrasive at times, but he was running out of options. Besides, it was only a short walk away, so he decided to go and check it out.

He was surprised to find he got a much warmer reception from Clive than he had from Shay.

'Fuckin' hell! Look who it is,' said Clive, marching over and giving him a handshake with greasy hands.'

Macca pulled his oil-streaked hand away and examined it.

Clive passed him a cloth out of a box and grabbed one for himself. 'Sorry, mate. I forgot. Here, use this.'

As Macca wiped his hand, Clive asked, 'When did you get out?'

'Just over a week ago.'

'How's it been?'

'Alright, y'know. Money's a bit tight. Where's Rob?'

'He moved on,' Clive replied. 'There's just me now. You looking for work?'

'Yeah. But not here.'

Clive chuckled. 'No, I didn't mean that. You ain't got the experience as a mechanic, have you? But there's summat you are experienced in.'

Macca smiled, more out of relief than anything. 'OK. Same arrangement as before?'

'Nah,' said Clive. 'It'd have to be the other way round: sixty to me, forty to you. I was never happy with the deal your mate wanted. But I suppose he was a bit persuasive, wasn't he?'

Macca remembered the day Todd had marched in there and demanded a sixty-forty arrangement. Out of fear, Clive had settled for his forty per cent even though it was clear he wasn't happy with it. Macca couldn't resist a wry grin, recalling how terrified Clive had been.

But now it was different. Macca didn't have Todd backing him up. It didn't stop him trying though. 'Fifty-fifty works better for me.'

Clive put down the cloth he had been using and said, 'Nah, it's sixty-forty or nowt. I'm not gonna be out of pocket again. Take it or leave it.'

Macca shrugged. He could have kicked himself for admitting that he was short of money. Clive would know exactly how short he was seeing as how he'd only been out of prison just over a week. 'OK,' he conceded. 'I'll take it. But I'll need some cash up front.'

Clive walked over to a cabinet at the back of the room and returned clutching a handful of cash. 'Here's fifty to be going on with but I'll deduct it from your first car.'

Macca took the money gladly. He walked home with mixed feelings. He was disappointed in himself for breaking his resolve and going back to crime so soon. But he was also relieved that at least he'd found a way to make a regular supply of income until something else turned up. He was determined that he'd still find a way to go legit and that thought lifted him.

By the time he arrived at his estate, he was feeling much more upbeat. But then he saw someone he thought he recognised. She was some distance away and wheeling a toddler's trolley, but it was her mannerisms that gave her away. The cocky way she walked and the slouch of her shoulders. By the time he had drawn closer to her, he was certain of who it was: Shell. And she looked thrilled to see him.

60

June 1996

As he drew even nearer to Shell, Macca took in her appearance. Her dirty blond hair straggled to her shoulders in greasy strands, and she was wearing a bright pink shell suit with black stripes. The jacket was open revealing a red cropped top and a midriff, which sagged over the top of her trousers. Shell was carrying a bit more weight than the last time he had seen her but that had been nearly seven years ago, and Macca guessed that it was down to the birth of her child.

She took a puff of her cigarette, then exhaled slowly as she appraised him with eager eyes. 'Well, well, haven't seen you for a while,' she greeted. 'When did you get out?'

'Just over a week ago.'

'How's it going?'

'OK, I suppose. Better than being inside.'

'I bet. So, what's it like being back at home with your mum?'

'Same as it ever was.'

'I bet it gets boring though, dunnit? I've got my own place now.'

'Oh yeah, is that where you live with your other half?'

'Other half? What you on about?'

'Your baby's father,' said Macca, his tone tetchy to convey that he was stating the obvious.

'Oh God no! I fucked him off ages ago. He's a right bastard. I'm on my own now.'

She flashed her eyes provocatively, but Macca didn't rise to it. He was tempted. It had been a long time since he'd been with a woman. But he wasn't desperate enough to go with Shell. Not again. He remembered what had happened the last time. He was just a kid then and hadn't known any better, but she'd become clingy afterwards.

Attempting to change the subject, he asked, 'How old is your little boy?'

'Eighteen months. And he's a little terror. Aren't you?' She addressed the child, bending forward to tickle his tummy. As she bent, she exhaled a plume of smoke over the child, but he giggled, oblivious to the health hazard. Then the child looked up at Macca, and he was drawn in by his large sad eyes. He smiled at the child and waved his hand till the child smiled back.

'What's his name?' asked Macca.

'Tyrone,' said Shell.

'He looks like a good kid.'

'Aw, he is really. But he can be a little bugger at times. He seems to like you.'

'Ha, maybe it's my charming personality,' said Macca, laughing.

'Hey, if you're doing nowt, why don't you come back

for coffee? You can get to know Tyrone a bit better if you want.'

Macca felt a moment of panic. He'd only asked about the kid to change the subject and now he had Shell thinking he was interested in him. Shit! If she thought he was going to step into the role of baby daddy, she was very much mistaken.

'No, I er, I've got stuff to do.'

'You working then?'

'Not yet, no.' Macca didn't want to tell her too much. He remembered how spiteful she could be, and he didn't trust her enough to confide in her about his arrangement with Clive.

'Well, what can you have to do that's so important if you're not working?'

'Just stuff,' he said. Then, attempting to change the subject again, he asked the question that he'd been dying to ask ever since he'd set eyes on Shell. 'Have you seen anything of Joanne?'

'No. She doesn't live round here anymore. Didn't you know?'

'Yeah, I knew she'd moved before I went inside but doesn't she still come to visit her family?'

'Not as much. Not since she got married.'

'What?'

'You heard. She got married.'

As she spoke, Macca noticed the self-satisfied grin on her face. She knew he was shocked. It was difficult to hide. And she was revelling in his despair.

'What's it to you anyway?' she asked. 'You two split up years ago. You're not still hankering after her, are you?'

'No!' he snapped.

Macca had been quick to deny his feelings for Joanne. He felt foolish to admit them. What had he expected? She was young and attractive. Who could blame her for moving on? She'd already told him she didn't want to be with him. Yet, like an idiot, he hadn't accepted that they were over.

But his denial couldn't disguise how he felt inside. All that time he'd been holding out hope that they would one day get back together. At times it was all that had got him through those miserable years behind bars. And now, to find out she was married to someone else, it was more than he could stand.

'I-I've got to go,' he said again, stepping away from Shell before she had chance to talk him out of it.

His pace was rapid, as though subconsciously he was trying to escape the turmoil he felt. Not wishing to be deterred, Shell shouted after him, 'If you fancy calling round, the offer's still there. And *I'm* single, not married.'

Macca kept walking. The thought of spending time with Shell was even more unappealing now. He just wanted to be alone with his thoughts. And his long-distant memories of the woman he still loved.

61

Aug 1996

Macca had been out of prison for two months. He spent many of his evenings stealing cars for Clive and his days either watching TV or playing on his games console. But he was bored. The only company he had these days was his mother and Clive. His mother had changed since his grandma's death and was only a shadow of the feisty woman she once was.

Lately Macca had been spending time at The Grey Goose. He still knew a few people in there, but they were more acquaintances than friends. Today he was standing at the bar, supping pints of lager and engaging in the odd chat with other customers, when a girl walked in.

She was quite attractive, with pointed features framed by a brunette bob. She wore dark eye makeup, which accentuated her eyes, and she was average height and slim. Her face looked familiar, and she smiled at him as she came to the bar.

When Macca returned the smile, she asked, 'Hi, how are you? I've not seen you for ages.'

Macca looked at her confused, trying to place her. 'Sorry, where do I know you from?' he asked.

'Just around. I used to see you in here a bit.'

'Ah, right. Yeah, I've been, erm, working away. But I'm back now so I've started coming in here again.'

They began to engage in small talk. Macca found out that her name was Nicola, and he offered to buy her a drink. Nicola excused herself saying she needed to find her mates and take their drinks to them, but she promised to catch up with him later. Macca could tell she was interested so he hung around at the end of the night and offered to walk her home.

To his delight she agreed. It didn't take long till they arrived. It was a flat in the middle of the estate and although it was surrounded by run-down properties, she kept it clean and neat inside. The furniture looked new, and the TV was huge.

'Wow! You've got a nice place,' he commented. 'Do you live here alone?'

'I do now,' she said, in a tone that didn't invite further discussion.

Macca guessed that she must have shared it with a partner who was no longer around. Maybe they had done the place up together. When she offered him a drink, he agreed. But he had other things on his mind. He wondered whether she was up for it.

She passed him his drink and sidled up next to him on the sofa, and he wasted no time in finding out. Putting his drink down, he turned to her and stared intently into her eyes, leaning in closer. He was pleased to get a response and soon they were sharing passionate kisses.

Macca let his hands roam along her body and she sighed contentedly. When he slid his hand inside her blouse and caressed her nipples, she softly purred. So, he carried on, letting his hands wander down and under her underwear. He slipped his fingers inside her, and she moaned with pleasure.

They were soon ripping each other's clothes off and within no time he was inside her, thrusting ardently. Macca felt mortified as he ejaculated within a couple of minutes. He saw a look of disappointment on her face, and he gathered his clothes together, hurriedly putting them on to try to hide his embarrassment.

'Jesus Christ! Is that it?' she demanded.

'Sorry. It's been a long time.'

'It must have fuckin' been,' she snapped.

Macca realised that this girl had another side to her. She'd seemed so nice when he'd been chatting her up, but now he knew how quickly her mood could change. He didn't intend to hang around while she vented her wrath so, once he was dressed, he raced to the front door muttering, 'I've got to go.'

He was glad to get out of the place. It had been such a humiliating experience and he hoped she didn't tell anyone in the pub. He might go elsewhere for a pint in future or perhaps he'd just front it out.

A sadness overcame him as thoughts of Joanne filled his mind. He wished she hadn't got married. He'd much rather have been tucked at home with her now, sharing cuddles on her sofa like they used to do while they watched a film together. Instead, he was making meaningless chat with pub patrons and having a one-night stand with a girl he didn't really want to be with.

He soon snapped out of his melancholic state and by the time he was home, Macca was seeing the funny side of the experience. At least he'd got his first post-prison sex out of the way. Perhaps he'd make a better performance of it the next time.

When he got inside the flat, he was surprised to find the light still on in the living room. Knowing his mum didn't like to waste electricity, he went into the room, intending to switch the light off.

'Bloody hell, Mum! You gave me a fright sitting there. What are you doing still up at this time?'

He noticed by the clock on the sideboard that it was turned twelve thirty. Then he saw that she had a drink in front of her too. That was also unusual for her. Generally, she only drank when she went out and that was rare these days. The look on her face told him there was something wrong.

'What is it, Mum?' he asked.

'I've been waiting up for you, love. It's your dad. I've had a call from him. He's in a bad way. It's his liver. He's dying. And he's asked to see you.'

62

Aug 1996

Macca didn't go to see his father straightaway. His father had never been there for him while he was living, so why did he want to see him now that he was dying? There was a time when he used to see him, but those visits had become less and less frequent so that as an adult he felt he hardly knew him.

The little he did know about his father was mostly from what Doris had said when she was having a rant. So, when he tried to think about him, the words 'useless article', 'good for nothing' and 'bloody boozer' spun around inside his head.

Macca deliberated for a few days. Finally, curiosity got the better of him and he agreed with his mother that he would go to see him in the hospice where he was staying. His proviso was that she should come with him.

When they arrived a few days later, Macca was surprised at the sight of the place as it was in lovely grounds. An amiable nurse greeted them at the door and led them through to Vernon's room, which overlooked the beautiful gardens. On the way they passed a common room where people were playing board games and watching TV.

Macca wouldn't have guessed at first glance that they were all suffering from terminal illnesses. They looked so happy. But, on closer scrutiny, he saw how skinny and pale some of the patients were. He put their happy outlook down to the friendly atmosphere in the place, and even though he wasn't close to his father, he was glad that he was ending his days somewhere like this rather than at home alone.

As soon as they got inside the room, it was evident to Macca that his father was closer to death than any of the people in the common room. He was almost unrecognisable from the man Macca had met years previously. His eyes were sunken in his face, which, like the rest of him, was skeletal and his cheekbones were prominent. Despite his skinny appearance, his stomach was swollen, and his complexion was sallow with a yellow tinge.

Macca stifled a gasp of shock as his mother approached the bed and said, 'Hello, Vernon.'

'Debbie. Mark. It's good of you to come,' Vernon replied, and his eyes filled with tears.

'How are you feeling?' asked Debbie.

Macca cringed at the stupidity of the question. How the hell did she think he felt? He wasn't exactly doing cartwheels, was he? Thankfully, his dad took the sting out of the question, forcing a weak smile then saying, 'I've felt better.'

Debbie attempted a smile back and then pulled out a chair and sat next to the head of the bed. Macca followed suit, tucking his seat just behind his mother's. When Vernon reached out his hand, Debbie obliged by taking it in hers and stroking it gently.

'It's good of you both to come,' Vernon repeated. 'I had no right to expect it really.'

'Shush,' Debbie urged, continuing to stroke his hand. 'Is there anything you need?' she asked.

'No, I'm OK. They look after me well here.'

'How long have you been like this?' asked Debbie.

Vernon attempted a shrug, which didn't translate well because he was lying in bed. 'How long's a piece of string?'

'What do you mean?'

'Gradual innit? I can't even remember when it started?'

'Can't they do anything for you? A transplant or summat?'

'No, according to the docs I'm not a good risk.'

He didn't elaborate but Macca presumed he was referring to the fact that he was an alcoholic.

'How long have you been in here then?' asked Debbie.

Vernon sighed. 'For Christ's sake, Debbie, what's with all the questions?'

'I was only asking!' she snapped.

Vernon looked remorseful then. 'Sorry, it's not your fault I've ended up here. I've only got myself to blame.'

Debbie didn't respond; neither did Macca. How could they offer him reassurance when he was telling the truth? Macca felt a stab of irritation because his father's irresponsibility had not only landed him in here, but it had caused suffering to those around him too. He'd known the damage he was doing every time he got drunk senseless and yet he'd still carried on doing it.

His father surprised both Macca and his mum when he said, 'Do you mind if I have a word with Mark alone?'

Debbie turned to Macca. 'Are you OK with that?'

Macca nodded. Not only was he OK with it, but he was determined that once his mother was out of the way, he'd stand no nonsense from his father, dying or not. If he started playing the pity card with him, he'd let him know exactly what he thought.

Debbie slipped from the room and Vernon urged him to move closer. Macca did as asked, but he threw his father a stony look.

'I-I believe you've just done a stretch,' said his father.

'Yeah. So, what's it to you?'

Vernon reached out his hand, but Macca refused to take it. 'I'm not asking anything from you,' said Vernon. 'I know I don't deserve it. I've been a terrible father and...'

'What the fuck do you expect me to say?' snapped Macca. 'You're not honestly expecting me to forgive you after how you've treated me, are you? After how you've treated my mum?'

'No. No, I'm not. Let me speak, son.'

Just then a nurse popped her head through the door. She must have heard Macca's raised voice because she asked, 'Everything alright, Vernon?'

'Yeah. It's fine. No worries.'

When she walked away, father and son locked eyes again. 'Listen,' said Vernon. 'I know I'm not one to preach. I've made a mess of my life. I'm a drunk and a thief, and I don't deserve any sympathy from anyone. But it's at times like this that you start thinking about things, y'know.'

He paused for a moment as though the little speech was tiring him out. During that time, he gazed across at his son. Then he continued.

'I wish I could leave you a proud man. I wish that in time to come you'd look back and say what a great bloke your dad was. But what will people remember me for, eh? For being a loser and a waster. The only people who thought I was a great bloke were those I was standing rounds to down the pub. And even they turned their backs on me when the going got tough.'

'What are you trying to say?' asked Macca, willing him to come to the point. The last thing he needed was an emotional farewell from a man who wasn't even worthy of being called his father.

Vernon grabbed his hand, his grip surprisingly strong for a dying man. 'What I'm trying to say is that I don't want you to go down the same road. Don't be like me, son. I've put your mum through enough. I don't want her to suffer the same from you. Make summat of your life so that when you reach the end of your days people can turn round and say how proud they were of you.'

He stopped to take a breather again before carrying on. 'It's not too late to turn things around. You don't have to go down that road. You were always a good kid. Make a change, son. Make your mum fuckin' proud! Don't be a waster like your old man.'

Vernon was crying openly now, and Macca was troubled to find that he was feeling it too. He tried to suppress his tears, pulling his hand away from his father's grasp just as his mother walked back in the room.

'What the bloody hell's going on?' she asked.

'Nowt,' said Macca.

Then he stood up and fled from the room in tears.

63

Aug 1996

Seeing his dad like that had hit Macca hard. He couldn't understand why, given that he hadn't seen him for years. A week later, after the funeral, he decided to visit Jojo. Macca didn't know what had driven him to do so now; maybe he had been subconsciously yearning for a proper father figure. But whatever it was, he was happy to be visiting him.

Macca still had the address Jojo had used when he'd sent him letters to Risley, so he called there first. The door was answered by a middle-aged lady who Macca assumed was Jojo's wife. She had a kind, rounded face but nevertheless she eyed Macca with suspicion.

'Is Jojo in?' he asked.

'Who wants him?'

'My name's Mark. I'm an old friend of his.'

'He's at the shop.'

'OK. Where's that?'

She was scrutinising him as she asked, 'Where do you know him from?'

Macca hesitated before replying, then decided there was no point in lying. 'Risley,' he said.

He could see she was already starting to close the door while speaking. 'I don't want him mixing with anyone from that place. He's put all that behind him.'

'I know. He told me. He was really excited about opening his jerk shop.'

Then there was a look of recognition in her eyes. 'Ah, are you Macca, the lad that shared the cell with him in Strangeways?'

Macca smiled. 'That's right, yeah.'

'He told me all about you.'

She smiled back so he assumed it was all good, which was confirmed when she gave him directions to the shop. It was a short walk away and within fifteen minutes Macca had arrived to find a large colourful sign outside that read, *Jojo's Jerk Shop*. He looked inside to find his friend standing behind the counter looking proud and upstanding.

Walking into the shop, Macca could smell the pleasant aroma of cooked meat and spices. It was so good that it made him salivate. The vibrant décor was inviting with bright lights accentuating the vivid colour scheme. There were about a dozen wooden tables in the front of the shop which were occupied by patrons enjoying tasty-looking dishes. Macca headed straight to the back to greet his friend.

'Bloody hell, look at you!' he said.

Jojo flashed him a wide smile before stepping out from

behind the counter and giving him a friendly slap on the back. 'Good to see you. How long you been home?'

'A few weeks,' said Macca.

'A few weeks? And you've only just come to see your old mate?' asked Jojo but his tone was jovial.

'Soz. I've been busy.'

'Oh yeah. Busy with what?'

'This and that. You know how it is.' Macca saw the disappointed look on Jojo's face, so he quickly deflected. 'My dad died.'

'Oh. Sorry to hear that.'

'Don't be. You know how it was.'

'Yeah, yeah, I remember you telling me. But it still gets to you, so you take care.'

Jojo accompanied this last sentence with a comforting pat on Macca's back. It touched Macca. *How does he know how I'm feeling?* he thought. *How does Jojo have this knack of always knowing exactly how I feel?*

Macca deflected for a second time, too uncomfortable to go into any more detail about his father especially in front of a shop full of people. He had a feeling it might upset him and then he'd feel a fool for caring too much about a man who didn't deserve it.

He resorted to the friendly banter they had shared when they were banged up in a cell together. 'Eh, is it true you're taking over the market for fast food restaurants in Manchester? Chinatown had better be worried,' he joked. 'You'll be buying up all their restaurants next.'

'You might scoff,' said Jojo with a smile. 'But I told you I'm going places and it's true. This place is doing great, and I've already got plans for a second shop.'

'Really? Where?'

'City centre. Like I told you in the big house, times are changing. People want to try something different.'

Adopting a serious expression, Macca said. 'Great. I know I take the piss but really, I'm pleased for you, mate. You've got a good set-up here. I'm bloody jealous.'

'You've no need to be jealous. In fact, you've turned up just at the right time. You see, I've found a building for the second shop, but I haven't found any staff yet. How about running it for me?'

Macca was flabbergasted. 'Me? But I haven't got any experience in running a shop.'

'No. But you've got experience in catering and cleaning. The rest you can soon learn. I'll show you the ropes myself.'

'I-I don't know what to say, mate. I mean, why me? Haven't you got family that want to help?'

'No. My kids have got their own careers. And neither of them lives in Manchester. And my wife, well, she's a homebody. She don't wanna be running no jerk shop. So, why not you? I know you'd make a good go of it.'

'Jesus, mate. That's great. I honestly don't know how to thank you.'

'Well, you can thank me by doing a good job and making sure my second shop does just as well as this one.'

'Sure. Course I will. And thanks for thinking of me. You won't regret it, I promise you.'

Jojo chuckled. 'I know I won't. I know what you're capable of. It's just a pity *you* don't know that yet. But you will.'

Before Macca got chance to ask him what he meant, a customer approached the counter and Jojo focused his attention on him. By the time he finished serving, the moment was lost, and Macca became absorbed in discussing more of the details with Jojo. The shop wouldn't be open for a few months yet but there would be plenty of preparation work in the meantime and Jojo wanted to put him to good use as soon as possible.

By the time he left the jerk shop and set off for home, Macca was buzzing with excitement. At last, he had been given a chance to turn his life around and it was all down to his good mate Jojo.

64

March 2004

After fourteen years Todd was finally released from prison, having had time added to his sentence for being heavily involved in the riots. He couldn't wait to get back out there. Fourteen years was a long time to serve behind bars and the world seemed like a strange place on the outside.

He'd come across the odd mobile phone during his later years in prison but now he was shocked to see so many people using one. Todd also noticed that people now listened to music on small devices called iPods and MP3s, but he didn't recognise any of the songs they played.

His mother had kept in regular contact with him while he'd been in prison, so he knew that his younger brothers were no longer at home. At this point, though, he didn't know why they had left. He was planning to catch up with them at some point, as well as his mates, but first he wanted to see his mum.

Sandra answered the door with a smile, but she also

appeared nervous. Todd flung his arms around her and gave her a kiss on the cheek. When he released her, he noticed her look of discomfort and realised that he had squashed her a bit in his over-enthusiastic embrace.

'Sorry, Mum. I forget my own strength sometimes.'

She laughed. 'Yeah, I think you were only half the size last time you hugged me like that.'

Todd was aware of his size. During his time inside, working out had become a regular pastime. He had always been big but now he was a very well-built man of thirty-four. It had helped him during his time inside; that and his refusal not to put up with any nonsense from anybody.

They walked through to the lounge to find his stepfather, Kev, sitting in an armchair. He had his newspaper open at the racing pages and a can of beer in front of him while the horseracing dominated the TV screen.

'Fuckin' hell! Look what the cat's dragged in,' he announced.

Todd retaliated, 'Fuck you! You little shit.' Then he walked over to Kev and stood over him menacingly.

Kev got up out of his chair. 'Don't you fuckin' speak to me like that in my house!' he said.

'Why? What you gonna do about it?'

Todd leant in even closer to Kev so that it was plain to see that he stood about seven or eight centimetres taller than his stepdad and was much broader. Kev looked tempted to lash out, his hand hovering precariously. But, on seeing the size of Todd, he seemed to think better of it and sat back down on his armchair, muttering, 'I'm not wasting my fuckin' time on you. The horses are on.' Then he leant around Todd's large frame trying to catch sight of the TV.

'Come on, I'll make you a cuppa, love,' said Sandra in a placatory gesture. She grabbed a packet of cigarettes with shaking hands then slipped one out and lit it.

'You can fuckin' get me one too,' ordered Kev.

'Don't' fuckin' speak to her like that,' Todd responded, determined that he wasn't going to tolerate Kev's nasty ways anymore.

Kev ignored him and focused on the TV, so Todd joined his mum in the kitchen.

Once she had finished making the drinks, Sandra said, 'I'll just take this to Kev and then we can sit in here and have a chat.'

'No, we can't, Mum. Why should we sit on the kitchen chairs? We can sit in the living room.'

'But Kev's watching his horses.'

'So what?'

Todd didn't wait for her to respond. Instead, he took his drink and some biscuits and strode through to the living room so that his mum felt obliged to follow. He plonked himself down on the sofa and, for a few minutes, he and Sandra made conversation while Kev looked up from his TV at intervals and scowled and tutted at them.

Todd was eager to catch up with all that had happened while he'd been away, so he ignored Kev and carried on. He could tell his mum was still nervous, but she needn't be. Now that he was back home, there was no way he'd let Kev harm any of them.

'Where are Ryan and Dylan now?' he asked his mum.

'Oh, Ryan's got a flat with his girlfriend. Remember, I told you he got her pregnant? And I'm not sure where Dylan's staying at the moment to be honest.'

'How come?'

'Because he got into some bad company. But Ryan usually knows where he is.'

Sandra's words were almost drowned out then by Kev yelling. 'Because I fucked him off; that's how come. I'm not having no fuckin' junkie in my house. And if Ryan knows where he is then that's because they're both as fuckin' bad.'

'You what?' Todd demanded.

'You heard. Both junkies and thieves. And if you think you're staying here, you've got another think coming. I've told her...' as he spoke, he pointed a finger dismissively in Sandra's direction '...I'm the man of this house and I'm not having no crooks staying here.'

Then Todd remembered that the house was originally rented by his mum and dad. It wasn't until later that Kev moved in with her. 'Well, seeing as how it's not your name on the rent book,' he said, 'you don't have a fuckin' choice. It's up to my mum.'

'She doesn't want you here either,' Kev snapped.

Todd turned to his mum. 'Is that right?' When she shifted uncomfortably but didn't answer, he persisted. 'Is that what you want, Mum, or is that what he's told you to say?'

'I just don't want any trouble, love, that's all.'

'Yeah, and we'll have nothing but fuckin' trouble if *you* move in. The police will never be away from the door. You lot are all the same: thieves and junkies. I don't wonder though seeing as how your own father was a fuckin' junkie who died of an overdose.'

Todd had heard enough. He sprang from the sofa and raced over to where Kev was sitting, despite his mother pleading with him to leave it. Then he hauled Kev up by his shirt collars and dragged him from his seat.

'Don't you dare have a fuckin' go at my dad. He was a better man than you'll ever be. And you'll never be a fuckin' father to me or my brothers. Do you understand?'

Kev didn't reply. Todd could see the fear in his eyes but guessed he was too proud to concede. It was his mother who stopped him. She ran over to them and, trying to wedge in between, she pleaded with Todd not to hit him.

Feeling bad for upsetting his mum, Todd let go and Kev slumped back into his seat. Todd would have left it at that but, seeing Todd respond to his mother's pleas, Kev chanced his luck, muttering, 'There was no fuckin' need for that. You're not in Frankland now.'

Todd snapped. After years of suffering at this man's hands and seeing his brothers suffer too, he'd had enough. He dragged him from the seat again and when his mother tried to get in between them, he warned her to stay away.

Sandra retreated as though she knew what was coming. And once he'd started, Todd found it difficult to stop. It was like someone had sounded the bell and he was fighting to the bitter end. He laid into Kev with ferocious blows. The first one bust Kev's nose but Todd carried on till the vermillion spray covered his fists, leaving bloody imprints on Kev's face each time he hit him again and again.

Todd was vaguely aware of his mother screaming at him, 'Stop, Todd, please! You're gonna kill him.'

But Todd had a thirst for it now. He was pumped up. On a testosterone-fuelled high. The endorphins racing around his body at full pelt. It felt good. The blood. The heavy impact of his fists on the man's slimy face. Kev's squeals of pain. And his look of terror. He had had it coming for years. And now Todd was letting him have it.

In the end it was a blow to the back of his head that stopped him. At first, Todd didn't know where it had come from, and he stood there dazed. He turned around to see a ceramic vase lying shattered on the ground and his mother cowering in the corner.

'I-I'm sorry, son, but it was the only way to stop you,' she muttered.

For a moment he stood and gazed at Sandra. Then, seeing her evident fear, he felt bad for making her feel like that. It wasn't about her. It was about Kev. Todd would never hurt his mother. But he was still hyped up. And he wasn't finished yet.

Todd stepped towards his mother and said, 'Right, now tell me, in your own words, do you want me staying here or not? Don't worry, I'm not gonna kick off if you say no. I just wanna know that it's your decision. So, what do you say?'

'I, yeah, course I do.'

'Good, that's all I wanted to know.' Then he turned back to Kev who was now a bloody mass slumped once again in his armchair. 'And you, if you ever dare to lay a fuckin' finger on any of my family again, you've got me to answer to.'

Once he'd said his piece, he needed to get away. The adrenalin was still pumping. He needed to walk it off and to get away from the sight of his terrified mother.

'I'm going out,' he said. 'Give me the spare keys. I'll be in later.'

He left, still with the blood on his knuckles and not knowing where he was going. He only knew that he needed to calm down and get his head around what he had just done.

65

March 2004

Macca was surprised to receive a phone call from Todd telling him he'd been released and had been home for a few days. Macca had had no idea, but he supposed that wasn't surprising really. The only other member of the gang still around was Shay, but Macca didn't have anything to do with him.

Macca and Todd were keen to see each other and have a catch-up. As Macca wasn't in work till that evening, he agreed to go for a lunchtime drink with Todd in The Grey Goose. Half an hour later he was there.

It was much quieter in the daytime and for a few minutes Macca sat at a table alone, nursing his pint and waiting for his friend to arrive. When he walked through the door, his features and demeanour were unmistakable. But his physique had changed.

'Fuckin' hell, look at you,' said Macca, eying Todd's muscles, which dwarfed his own even though he still made regular visits to the gym.

He hadn't seen Todd much since he'd been inside, as visiting orders were reserved mainly for family, and he was amazed at the change in him. Todd had always been a big strong lad but now he was so ripped that his biceps were bulging out of his shirt sleeves and his chest was so developed that his shirt buttons were straining to stay fastened.

'Well,' said Todd. 'There's fuck all else to do inside. Besides, it helps me, dunnit?' As he spoke, he tapped the side of his head.

'What do you mean?' asked Macca, not picking up on the non-verbal clue.

Todd looked uncomfortable for a moment before he answered Macca's question. 'I just get so fuckin' angry. But, when I've done a gym sesh, it calms me down. It's so bad in there. Locked in a shitty little cell with some nutjob that you feel like killin' half the time.'

'I know what you mean. I still use the gym myself.'

'Yeah, but with me it's different. It's like I need it to keep me calm. I blame that bastard my mum's shacked up with. Anyway, he got what was fuckin' coming to him when I got out.'

'How d'you mean?'

'Started giving me grief as soon as I got home, didn't he? You'd have thought he'd have let me and my mum have a bit of a chat seeing as how I've been away a long time. But no, he had to fuckin' start; first calling me and my brothers thieves and junkies, then having a go about my old man. That was when I fuckin' lost it. What a shithouse to have a go at a man who's not here to defend himself anymore!'

Macca let him rant till he had got it all out of his system.

Then he asked, 'How are your brothers? I've not seen either of them for a long time.'

'No, that's because they moved out, thanks to that twat. Ryan's shacked up with a girl but I ain't seen Dylan yet. They're both druggies from what I've heard. I was hoping they'd be up for doing a bit of work with me but fuck that. I'm not working with any junkies even if they're my brothers. What about you? What are you up to nowadays?'

'I've gone legal.'

'You're fuckin' joking, aren't you?'

Macca laughed. 'No, straight up.'

'What are you doing?'

'I'm running a fast-food shop.'

Now it was Todd's turn to laugh. 'Come on, mate, seriously. You can't be earning much doing that.'

Before he responded to Todd, a thought flashed through Macca's mind. He was recalling the time when Leroy died. Todd and the others had all done a runner and Macca had protected them from the law by not disclosing their names. Although it was his own decision to stay, he felt he owed Todd nothing. He'd paid his debt to society and now he wanted to be free of all that. He didn't want the hassle anymore of always having to watch his back.

'I do alright,' he replied defensively.

He was determined not to be talked out of working for Jojo. Things were going well and, although he still liked and trusted Todd, he much preferred being on the right side of the law.

'The place is a goldmine,' he continued. 'It's a jerk shop,

and the owner's given me a chance to buy a share in the shop. He's getting near to retirement, so he doesn't want to be running the shops forever.'

This captured Todd's interest. 'What? You mean there's more than one shop?'

'Two at the moment, but who knows what might happen in the future? They're really popular.'

Macca could tell he was gradually earning his friend's respect, especially when Todd said, 'Fuckin' hell! Who'd have thought that? You, a businessman?'

Then he gave Macca a friendly slap on the back. 'Good on you, mate. I don't blame you for wanting to go straight. I wish I could but there's nowt out there for me. Who are you in business with anyway?'

'An old mate of mine. He's West Indian descent so he knows all about jerk shops.'

'It's not that old bloke you were inside with, is it?'

'Yeah, Jojo's his name.'

'Jojo. That's it yes. Seems like a decent bloke.

Macca smiled. 'He is. In fact, he's been like a dad to me at times.'

Todd nodded but didn't respond. Macca already knew the story about what had happened to Todd's dad, but he also knew that Todd wasn't one for showing his emotions.

'I tell you what,' Todd said after a few seconds, 'you might not be up for working with me but why don't we go for a night out for old times' sake?'

Macca thought about it for a moment. He couldn't see any reason why he shouldn't. Although he and Todd now operated on different sides of the law, it didn't mean he couldn't stay friends with him. So he said yes, but he knew that although Todd was still his friend, they would never be as close as they had been as kids. Their lives had changed now, and they were both headed in different directions.

66

March 2004

Macca and Todd decided to go into Manchester for their night out rather than stay local. Macca couldn't blame Todd for wanting to experience the full delights of the city centre after being locked away for so long. It was rare for Macca to get a Friday night off, but he'd persuaded one of his staff to step in for him by offering him a financial incentive.

They started off in Sinclair's Oyster Bar and The Old Wellington, and Todd was amazed to discover that the two old medieval pubs had been moved to a different location after the Manchester bomb of 1996.

'How the fuck did they do that?' asked Todd.

'Piece by piece from what I've heard. It took ages. They're better where they are now though, don't you think?'

'Yeah, great,' said Todd, looking at the area surrounding the two pubs, which had been redeveloped.

After visiting the two pubs, Macca and Todd took a short walk to The Printworks where they found a lively bar. The bar was packed with the typical Friday night crowd and it amused Macca to see the look on Todd's face every time a scantily dressed girl walked past him.

'Fuckin' hell, mate, pick your tongue up off the floor,' quipped Macca as a group of girls hovered close to them.

Todd laughed. 'It's been a fuckin' long time. I bet you were the same when you got out.'

Macca joined in his laughter. 'Yeah, you're not wrong there.'

'So, how's it going now, mate? You never mentioned whether you were seeing anyone.'

'That's because I'm not. I mean, there was a girl I was seeing for a few months. We broke up a couple of weeks ago. She was too fuckin' clingy and I couldn't hack it.'

'Ah well, no worries. Play your cards right and we could both get a ride tonight, mate,' said Todd nodding at the group of girls as he spoke.

Shortly afterwards Macca went to the bar to get some more drinks. As the place was so packed, he had to fight his way through the crowds and queue at the bar for a while. It was sometime later when he returned to the spot where he had been standing with Todd. To his dismay Todd was no longer there. Neither were the group of girls, and Macca wondered whether Todd might have left with one of them. He dismissed the idea as soon as it had occurred to him. Todd wouldn't go off anywhere without telling him.

Macca found a small standing table on which he placed the two pints he had bought. Then he looked over to where they had been standing previously, hoping to catch sight of Todd. There was no sign of him, so Macca gazed around the bar.

It was still packed, but Todd was so tall that he hoped he might still be able to spot him.

When a group of people left, a gap emerged in the crowd. Macca continued to scan the bar, gazing through the gap. He still couldn't see Todd but then he spotted a familiar face.

'Oh my God!' he uttered, causing a few girls to flash curious glances his way.

But Macca was oblivious to the girls. There was only one girl he was interested in, and to his amazement, she was staring back at him. At first, he thought he might be mistaken. She looked older, her face having lost the roundness of youth, and her hair was different. It was now straight rather than permed but was still that lovely natural shade of chestnut brown.

As he gazed in awe, to his amazement she smiled. But he didn't smile back; he was too dumbfounded. Macca knew he could never pass up an opportunity like this, so he walked towards her, his heart pounding. She watched ardently as he made his way through the crowds.

He had almost reached her when he remembered what Shell had told him. Joanne got married. But it was too late to turn back now. She was still watching him expectantly so he decided the least he could do was to say hello and ask how she was.

Joanne broke away from her crowd of friends as he reached her. 'Bloody hell! I thought it was you,' she said. 'How are you?'

'I'm good, really good.'

'Great. And your mum?'

'She's good too. We lost my grandma and I think she struggled at first being on her own, but since I've been home, she's getting back to her old self. What about your family?'

Joanne smiled again. 'Aw, sorry about your grandma. Yeah, my family are all good.'

Macca felt self-conscious as he attempted to make polite conversation. He'd adopted a formality that was at odds with how they used to be. But he couldn't help it. She looked stunning. So classy. So wonderful. And he felt awkward around her. Joanne was too good for him, always had been, and he had a dismal feeling that she couldn't wait to break away and rejoin her friends.

'I suppose your sister is married by now, isn't she?' he asked for something to say.

'Yes, she is.'

'That makes two of you then,' he said with an unfamiliar tremor in his voice.

'What do you mean? I'm not married anymore. I got divorced.'

'Oh, sorry,' he said but he failed to hide his glee. Macca's eyes brightened and his voice shot up an octave. 'I didn't realise. I thought you'd still be with him.'

'Oh no. That ship sailed long ago. He was too possessive for one thing.'

'I don't understand guys like that. It's not like you would give him any reason to be jealous. I always trusted you.'

'I know, but some people are just like that and, to be honest, it didn't help when he found the letters.'

'What? You mean the letters I sent you? Did you actually keep them?'

'Yeah, fool that I am. In fact, I've still got them.'

Macca didn't know what to say. He was gobsmacked by her revelation.

'What about you?' she then asked. 'Did you get married?'

'Oh no. Not me. I never met anyone I wanted to marry.' Then, realising what he had said, he tried to backtrack. 'Well, at least, not since you.'

He felt foolish. Was he coming on too strong considering it was the first time he had seen her for fifteen years?

He decided on a swift change of subject. 'What are you up to these days?'

'Still hairdressing but I'm a fully qualified stylist now and I moved to another salon for better pay but it's still in the centre of Manchester.' She nodded towards the crowd she had been standing with. 'Those are my colleagues. We're on a works night out. What about you? I hope you're not still getting into trouble.'

Macca smiled. He knew this was his chance to prove to her that he'd changed. 'No, I'm not. I had enough of that life. I'm part-owner of a jerk shop now.'

He'd bigged it up a bit knowing that Jojo had only just offered him the opportunity to buy a small share, but he wanted to impress her. It mattered to him that she should view him in a different light.

It seemed to be working as she said, 'That's good to hear. Well done you. I bet it was difficult to make the change after… well, y'know… after what happened.'

'Yeah, it was but thank God a friend of mine gave me a chance. I'm so glad I met him. I've got loads of plans for the future. I'm going to diversify.'

'Ooh,' she teased. 'Diversify, that's a big word for you. How?'

He smiled and for a moment it was like old times. They had always had good banter and now she was teasing him just like she used to. Brimming with enthusiasm, he was about to tell her all about his plans when Todd turned up.

'Fuckin' hell!' he said to Macca. 'I've been looking for you all over the place. I might have known you'd be chatting someone up.' He looked at Joanne then did a double take. 'Fuckin' hell!' he repeated. 'Joanne. What are you doing in here?'

Macca glanced from Todd to Joanne, awaiting her reaction. But it wasn't favourable. She tutted before addressing him. 'I thought it was too good to be true. I suppose you're gonna tell me he's your business partner now, are you? You must think I'm an idiot to fall for all that crap about you going legal.'

Then she walked away. Macca called after her, 'No! I wasn't lying. I have got a jerk shop.'

Joanne bypassed her group of friends in her haste to get as far from Macca and Todd as possible. He watched as one of her friends broke away from the group and went to follow her. Macca decided to pursue her too but as he tried to move, he felt a restraining hand on his arm. It was Todd.

'Forget it, mate. She's fuckin' married anyway.'

'No, she isn't fuckin' married! She got divorced.'

'Why are you bothered what she thinks anymore?'

But Macca *was* bothered. In that few moments all his feelings for Joanne had come flooding back. In fact, they'd never gone away. She was the love of his life and he realised that he would never love any woman the way he loved Joanne.

Todd's hand had now dropped from his arm, and Macca thought again about following her. To hell with what Todd thought! For a moment he searched the crowded bar, deliberating over what to do. But there was no sign of her. She was gone.

SEVEN YEARS LATER

67

May 2011

Macca carried on through the estate on his way to Todd's house. As always when he visited the estate these days, he noticed its decline. The boarded-up houses. Other properties inhabited but nevertheless run-down. The rubbish stacked in people's gardens. The weeds, mouldy walls and rotting gates. Thank God he no longer lived here! After all these years it seemed another world away.

The two young lads who had attacked him were still on Macca's mind as he walked away from the late-night convenience store wearing a wry smile. To think they'd tried to mug *him* of all people. They'd probably got the shock of their young lives when he'd responded by laughing at them. He hoped they would find the right path in life, but he had to acknowledge from his own experience that the odds were stacked against them.

On the way to Todd's house, he couldn't help but swing by his grandma's old house. He'd not been there for years, and he was curious. He remembered how she had always kept it so neat. In the summer she would sit on a chair in the tiny front garden, reading the paper, or admiring her roses as she chatted to her neighbours.

As he drew near, he could see that the low, sturdy fence that bordered the path to the front door was still there although the paint had peeled and faded, and one of the fence panels was at an odd angle. Instead of seeing his grandma in a chair he saw three youngsters sitting on the fence, one male and two female. The sound of lively conversation came to an abrupt halt when he passed the house.

Macca couldn't help but stare at the exterior. The roses were long gone and there had been an attempt to create a small lawn, but it was now overgrown and full of weeds. The windows were filthy, and the door had been painted in a lurid shade of lilac. The three youngsters eyed him warily and, once he had passed, their conversation resumed.

Seeing his grandma's old house stirred a feeling of sadness in him. How it had changed, and not for the better. It somehow felt like an insult to his grandma's memory. Doris. How she had tried to keep him on the straight and narrow! If only he had taken notice of her, he could have saved himself a lot of heartache. He was still mulling it over when he bumped into Shay.

It was a shock. He'd not seen him for years. Like Macca, Shay was approaching middle age. Knowing he was a bit older than himself, Macca put him at around forty-one, forty-two. Not that old really, but the years hadn't been kind to him.

What was once a kink in Shay's brown hair now resembled greasy straggles and it was streaked with grey. He looked haggard with his pale, drawn complexion and his sunken cheeks and jowls. In fact, the only part of his face that showed any vitality was the dilated pupils of his eyes. But Macca knew that this was synthetic rather than natural.

His face wasn't the only part of him that screamed of a lack of self-care. Shay's saggy, stained jeans hung from his skinny frame so low that they were concertinaed from the knees down. Macca wondered how they defied the law of gravity as there seemed to be nothing holding them up apart from Shay's protruding hip bones.

'Wow! Look who it is,' said Shay. 'How's it going, mate?'

As he spoke, Macca became aware of his twitchiness, which he recognised as a symptom of cocaine abuse.

'Good,' said Macca, but he didn't ask Shay how *he* was. That was obvious from his appearance.

'Have you heard about Todd?' asked Shay.

'Yeah, that's part of the reason I'm here. I'm on my way to see him now.'

'You fancy coming in for a drink before you go round? You might fuckin' need one! I've got a house now. It's on the way to Todd's.'

Shay's words disturbed Macca. He'd heard that Todd had been attacked outside a city-centre pub after a disagreement with another customer and had spent some time in hospital.

As with Shay, Macca hadn't seen Todd for some time. Macca's mother had also moved away from the estate and was now living in a retirement apartment near to him. Therefore, his visits to the estate were infrequent.

From what Macca knew, Todd was still involved in a life of crime and had a reputation for fighting. Macca had deliberately kept his distance. He was no longer immersed in that lifestyle and had been relieved when Todd had accepted that, and they'd gone their separate ways years previously. But when Macca heard about the attack, he knew he had to pay Todd a visit if only for old times' sake.

'I can't drink, I'm driving home. How bad is he?' asked Macca.

'Bad, mate. Bastards did him over good and proper. Broke five fuckin' bones as well.' Before Macca had chance to comment on Todd's injuries, Shay said, 'Eh, at least come and have a cuppa. You can meet the wife and kids. It's only round the corner.'

Macca couldn't think of a suitable excuse to get out of going to Shay's, especially as he was going to pass it anyway. 'OK,' he said. 'But I can't stay long.'

They soon arrived at Shay's home. Like many of the others on the estate, it was run-down. In the front garden, two young children played on some battered plastic toys. When they saw Shay approach, they ran to him.

'Have you got us some sweets, Dad?' asked one of them, a little girl of about five with a runny nose and torn jumper.

'No, stop mithering. This is a mate of mine: Macca. Say hello.'

But the little girl stuck out her tongue then ran to join her brother once more.

'Little sods,' muttered Shay as he pushed open the front door, which had been left unlocked.

It was then that the smell hit Macca. It was a foul, rancid smell and he knew that he couldn't face going inside the house let alone drinking out of cups that were probably manky.

'Actually, mate, I've just remembered there's something I need to do after Todd's so I can't stay.'

He turned back but before he had chance to break away, Shay called out to him, 'Hang on a minute. I need a word.'

Macca reluctantly walked back to Shay who then asked. 'You couldn't spare a few quid, could you mate?'

'No, sorry,' said Macca, shaking his head.

Before Shay had chance to argue, Macca walked away without stopping. He felt a pang of guilt as he saw Shay's children stare after him with slack jaws. But he knew that those children wouldn't see a penny of any money he might give to Shay. It would all go on drink and drugs.

He wondered what future Shay's kids would have. Would they also become involved in a life of crime? Or even drug abuse? It perturbed him to acknowledge that in all likelihood the answer to both questions was yes. Unfortunately, it was the case for many young people on the estate. Without the correct influences, the cycle of neglect, lawlessness and underachievement would prevail. After all, hadn't Shay had a similar childhood and what had he done with his life?

Once he had passed the house, Macca made a note of the number and the name of the street. He would arrange for a food parcel and some clothing vouchers to be sent to Shay's wife and kids as soon as possible.

Then he carried on to Todd's house. Two minutes later he arrived. Todd still lived in the same house he had lived in back when they were teens, but it wasn't quite as neglected as some of the others Macca had seen. Todd's mother was now elderly and from what Macca had learnt, there were just the two of them remaining at the property. Todd's stepdad had left a long time ago.

Sandra answered the door and although she gave Macca a warm hug and a friendly greeting, he could tell from her face that she was under strain. But nothing could have prepared him for what he found once he stepped inside the house.

68

May 2011

They walked into the hallway and Sandra paused, turning to Macca and speaking in a low voice and clipped sentences. 'Terrible what they did to him, y'know. Witnesses said there were four of the buggers. Followed him outside the pub. Used his head like a football, they said. And all because he'd had an argument with one of them.' Then her voice dropped to a whisper. 'He's a bit out of sorts today. But I'm sure he'll soon perk up when he sees you.'

A feeling of dread descended on Macca. Why was she talking about Todd like this, as if he was a troublesome child? She pushed the living room door open and encouraged him to follow her inside.

The sight of his friend shocked Macca. Todd's features were distorted, and his enlarged head hung slightly to one side, so that he almost resembled a cruel caricature of Todd rather than the man Macca remembered. He had food stuck in his hair and slathered around his mouth. Despite his alarm, Macca tried to front it out. 'Hi, mate, how are you?'

Todd was sitting in a high-backed chair. Over him was a tray on a stand with wheels, like the type used in hospitals. Macca realised he had arrived at feeding time. There was a plate in front of Todd, which was almost empty. It was hard to recognise what the meal had been as it was sloppy rather than solid. With his right hand, Todd was waving a food-laden spoon and Macca could see that bits of it had landed on the floor. Fortunately, there was a plastic cover under the chair.

By way of response, Todd grunted, but he had become excitable; as well as waving his arms about his eyes had lit up.

'He recognises you,' said Sandra. 'That's why he's getting excited.'

Her voice was raised as she tried to compete with the sound of the TV in the background. She stepped up to Todd and took the spoon out of his hand.

'Look at the mess you've made again,' she scolded. Then she turned back to Macca. 'Have a seat. I'll get you a drink in a minute when I've sorted him out.'

'Do you want me to switch the TV off?' asked Macca.

'Oh no, don't do that,' she said. 'He likes it on while he's eating. In fact, he goes bloody mad if I switch it off. That's why he eats in here, so he can carry on watching TV.'

'Ah right,' said Macca, assuming that they only had the one TV.

He plonked himself down on the sofa, feeling awkward as he watched Sandra wipe round Todd's face and then pull the tray away.

'Actually, would you mind doing me a favour while you're here?' she asked. 'I need to take him to the toilet.

He's not been for a while and the carer's rung to say she'll be late. It's a bugger trying to lift him myself. You wouldn't give me a hand, would you?'

'Sure,' said Macca, getting up off the sofa.

He helped Sandra to lift Todd who now stood at well over six foot and was still carrying a lot of muscle. Even to him, Todd felt heavy, and Macca's heart went out to his poor mother whose life now seemed to revolve around caring for her grown-up son. They walked slowly and unsteadily across the room. As they did so, Todd let out a series of undecipherable noises, some of them ear-piercing shrieks.

Sandra must have detected the alarm on Macca's face because she said, 'Don't worry, that's just him trying to speak. He gets frustrated at times. But he understands what we're saying.' Then she raised her voice and directed a question at Todd. 'Don't you, love?'

Macca thought he could detect a slight nod of the head from Todd. They arrived at the lounge door and Sandra directed them to an understairs toilet in the hall, encouraging Macca to turn Todd so he was facing in the right direction.

When they arrived there, Macca hovered awkwardly, wondering if Sandra needed any further help. To his relief, she must have detected his embarrassment because she said, 'Thanks, Macca. I can take it from here, but I wouldn't mind a hand bringing him back. I'll shout you if that's OK.'

'Sure,' said Macca, feeling relieved to dash back to the living room but at the same time guilty.

He had left Sandra to handle putting Todd on the toilet herself because he couldn't face seeing his friend like that. While he sat in the living room waiting for Sandra to call him back, he felt his eyes flood with tears. He tried to fight them back, knowing it wouldn't help Sandra to see him like that.

It had been too much. To see Todd like that was like a punch to the groin. He had been so strong, so vibrant. And now he was like a shadow of the man he once was, all because of a disagreement in a pub. The sight of him was too distressing for Macca, but he wanted to help.

When Sandra shouted him, they brought Todd back to the living room and sat him in a comfy armchair in front of the TV. Then Macca offered to help Sandra clear up the mess Todd had left and give her a hand with the drinks. She waved away his offer of help but asked if he would sit and watch Todd while she went through to the kitchen.

Those few minutes were like mental torture. Macca watched his old mate whose gaze was fixed on the TV screen. Todd was watching some old cartoons and squealing with laughter at the antics of the animated characters. He was so engrossed in what was happening onscreen that Macca wondered whether he was even aware of his presence anymore.

Macca's mind flashed back to the past, reflecting sadly on Todd's life. He surmised that Todd had lost his temper with somebody in the pub over something or other and lashed out. That had always been Todd's way. He was an angry man, and with good reason. Because he had grown up being physically and verbally abused by a man who resented his presence. And hitting back was the only way he knew.

The sadness of it all got to Macca and when Sandra came back with his coffee, he downed it as quickly as possible so that he could make his escape. She attempted polite conversation, telling Macca Todd's favourite programmes and filling him in on the carers who visited and their various attributes.

Once his coffee was finished, Macca got up to go. He walked across to Todd. 'Right, mate, I'm off now.'

Todd looked at him momentarily but this time there was no recognition in his eyes, which soon flashed back to the TV screen.

'I'll come with you to the door,' said Sandra.

They both knew it was a pretext to speak to him alone. 'I'm sorry it's been a shock,' she said. 'I didn't know how much you knew.'

Her regard for his feelings in the face of all she was going through touched Macca. Tears filled his eyes again, and he couldn't wait to get out of the door. 'I've got to go,' he muttered, grabbing the handle and turning it, then walking outside to a feeling of relief as the air brushed his tear-stained face.

With his back to Sandra to hide his tears, he shouted, 'I'll get you a TV for the kitchen so he can eat in there.'

As he dashed back to his car in floods of tears, an ironic thought came to him. He hoped he didn't bump into the two troublesome youths again. He dreaded to think what they would make of his hardman image if they were to see him in this state.

69

May 2011

On the drive home Macca couldn't take his mind off the sight of his old friend. He really felt for him, but he felt for Sandra too. She was getting older now and he could tell it was a struggle for her. And what would happen to poor Todd once she was gone? He knew Todd had brothers but although Sandra had mentioned carers coming in, she hadn't mentioned Todd's brothers. And Macca didn't like to ask.

Macca knew he wouldn't be able to help Sandra in the physical sense. He had too many responsibilities of his own with a wife and two kids plus his businesses. But he vowed to himself that he would help in any other way he could. Financially, he was able to provide support and he was determined to ring Sandra once he was feeling calmer and ask her what she needed.

Then other thoughts came to Macca. Out of all his friends off the estate, he was the only one who had made something of his life. He reflected sadly on what had happened to each of the mates he had formed a gang with back when he was a teenager. Leroy and Spinxy were both gone. Shay was a messed-up junkie. And now Todd.

But Macca tried not to dwell. Instead, he considered how lucky he had been to survive it all. Not only had he survived but he'd thrived. Macca often thought about how proud his grandmother would have been if she'd found out how he'd turned his life around. He'd also lived up to his father's dying wishes.

Macca had expanded his share in the jerk shop he had run. In fact, he had bought both shops from Jojo when he had retired. But he'd also fulfilled his plans to diversify and now had a chain of late-night convenience stores, one of which he had been visiting when the two youths had tried to mug him. How ironic that Agnes, who had once given him a clip round the ear for shoplifting, now worked in the store owned by him.

He didn't visit that store too often, which was why he'd seen nothing of Todd or Shay for years. The area brought back bad memories. But now, despite the bad memories, he vowed to himself that he would go back regularly and visit Todd and Sandra whenever he was there.

It wasn't long before Macca arrived home. He lived only a few miles up the road in the middle-class suburb of Heaton Moor, but in terms of the area, it could have been a million miles away. Here people were mainly professionals, and they took a pride in their homes and gardens in contrast to the shabbily neglected homes in the area he had come from.

Macca resolved to put things behind him for now and concentrate on his loving family. He drove his four-by-four up the drive then let himself into the house. His two young children greeted him at the door. The eldest, four-year-old Elise, shouted gleefully, 'It's Dad!' while the youngest, two-year-old Joseph, clung to his jeans.

'Let me in, son,' he said. 'Otherwise, you won't get your treats.'

He walked into the kitchen and plonked down two packets of sweets, which he'd grabbed from his shop. There his wife was waiting for him.

'Want sweeties,' grumbled Joseph, attempting to reach up to the work surface.

'No, you can wait till after tea,' said Macca's wife. 'For God's sake! He's been cranky all day. Where have you been till now? I thought you'd have been home long ago.'

Macca could see she was stressed but he didn't rise to it because he was grateful for what he had. Normal family life in a lovely home with a loving wife and two adorable children. Instead, he went up to her and put his arms around her, planting a kiss on her cheek.

'I've missed you,' he said. 'It's been a trying day, but I'll tell you about it once the kids are in bed.'

She pulled away from his embrace and stared inquisitively at him. 'What's come over you?'

'Well, I suppose I'm just grateful for what I have, Jo. And I'm so glad I pursued you after that night in Manchester.'

She smiled and he knew he was winning her round. It was so easy to do because they had a loving bond that no amount of family stresses and strains could break. 'Pursue me?' she joked. 'You were like a stalker. How many salons did you go to before you found me?'

He laughed and the children, picking up on their banter, joined in. 'Oh, just about every one in the centre of

Manchester. And I'm so glad I persuaded you to come for a drink with me and at least hear me out.' Then, seeing the grin on her face, he added, 'Eventually'.

'Anyway, I was thinking,' he continued. 'About that bigger house you'd like us to buy, would you like us to view a few this weekend?'

'Yeah… but… I thought you said you were too busy with the businesses?'

'No, it's fine. I'll make time. You're right, the kids could do with a bit more play space and we can afford it, so why not?' She smiled again and he said, 'Anyway, let me give you a hand with the dinner, and get these two little monsters fed so they can have their sweets.' As he spoke, he lifted his son and ticked his tummy till he squealed with delight.

70

May 2011

Macca walked through the doors of Manchester Royal Infirmary and looked at the details he had been given by Jojo's wife, Kadene. He'd received a call from her that morning to say that Jojo was in hospital so he rushed there as soon as possible knowing that Jojo had been in ill health for some time. It seemed that all the bad news was coming at once. First Todd, and now this.

He made his way to the appropriate area where a nurse directed him to a side ward. Jojo was lying in bed looking frail with Kadene sitting in a bedside chair. She got up to meet Macca as he walked through the door.

'How is he?' he asked.

'No need to whisper. I can hear you,' shouted Jojo, his voice surprisingly strong considering the state of him.

Macca looked across the room at Jojo who was attempting to sit up in bed. Then he walked towards him. 'You don't change, do you?'

Jojo managed a smile. 'I'm too old to change now.'

At the sight of him struggling, Macca said, 'Don't sit up on my account. It's fine. I can still see you.'

'Good,' said Kadene. 'He gets tired easily. That's why he's lying down.'

'Erm, hello,' said Jojo. 'I'm still here, y'know. I might be on the way out, but I've still got all my faculties, for the moment anyway.'

Macca saw the look of distress that crossed Kadene's face, but she quickly tried to disguise it. 'Stubborn old mule,' she said but the words had a note of affection in them.

'Kadene, do you mind if me and Macca have a word alone?' he asked. 'We need to talk business.'

She nodded solemnly and left the room. Macca wondered what Jojo might have to say that he couldn't say in front of his wife. He didn't think it could be business-related as Macca was now sole owner of the jerk shops, and the late-night stores had been Macca's own investment. Jojo and Kadene had enjoyed their retirement with the proceeds of sale until Jojo got cancer, which he had been fighting on and off for years.

'I didn't want to say this in front of Kadene,' said Jojo. Then he scrunched his face as though in pain before taking a deep breath and carrying on. 'I'm not coming out of it this time. Can't say I'm sorry. I'm tired of fighting to be honest.'

'Don't say that, mate,' Macca protested. 'You can't just give up.'

Jojo smiled wryly. 'I haven't given up on life, Macca, it's given up on *me*. They've done everything they can now. The doctor told me as much.'

Despite Jojo's evident fragility, Macca was shocked. He couldn't believe how courageous Jojo was being to talk about the end of his life with such impassivity. And, despite his own feelings of upset, he decided that if Jojo could be brave, then he could too, at least till he got outside.

'Does Kadene know?' he asked.

'Oh yeah, and it upsets her. That's why I didn't want to tell you in front of her. Oh, I know she tries to hide it, but you can't kid a kidder, can you?' Jojo winced again. 'It'll be a matter of days from what the doctor says.'

This time Macca couldn't hide his shock. 'You what? But... but...' There were so many things he wanted to say to Jojo, this man who meant the world to him. And, knowing it might be the last chance he got, he began, 'I want to thank you, Jojo, for everything you've...'

Jojo held up his hand to silence him. 'No need.' Then he grinned. 'You did most of it yourself anyway.'

'I couldn't have done it without you, Jojo.'

'Oh, you'd be surprised. Now, I want you to promise me that you'll take good care of those two kiddies and that lovely wife of yours. I don't want you getting up to no good when I'm gone.'

'No, course I won't,' said Macca. 'I'll never let her down again, and that's a promise.'

'Good,' said Jojo. 'Anyway, it's time they were topping up my medication. Do me a favour and press that buzzer for the nurse, then tell Kadene to come back in.'

Macca did as he was asked knowing that Jojo had saved them from an emotional scene as they had both been on the verge of tears. The nurse was soon in the room, and she gave Jojo a dose of medication. While she tended to Jojo, Kadene stood calmly observing with Macca in the background.

Once the nurse was gone, Jojo closed his eyes and muttered, 'Goodbye.'

Macca panicked, turning to Kadene. 'He's not... he's not gone, has he?'

Kadene smiled. 'No, not yet. It's the morphine; it sends him to sleep. Well, that and the cancer. It tires him out.'

Macca blew out a puff of air. 'Right, well, I suppose I'd better get going then.'

He hugged Kadene and then approached the head of the bed where he hovered awkwardly for a few seconds. Then, deciding this was no time for macho pride, he leant forward and gave Jojo a gentle kiss on the forehead. Then he pulled away, wished Kadene goodbye, and left the ward.

Macca waited until he was outside before he gave release to his emotions, just like he had done a few days prior when he'd visited Todd. He felt deeply sorry to be losing Jojo who had meant so much to him. And his heart cried out to Kadene who would no longer have such a good man by her side.

By the time he reached the car he was crying openly, his shoulders juddering as mighty sobs racked his body. He had known Jojo for only part of his life but, in that time, he had been everything to him: father, confidant and friend.

It was the following morning when Macca received a call from Kadene. Her voice was shaky and as she spoke to him he could tell she was fighting back tears, her composure of the previous day now gone. He had a strange feeling in his stomach as dread consumed him. He knew what she was going to say before she said it. But he had to hear it, nonetheless. He had to be sure.

'Is he OK?' asked Macca, trying to help Kadene when her words wouldn't come out.

'No.' She paused a moment before taking a juddering breath then adding in a broken voice, 'He's gone.'

'I'm so sorry,' said Macca, feeling her sorrow.

'I know. I know. Sorry, Macca, but I've got to go. I've got to make more calls.'

'OK, I understand. If there's anything I can do…'

But she cut him off and he could tell by the tremble in her voice that it was getting too much for her. 'I'll be in touch,' she cried. 'About the arrange…'

Her voice choked on a sob, so he didn't catch the rest of the word. But he understood what she meant. The funeral. She'd be in touch about the arrangements for the funeral. Before he could say anything further, the line went dead. Macca looked over to see Joanne staring at him with an expression of sympathy. His eyes filled with tears and she raced across the room and put her arms around him. Macca didn't need to say anything. She knew.

71

June 2011

'You sure you're alright driving?' asked Macca as Jo brushed some fluff off the collar of his smart black suit.

'Yeah, course I am. You'll want a drink, won't you?'

'I could do with one now to be honest.'

Joanne smiled. 'You'll be alright.'

Macca attempted a smile, but she could see how tense he was. 'Will everything be OK at the shop?'

Joanne knew he was referring to the hairdressing salon he had helped her buy rather than to any of his shops. 'Yeah, course it will. I've told you, Angela's running it today. She's more than capable.'

He nodded, then she could see another thought had occurred to him. 'What time did you tell your mum we'd pick the kids up?'

'I didn't. She knows it will take as long as it takes and if we're late back, I'll give her a ring and they'll stay over.

You know how much they love it there. Now come on, stop worrying and let's get going before we're late.'

She tapped Macca gently on the back to encourage him to leave the house. He had been dreading today, but Joanne knew he would be fine. Macca had achieved so much in recent years, and she was thankful for that. In particular, she was happy with the way he had finally won her parents round and gained their respect.

Joanne drove steadily until they arrived at Southern Cemetery where Jojo's funeral was to be conducted. She parked the car, and they made their way towards the crematorium where they were greeted by Jojo's son, Chilton, and Jojo's daughter, Jada. She had only met them twice previously and had found them pleasant but not particularly close to their parents as they both now lived in other parts of the UK.

Jojo had told Macca on the quiet that his past would always stand between him and his kids, no matter how much he tried to make amends. They had never openly criticised him, but Jojo had felt their disapproval. She didn't know whether that had been paranoia on his part or whether they hadn't been able to see past the childhood memories they had of him flitting in and out of prison.

Next, Joanne and Macca met Kadene near the entrance. Her face appeared moist and her eyes puffy as though she had already shed many tears. But she held it together while she greeted everybody and gave Macca in particular a warm hug. Joanne admired her resilience. It was something she would have found impossible if she had been in her position.

As they all began to file into the crematorium, Joanne

could feel Macca tense. 'It's OK,' she whispered. 'You'll be fine.'

Then they heard the song that was being played – 'Don't Worry, Be Happy' – and Joanne smiled at Macca in acknowledgement. He'd told her how often Jojo had played it during their time in Strangeways and what effect it had had on him. Having met Jojo a few times, and having heard many tales about him, she knew that it summed up his outlook on life. Noticing the many confused faces of the other attendees, though, she could tell that most people weren't aware of the song's relevance.

They sat on the second row directly behind Jojo's family and as the celebrant went through the various stages of the funeral service, Kadene and Jada were fighting back the tears. Chilton stood tall and proud while he took in the words of the celebrant. But Macca's mind was elsewhere. Joanne could almost read his thoughts as he focused on memories of the man he had loved.

Eventually it was time for the eulogy. She gave Macca's hand a gentle squeeze of encouragement as he stepped into the central aisle, then made his way to the front clutching the list of bullet points that he had prepared beforehand. She knew he was nervous, which was why he had been uncharacteristically fussing so much before they had left the house.

Despite his successes in life, Macca wasn't used to public speaking, and he had agonised over his speech for days. Joanne also knew how important it was for him to get it right. He had been disappointed at not being able to tell Jojo how much he meant to him while he was still alive, so for him this was his chance to pay tribute.

As Macca cleared his throat, Joanne was surprised to find that her palms were sweating until she realised that she was feeling anxious for him.

'I, erm, I'm a good friend of Jojo's,' Macca began with a tremble in his voice. 'We met over twenty years ago. I soon became close to him, and we've been good friends ever since.

'I want to start by offering my condolences to the family, in particular to Kadene, his widow, and to his children, Chilton and Jada. I know how much Jojo meant to them and how much they'll miss him.'

As soon as he spoke the words, Kadene broke down into uncontrollable sobs. It was as though the tenuous control she had held over her emotions up to this point had finally broken. Jada turned to her mother and took her in her arms, her own tears flowing too.

Chilton looked towards the two women then turned his head forward again, but Joanne could see the rise and fall of his shoulders as though he had taken a deep breath to steady himself. To Joanne it was an acknowledgement of how much feeling Jojo's children had for him despite his criminal past.

Looking towards Macca, Joanne could see that the emotional reaction to his words had flustered him. He fiddled with his tie while he looked down at the bullet points he was clutching with shaking hands. When he looked up again, she gave him an encouraging nod of the head, willing him to continue.

'I've known Jojo for over twenty years,' he repeated. 'He wasn't always the man he is today, and I know he had a lot of regrets. Not everyone knew the true Jojo. He did a lot of bad things in the past and unfortunately that might be what some people remember him for rather than for the way in which he turned his life around.'

Jojo's children were paying ardent attention to Macca now and Joanne was pleased at the way he held their gaze, aware that he was gaining in confidence.

'When Jojo came over to the UK there were few opportunities open to him. Like a lot of young men from deprived backgrounds he drifted into a life of crime because it was the only way in which he could provide for his family. But it was his intention for many years to find a way in which he could make a living legally, although it wasn't easy with no qualifications and limited experience. Through his determination and strength of character, Jojo eventually found a way.

'Jojo was a religious man, and he found great strength through his religion. In fact, he often told me that it had helped him to see the light.

'He was very proud of his children's achievements and talked about them often. His hope was that they would one day be proud of him too.'

Joanne saw Chilton nod and she couldn't help but feel touched. Jojo would have been so pleased to know that his son had finally recognised the good he had done. Then Jada let out a sob, but Macca continued, undeterred, clearing his throat before he came to his next point.

'I know how Jojo felt, because he spoke to me about it often and because I went through similar experiences myself. Jojo didn't just turn his own life around, he helped me turn mine around too. He gave me a start and encouraged me to invest in his jerk shops. Thanks to him, I'm now a successful businessman and I know that, without his help and guidance, I would never have achieved any of that.'

Joanne heard his voice crack then, so she gave him another nod of encouragement. Pulling himself together, Macca carried on with his speech.

'In honour of the great man that Jojo was, I have decided to name my shops after him. So, each time any of you pass one of "Jojo's convenience stores" you will remember what a wonderful man he was. Because it's down to Jojo that I managed to set up the shops in the first place.'

Macca gazed around at the attendees before lowering his voice for his closing words.

'Thank you for allowing me to share my memories of my wonderful friend Jojo, one of the greatest men I ever met.'

He walked steadily back to the second row, and Joanne smiled at him as he met her gaze. When he slipped into the seat beside her, she gave his hand another squeeze.

'You did brilliantly,' she whispered, and his face lit up despite his sorrow.

Joanne had never felt prouder of Macca. He was now the man she had always wanted him to be, and she had never for a moment regretted the day she had agreed to marry him. She gazed at her handsome, determined and resilient husband and knew that although his mentor and father figure was now departed, Macca was going to be absolutely fine.

Acknowledgements

First, I would like to thank my publishers, Head of Zeus, for their support not only with this title but with the whole of my back catalogue. Special thanks go to Martina Arzu for your thought provoking and very useful suggestions, Matt Bray for your excellent cover design, Helena Newton for a wonderful job on the copy edits and Yvonne Doney for the proofreading. Thanks also to all the other Head of Zeus staff who work so hard in the background.

Thanks to my agent, Jo Bell, for your support, and to the staff at Bell Lomax Moreton including Sarah McDonnell and John Baker.

I conducted a lot of research for this novel relating to arrest and imprisonment, the Strangeways prison riots of 1990, and other areas of the novel. Apart from reading online articles, watching videos, and reading books, a number of people were very helpful with my research, so I want to thank some of them individually:

o My author friend and ex-police officer Roger Price for information relating to police procedure.
o Brian Goodyear for your insight into life inside Strangeways in the 1980s.
o My author friend and ex-police officer Mark Knowles for information and advice relating to police procedure.

I would like to point out that if any information, particularly that relating to police procedure, is factually incorrect then the fault lies with the author and not with the aforementioned people. I have also used a little poetic license in some areas of the novel.

Big thanks to the crime reading community including book bloggers, reviewers and everyone who reads, rates, and reviews my books. Your input makes a world of difference. Thanks also to all the readers who continue to buy and recommend my novels. I appreciate each and every one of you.

Last but not least, I would like to thank my family, friends and loved ones for your encouragement throughout my writing journey.

About the Author

HEATHER BURNSIDE spent her teenage years on one of the toughest estates in Manchester and she draws heavily on this background as the setting for many of her novels. After taking a career break to raise two children, Heather enrolled on a creative writing course. Heather now works full-time on her novels from her home in Manchester, which she shares with her two grown-up children.